RISE

RISE

BRIAN GUTHRIE #18

Nate,
You Made my Day!

INKSHARES

Published by Inkshares, Inc., San Francisco, California
www.inkshares.com

Edited and designed by Girl Friday Productions
www.girlfridayproductions.com
Cover design by Paul Barrett
Illustration by Chris McElfresh

ISBN: 9781941758830
e-ISBN: 9781941758847
Library of Congress Control Number: 2015955810

First edition

Printed in the United States of America

To the broken, the shattered;
Those whose world has been torn apart.
To those hiding in a dark room, longing for the light;
Those who have lost hope.
This story is for you.

CONTENTS

Note from Logwyn, scribe recruited to record these events: The following interviews were conducted at different times in different locations. The placement of each is meant to preserve the chronology of the narrative.

CHAPTER 1

PAPER

I suppose this all started with paper. Real paper. I could not recall the last time I had seen a fresh batch of it. That close to the core, one rarely found supplies of this sort; they were hard to come by even for researchers like me. "Only the bare necessities for those sworn to protect." How many times had I had those words thrown in my face? Still, someone must have seen my request. How else had this package of crisp, white paper been delivered? The first thing I did was pull a piece free, hold it close to my nose, and inhale slowly. If I closed my eyes, the faint odor made me believe I was pressing my face close to a real tree standing before me, a soft breeze shifting my long hair around as it moved past. Well, I pictured what I thought was a tree. It was a pleasant dream.

A cough interrupted my wandering thoughts. I quickly lowered the paper and opened my eyes, brushing a strand of my hair from my face. There in the doorway stood a figure I'd never seen before. He stood at least a full head taller than me, and I was considered tall at 172 centimeters. He wore long, flowing silver robes; a hood covered his head and a cowl most of his face. A slit cut across it revealed dark skin and black eyes, which were locked on me. My heart accelerated slightly, and a tingly feeling ran up my side to my chest. He hesitated in the doorway, hands clasped behind him. I tossed the paper behind me and bowed my head as my cheeks warmed, not wishing to stare at the strange figure waiting before me.

"May I enter?" he asked, his voice deep and rough.

I looked up and nodded. He stepped forward to the table that dominated the room's center, the door sliding shut behind him.

"Feel free to stare," he muttered, eyes roaming around the space. "I find it helps you lot get past the startled stage sooner."

As his black eyes darted around, I felt self-conscious about the clutter. My eyes followed his around my messy office, taking in random articles of clothing, a hairbrush, and a tin of moisturizer, and I wished I'd taken a few moments earlier in the day to tidy up a bit.

"Your robes are an interesting choice, considering the heat," I said, words racing out of my mouth. I closed my eyes tight and took a few deep breaths.

"And a perpetual curiosity to you core lovers," the man said, moving to stand by the table holding the paper. "Quite a prize here."

I must have looked confused, for the man arched an eyebrow and nodded at the table. When I looked around, all I saw was the paper.

"This?" I asked. "Yes, it is. I have no idea where it came from, either."

"Such a lovely day," the man said, moving past the table to stand near the room's lone window. "Join me? Seems a lot less windy than usual for this time of day, don't you think?"

I didn't move. I had no idea who he was. My first thought was to move toward the door, not the window.

"Don't you agree, Logwyn?" he asked, nodding toward the window. "About the wind? Seems very calm for this late in the day. The night shield will be up in a few chrons."

I turned my gaze to the window, puzzled as to why he would want to discuss the weather with me. In the distance, I spied another shell, too small to support a population, orbiting the core just below ours. Aware of the man standing next to me and his question, I searched for some kind of response. I settled on a nod and started to reply, then stopped. He'd called me by name.

"Truth be told," he said, looking toward the door and dropping his voice to a low murmur, "I'm not here to talk about the weather. I'm here to discuss that prize you just received."

I moved back toward the desk that stood along one side of the room, my eyes narrowing.

"I gather you're getting suspicious right about now," he said, his voice still low. "Good. Don't lose that. You're going to need it."

"How do you know my name?" I asked.

He smiled. "If there's one thing you can count on everywhere, it's the bureaucratic urge to account for everything." He glanced around the room, taking in the table, my desk, and the wardrobe along the far wall. "Especially who works in what office."

"You looked me up?"

"I needed to find you, and, frankly, you're the only woman with that name in the index."

"Why?" I moved around the table.

He nodded at the door. "Go ahead. The door's not locked."

"Who are you?"

"I'm a friend of your Queen." He looked back out the window. "As difficult as that may be to believe."

"The Queen doesn't have friends. She hardly ever comes out of her cave anymore."

He shrugged. "So, you don't know what she does or who she talks to." He smiled at me. "Or who she is friends with."

I bowed my head at him, conceding the point, and nodded at his garments.

"Those are not from our shell."

"Nor mine, I'm afraid," he said, shrugging. "However, it's an effective disguise on most shells I visit."

"How? You stand out. That can't be what someone wearing a disguise wants."

He chuckled. "Down here, I'll grant you that much." He looked at the ceiling for a moment. "Up there, on other shells, you'll find these cloaks carry a lot of power and weight." He held up a hand. "Not that I'm here to flaunt that power. I just didn't have time to change before I came."

"Why are you here?" I asked, looking back at the paper.

"Right, let's get to the point." He stepped away from the window and picked up a single sheet of paper from the table. "As I said, quite the prize. Getting this here was no small feat, I can tell you."

I looked back and forth between the paper and the stranger. "Pardon me," I said, holding his gaze, "but isn't this a violation of the import codes?"

The man leaned close, his dark eyes turning to look at me as he waved me closer. "It can't be a violation if it wasn't imported."

I opened and closed my mouth several times, trying to fathom how else the paper might have come. Nothing got to this shell except from the matter reforger or by import. Both of those required months of waiting to get anything beyond the necessities.

"An impressive bit of work, this is. I can't recall ever seeing a single sheet in existence, and here she's made an entire stack of it. The first is the most complex, as you know. I'm sure if I tried it would take me twenty-four chrons just to make the first sheet." He grinned at me. "I'll wager she did it in twelve."

I stared, my mouth hanging open slightly. Twelve chrons? At that point, I would have needed roughly thirty chrons to duplicate one sheet from the completed pattern, and whoever had done this had made one from scratch in half a day.

"Who?" I asked again.

"You can't figure that one out?"

I shook my head. "I can't think of anyone powerful enough to—" I stopped, my eyebrows shooting up. "The Queen?"

He arched an eyebrow. "The light dawns."

I looked at the paper. "We hardly ever see her anymore. Why would she make something like this?"

"She made it for me," he whispered.

That made me pause. I had only ever seen the Queen once in my lifetime, cycles in the past, the day I'd failed my test. It wasn't a happy memory for me. As it was the only time I'd ever seen her in person, I'd hardly forgotten it.

"How long have you known her?"

"For a very long time." He stopped speaking, his eyes locked on the piece of paper in his hand.

"Did she make all of these?" I asked, finger running down the stack of paper.

The stranger chuckled. "No, once she had the original, duplicating is permitted with a matter reforger, I'm sure." He shook his head and waved the piece of paper at me. "Still, I didn't come here to brag about the Queen's abilities," he said, placing the sheet back on the table. "I have a task for you." He frowned, looking back out the window. "Not an easy one, either."

The stranger stood silent for a moment, his eyes glazed over. He shook his head and refocused on me, reaching into his robes.

"You know what this is, correct?"

He held out an object. I took it and discovered it was an envelope, made from paper and sealed with what looked like a hard, red substance.

"Inside you'll find instructions." He nodded at the envelope. "I thought it best to avoid using certain devices. What's in it is of a delicate nature."

I turned it over in my hand and found my name written across it.

"You know how to write, correct?"

I looked down at the paper. "Yes, but I won't have anything to write with much longer. I'm on my last pencil, and it will take me much longer to make more. Pencils aren't high on the reforger priority list."

The man smiled, held out a small, cylindrical case, and set it on the table between us. He nodded for me to take it.

"I think you'll find this more to your liking."

Inside the case lay a finger-length, cylindrical device made from solid metal. One tip ended in a point, the other rounded smooth. I held it up and shifted it to rest on my fingers like a pencil.

"Correct, it's a writing device. It doesn't have a name yet, but I'm told it's a never-ending pencil, for lack of something better," he said, pointing at the package that once held the paper. "Try it out. It will write on any surface."

I drew a scripting symbol on the packaging, careful to leave the powerful construct incomplete so as not to cause some freak accident. The script looked wet at first but was dry when I brushed a finger across it. I tried it on the smooth metal table and found the same result.

"Do I want to know how long it took her to create this stylus?"

"She didn't make that one, but I'll tell you who did now that you've named it," he said, stepping closer to the table and lowering his voice. "I took it from someone who I am quite certain will be up in arms about it, especially if he hears you've given it a name." He burst out with a hearty laugh, the first emotion I'd seen from the man. "Now, here is where I leave you, but I must give you one word of warning. For this project, I'm sorry to say, you can't use the computers, not for any part."

I looked up from admiring the stylus to stare at the stranger.

"I can't use the computers?" I asked, looking behind the man.

Had we been in most any other room, a large, silvery display panel would have met my eyes, but not in this one. It was part of the reason I had chosen this space to work: To get away from the machines. To hide from the nagging feeling someone or something was staring at me from behind the panel.

"No, I'm afraid not."

"You haven't told me what it is you want me to do."

He pointed at the envelope. "Everything I can tell you is in there."

I looked up at him. "You never told me how you knew to look me up."

He took in a deep breath and let it out. "Some questions have to wait for their answers."

The stranger turned to leave, but I called out to him. "What's your name?"

He didn't answer. He walked out, the door sliding shut behind him. I turned the envelope over in my hand and stared at the red substance pressed to the side. I ran a finger over it. Whatever the red stuff was, it had solidified and turned smooth. A single image lay compressed into the center: an O. A memory tickled on the edge of my consciousness, then flitted away. Shrugging, I used my fingernail to separate the substance from the envelope, freeing the flap. I pulled a piece of paper out and began to read:

> Logwyn, your Queen needs your help. She is on the brink of a choice, one that has far-reaching consequences for us all. I do not believe she'll make the right choice in her current state of mind. She is about to send for you to request that you complete a task for her. When she does, you must tell her one thing when she asks if you will complete the task for her. Tell her you know her secret. The secret no one else knows. What that secret is is hers to tell in her own time. She will challenge you. When she does, show her and only her the item I left on your table.

I stopped reading and looked around. There sat a metallic box the same color as the table. A single sheet of paper lay across it, blocking half the box from my sight. The paper the stranger had held. I looked back down at the letter.

> Show no one else what lies inside this box, not even yourself. Keep it secret from everyone save for the Queen. Only reveal you have it at your direst need.

> A Friend

> PS: Do not trust any computer terminal you happen upon.

I set the note aside and moved to stand over the box. It measured just longer than my arm from elbow to fingertip and a bit wider than my wrist. How I'd missed him placing it I still don't know. A small magnetic clasp held it closed on one side. I moved to open the box, pausing to glance at the note. He said to show her what lies within. What could it be? My finger toyed with the clasp as I pondered what might lay inside.

A moment later a messenger appeared, delivering a summons to see the Queen. He found me standing over the still-closed box. After he left, I eyed the summons and the note, my hand still resting on the metallic box. What did the strange man want? What did the Queen want? And why all this secrecy?

It took me several months of work to find those answers. To find that they boiled down to a friend caring for another and trying to help his friend recover from a loss. It took even more for me to understand the need for secrecy. To truly comprehend the danger the box in my possession brought with it. Not just to me, but to everyone. And not just danger. Power. Had I known then the implications that box carried with it, I might have thrown it into the core.

But at that moment, I didn't know any of that. I needed more information, and only one source lay open to me. Before I'd finished thinking the thought through, I found myself walking out the door—paper, stylus, and a still-closed box all tucked away safely in a travel sack.

Finding the Queen is easier said than done most days. Being the oldest and sole eternal of our bunch, she had always carried a massive burden. Ours was the only civilization still in existence that had complete records going back to before the Shattering that nearly destroyed the world. That knowledge was closely guarded, locked away in the network that controlled everything and kept us alive. Water, gravity, even the night shield that let us sleep all came from that network. As such, it was a closely guarded thing. A task our society had carried for centuries, since just after the war of the Ancients had resulted in the Shattering. And all throughout that had stood the Queen. Always present, always carrying out her duties. When not required for disputes and various royal obligations, she spent most of her time in seclusion deep in our shell's cavernous belly. Once she went down there, we would not see her for days, sometimes dozens of them. High ones would venture below to meet with her on occasion and bring back her words of wisdom to guide our race. It had been that way for as long as I'd been alive and, from what the public records we kept showed, for much longer than that. Since her coronation millennia ago, the Queen had been a recluse, speaking only when necessary, avoiding the details of our world while guiding us from the background. Many had questioned this method of governance over the centuries. Some had tried ousting her. We don't talk about those days anymore.

Needless to say, as a scribe given the chance to speak to her, I was overwhelmed with excitement. Soon, I would stand with history, our history, and I didn't even know why yet. No one had been invited down to her abode in my lifetime, outside of upper-level officials, and even those visits were rare. More and more over the centuries, she had isolated herself. No one really knew why, beyond rumors of her aging or being ill. The fact that she was still around so many hundreds of cycles later proved most of those rumors false, yet they persisted. As a scribe, the thought of being in the same room as the Queen should have filled my mind with questions about her past, about the world as it had been long ago, before the Shattering. At the very least, it should have preoccupied me with silly things, like whether my hair was suitably combed out or my robes of fine enough quality to be in her presence. Instead, I could think of nothing more than the conversation I'd just had. That and the metallic box resting in my sack. When I found myself standing at the entrance to the cavernous tunnel leading to her domain below, I was distracted enough to not move. The guards didn't seem inclined to fly down from their posts along the walls. They just stared at me with their yellow eyes, their long, sinuous necks turning and twisting as they watched for anyone attempting to disturb the Queen's reverie.

No, I wasn't stuck for fear of them. Or fear of going down into the gaping maw that reminded me of a black hole sucking in all the light. Really, I couldn't say what had me afraid, but I was. So, I stood there, clutching my travel sack in one hand, glancing up at the guards. They weren't nearly as majestic as the Queen, yet still intimidating. I remember entertaining thoughts of being a dragon when I was younger. In my mind, I held an imposing form as a dragon. That dream had been denied me long ago on the only day I'd met the Queen, and, to be honest, I didn't care that much. However, that thinking was frowned upon in our society. So, whenever I was out in public, I maintained the proper reverence for those blessed with that form. It made me long for my room. So many people and their put-upon airs. Regardless, in most of the dwelling areas inside the shell, I rarely saw those blessed with the transformation. Preferred form or no, the inhabited parts of our shell were as priceless as they were Ancient. The Ancients' civilization was once the greatest the world had ever known, and it was their technology that had altered everything about the world—had even been used to nearly destroy it. Now all that remained of the Ancients were their buildings and the network. We couldn't have dragons destroying the few remaining Ancient structures we possessed.

A cold breeze whipped past me, sending chills down my spine and making me quiver, bringing me back to the issue at hand. I looked up to find the guards watching me. A bemused expression twisted their hideous faces into an even worse state.

"Is the Queen below?" I called up.

The guard on the left nodded, his head dipping up and down. "And she's expecting you, scribe. So, get to it else we'll have to take you down ourselves."

I sniffed at his suggestion and shook my head. "No, thank you. I'll walk on my own."

Both guards barked out laughing, small puffs of flame slipping out as they did.

"Are you daft, scribe?" the guard who had spoken before asked. "You've been around your computers too much."

The guard on the right took to the air and glided down to land beside me. "No one walks into the Queen's domain," he whispered, sidling close enough for me to feel his body heat through my cloak. "Not out of respect or anything like that, mind you."

The other guard landed to my left and moved in as close as the other. "No, you have to fly, scribe. There's no other way in." He nodded toward the black tunnel reaching toward us, reminding me of an image I saw of an extinct creature called a snake lunging to swallow a meal. "Just beyond the edge of the light, see? The floors all drop off."

"It's a giant cavern in there," the guard to my right continued. "And to meet the Queen you have to find her."

"You have two choices, scribe," the other guard said. "You ride the platform, blind, or we fly you down." He leaned close to me, and a sulfuric odor wafted past me as he spoke. "Also blind."

"I'll take the platform, thank you," I whispered, grasping my travel pack and shifting past them.

I jumped as the two of them burst into laughter and took to the air, returning to their perches. They muttered back and forth about scribes and emitted what sounded like a few colorful phrases directed at people like me. I felt my skin flush warm, despite the cold wind shifting around me. The light behind me illuminated just enough of the tunnel for me to see the end of ground and the metallic platform that awaited me. Beyond, the air was blacker than I'd imagined, causing me to pause and stare for a moment into the heart of our floating shell. I took a deep breath, closed my eyes to center myself, and climbed on. The device rose, wavered a bit, and then dove down into the black maw, taking me with it into complete darkness.

CHAPTER 2

THE QUEEN

I floated on the platform through the dark space, my ears tuned to my surroundings. The guards proved correct on two counts: it was indeed a giant cavern, and pitch black to boot. The trip did not take as long as I thought it might. As the platform descended, I began to worry if the platform would fly out the bottom of the shell. No light came into view, so I assumed the cavern's floor remained sealed. I began to wonder, nonetheless, if the bottom would ever come, when the platform's movement began to change. It altered its descent, shifting to slow and coming to a soft landing in the silent blackness. The sound of my touching down echoed through the open space all around. I sensed the cavern walls in the distance. Still no Queen.

I looked around me, listening in every direction. How different this place must seem to those blessed with the form. It probably wouldn't have helped. If she was there, the Queen was motionless, appearing as rock or wall.

"My Queen?" I called into the silence. "My Queen, you sent for me?" No answer. "My Queen, it is Logwyn. You sent for me. I've come per your request."

Something shifted behind me. A voice tickled past me from the other direction.

"It's a tricky thing, Logwyn, trying to sense someone who doesn't want to be found."

That voice had come from two directions. Trying to decide which direction to respond to, I settled on the middle.

"My Queen, my apologies for disturbing your quiet and intruding into your domain," I began.

The Queen silenced me. "I called you here for one reason, dear scribe," she said, her voice coming from two new directions this time. "The network has been sabotaged, and unless I can find a way to fix it, our people will die."

It took a moment for the full implication of her words to hit me.

"Not just our people," I whispered. "Everyone." I tried to look around the room. "Is it just the water that's threatened?"

"No, Logwyn. The entire citadel network and all that they control would go down."

I hissed, running a hand through my hair. "The shells would fall down into the core."

"You appreciate the danger, then." The Queen shifted in the darkness. "And the need for secrecy. This place is one of the few that is isolated from people and the network alike. I think you, in particular, will appreciate the uniqueness of that."

My instinct was to nod, despite the dark room.

"Your mind is preoccupied, Logwyn," she stated, her voice shifting directions to come from just ahead of and behind me. "Speak."

"The reason for summoning me?" I asked, hugging the sack close, the words of the stranger's note at the forefront of my mind.

The Queen chuckled, the sound echoing all around. "Yes, my summons. I need your help to find some answers. And for that I need your skills. So, to begin, tell me of your progress on your project."

"My project? You mean the compilation? You know of that?"

"Keeping tabs on people who ask as many questions as you do is of interest to me, Logwyn," the Queen answered. "Especially when they make as much use of the network as you have." The Queen paused, and I heard something that sounded like a claw clicking on the cavern floor. "A point that is odd enough considering your feelings toward the machines."

My mind tried to find some response but failed. The Queen rescued me.

"Cat got your tongue?" she asked, her voice coming from ahead of and behind me.

"I'm just stunned you would take the time to notice me. Or my project."

The Queen made a clicking sound into the darkness. "Few things please me these days, Logwyn. Keeping tabs on worthy projects put forth by our people is one of them. It just so happens that the skills you've employed in completing your project are critical to helping me solve what is happening to the network."

I contemplated her words. "You want me to interview someone?"

"See? Intelligent to boot," the Queen said, chuckling, the sound echoing across the dark room. "Considering your project, it is not that much of a stretch."

"Your Highness, I struggle to see what you would need me to compile. I've spent my time researching mostly mundane people."

"No one is mundane, Logwyn. No one."

I bowed my head. "Forgive me, my Queen. It's just that, in comparison to one such as you, the people I've interviewed or researched are relatively mundane."

"To me, especially, no one is mundane," the Queen whispered, and the warmth of her presence drew near.

"My apologies again. I didn't mean to offend."

The Queen remained silent for a moment.

Finally, she said, "You didn't offend me, dear Logwyn. It is just tiresome when our kind believes we are better than the rest of the world or sells ourselves short to the point we paralyze our society when action is needed."

Her words confused me, so staying quiet seemed the best action. After a moment, she continued.

"Logwyn, I need your help to find the answer to this puzzle. Something is escaping me. Something vital. Something that may be the answer to much that is going wrong in our world."

The metallic box in my sack felt very heavy all of a sudden. I clutched the pack close and waited for her to continue.

"Our people rely so much on the network. The computer is so powerful." The Queen sniffed into the darkness. "But something is wrong with it. Something I can't quite figure out, despite my very lengthy efforts."

"It seems to be functioning as it always has."

The Queen sniffed again. "When you've been around it as long as I have, you notice things others don't. No, something is wrong with it. Something you can appreciate."

The warmth of her presence flooded over me as she lowered her giant, invisible form. I knew from previous sightings the Queen's dragon form stood as the largest ever recorded, even in the Ancient world. That body drew close, not touching but pushing down nevertheless, weighing heavily on me. Her next words came as a whisper in both of my ears.

"Information is missing from the network," she whispered.

"But that's impossible," I blurted out. "The computer has all of the knowledge ever gathered."

"And much more, trust me," the Queen went on. "But some of it is missing. It appears to be random, but it is not. I've tried to find a pattern to it, but it is changing. Like someone or something is altering the data, shifting it around to keep it hidden."

I frowned, looking down despite still standing in the dark. "What kind of data are we talking about?"

"Very old information," she answered, her voice quiet. "The kind that once nearly destroyed this world."

"Who would have that kind of access?" I asked, my mind reeling from the implications. "The network is built on the most powerful quantum system ever devised, powered by the endless energy supplied by the singularity core of our world. And that computer was locked away in a secret place known only to . . ." I tried to glimpse her. "To you. As the Queen."

"Exactly. So, if I say something is wrong with it, trust me."

I bowed my head. "Forgive my rambling."

"Don't apologize for your curiosity and instinct. I have my theories as to how it is happening, but I need an outside perspective. Your instincts may be the key to solving what is wrong with the network." The Queen's warmth increased, and the sound of her long, lithe form twisting around me in the darkness filled my ears. My body twitched despite my best efforts at not reacting. "Solving that is of the utmost importance. Many lives depend on it, and not just here on our shell."

My eyes shifted, looking around the dark space surrounding me. This cave, judging by my flight time down, had to be near the bottom interior of the giant landmass floating around our world's core: a fragment of what once was the crust of a planet. Dozens more orbited at higher altitudes, each with a citadel on it and a population of survivors now grown to full-sized civilizations.

"It's affecting other shells?" I asked.

The Queen murmured, "Indeed. And it's been getting worse for several cycles now."

"Why wait until now to do this?"

The Queen chuckled. "You assume I've been doing nothing?"

I shook my head, grinding my teeth together. "Apologies, that's not what I meant."

"Trust me, Logwyn, much has been sacrificed in trying to fix this problem. Much."

Silence fell, and my mind wandered back to the box in my sack. The stranger had been very specific. The Queen needed to ask me to complete the task for her. I held my tongue even as my hand gripped the sack a bit tighter.

"For what you are about to do, you cannot trust the network. Swear to me from this point forward everything you hear and learn will remain free from that cursed machine."

"How can I help you find a problem in the network if I'm not allowed to use it?"

"The answers you seek won't be found within the network," she answered.

A frown twisted my face at those words, but I had no time to respond.

The box seemed heavier to me at that moment. The stranger's words echoed in my head.

"Will you complete this task for me? Your agreement is paramount before we can proceed."

I took a deep breath. "My Queen, forgive me, but someone required me to say these words." My heart pounded in my chest. "I know your secret."

The silence that fell seemed heavier than the box in my bag. Her warmth began to wane like fire shifting from a strong wind.

"I have many secrets," she said. "When you have lived this long, they gather around like grandchildren." She barked once in laughter. "Not that I have any of those."

A different tack seemed in order. "Not just any secret. The secret. Your most important one."

That attempt seemed to hit closer to the mark, as she didn't respond. Her next words ended that hope.

"Nothing I hold that dear is a secret."

Mindful of the stranger's warning, I made my choice.

"There is something you must see," I whispered, reaching into my sack to pull out the box.

The Queen did not answer as I set the sack down and held the box out before me.

"What is this?" she asked. "A trick?"

"I hope not," I whispered to myself, flipping the latch and lifting the lid.

Even though the room was dark, I had no doubt she could see. The hiss, followed by the withdrawal of her warmth, confirmed that suspicion.

"Who gave you this?" she whispered, her voice tremulous.

"I don't know. He never gave me his name."

"Do you know what it is you hold?" I shook my head. "He made you promise not to look?"

"No, he left it in my care secretly and instructed me in a note not to look."

The silence that followed stretched on forever. My arms began to tremble at holding the box out.

"And you didn't look. So trustworthy." The warmth began to return. "You may put that away. Did he instruct you to keep it secret?"

I nodded, lowering my arms and flipping the lid closed. "I was only to show it to you." To this day the reason I kept the rest of his warning to myself has eluded me. "And only after you asked me to complete your task for you."

"Did he give you anything else?" she asked.

"A package full of paper."

A soft chuckle rolled past. "That devilish Nomad."

"Do you know him, my Queen?" I asked.

"Indeed. You may trust him. With your life."

"My Queen, please forgive my boldness."

The Queen shifted around me. "Do not apologize for such things. You simply followed the words of someone who at this moment is wiser than both of us. Blindly maybe, but you still took the wiser course."

Taking a gamble, I asked, "Might you tell me what it is in this box?"

"No," she said, her voice firm. "For now, it is best that no one, not even you, knows you have it. Not yet." The clicking noise touched my ears. "Until we know more about what is going on with the network, specifically who is doing it, it is not safe for anyone to know about that. Trust the Nomad and your Queen in this matter. If what we fear is wrong and we can't find a way to prevent it from happening, what you carry may be the only chance we have of reversing the damage."

"And what is happening?" I asked.

"As I said, someone or something is degrading the network, making it harder to use and decreasing its efficiency to the point the shells are going to start seeing problems. Water shortages. Power outages. Rationing of reforgers." The Queen rumbled in what I interpreted was a growl. "Government seizures of power and other actions taken to focus the blame elsewhere so they don't get ousted."

Another silence fell. The warmth of the Queen's form shifted.

"So," she spoke into the darkness, "you never answered my question regarding the task."

I held my tongue for a moment before nodding. "Agreed."

Her warmth left as she moved away. Something clattered to the ground before me and began to glow. It was a small padd.

"This is the only device you may use," the Queen said, her voice echoing down from a single point above me. "It will record the words you hear and allow you to transcribe them to the paper our friend gave you." She laughed slightly. "Do you have something to write with?"

"Yes, a stylus."

"I don't recognize that word. Where did that name come from?"

I shrugged. "A word from our distant past. It came to mind when it was given to me."

"Did we once use them?" she asked.

"Yes, my Queen," I replied, reaching to pick up the padd. "Back before the Ancients and their technology took over the world, what they called styluses were in common use with the technology of that age."

The Queen chuckled, a warm sound that radiated past me. "You are perfect for this task."

"You haven't told me what that task is."

"Considering what you just showed me, that task has changed. I had thought the item you carried lost. It would seem even friends as close as the Nomad and I keep secrets from each other. Be that as it may, that item only works when whole and is only as powerful as the person wielding it. You see, what you carry in that box is only a fragment of a larger piece. I suspect I know where one of the two other pieces is, but, to confirm that, you're going to have to talk to someone else."

"Who?"

"Another very dear friend of mine," the Queen answered. "She will be here presently and will be reticent to speak of the object. You're going to have to draw her out, get her talking. The device will record the words you hear, and you may use the stylus to transcribe them to paper later. The device is already on. It is recording everything we say."

The Queen chuckled. "It wouldn't surprise me if our mutual friend carried it with him earlier. He did come to visit me twice today, and when he left with his paper he might have pilfered this from me."

"So, you need me to find the rest of whatever it is I carry? And to do so by talking to people?" I asked, waving the glowing padd around.

"Your task is a bit more complicated than simple interviews," the Queen said, her tone flat. "It was my hope to keep this much simpler for you. But our mutual friend is correct in what he's not saying outright. I believe the Nomad was trying to tell me this earlier and I wasn't listening. So, he used another tactic, bringing that fragment into this. To help me with the larger problem, you need to start much earlier. That may be the only way to figure out what happened to the last remaining piece if the second is indeed where I suspect it is."

Her words confused me further. I said as much to the Queen.

"You'll remain so for quite some time, most likely," she stated. "But it is necessary. The benefit of outside eyes is paramount. My proximity to the problem is a hindrance."

"And where do you suspect this other piece is?"

The Queen let out a long breath into the cave.

"In the hands of a broken man," she whispered.

Something in her tone told me that man was very important to her. At that time, I had no idea how right I was in that feeling.

"I'll help in any way possible."

The Queen chuckled. "Remember those words when you're talking to some of the people you will inevitably have to interview. Particularly a certain annoying old man."

"Do you have names for me to start with? Typically, I at least start with that much."

"You may have four names, actually. In no particular order. Micaela, Quentin, Suyef, and Nidfar." The Queen paused after that last name. "Although that last one might be a lost cause at this point. To be honest, the only one on this list I can say for sure you might find is the first one."

"How so?"

"Because she's the one I brought here. And she's already arrived."

I looked around. "In this room?"

The Queen chuckled slightly. "No, in my retreat nearby. Heed my warning: she will be very reticent to discuss these matters. You will have to draw her out."

"She's your friend?"

"A greater friend than you could possibly imagine," the Queen replied. "All in good time, you'll understand."

"So, convince her to talk to me and record her words to paper? All so we can find the other pieces to this thing I'm carrying and hopefully find the answer to why the network isn't working properly?"

A sound like the Queen landing nearby greeted my ears, a soft thud for such a giant creature. "Somewhere in her words is the clue I'm looking for. She may not have all the answers. Trust your instincts. Find the others if you can, and when you do, convince them to talk to you," she said, her voice just a hair above a whisper. "I'm afraid that's all I can tell you for now."

"You left out a lot."

She didn't answer.

CHAPTER 3

THE FIRST NAME

Our interview ended at that moment. The Queen's presence left just as light flooded the chamber ahead. Shielding my eyes against the brightness, a stab of pain in my head, I blinked my way toward the opening, the Queen's padd now in my travel sack. As I neared the light, it turned out to be a door that better suited my human form. I pondered why the Queen would need such a place down here when she had her own illustrious quarters above in the main city. Shrugging, I walked through the door into a small chamber, my travel sack flung over my back. The walls were a soft gold color, save for the left wall, which was a deep red. The floor lay bare. Two chairs sat to my right near the wall, small, lighted alcoves over each feeding soft light up toward the ceiling. A desk stood to my left, a single book lying open atop it. My eyes widened at the sight of the ancient tome. It appeared to be a religious text, translated into the Ancient tongue.

"So, not as ancient as you seem," I whispered, looking over the script and lifting the edge to see the binding. "Still, old enough."

I set the book down and moved in front of the desk. Another door stood opposite the one I'd entered. Stepping near caused it to slide open, revealing a larger living chamber. A single table with two benches stood in the center. To the right I saw what appeared to be a kitchenette, to the left a sitting area with a large leather sofa. The book had been one thing, a leather sofa altogether another. I stepped near and ran my hands along the smooth, dark-brown surface. A window stood beyond the sofa, and I forgot entirely about what my hands touched.

Beyond the window, the blinding core shone far below. Above, giant broken stalactites reached down from the bottom of our shell toward the world's center like the teeth of some horrific monster. Each hung like a pillar, massive in girth, and disappeared at the top into the broken, solid landmass floating in the heavens. In the distance, another, smaller shell orbited. This close to the core, several similarly sized shells orbited in proximity to each other. Ours was one of the lowest. Far above lay much larger shells, some filled with large populations of people. I stepped around the sofa toward the glass, stunned at the beauty our broken world offered us.

"I see you enjoy the Queen's view," a quiet voice said from behind me.

My head spun, and shame for my intrusion colored my cheeks red. There stood a beautiful woman, red hair hanging straight down over one shoulder, blue-silver eyes on me, small red lips formed into a smile. She wore a rich, turquoise dress that clung close to her svelte form, sleeves reaching down to cover part of her hands, collar cut to accentuate her neckline and adorned with a thick, intricate embroidery. At her waist, she'd cinched a simple yet elegant silver belt covered in intricate symbols etched into the precious metal. A thin line of embroidery reached down the dress from both shoulders, highlighting her shape as it ended at the bottom of the gown. One of her thin eyebrows arched slightly.

"Nothing to say?" she asked.

I coughed and bowed my head, eyes darting to the belt. "Forgive my intrusion, High One. The door opened, and I assumed the Queen meant for me to enter."

"Yes, she did, or you wouldn't be here," the woman said, moving around the room to join me by the window. "Are you enjoying the view?"

I looked back outside to avoid staring at the newly arrived woman. "Yes, it's amazing what beauty this shattered world offers us now."

The woman let out a long breath. "Yes, it is."

I looked over at her to find the woman staring out the window, her eyes moist. She blinked, and a tear fell down her cheek. A thousand questions came to mind. What did she see out that window that made her feel that way? I looked again at the shell orbiting. Later I learned that something did happen on that landmass. And more happened farther down in the core. But at that moment, I simply pondered the possibilities.

"My name is Logwyn," I stated, eyes still on the shell below us.

"Micaela."

"Pleased to meet you, High One."

"Don't call me that." Her tone drew my gaze, and I found her blue-silver eyes locked on mine. "Please."

"Yes, Micaela."

"So formal," she muttered, dropping her hand and looking around the room. "Why?"

I looked down at her belt. "That is a rare item. Silver is hard to find these days, as are other precious metals. To have so much in a single piece is something usually only seen among High Ones." I nodded at the door behind me. "Those that comport with the Queen."

"It's been in my possession for a long time, and in my family's even longer." She moved near the leather couch. "I've always loved this piece."

"You've been here before?"

Micaela nodded. "On several occasions. My duties keep me away, but I visit whenever possible."

"Did you wait long?" I asked, thinking of my delay to look at the book in the foyer.

"No, the Queen sent for me recently, and I'd only just arrived," the woman said, moving to sit on the sofa. "Please, join me."

Easing myself onto the priceless piece of furniture, a small part of my mind wondered if the Queen had fabricated it, too.

"Did she mention the reason for her summoning you?"

The woman shook her head. "I just arrived," she said, lowering her voice, her eyes darting about. "She's a bit paranoid about certain things."

A glance around the room revealed a lack of any Ancient technology. "Yes, the network."

Micaela arched an eyebrow, tilting her head as she did. "A bit more than just the network, but that'll wait till later." She looked at my sack. "That's an odd thing to see one of you carrying around."

My hand gripped my travel sack tight. "They have their use."

"Agreed," Micaela said, smiling. "But as most of you tend to stay in your blessed form."

My eyes dropped to the floor, hands shifting to the edge of my sack.

"How long has it been since you tried?" Micaela asked. When I looked up at her, my brow furrowed, she went on. "The blessing. How long since you tried to take the form?"

"Fifteen cycles, High One." My mind wandered off. She frowned at the moniker but didn't say anything, so I continued. "There's been no reason to try again."

"Not once?"

I shook my head. "I failed and missed the blessing. Seems pointless to try again or pine over it. Not all of us are that lucky."

Her silence drew my attention. She sat there, eyes locked on me, a frown on her face.

"Did my words offend you, High One?" I asked, bowing my head.

"Besides your refusal to call me by name? No, they're just confusing." Micaela waved a hand at me. "My apologies, you don't want to talk about it." Her eyes narrowed as she looked out the window. "It's just a different way of thinking."

Another moment of silence followed. I shifted the sack and felt the mysterious box move inside. My mouth opened to speak, but then I pursed my lips, uncertain of how to proceed.

"Out with it," Micaela said, her eyes turned back to me. "I know a question when I see one."

"I'm not sure where to begin" I admitted, putting on my best smile in hopes of hiding my nervousness.

"The beginning?" she offered.

I nodded at her. "Okay, it starts with a Nomad sending me to talk to the Queen."

I recounted the events of that day to her. She listened in silence, nodding once or twice, eyes never leaving me. When I finished, she tapped her lips.

"The Queen is right about Suyef," she said after a moment. "You can trust him." She pointed at my sack. "As to that item, you can leave that where it is. I don't need to see it."

"But do you know where the rest is?"

"I know where one part is. Well, I suspect I know." She shook her head. "But the other. Let's just say if it's where I fear it is, it will cause problems."

I frowned. "And where is that?"

"In the hands of an insane man." She looked toward the window.

I watched her for a moment, then placed a hand on the pack.

"The Queen thinks you can help me find those pieces," I said.

"I suspect there's more coming," she replied.

I nodded. "She believes those pieces are the key to saving the network."

"Yes, she's been hinting at such a problem." She glanced at me. "And she thinks you can help. Why?"

I shrugged. "I'm just a scribe. I study people and their stories. She believes you have the answer."

"My story?" She glanced over my shoulder toward the foyer. She scrunched her nose slightly. "It's not a tale I like to tell." She spied my hands gripping the edge of my pack. "You've got what you need to hear my story tucked away in that sack of yours."

There didn't seem to be any point in hiding that fact, so I pulled the padd out. I placed it between us and activated the recording software.

"It's unclear what we're supposed to be recording, but the Queen did seem adamant it happen."

Micaela smiled. "She usually is when she sets her mind to something." She looked at the padd. "So, just talk? Now?"

I waved her on. "By all means."

The woman nodded, her eyes wandering back to the window. My back began to hurt, and shifting on the sofa didn't help. Micaela noticed and nodded at the table.

"Would you be more comfortable there?"

I glanced at the table and fingered my sack. "Maybe."

Soon, we sat across from each other at what turned out to be a solid-wood table. My hands ran along the surface, marveling at the feel.

"You don't see much wood around here," Micaela stated with a smile, eyes twinkling.

"It's so rare these days," I whispered. "Trees vanished long ago, you know. The fact that some of this still exists is amazing. This must have cost the Queen a fortune."

Micaela nodded, looking down at the table. "You have no idea," she whispered.

My eyebrow arched.

She smirked and shook her head. "Where were we?" she asked, waving a hand at my padd on the table.

"The network. The two remaining pieces."

"Perspective," Micaela muttered.

"Mine?"

She nodded. "Outside perspective. You said you're a scribe?" It was my turn to nod. "So, outside perspective coupled with a curious mind used to noticing details."

I frowned and looked down at the padd. "She gave me some other names along with yours."

"I'll bet she did," Micaela stated, running a flat hand across the table. "One is Quentin, yes?"

The fact that she knew his name surprised me, but it shouldn't have. It stood to reason that if the pair of them knew about the missing pieces, they'd know each other. Just how well they knew each other I didn't suspect at the time.

I nodded. "And Suyef. And a strange name."

"Nidfar," Micaela said, arching an eyebrow.

"Clearly you all know each other," I said.

"Inseparable, in some ways." Her gaze hardened. "Sometimes painfully inseparable."

"Like with Nidfar?" I ventured a guess.

"No, he's just a nuisance. And he will prove the hardest to find. He's a crazy old loon who vanished on . . . well, let's just say he disappeared. And at an inconvenient time, all things considered."

"Do you have any idea where I can find him?" I asked.

She nodded. "One of his towers on Colberra or the Nomad shell."

"And Quentin? Is he an 'inseparable' friend?"

"He was once. Now I don't know anymore." She looked away. "I suppose that foolish man is still a friend. A close one at that. Only those closest to you can hurt you so much."

"Do you know where he is?" I asked.

Her head moved up and down, very slowly. A tremor of emotion broke through her clearly practiced calm.

"But you aren't going to tell me where he is?" I asked.

"Where he is isn't your problem when it comes to Quentin," she stated. "It's the fact that in his current state, he's all but useless."

"And what state is that?"

"He's dead," she whispered.

I frowned again. "How am I supposed to talk to someone who's dead?"

She continued speaking in a whisper. "Well, as good as dead."

My head cocked to one side, but I held my tongue.

She arched an eyebrow. "Confused yet, dear scribe?"

I nodded.

"My part in this story I can tell you, but for his part, there is only one person who you might find answers in. Suyef. If anyone knows where Quentin is or if he's even still alive at this point, it's him."

"Where might he be found?"

"Probably on the Nomad shell." She looked over at me "Have you ever been there?"

"No, but I've always wanted to go see it. We have an interesting relationship with them, our society." I pointed up. "They're really the only of the other people in this world we speak to at all."

She nodded. "Yes, a distant connection in the past, I believe."

"The Nomads claim a direct descendance from the Ancients, which our society does as well." I shrugged. "Theirs is less solid, but it's there."

"They're a secretive people, but honorable. They distrust my people, the Colberrans, but that's to be understood considering their history." Micaela smiled. "Did he wear those silly robes again?"

I nodded. "Said they were a disguise."

"More like a crutch." Her head tilted to one side. "Still, if he's wearing them, that means he came from Colberra to here."

"Is that important?" I asked.

She shrugged. "Maybe. It could mean Quentin is doing better or that he's finally gone. I don't know anymore." She let out a long breath. "I don't see those two that much anymore. And no one has seen even a whisper of Nidfar in nearly half a cycle."

"Why not?"

"Time. Disagreements. Many reasons." She focused on me. "None of which help you start this quest of yours."

"I disagree." I pointed toward the Queen's cave. "She thinks all four of you know something about the missing pieces. So, start there. Tell me about how you met."

She leveled a questioning look at me.

"I like to take my own notes."

She fell back into silence with me waiting, not looking at her out of respect. After a moment, she nodded and sat upright.

"How we met," she said. "That's not a short tale. But if the Queen believes the answer to her puzzle is in it and you want to hear it, well, here it is." She paused, a finger tapping the table, lips pursed in thought. "This is the story of how I met Quentin and Suyef. And how my world ended."

CHAPTER 4

THE ILLNESS

I guess this story begins with a question: When did I lose hope? It's not something most people think about. Can you think of a time when you had hope, then started losing it? Can you quantify it? Well, I know when it started to fade.

My family lived on the outer edge of the Colberra shell. My father and mother both worked in the one industry that mattered: water extraction. As they made their home in what is called the Outer Dominances, water came at a premium and people with my parents' skill more so. Sure, the outpost had a water station connected to the shell's water network, but that had proven unreliable in recent cycles. Even before my parents moved to the outpost, the water supply from the network had begun to dwindle. Not in a noticeable amount at first, mind you. Most people would not have noticed the drop in output, but my father discovered it soon after he and my mother moved there.

See, my father had a particular knack for technology. We never understood where it came from, but he could make the network systems do things no one else could. He was very quiet about it, as it wasn't good to flaunt such abilities. You never knew when the Seekers, our shell's police force, might take offense or get suspicious. So, he kept it to himself. I remember asking my mother about it, and she just shrugged.

"He's always been that way, dear," she said in answer to my question, when I was about ten. "Something between him and those machines, it just works."

I tried pushing him for an explanation of how he did it, and he'd just smile, rub my head, and send me off to study. I persisted one day, and the look in his eyes still haunts me. They were empty, hollow, staring right through me. He sat like that for a long moment, then blinked and looked away. I swear he wiped a tear away. He just waved me off, telling me the answer lay in my studies.

So, I studied, but not the normal stuff like arithmetic, reading, science, or history. We did those, too. No, my siblings and I learned the code. The language of the machines. Dull, boring stuff. We would spend entire days just creating code on paper, forming constructs, learning symbols, and making sentence columns from them. My parents never ran out of the paper, even though we never figured out where they got it. One of my brothers, Donovan, insisted they just erased what we'd been working on the day before and reused the same sheets. Seeing as we never saw our work again after completing it, he might have been right. All four of us—me, the eldest, down to the youngest, my sister, Jyen. We all learned the code.

We learned other things, too. My father, he could find things in the network most people couldn't. That included some things from history most people don't know. Early on, it became apparent I'd inherited my father's knack for working with the network. Maybe it came from all those chrons drawing code on paper; I'm not sure. Soon, my father began giving me coding projects, having me create programs inside safe working environments he called sandboxes. Many a happy afternoon was spent making simple programs to do useless things on a side section of giant touch screens we called terminals. We even made games for Maryn, my other brother, and

Jyen to play on the rare occasion my father allowed them near a terminal.

Yes, we were a happy family. Then the illness came.

Most people didn't realize they had caught the disease. The symptoms were subtle, often mistaken for some other illness. Muscle weakness, fatigue, cramps were just the start. Later came the headaches and eventually the seizures. Vomiting followed soon after. Near the end, eye control weakened, the stomach began to bulge, and most bodily functions shut down. By the time most realized the truth, it was too late. Not that knowing sooner would have helped. It was an old plague, one from the time of the Ancients. Some say it was the plague that wiped out the Ancients. Others say they made it themselves to limit the population after the Splitting. I didn't know if I believed that, but I did know we'd never found a cure for it.

There was no pattern, no way of figuring out who would be next. It didn't come all of a sudden, like the plague. It was slow. At first, no one really noticed anything was amiss. Little old Marie, a kindhearted lady who lived up the street from us, caught it first. Walking past her house, we could always smell fresh bread baking in her convection oven. Then it stopped, and we knew it was serious. Before you knew what to think, she was gone. We had no proof she died, but everyone assumed she did. One day, her house stood empty, and her only relative in the town refused to discuss it. There were rumors, though.

You must understand that paranoia dominated the people's emotions in that part of the shell. They believed the government ruling the Central Dominance in Colberra Citadel was after them. They were a very isolated sort, and they liked it. It was true all along the Outer Dominances. For cycles, the central government had been trying to find ways to get the people to give up living in these regions. At least, that's what the people out there would tell you. My father had his own opinions about the issue, but he kept those to himself. He didn't do it out of fear of the people, but because he feared the Seekers. Who didn't?

When the illness began, that was when we first saw them. Seekers, come from the Central Dominance. You could spot them anywhere. Long, silvery-colored cloaks, billowing in the wind as they strode through the streets. The empty streets. No one got in the way of a Seeker, because those that did often disappeared. People said Seekers didn't come out to the provinces unless trouble was starting. Some said trouble started when the Seekers showed up. All I know is they came when the illness did.

At first, we ignored them. As long as people stayed out of their way, the Seekers left the people alone. As much as the residents disliked having them there, they knew better. Seekers were the hand of the government, the power behind the force that governed the shell, and the most elite fighting force in the history of Colberra.

Established centuries before almost as soon as the history records on our shell began, the Seekers originally served one purpose: to protect the citizens from the Wilds, a vast region to the west of where I grew up that had nearly been destroyed by a collision with another shell. The Seekers, wearing bright silver robes to help them stand out in the wilderness region, were established to go into the Wilds and seek out survivors. After some time had passed, they become a glorified border-protection organization, a role that chafed at their leadership. They lobbied for a new role in society, and the Central Dominance obliged, transforming them into a military and police arm of the government. They became the law and could change it as they saw fit. Most of the time, they enforced established rules, as written by the Central Dominance. Sometimes the Seekers would bend those rules to their own liking and benefit. When someone threatened the peace of the land,

Seekers came. When disaster or disease struck, Seekers came. And when they came, everyone got out of the way.

We could only stay out of the way so long. As the illness spread, people began to get nervous. Even with their reputation, or maybe because of it, people in the Outer Dominances distrusted most things from the central city-state. The Seekers were no exception to this distrust. Rumors spread that the Seekers had brought the illness with them, that they spread it on purpose, that the Central Dominance was trying harder to get the people to leave.

My father thought they were all wrong. He didn't share what he believed, but I could tell he didn't like the way they talked. Soon, we weren't allowed to leave the house. At first, we thought it was to keep us out of the way of the Seekers. Now I think it was to keep us away from the people.

Either way, it didn't work. The illness was spreading. No one knew what was causing it, and the Seekers weren't very forthcoming with details. Somcone would get ill, and they'd disappear. It became clear to us very quickly the Seekers were there to contain the illness. Well, it became clear to me. My father was skeptical, but he always encouraged us to think things through.

"Why else would they be here?" I asked one evening as we sat to dinner. "Old Marie got sick, everyone knows that much. Then she was gone. The Seekers didn't come until after she got sick. But no one remembers if they showed up before Marie disappeared or not."

"I'm not saying you're wrong, my sweet." My father took a sip of water and pointed at me. "But I'm not saying you're right, either."

Normally, we would go on like this for a while, him encouraging me to think through to a conclusion. Not that night. His mind was somewhere else.

The next morning, my sister Jyen was dizzy and unable to stand up. She complained of a headache. Then she began to vomit. At first, she just couldn't keep any food down; soon she began to dry heave. It went on for a couple days. My mother insisted it had nothing to do with the disease. There were no rumors of vomiting going around the settlement. Still, they kept my sister isolated. You can never be too careful with Seekers.

Her condition worsened. Jyen needed a doctor, but we couldn't take her to one. If we sent for one, the Seekers would get wind of it. We took turns caring for her. If it was contagious, my mother argued, it was too late. I remember sitting in her bedroom, holding her head in my lap, a damp washcloth in hand, massaging her forehead. She asked me to tell her stories, so I did. Every story I could think of, silly ones to make her laugh.

One morning, about a week later, someone knocked at our door. My father answered it, and the look on his face told us all who it was. I ran up the stairs and into my sister's room, where she lay sound asleep. It was the first time she'd really slept since the illness came. My mother sat by her bedside, a finger brushing at her hair.

"She's through it now," she said, a slight smile touching the corners of her mouth.

I tried to say something, to warn her, but my father grabbed me from behind. I kicked and pulled, twisting to get away. A Seeker strode past, silvery cloak billowing around him. He wore a spectacle device across his eyes, the sun glinting on the screen as he entered the room. He approached the bed where my mother sat.

"Mom!" My voice was hoarse. "Mom, don't let them take her."

She just stood and moved away. My father held me despite my struggling to get free, to go to my sister. He wrapped his arms around me. The Seeker stood over Jyen's quiet form for a moment, voice murmuring just quietly enough that we couldn't hear what he said. Something beeped, and I saw a line of blue light scan over her body. After that, he turned to look at my father. He said nothing, but my father stumbled just a bit. He pulled me back out of the room, my mother following behind.

"No!" I screamed, kicking at my father, clawing at his face. "No, they can't take her! She's better now! Mom, please. Please make this stop. Please!"

She just stared at me, her eyes blank. She moved slowly, head tilted to one side, mouth hanging open. That stilled me. The look on her face. No tears, no audible cries. The silent cry of a mother who has lost a child.

They took Jyen that day. They gave us the name of a hospital in the central district she would be taken to, along with instructions for applying for travel papers. Those papers never came. We never saw her again.

My mother was never the same. Something inside her died that day. My father did his best to take care of us, but he seemed lost, distracted. I remember walking into the kitchen to find him standing over the cooking glass, staring at the wall. Whatever he had been preparing lay ruined, the smell filling the house and drawing my attention. So, I took over some things. That's the day life asked me to grow up. We needed a mother, so that became my role.

My brothers, thankfully, didn't seem to mind me doing that. Maryn, the youngest, was seven cycles old, Donovan, the next oldest, two cycles my younger. We all grew up a lot that season.

My father finally returned to his work, although he spent less time away from the house. My mother still mourned, he told the citizens. We all had no desire to go out after the Seekers took my sister. Donovan suspected someone had ratted on us and brought the Seekers to take her. Trying to reason with him was no use, as he became very stubborn and angry. He never said anything where Maryn could hear. My only hope lay in my father talking some sense into him, but he would just grunt and go back to work whenever I mentioned it.

So, we lived, a sad, broken family trying to put things back together. Each day left me more tired than the last, filling me with dread of what the next day might bring.

One day, my mother stopped eating. Nothing we did could convince her to eat. She would sip water, so I tried making a broth for her. She just turned her head away and rolled over, ignoring my pleas to eat. Soon, getting her to drink water became a chore. And the fits began. She would just scream, howling cries that echoed through the house. Sometimes my ears convinced me my sister's name was in those cries.

My father and I tried to calm her. Donovan did his part and kept Maryn away from her. When a fit came on, he'd gather our younger brother up, and they'd vanish out the door. Still, Maryn knew something was wrong. We all did. We begged my father to find some help for her, but he refused. The Seekers would come take her for sure, he insisted.

A week after the fits began, his fear came true. The Seekers took my mother away.

I held up a hand and Micaela paused.

"Was she actually sick?"

She shrugged. "Who knows? It didn't matter to them. Something was wrong with her, so they took her away."

"Didn't the people in the settlement do anything?"

She chuckled softly. "Those people. They're all talk." She leaned forward, pointing a finger at me. "They claimed to be frontier types, rugged, tough, not needing the trappings of civilization to survive." She smacked her hand down on the table. "Hypocrites! All of them. As soon as the Seekers showed up, they all got in line and bowed their heads. Not one dared stand up to the Central Dominance, not openly. They were all talk."

She stopped speaking, breath racing through her nose as she stared off toward the window.

"Did they tell the Seekers about her?"

She shrugged. "Probably. Who knows how they knew? Those buildings had thick walls. You couldn't hear her outside." She closed her eyes and sank down in her chair. Her shoulders slumped forward. "They heard her that day, though."

Her screams echoed throughout the streets as they left. Maryn and Donovan spent the day out of the settlement. Feeling helpless, I went to find them and wandered the desert. A small canyon, a gully hollowed out by the wind near a tall rock outcropping, opened up before me after much walking. From atop the formation, I could see for leagues, from the central mountains in the north to the edge of the shell to the south. I sat there for chrons, watching the core-light reflect off the distant water shield protecting us from space overhead. That shell orbits higher than any other does, so we can see the water shield. My mind wandered, pretending it could see the surface in detail, imagining waves crashing down on the surface. I pondered what it must be like to sail along the water, as legends told the ancient world had done.

Not anymore. Humanity didn't have boats. And I had no mother. In that moment, I felt more alone than ever, and my heart broke under the weight of it. I curled myself into a ball and wept. The tears flowed until there were none left and I just lay there.

Eventually something clicked in my head. Maybe it was the thought of my brothers looking for me. Maybe the thought of my father and how he must feel. To this day, I'm not sure what it was, but one thing was certain: they needed me.

So, I dragged myself down from that rock and made my way home. My brothers had returned from the desert. Maryn sat weeping in a corner, Donovan standing over him. My father sat nearby, head in hands. My family, or what was left of it.

In that moment, yes, I could have quantified hope. Three. Three people was all the hope left to me. Yet even that was fading. I knew if any more of my family was taken, hope would not last.

Little did I know how much I would lose.

CHAPTER 5

WRONG QUESTION

After that, my father became very distrustful of the network. As much as he loved the system, he became more and more suspicious that someone was using it to monitor everyone. He had no proof, try as he might to find any, but that didn't stop him from acting. Soon after they took my mother, he woke me up in the dead of night, told me to pack my belongings and get ready to leave. I stumbled around in the dark, cramming everything necessary into one bag before leaving to check on my brothers. We all met, bleary-eyed and blinking in the hallway, bags in hand.

My father led us out of the house into the night. The dim core-light reflecting off the water gave us means to see, but just barely through the night shield. We slipped from the settlement into the desert, my father refusing to tell us where we were going, just grunting and continuing to move. We traveled for a long time, but one thing was clear: we moved in circles, the settlement always to our left. Just when the night shield was about to lift and the full core-light return, my father stopped walking. On the last circuit, we'd moved closer to the settlement, and now we stood, quiet as the night, backs pressed against the smooth wall of the settlement's primary water control station.

Most people avoided the structure standing along the settlement's northern edge. Reaching twice as high into the sky as the settlement buildings, a Seeker outpost stood adjacent. Why we were here, only my father knew. After several moments at that wall, my father motioned us to wait and moved toward the entrance. A single door granted access into the tower on the settlement side of the building. We waited, straining our ears for any sounds.

My father returned moments later, padding along in soft-soled shoes. A breath I hadn't realized I was holding slipped out. He waved at us to follow, then slipped back toward the entrance. We made our way into the structure, and the door slid shut behind us, its outline almost disappearing into the wall. The main floor of the control station held a single large network touch screen. The translucent panel stood before me, facing away toward a chair. Beyond the terminal, a set of stairs spiraled up to the second floor. The Ancients that designed the stations long ago had lacked imagination. We would find the equivalent to living quarters: kitchenette, washroom, and several sleeping quarters on the floor above that. They meant the station to be self-sustaining, as it was much older than the settlement and meant to stand alone.

My father held a finger over his mouth, then nodded toward the stairs. All of us ascended to the second level, where my father touched a panel, closing a door hidden in the floor.

"We'll be safe here," he said. "Micaela, figure out what supplies we have. Donovan, get Maryn settled in a bed. He looks dead on his feet. I need to think."

"Why are we safe here?" I asked, not moving. "Are we in trouble?"

My father shook his head. "No, not in trouble. Just safer here." He sighed. "No unwanted eyes."

The place looked sufficient, but drab and very simple. I couldn't put my finger on it, but Donovan saved me the trouble.

"No computers."

Looking around proved him correct. This had to be the first room I could recall that didn't have a network access panel of some kind.

My father nodded. "And a little privacy to boot. Get to it."

We settled in to the water control station. My father made appearances of returning to the house over the coming few weeks. When asked how long we would have to stay in the control station, he would say, "Until the eyes go away." I pressed him for some meaning, but he never offered more than that.

A routine of sorts took over our lives. We'd start each day with our lessons, but my father would interrupt Donovan and me—one of us in the morning, the other in the afternoon—to help him with a problem. Beyond these occasions, he forbade us going near the network station, a point of contention between him and me, you can imagine. That machine held a special draw for me, so full of knowledge and possibility. Still, he insisted, and despite my disappointment, I acquiesced to keep things calm. When my turn would come, however, I would leap at a chance to be near the terminal, even if for but a moment.

It was then that my father gave us a puzzle to solve. When we pressed him for details, he simply stated that the survival of our settlement could very well depend on it. Father would show us data, information that was related, but he couldn't tell us how because at the time he didn't know. He'd let us look for as long as we needed, then take us away. Each evening, as we ate, he would ask us what we learned from the information.

"Honestly, I'm having a hard time seeing a connection," Donovan said at dinner one evening. "A little context would help."

My father just sat there, eating in silence. Donovan shrugged and looked at me. I decided to try a different tack.

"Maybe if you told us why you want us to look at the data, Father." He paused to contemplate my statement. "We just want to help, and to do that we need a little nudge."

"I already told you that all our lives depend on that information," he stated, and returned to his meal. "I'm wary to tell you more because anything beyond what I've already told you is conjecture and I don't want to twist your perspective."

I pondered his words, shuffling the data in my head. "Water?"

He smiled, a small act just touching one side of his mouth. It was the first time he'd done so in weeks.

"Bingo. Now you have your context. Now, take that and piece it together with what you've learned and see what you come up with." He pushed his plate away and stood up. "I've got a bit more work. Chores before anything else."

He left us and returned to the workroom below.

"Nice guess," Donovan whispered.

"It wasn't a guess. It's the only answer to his clue."

Donovan frowned. "Still doesn't help me with those numbers."

"Me, either." I spooned a bit of soup into my mouth, hardly noticing the taste. "But there's something there. Why else put us to it?"

Donovan shrugged. "He may not be right in the head. There may be nothing to what he's showing us."

I glanced at our younger sibling eating at the end of the table and glared at Donovan. Maryn seemed oblivious to the dinner topic.

"He may be sad, but Father's just as sharp now as he's ever been," I retorted.

"Calm down, sis. I didn't mean anything by it." Donovan glanced at Maryn. "But he has been acting odd. Moving us here, for example."

"He's scared. We all are."

Donovan nodded. "But he's the adult. He's supposed to set the example."

"He's doing the best he can. He just lost his wife and daughter. You think you feel bad; imagine how he must feel."

Maryn looked up from his food. "I miss Mommy."

That ended our conversation. Donovan cleared the table while I took Maryn and put him to bed. I went to my room, one of the three in the building, and lay down myself. I stared at the wall for chrons, contemplating numbers, water, and my mother. Just as sleep began to take hold, it struck me.

I pushed myself out of bed and went downstairs. My father sat at the network screen, staring at a large data set. The now-familiar script of the computer screen dominated the panel from one side to the other.

"A thought, my dear?" my father asked, not taking his eyes from the panel.

"Someone's stealing our water."

My father stopped what he was doing and turned to look at me. "Explain."

So, I did. He brought up the numbers and listened to why I thought it referred to our water. I extrapolated the data out to the potential conclusion.

"The only thing I don't get is, why?"

"I can think of only one reason someone would want to steal our water," he said.

I shrugged. "Forcing us all to leave?"

He raised one eyebrow.

"They want us to die?" I asked.

This time he shrugged. "Either one is a good reason, assuming they're doing it on purpose. They could simply not know it's happening."

"Or they do, and they can't stop it?"

He nodded. "Also possible. Or they do, but they have to do it. The point is, there are a lot of reasons why it could be happening.

But whatever the reason, we're still confronted with a dire situation. Especially if it's who I fear it is."

"And who is that?" I asked.

"The only people that stand to benefit from us not leeching their water," he said, pointing toward the north wall of the room.

I frowned. "But why would the Central Dominance want us to run out of water?"

"They aren't the only one that benefits."

I looked over at him. "Seekers?"

He nodded. "The less of us out on the edge, the easier they can control us."

"But they already dominate the shell. Why would they need us to leave the outer edge? What threat are we?"

He nodded at the panel. "Access to this, for one."

"Don't they have access to the network in Colberra City?" I asked.

"Yes, but only panels hardwired into the water system can bypass the controls the Seekers and the Central Dominance place on the network."

"So, why not just force us to leave?" I nodded at the panel. "They could easily overwhelm us if this thing is a security risk to them."

He chuckled. "You forget the politicians. While they may agree with the Seekers, they have elections to worry about. The populace of the Central Dominance may not be as independent thinking as those of us out here on the edge, but they understand unfair treatment when they see it." He held up his hands. "That's the only reason I can come up with for their lack of action."

I nodded. "How long do we have?"

My father sighed, rubbing a hand over his face. "It's hard to tell from here. Cycles, possibly, unless the rate of decline suddenly accelerates."

"The data shows it's been steady for cycles now," I said, pointing at the panel.

He raised his eyebrows and pursed his lips in thought. "And that leads us back to why. If the decline's intentional, it's been at this rate to hide it. If it's not, then who knows why the rate's been consistent. Whatever the cause, we need to assume the rate can suddenly change."

"What do we do?"

He smiled, another small one, gone in an instant, but I did see it. "We find a way to steal it back."

So, we set to it. Over the coming weeks, we worked together to break apart the network coding and figure out how it worked. I say "we," but the lion's share fell to him, as he understood the system better. He kept me there for a set of fresh eyes on the rare occasion when he got stuck. I didn't complain, as it let me near the network, even if vicariously.

Donovan took to keeping Maryn out of our hair. The two of them became almost inseparable up in the water tower. Once the Seekers lost interest in our settlement's supposed outbreak and left, my father let us leave the station. The two of them would escape into the desert for chrons on end. I chose to stay with my father. The work helped me not think of those lost to us, during the day, at least. Nights were a different matter, involving many tears and no sleep. It was the only time for tears. The rest of the time, my family needed a strong face. Well, it seemed they did.

Several weeks later, my father cried out in surprise. Lying on the cold floor behind him, I had just closed my eyes, the code dancing in my mind from all the time spent staring at it. He stood partway, hands raised overhead.

"I think I've done it!" he said, waving me over and sitting back down.

I scrambled to my feet. My father highlighted the bit of coding we'd wrapped our brains around for the past three days.

"The control code?"

"No, that proved impossible to alter, as you said," he answered, nodding at me. "So, I tried something else. This is how the system determines how much water is needed at each control point." He nodded again.

Understanding came over me like a flame lit anew. "You tricked the algorithm into thinking we need more?"

He smiled. "Better. Keep going."

I went back to the coding, following each line back to its connection to the main control code. Then I saw it.

"Here." My finger hovered over a symbol joining one random code line I'd passed over at first. "This is a connecting symbol." I tapped the new column of symbols. "And that line is code for another control point." My father raised one eyebrow but remained silent. "But we're the end of the line. Why does this have another control point beyond us?"

He just sat there, not answering. I stared, then looked back at the code. "Oh, brilliant, Father. You tricked the system into thinking there's another control station beyond us that needs more. Not much, as we don't want it to stand out."

"Exactly." His grin split his face open.

"So, what do we do with the extra water?" I asked.

"For now, nothing." He used his fingers to grab a different section of code and pull it to the front. "My calculations show that even with the new water rations, it will take close to a cycle before our storage tanks are back to what they were before the decrease began."

"And what then?" I looked down at him, one eyebrow cocked.

He shrugged. "Either we find some new storage, or we adjust the rate again."

A map of the settlement appeared at a touch of my finger. "New storage won't be easy to hide." I pointed at the four main tanks distributed around the settlement, each branching out from one main line that left the control station. "Those are the largest structures around. If we add another, someone is bound to notice."

The screen went clear. My father's hand lifted from the only button on the desk before him, the control switch.

"That's a problem for another day," he said, standing. "Go. The core won't dim for several chrons. You need some light."

I stood, staring at the translucent screen. "Father, what you just did. I've never seen such complicated coding." He nodded once. "You've been teaching me the code for cycles, but I only barely grasp it."

"Don't sell yourself short, my dear," he said, leaning close and placing a hand on my shoulder. "You've got just as much of a knack for this code as me. Don't neglect the connecting symbols. Where they go and what they are play a key role."

I stuck my tongue out at his reminder of my weakness in the language. "They don't teach this stuff in school," I pointed out. "Where did you learn how to do that?"

He met my gaze for a moment. His feet shuffled as he ran his thumb and forefinger through his black and white mustache.

"Let's just say I had a good teacher."

"Out here?" I asked, not bothering to hide my doubt. "Where most people avoid using the network machines when they can?"

He contemplated me for a moment. "Just because you think we're alone doesn't mean we are." He held up his hand. "Now go. I need some time to myself."

My father never answered that question, and not for lack of effort on my part. I brought it up at every chance. Never where my brothers could hear, just in case he didn't want them to know. Surprising him with it didn't work, nor did dropping it in an otherwise normal conversation. Confronting him failed as well. He would just smile and change the subject.

One day, I managed to corner him. Anger twisted that conversation, as I insisted he stop hiding whatever he kept secret and opined that he didn't trust me. The look he gave me at those words—well, let's just say I never tried that line of reasoning again.

Still, something must have gotten through, because one day, instead of employing his normal evasive tricks, he turned the tables on me.

"You're asking the wrong question, Micaela," he said. "Stop focusing on a distant problem and focus on the one at hand. If we don't fix that one, the other one won't matter."

From then on, that was his response, one that infuriated me even more. I got so fed up with this answer one day, it drove me out to the desert. I stormed right out of the control station and, without realizing it, found myself out in the open, away from the settlement. I pulled my cloak scarf around my head and torso and stared up at the very same rock outcropping I'd come to before. The rock face looked to be glaring down at me, looming large overhead like the problem I now faced. And it seemed just as useless as my father was in figuring out a solution. I couldn't fathom at the time why he would insist on being so infuriating when it came to those questions. Considering what happened next, I suspect he knew what was coming. That someone had tipped him off and he was trying to catch me up to where he was in the problem without just handing me his answers. He wanted me to find them on my own. Still, at the time, it felt more maddening than helpful.

Glancing down from the rock face, I saw the gully below. Curiosity compelled me down, out of the ever-present wind. The rock face felt rough under my hand. Near my feet grew the only plants that managed to survive the desert: yucca and small cacti. The crevice extended several hundred meters in different directions, a spiderweb of stone hallways hidden from sight below the outcropping visible above. Keeping it in view, I made my way inside the crevice to the nearest point below the rock formation. There it ended in a wall of rock, forming a small circular alcove with a large stone surface jutting up from the middle of the floor.

To this day, I'm not sure what possessed me to do what I did next. Stepping near the stone jutting up from the floor, I unclasped the necklace given to me by my mother on my last birthday before she was taken. I placed the piece of jewelry on the center of the surface, rested my hand on it for a moment, my eyes closed, then turned and walked away. Inside, a small piece of me fell away, like a feather falling from a bird one might see in a zoo. It's not that my spirit felt lighter or happier. It just felt . . . different. Settled. Maybe a bit more complete.

That feeling ended when I returned to the control station.

"Why do I get the feeling another member of your family is about to vanish?" I asked, holding a hand up for Micaela to stop.

"Sensing a theme here, Logwyn?" Her voice took on a sour tone.

I stood up and stretched. "Who is it?"

"Guess."

I yawned, brushing some hair out of my face. "This is where you really grew up, isn't it?"

She nodded once, very slowly. Her eyes moved away, looking around the room.

"I suppose I already had. It's not like life gave me much of a choice." She looked back at me. "They needed me, so I stepped in."

I looked at her, but my mind wandered to the Queen. Someone else who'd been given no choice.

"I see why you are friends with the Queen."

She smirked a bit. "The Queen has no friends. Just people she tolerates." The smile faded. "What friends she did have left her long ago."

I moved back to my seat. "The control station?"

When the door slid open, I noticed several odd things. The network station stood empty. That was the first thing. Donovan sat on the floor beyond the chair. That was the second. Maryn was not with him. The third.

"Where's Father?" I asked, the door closing behind me.

Donovan just stared at the screen, not answering.

"Donovan?" I waved from behind the panel. Nothing. "Donovan?"

I moved around the panel to stand next to him. He just sat there, eyes locked on something. Following his gaze led me to a small flashing icon on the screen. I touched it with my finger, and my father's face appeared, dominating the room.

"If you're looking at this, someone has discovered us. Micaela, although I know better, I'm going to tell you this anyway. Forget your question. Forget the right question. Forget about all of it. Look after your brothers. They need you, now more than ever. Take care of each other. We will see each other again, I promise you that. I love you all."

His face vanished from the panel, which returned to the blinking icon. We waited in silence. After several moments, my brother managed one word.

"Seekers."

CHAPTER 6

TOO CLEVER

I must preface the next part of the story with this: usually, I listened to my father. This time, however, I did not; judging from his message, he knew I would not. I let it lie for a few days, more out of concern for my brothers than anything else. Donovan, after recovering from his initial shock, took to being very angry. Maryn became distraught and nearly unmanageable. Trips into the desert with Donovan seemed to be the only thing that would calm him.

Walks only sated Donovan's anger so much. Once back and with Maryn tucked away in his room, he would go down on the work station and begin searching. At first, I left him to it. However, after several days of him doing this, I began to grow suspicious of what he was doing. When I asked him, Donovan would mutter to himself and walk away. If I tried to peek at what he was doing, he would turn it off, changing to some mundane task we both knew he wasn't the slight bit interested in. Trying to find my way to what he was doing on the terminal proved frustrating. He may not have always enjoyed working on what my father had trained us to do, but Donovan had learned well enough to hide his work.

After several days of growing frustration, I cornered Donovan before he could escape with Maryn. Our brother slipped out the door, oblivious he was alone.

"What are you doing, Don?" I asked.

"Nothing!" he replied, and tried to go around me.

I put a hand on his chest. "Donovan, please. I just want to know what it is."

He tried to push past me. I held my ground, though, and he stopped. His jaw tightened, and he breathed hard through his nose. After another few moments, his body relaxed and he leaned away from my hand, which I let drop.

"I'm looking for Father, Mother, and Jyen," he whispered.

His voice lowered as he said the last name. I felt my heart skip and my face go numb.

"Donovan, she's gone," I whispered.

"And who told us that?" he asked, looking up at me. "Who took them away from us?"

"The Seekers, but that doesn't mean they lied," I said, knowing I didn't believe the words myself.

The glare returned as he puffed up his chest.

"Well," he stated, "until proven wrong, I'm not trusting the word of a Seeker."

After that, he stormed out. I didn't notice him on the station that evening, but I knew he would return to it. Once he got something in his mind, he didn't let go of it. I had other, more pressing things to worry about, but somehow I knew his search was going to come back to haunt me.

We also faced the predicament of whether we should stay in the control station. Donovan thought it would be best if we moved back to our house, an idea Maryn agreed with wholeheartedly. I was less sure. We agreed we couldn't continue living in the station, but I argued the house seemed even less secure. We remained at an impasse on this point for several nights before Maryn, of all people, stumbled on the solution.

We sat around the table, munching on a light meal. Maryn sat chattering about his day and the grand adventures he and his brother had gone on. I listened, sort of, preoccupied with the problem at hand, when something he said caught my attention.

"Wait, you went where?" I asked, interrupting his chattering.

"Which part?" He screwed his face in thought, trying to remember his words.

I searched my memory for his words. "Just before you battled the giant lizard dragon."

"We assaulted a guard tower protecting a secret tome," he said, grinning. "Donovan stunned the wizard, and I snuck the old book out the back door."

"Tower?" My eyes shifted to Donovan.

He furrowed his brow. "I think we were near one of the outlying water stations."

Maryn shook his head. "No, we were right under the giant pipe, remember? The lizard dragon used it to hide behind before he sprouted wings and took off."

"So, a relay station?" I looked between them, both nodding in answer. "And you got inside?"

Donovan shifted, spooning some pea soup into his mouth. Maryn grinned.

"Yep, Dono used all those pretty drawings you've been working on to make the panel slide right open," the youngest boasted, pointing at his older brother.

"You weren't supposed to tell her that part."

"I don't care how you got in. Just tell me what's inside and if anyone saw you." The two shared a look. "Now out with it."

"It looks like this place," Donovan said, looking around the facility. "Control level, second-floor living space, only two rooms above that instead of three and they're on separate floors." He shrugged, spooning some more soup into his mouth before adding, "It's taller than this one. So, it has two floors more than this station."

Maryn nodded, his eyes big and a smile splitting his face. "We climbed all the way to the top floor. That's where the wizard hid the tome. While Dono fought him, I stole the book so we could get out of there."

I arched one eyebrow at Donovan, a smile tickling at the corners of my mouth. He hunched over and concentrated on his almost-empty bowl.

"Can you remember which one you were at?" I asked.

Donovan nodded, looking up from his bowl. "You're not thinking of moving there, are you?"

I shrugged. "It's a possibility."

"That's pretty isolated," he countered, pointing a spoon at me. "If they came back, you'd be setting us out pretty far from any help."

"What help do you expect to get from these people?" I asked, pointing in the general direction of the settlement. "They move out of the way whenever the Seekers come."

Donovan opened his mouth to respond, then snapped it shut. The spoon remained pointed at me. "The settlement will see us," he said, dropping the spoon in his bowl.

I smiled. "So, we make ourselves invisible."

Pulling off that stunt proved far simpler than it sounded. The people only took notice if something changed. When we moved to the control station, people were bound to notice, because everyone notices what goes on around water stations, for good reason. Moving back out of the facility would get attention. We just needed to make it look like we were moving somewhere different.

We concocted our ingenious plan. Each day, Donovan and Maryn would continue their excursions into the desert. Every time they went out, they snuck a few supplies—water and nutrient packs, clothing, and medical kits. At some point during their day, they would stop by the relay station and stash our supplies in the upper chambers. Meanwhile, I returned to our house with obvious bundles designed to look like I carried more on the way to the house than on the return trip. In truth, unfolded blankets filled my pack, making it appear overstuffed. At the house, I refolded the blankets to be smaller and put some supplies and things from the house in to sneak back to the control station and out to the relay tower. While at the house, I made a point of going for some supplies in the settlement, taking them back to the house. Those, too, made their concealed trip to the relay station.

This ploy took a lot of time to pull off. All that while, I followed my father's warning. The problem we'd discovered remained untouched. At least, on the computers it did. My mind rarely focused on anything else beyond our smuggling operation. The same was true for Donovan and his search. We were so busy smuggling our stuff, I never saw him on the terminal in the water station. That didn't mean he wasn't busy out at our soon-to-be new home doing the same, but I couldn't control that. I just had to hope he was smart enough to not poke around in places he might get caught.

Several days later, Donovan, Maryn, and I gathered around the oval table for one last meal in the control station. Once done, we left the tower and returned to the house. Core-set, the time when the shield generated by the citadel surrounded the shell and provided us with an illusion of night, was still a chron or so off, and the citizens could not help but notice us. We made our way, loaded down with bedding and a few prized possessions, back to our home.

That night, we kept the windows closed and sealed against prying eyes. Just past core-set, we dimmed the lights and gathered in an upstairs room to watch the settlement. Here and there, lights in windows began to go out. Maryn curled up at my side, head on my lap. He soon fell asleep as my hand stroked his hair. Donovan stood leaning against a wall, arms crossed, his forehead creasing as his eyebrows furrowed.

"I'd ask what you're thinking, but I could probably guess," I whispered, running a finger over Maryn's forehead.

Donovan didn't answer but looked down at our brother before returning his gaze to the window. "You know I think this is your fault." I looked up and held his gaze, staying silent. "Well, yours and Father's."

"Which part?"

"Why we're forced to abandon another home." He nodded out the window. "Why we're standing here waiting for them to go to sleep. This predicament."

"How is it my fault?"

He turned his head back to me, eyes on mine. His jaw clenched, and after a moment, he looked away.

"You two just had to go meddling with things you didn't understand," he whispered.

"You're going to lecture me about meddling?" I retorted.

"The point is you were digging around with something you knew they had to be watching," he stated, waving a hand at me. "Just had to keep digging for an answer you didn't need."

"The problem we found is a lot more important than you think." I nodded out the window. "To all of them, too. Not that they know that, of course."

"And didn't you think about what might happen if someone noticed? Or hadn't you had enough of Seekers meddling in our lives?"

"Father was so secretive about it," I muttered, shifting to rest my back against the window frame and stretch my legs out across the window seat, Maryn sound asleep on my lap. "Is it that far of a stretch to assume he'd taken care to hide what he was doing?"

"Clearly, he didn't."

I glared at Donovan. "You could have said something to him instead of taking it out on me. Did you bother bringing up your little theory to him?"

"I tried." My brother scowled, crossing his arms over his chest and leaning against the far window frame. "He just hounded me for my answer to his question. You got further with that than I did."

"I beg to differ; you caught on that it was the water."

He shook his head. "You're remembering wrong. You guessed it was water, and you figured out the rest. The whole thing bothered me, and I tried to explain that to him, but he wouldn't listen."

"Donovan, you can't blame yourself. You shouldn't even blame him. Be mad at the Seekers."

"There's anger to share with them, too." He let out a long breath, the kind you do when you're trying to calm yourself. "Plenty for them." He turned his gaze to me. "But you two brought this one on us. Inadvertently, maybe, but you still did it."

"Blaming me for this isn't going to make it any better," I whispered, looking away from him and out the window. "Nor will it bring any of them back."

"They aren't coming back." He clenched a fist. "Unless we find them ourselves, they're gone forever."

He said it with such finality. A weight settled down on my soul, a statement of fact my heart didn't want to acknowledge. To distract myself, I tried to find something out the window to focus on in the dark settlement. I blinked, easing myself up.

"It's time."

All things considered, the actual act of sneaking out of the settlement to the outlying relay station proved uneventful. Moving under cover of core-night, we encountered no one as we made our silent way out into the desert. Maryn slept the entire way, carried on Donovan's back and tied on just to be safe. We carried no packs or anything that might reveal our intentions to the random person looking out a window at that chron. Not that we needed to have worried. The settlement slept soundly.

I'm sure they must have noticed we disappeared. Maybe that's what drew the Seekers back. Maybe it was Donovan's meddling, a point of contention between us as he persisted in pursuing his theory after we moved. Still, I had no proof it was his fault. To this day we never figured out who was to blame, if either of us. What I do know is that, for several days, we lived in that relay station, thinking ourselves very clever. Our supply gathering had been thorough, thanks to Donovan's foresight. He and Maryn continued to spend most of their time roaming the desert. Worry twisted at me that they might draw attention to us, enough so that one time I attempted to follow them. I lost them five minutes out of the station and stopped worrying. A little.

And what did I spend my time doing when caring for my two brothers didn't occupy me? I tried to resist the puzzle, to follow my father's last bit of advice to us. I couldn't do it, however. Arguing with myself over my actions, my reasons, trying to rationalize what needed to be done, only helped so much. Part of me said someone needed to make sure my father's program continued to operate and remain hidden from prying eyes. The settlement needed the water, after all. Part of me wanted to know who was doing it and why. Yet another part hoped the answer to where my father had been taken could be found.

So, searching the database occupied my attention during those days alone. I made sure my research remained hidden and diverse, hoping it might throw off any prying eyes. My research included everything from current events to folktales to cooking recipes. I got myself lost in the vast network of information, all the while trying to search for the necessary data. Research of current water usage got buried in historical reports on how the water system came to be. Events of modern interest in the Colberran main city swamped my work in hopes of discovering more about the Seekers and what they do. I brought up cultural studies of the Outer Dominances in order to study population and water-usage trends there. It was tedious work, and it had to be finished by the time my siblings returned.

Oh, I thought that was being clever. My work had to have remained hidden. Oh, how naive I was.

The Seekers returned less than a month after our move to the relay station. Inconveniently for me, they arrived during one of my trips back into the settlement. In order to at least hold off the citizens' curiosity about where we had gone, Donovan and I took turns every few days sneaking back during core-night to our old house and being seen doing business during the day. We never did figure out if it did any good, but we were young and full of our well-conceived plans.

One day, as I strolled back to our house, a sackful of food-stuffs on my arm, the telltale cloaks of the Seekers one street over greeted my eyes. I looked away and, once out of sight, hurried my pace. It was impossible to tell if they had seen me or not, nor was I even sure they were looking for me. Still, the risk was too great to take a chance on either. I rushed as discreetly as possible back to our house and, once inside, locked the door. Core-set was several chrons away. To keep from worrying, I busied myself cleaning dust off the furniture and re-situating my travel sack over and over. Cleaning enabled me to peek through the window sheers drawn closed throughout the house. My efforts to look outside revealed no sign of the Seekers. Gradually, as the day passed, I began to relax.

As core-set came and the settlement went to sleep, I made my way back out into the desert. To be safe, the route I chose left the village heading west, the central mountain range to my right, the edge of the shell to my left. I traveled almost a chron before doubling back around to the north. Even in the dim core-light, the water pipe dominated the skyline stretching from the mountains to the settlement. Once under it, I made my way along the pipe toward the relay station.

When I arrived, however, the Seekers were already there. I huddled near a rock outcropping, looking down at two of their mounts. Each of the long, thin, single-seat hover-bikes had a bulbous nose in front, with a swooping tail in the back. The machines floated a few feet off the ground just under the tower, their riders nowhere in sight. I stared down at the station at a complete loss as to what to do, when something large moved just over me. I rolled to my right, but something heavy leapt atop my body and pinned me on my back, an air-pulse gun aimed at my face. Beyond the weapon stood a Seeker, cloak shifting in the swirling desert winds, dark face mostly concealed behind a cowl.

"Do nothing sudden, and I won't have to discharge this and carry you," a calm, male voice said to me in an unrecognizable accent.

I nodded, and he moved off, allowing me to stand. He waved the gun toward the relay station, and we made our way there in silence. At his signal, I entered to find Donovan and Maryn sitting on the entry level against the wall to my right. Another Seeker stood guard over them, his white face also mostly concealed. My captor pointed, directing me to sit next to my siblings.

"Found her on the rise coming from the settlement," my captor muttered, stepping near his counterpart.

"Out a bit late, aren't we?" the second Seeker asked me. I kept silent. "Talks as much as these two. See anyone else?"

"No, she's the one our sensor picked up," my captor answered, shaking his head. "Been tracking her since she left."

I glanced at my brothers, and Maryn moved to sit in my lap. The Seekers ignored him.

"If we picked her up, you know the rest did," the second Seeker muttered. "They'll be coming our way soon."

My captor shrugged. "Or expecting us to bring her in." He pointed at Donovan and Maryn. "They won't be expecting them, though. Only what their sensor told them: a lone person sneaking off into the desert."

The second Seeker eyed my brothers, his blue eyes not moving from us. "If we take her in, they'll find out about these two soon enough."

I glanced at Donovan and mouthed the word *if.* He shrugged and nodded at the Seekers.

"If we stay out here too long, they'll start wondering anyway and come looking." My captor pointed at me. "She fits the description of the woman they're looking for." He nodded at my brothers. "And she has two siblings."

Unable to stay quiet, I asked, "Who's looking for me?"

The two Seekers stopped talking and looked at me, neither speaking at first. The second Seeker nodded at my captor and stepped forward. My captor left the building, leaving us alone with the other Seeker. He stepped nearer and squatted down before me.

"They're looking for you . . . Micaela, is it?" he asked, cocking his head to one side. I nodded in answer. "And I guess this is Donovan?" He waved at Maryn in my lap.

"I'm Donovan," my brother piped up from beside me.

"Oh, my apologies," the Seeker said, looking at my other brother. "So, you must be Maryn."

We all remained quiet, uncertain about what to do or say.

"As I was saying, the Seekers are technically looking for all three of you. They were quite bothered when they couldn't find you in the settlement." His eyes glanced at the ceiling. "Ingenious little place to hide. Maintenance crews won't be by here for another, what, quarter of a cycle?"

"They just came here a couple of weeks ago," Donovan said.

The Seeker looked at my brother. "Ah, so a half cycle." He looked back at me. "As I said, ingenious."

"Not nearly so, if you found us."

He chuckled under his cowl. "That was random chance." He nodded at Donovan. "Your siblings here led us on a wild hunt tracking them. My partner outside even had a bit of a challenge at some points, and that's saying something for him."

"Couldn't you just use your tracker to follow us?" Donovan asked.

The Seeker nodded. "Sure, but my partner doesn't like those machines. Avoids using them when he can." He shrugged and turned his gaze back to me. "He does what he wants. He's survived on this shell long enough to earn that much."

I opened my mouth to ask a question, then stopped. What did he mean, survived on this shell? I was about to ask, when the door opened and my captor returned.

"They're coming."

CHAPTER 7

HARD TRUTHS

"How much time?" the second Seeker asked.

"A matter of minutes." My captor exited, and the door closed.

"Right, we don't have much time." The second Seeker knelt before us. "I need to know one thing before the Seekers get here."

"You keep referring to them like you aren't one of them," I commented.

His eyebrows raised in unison, eyes locked on mine. "I'm not, but that's not important right now. What is important is who you are." He looked at each of us in turn. "Which one of you has been accessing the water-usage data on the network?"

Donovan tensed next to me but kept his mouth shut.

"I'll judge by your reaction you at least know what I'm talking about. Was it you?" he asked my brother. Donovan shook his head. "You?" He turned his gaze to me. I held my tongue. "Fine, keep your secret. From everyone. Don't trust any of the Seekers. They'll just as soon kill you as take you to join your father."

"What do you know about our father?" I asked.

"Enough to know he's probably the brains behind your little water-stealing program."

I shook my head. "We weren't stealing water. Someone is stealing it from us, and we were trying to stop it."

"Be that as it may, the Seekers coming don't agree with you." He looked over his shoulder as my captor came back inside, two fingers held up. The second Seeker nodded, then looked back at me. "Don't volunteer any information. And do your best to play along."

"You expect me just to lie to a bunch of Seekers?"

"Not lie. Equivocate. Dissemble. Dodge. Just avoid the truth."

I frowned. "That can't be as easy as you claim."

He reached out, patting me on the shoulder, and said, "Don't sell yourself short."

A chill rushed down my back at his words. My father's words. Words he'd been saying to me for cycles. I glanced at Donovan, who shook his head and shrugged.

The second Seeker stood up, made sure his cowl and hood remained in place, and then took a position standing over us. We all sat or stood for a moment before the door slid open and three more Seekers walked in, pulse guns drawn. They scanned the room; one signaled for the other two to search above as our captors stood watching. After a few moments, the two Seekers returned from their search, shaking their heads. The third Seeker stepped partway out of the door and signaled to someone outside.

Two more Seekers walked in, but only one drew my eyes. He stood a head taller than the rest, and his cloak, while the same silver as the others', had solid-black trim along the edges. The cowl covering his face was striped gold and black, and he had eyes of solid black, visible through a small cut in the cowl. When those fell on me, another shiver went up my spine. Only when he looked away did I start to breathe again.

"Ah, our two Off-shellers beat you here, Squad Leader," the man said, his voice rough, though muffled by his cowl. "How disappointing."

The man standing next to him lowered his head, shoulders bowing.

"Still, you're not a complete waste," the man with black eyes muttered, stepping into the center of the room. "Off-shellers, are we to assume three children are enough of a threat to warrant you standing guard over them?"

I glanced at our two captors, trying to fathom why the man with black eyes would insult them so. The first had dark skin, so the term was accurate for him. But the other looked for all the world like a Colberran.

The second Seeker, Blue Eyes, shook his head. "One is a child; the other two are adults." He pointed at Donovan. "This one is old enough for conscription, unless I miss my mark."

"Bah, these three weaklings hardly warrant both of your attention," Black Eyes stated, not even bothering to look at us. "Why didn't you send someone back to get us?"

"We've hardly been here long enough to do that." Blue Eyes held his head up, staring into the hard, cold, black eyes of the Seeker in charge. "This one"—he pointed at me—"was in the settlement. You can imagine Suyef's and my surprise she made it out this far."

The squad leader jerked his head up, eyes flaring. "I've had enough of your insolence, Off-sheller!"

Black Eyes raised one finger, and the squad leader fell silent. His hands clenched into fists at his sides.

"As you know, our sensors aren't functioning inside the settlement. Squad Leader Pollan here decided to take the initiative and leave the settlement to see if they would work in the desert." Black Eyes moved to stand over us. "Needless to say, they did."

"We were just about to bring them in," Blue Eyes said, shrugging. "Figuring out how to mount two speeders with five riders would have proven . . . difficult."

Black Eyes held up a hand. "Enough of your excuses, Quentin. I don't really care. You're only here because your orders protect you." He glanced over his shoulder at our captors. "Be silent, for once."

Blue Eyes, or Quentin, as his name appeared to be, opened his mouth to reply, but Suyef, my captor, touched his arm, and Quentin's mouth snapped shut.

"So," Black Eyes said, squatting down to stare at me. "These are the progeny of our leader's current distraction." He chuckled. "I'm sure it will lighten your hearts to know your father is alive and well. For now."

He stood up, glowering down at us from behind his cowl. Beside me, Donovan gave a start, bumping against me. The Seeker glanced at him, then back at me.

"Cross me," he continued, "and I can assure you, His Eminence hears my words. I can make your father's stay in the Central Dominance quite uncomfortable."

I stared up into those cold, black eyes, waiting for him to go on. He looked over at Donovan and Maryn and then back at me.

"Which of you is most likely to talk?" he asked, turning and walking away.

The three Seekers that had investigated the tower before Black Eyes arrived remained positioned around the room. The squad leader, Pollan, stood before the door, and Quentin and Suyef remained off to my right. Black Eyes clasped his hands behind his back as he came to a stop before the network terminal.

"Better yet, which one of you will show me what it is your father's been up to out here?" He looked over his shoulder toward us. "We know you've been meddling in things you shouldn't."

I gripped Donovan's arm and dug my fingers in for silent emphasis to let him know what I thought the Seeker meant. He shook his arm free, and I could feel him looking at me.

"We know your father is the guilty one." He turned to face us, and a small smile danced across those eyes. "And we hardly want to make you children . . . uncomfortable. A journey to Colberra City will be difficult, for sure. Being from out here, the altitude in the Central Mountains might be a bit much for you. And the city itself." He looked at Donovan. "Have you ever been?" We shook our heads. "Well, it might be worth going just to see it, but you won't be tourists. You'll be Seekers' guests until His Eminence has what he wants from your father." He stepped away from the terminal and stopped a few paces from us. "So, will you tell me what I want to know, or shall we go north?"

I glanced at Donovan. He glared at the Seeker, his jaw set in a very familiar way: stubborn defiance. I looked back at Black Eyes and shook my head. The tall man looked at the ground.

"Off-shellers, did you find out anything before we got here?" His voice turned hard and cold.

"As I said, sir, we arrived just before you," Quentin repeated. He pointed at Donovan. "The two males were out in the desert when Suyef spotted them on our patrol. We tracked them to this station. I took charge of them while Suyef conducted a search for anyone else. I wasn't in here very long before he came back saying he'd spotted movement west of here." He pointed at me. "That was her."

Black Eyes turned to face Suyef. "Let me guess, refusing to use our sensors again?" Suyef shrugged. "I'm telling you, Off-sheller, you keep this up and we'll ship you back to your own shell."

I tucked that bit of information away for later. I knew something had seemed different about him the moment I saw his dark-skinned face. For his part, Suyef remained quiet, standing close to Quentin. The pair seemed an odd set, facing the imposing figure.

"Someday, you'll cross that line enough for me to do something to you," Black Eyes growled. "Both of you." He turned away from our two captors. "Squad Leader," he barked out, "secure this facility. You two"—he pointed at Quentin and Suyef—"take the prisoners upstairs and put them in one of the sleeping quarters. Since you caught them, you get to guard them all night. We'll take them north tomorrow."

My upheld hand stopped Micaela from continuing her story.

"Am I to assume these two are the same ones the Queen mentioned?" I asked, tapping a finger on the piece of paper I'd jotted down the names on earlier. "Quentin being the one you said was dead?"

"It is," she said, shifting in her seat and resettling her dress around her legs.

"Can you tell me more about him?"

To this day, the look on her face upon hearing that question still haunts me. Her eyes locked with mine as a storm of emotions raged across her face. Her eyes hardened, then softened, shifted, then held mine again. Her lips compressed, opened, then trembled a little. One hand clenched her dress into a ball, then released and smoothed it out. Her chest rose and fell in quick breaths; then it slowed. Finally, she shook her head.

"We'll get to him in good time," she whispered. "Let's just say that he and I—our lives are very intertwined. And there are times when that is a bad thing."

I stared for a moment before nodding and waving her to continue. A new note appeared next to the man's name as a reminder to ask him what he had done to warrant such an emotional reaction in Micaela. There clearly was more to the story, but she didn't want to tell me just yet. Instead, she continued where she'd left off.

Our captors marched us upstairs into Donovan and Maryn's room. Suyef moved another mattress in for me and took up watch near the door. Quentin stood with him, and the two conversed in low whispers. After a few moments, he moved to sit against a wall. He didn't say a word, just sat there, staring at the floor.

"Why do they call you two Off-shellers?" I asked.

He looked up from his thoughts. "We're from another shell."

"Off-shellers aren't exactly welcome in Colberra nowadays," I stated. "Seekers, in particular, discriminate against them."

Quentin laughed. "That's putting it mildly."

"So, why call you that?" I asked, turning my gaze to Quentin.

He shifted under my stare. "It's a power thing. That, or he's being picky about my birthplace."

He pulled the cowl and hood from his cloak back, revealing short brown hair, a long nose, and a beard equal in length to his hair. His face reminded me a bit of a statue's: straight lines, high cheekbones, and a strong jaw. But his eyes, the same color as the water high above our shell, did much to soften his appearance.

"I'm from this shell, just not born here." He nodded at Suyef. "I was actually born on his shell."

I arched one eyebrow. "Are your parents Colberran, then?" He nodded. "What were they doing on another shell?"

"Expeditionary Forces," he replied, reaching into his collar and pulling out something on a necklace. "Both of my parents were Civil Defense." He held up a pair of metal tags with small print engraved on them. "That's how they met."

"And they were assigned to this man's shell?"

He shook his head. "My mother volunteered for it. My father, well, he ended up there under very different circumstances." He shrugged. "That's a story for another day. Suffice it to say, Expeditionary led them both to his shell, and it suited them. As Colberran as they may be, they've never been at home here." He chuckled more to himself than anyone else. "They're not even on this shell now. Off helping our Expeditionary Forces establish another base on a different shell."

I glanced back at Suyef. "So, Off-sheller is meant to set you two apart from the rest." Quentin nodded. "Why join the Seekers if they treat you so?"

"Resources, Micaela, resources," Quentin stated. "Now, before we get too far off topic, shall we continue our discussion?"

I didn't bother hiding my confusion. "Our discussion?"

"What you and your father were doing here."

My eyes narrowed. "You said I should just keep all that to myself. Not share it with Seekers at all."

"No, I said keep it from the others," he pointed out, nodding toward the door. "They're the ones who can make your life difficult."

"You wear the same uniform."

"Only out of necessity, but I don't expect you to believe me." He pointed at Suyef. "The fact that he's not from this shell should clue you in we're a bit different from the rest. We can save that for later. We noticed your little addition to the coding."

I glanced at the other Seeker, but he remained silent. "He doesn't talk much, I guess."

Quentin barked a laugh. "You just haven't found the right topic. Once you do, he'll talk, but only as much as necessary." He glanced over at his companion. "You are being a bit quiet, even for yourself."

Suyef glared at Quentin. "When I have something worth saying, I will."

"And that's what you get most of the time. I think he's got a thing where he saves up all his words for when he needs them. Like a mental count in his head how many he's allowed to use most of the time."

Suyef rolled his eyes and went back to staring at nothing. Quentin burst out laughing. I took a moment to look at my brothers. Maryn lay asleep, and Donovan sat over him, silent as Suyef, his eyes darting back and forth between our guards and the door.

Quentin's laughter died down, drawing my gaze. "Anyway, where were we?" He squinted, then snapped his finger and pointed at me. "Water program. Ingenious solution, there. Your idea or your father's?"

I held my tongue. Little reason existed to trust either of them; this in spite of the fact they appeared to have helped hide our secret and roles from Black Eyes. Still, their knowledge of us gave me pause.

"I'll assume both. Keep that from them, too." He pushed off the wall and knelt before me. "Don't volunteer any information around them. Colvinra is a high-ranking Seeker and a Questioner to boot. He likes to make people squirm and isn't afraid to cause pain. He's very good at hiding his handiwork, so don't expect the no-harm orders to hold sway with him." He glanced at Donovan. "Keep your mouths shut and your heads low. I'm not sure where they plan on taking you, but it won't be a normal Seeker facility."

I shared a look with my brother. "If they want information about my father, wouldn't it make sense to take us to him?"

"Normally, I'd agree," Quentin said, nodding. "But we can't even figure out where they are holding him, and between the two of us we're pretty good at finding information like that hidden on the network. Something is keeping his location secret."

"Seekers?" I asked, glancing at my brother.

He shook his head. "They could not care less about what's visible on the network. Most people can't access it, and those that can are generally loyal to the Colberran government and, in turn, the Seekers. No, this is something else." He pointed at me. "Just remember, don't offer up any information to Colvinra. Make him take you wherever he's going to take you."

"Why are you helping us?" I asked, keeping my eyes on his.

He shrugged. "I like the underdog." He smiled. "Plus, you're right. Someone is stealing your water, and that needs to be fixed."

"So, why not help us escape from the Seekers?" Donovan asked, his voice quiet but firm.

Quentin looked at my brother, pursing his lips in thought. His eyes began to move around the room as he contemplated Donovan's words. He turned to look at Suyef, eyebrows raised. Suyef shook his head.

"You have to admit, we could stand a chance," Quentin persisted, nodding at the door. "I have no doubt you could handle that squad."

"And you think you can handle a Questioner on your own?" Suyef asked.

Quentin shrugged. "I'm getting better."

"No, we didn't come here to rescue them. We take down a squad with a Questioner, and we draw too much attention to ourselves." Quentin opened his mouth to reply, but Suyef cut him off. "No, Quentin, we can't do everything."

Quentin's mouth snapped shut, and I saw something in his eyes. He wanted to argue the point and might have. I eyed Suyef. I can't say that at the time I understood what I'd just seen, but it made me think.

"I don't understand," Donovan muttered. "You're Seekers. Can't you do something?"

Quentin chuckled as he looked over at my brother. "No, Suyef's correct. Have you ever seen a Seeker fight?" Donovan shook his head, as did I when Quentin looked at me. "Let's just say a pair of brand-new Seekers fresh from their academy is a formidable duo to defeat." He pointed at the floor. "There are five of them down there, four of them from the same squad. Those four haven't been apart since they left the academy." Quentin shifted and pointed at Suyef. "Now, my friend here could easily handle a pair of them, and with my help probably the whole squad." His voice dropped to barely above a whisper. "But he's right. Only a fool takes on a lone Questioner. No one tries it when that same Questioner has an entire squad of Seekers to back him up." He shook his head and spread his hands. "I'm sorry. I wasn't thinking when I suggested we might take him on. Had we found you sooner, maybe we could have helped you stay hidden. For now, until something else comes along to change the game, you're Colvinra's."

"So, that's it, then?" Donovan blurted out, his tone elevated and fist clenched. "You're just going to let them have us?"

"Until we see reason to risk our lives to rescue you and a more viable means of doing so, I'm afraid we have to wait," Quentin replied, shrugging and looking at me.

"Considering you were just trying to convince your friend to try, it's hard to take you at your word," I said.

"Sorry, but he's right. There's not much we can do. Yet."

"You could help us escape," my brother hissed. "Get us away from here before they take us like they took Mother, Father, and Jyen."

"Seekers took your mother, too?" Quentin asked, glancing over at me.

I nodded, looking down at the floor. "And our youngest, my sister. They were sick and a threat. Or so the Seekers said."

"And they said they took them to a hospital?"

I nodded again.

"Did you ever get to see them there?"

I shook my head. "They promised travel papers, but the papers never came."

Quentin glanced at Suyef. "Have either of you ever known any-one to get permission to go to a Seeker hospital?"

"No," I replied, feeling a chill go down my spine as the pair of them traded looks. "Why?"

Quentin turned his gaze back to me, and the look in his eyes sent a tremor of fear and sorrow through my body.

"Seeker hospitals don't exist."

CHAPTER 8

A RAID

I slept little that night. The conversation with Quentin and Suyef died after his statement about the hospitals. I wasn't sure if he could be believed or not. The look on his face before he told me, however . . . That gave me pause. He seemed to dread telling me; he wore the look of a man come to tell you someone close to you has died. And that is what it felt like. The raw wound stabbed into my heart when Jyen had been taken, and ripped open anew when my mother left. I did my best to hide it so as not to wake my brothers. They seemed to sleep that night.

Quentin could tell his words bothered me. He tried twice to comfort me, but words failed him. I had nothing to offer him anyway. After a few attempts, he gave up and left the room. Suyef remained on guard the rest of the night. When morning came and the door slid open, the two were gone. I looked for them as one of the other Seekers led us down. Colvinra, sitting at what had been our table with his cowl and hood removed, must have noticed me searching.

"You'll not find your friends here," he growled, his voice sounding even gruffer in the morning. His nose hooked down to a sharp point, and his lips were so thin they almost weren't there. "I've sent them off on their mission, where they belong."

The three of us huddled close and remained silent.

"Still not much of a talker, eh?" He sniffed and grimaced. "By the core, I can't stand the smell of you Edgers. I'll be glad to be done with the lot of you and back in the Central Dominance, where we belong." He grinned, a wide, evil thing that made his face even more ghoulish than did his all-black eyes. "And from what I hear, soon you won't have much of a choice but to move to more civilized parts of the shell." His gaze locked on me, and the smile vanished. "Your father's bit of thievery notwithstanding, of course."

Donovan tensed next to me, and I laid a hand on his shoulder. His muscles tightened under my touch, but, to my relief, he relaxed and remained silent.

"Still won't talk," he whispered, tapping a finger on the table. "Very well. Squad Leader, get them mounted. We leave when I finish eating."

The squad leader led us outside, where we found five of the elongated Seeker speeders waiting. I looked around once my eyes adjusted to the bright morning core-light but saw no sign of Suyef, Quentin, or their speeders. The morning winds whipped my hair about, and I pulled my red body scarf up around my head, the long ends hanging down and shielding my body. Donovan and Maryn donned theirs as well, and we followed the Seekers over to the speeders. Up close, the machines looked impressive and frightening at the same time. Twice as long as I was tall, these had long seats to accommodate two riders. A Seeker mounted each bike, lying down and settling their chins onto a cushioned extension of the seat. We climbed aboard behind them, the grooves on each side for our legs making it so we had to lie on our captors, legs flung back on each side at a downward angle behind us, arms wrapped around their bodies.

I situated Maryn with his Seeker, strapping him in with a harness of sorts the Seeker offered me to ensure he was secure. After that, I made my way to my mount. Once situated, the six of us waited for several minutes before Colvinra and the squad leader emerged and mounted.

"We head east first," Colvinra called to the Seekers. "You know the dangers we face. If we are attacked by raiders, split and meet at the rendezvous point. Squad leader and I will deal with them." He paused, staring off in the direction of the edge. "If it's anything else, hope your speeder is faster than it."

I glanced at Donovan, confused. He mouthed the words *anything else* to me, and I shrugged. My riding companion shifted to look over his shoulder at me.

"Keep a tight grip on my back. If you fall off, you'll die." His tone was flat and emotionless. "I'm not going to get in a wreck trying to save you, girl."

"Got it," I said, huddling close and getting a good grip on his torso.

Donovan appeared to receive his own instructions as he huddled closer to his Seeker, eyes determined.

The squad leader ordered them to move out. The speeders lifted off the ground and vaulted forward, slicing through the air with hardly a sound from the machines. The desert landscape flew past, the control station falling away behind us. Far off to my right stood the settlement, the edge several miles distant beyond that, and to my left loomed the Central Mountains, dominating the shell. They hardly moved, despite the speed with which we soared past the terrain. Small shrubbery, stunted trees and the like, raced past, and rock formations that had stood far on the horizon from the settlement zipped past, looking shorter and rounder than my memory recalled. Before long, we traveled past the familiar lands I'd once gotten lost in. Angling my head a bit brought the tall rock formation I'd visited twice before in sight. I knew my mother's token still lay there, and part of me wished there'd been time for one more trip to get it.

We rode for a few chrons before the Questioner called a stop. We wolfed down a quick bit of nutrient gel and a swig of water from packs the Seekers offered us before remounting and heading off. I saw no sign of anyone for miles, but the Seekers still flew about like men expecting a surprise. They dodged back and forth, keeping to gullies and washes, staying away from ridges unless forced there. I craned my head in as many directions as possible but saw nothing. Who were we hiding from? Who would the Seekers be worried about? They were the preeminent power on the shell. If something scared them, it must be quite awful.

I figured it out later that first day. As we cleared another ridge, darting down the other side into a long gully that ran away from the descending slope, my Seeker steered his mount near Donovan's. As I looked over to check on him, a shadow crossed over the mounts. The Seekers both flinched, glancing back behind us. I looked the other direction but saw nothing. Donovan cried out and looked up, his mouth hanging open. I followed his gaze to see, but the Seeker on my mount jerked us hard to the left. I tightened my grip on his torso as my stomach shifted the other direction and the muscles in my neck cramped up. He finished the turn, and I twisted to look up, the speeder slowing to a halt. Nothing was there save for the water shield high above our shell, the only thing between us and the cold of space. The Seeker turned our mount slowly as all five mounts moved away from each other before stopping, their riders scanning the horizon and the skies above.

"What was it?" I asked the Seeker, but he just held up a finger.

The next instant, something rose up from the edge. It loomed high in the sky, filling the horizon with its long neck and giant, translucent wings. Soon, more followed the first. I felt my stomach drop as my jaw fell open.

A dragon raid.

Micaela paused at my signal, my stylus busy jotting down notes.

"Had you never seen a dragon prior to this?"

She shook her head. "Not enough to remember. My father told us of a raid that occurred when Donovan and I were very young, probably fifteen cycles before this one. I was only five, Donovan four. My brother seemed to recall it more than I, but more from what he heard than remembered. That's how he made up all those stories for Maryn." She paused, staring off to one side. A small smile crept onto her face. "He had our little brother convinced he was an expert on dragons. The two of them would have grand adventures in the desert battling the monsters of their imagination."

I held my tongue, not wanting to interrupt a moment of pleasant memories. All too soon, the smile faded and she glanced at me, a single eyebrow rising.

"My guess is that this first encounter didn't go so well," I said.

She nodded, a slow motion that carried a perception of weight. "That's putting it mildly."

Not much is known about why the dragons come and take people. No one has ever come back to tell us. Some assume they take us for food. Others to be slaves. Either way, Colberran history is filled with their raids, flights of dragons coming up and attacking the outer settlements. At one point centuries ago, the Seekers passed themselves off as our protection against the beasts. After another raid wiped out an entire army of the men, the government backed down on that protection. It had been many, many cycles since a raid had happened in our region of the outer edge. I was so little I hardly recalled any details. Stories passed down warned us of what to do. They all amounted to the same thing: hide. It's your only chance. The Seekers clearly had other ideas.

They scattered in every direction. Donovan's mount soared off toward the mountains in the north as my own split off the way we'd just come. I spun my head around to the left and saw Colvinra and the squad leader shooting off toward the edge and the dragons. A shadow drew my eyes up and made me forget about the Seekers.

A flight of dragons, greenish in the scales, spread out above us. Bodies long and lithe, with stunted arms and long sweeping tails, they flew on wings translucent green to match their scales. The beasts swept past us and turned in the air. Two bore down on us and forced my Seeker to turn the mount down the ridge as he tried to escape. Yellow-tinted bone structures jutted out above their eyes and swept back like hair frozen in place. Their golden-yellow eyes did not blink as they flew past us, pulling up into the sky with a pump of their wings.

The Seeker downshifted his mount and pulled it hard to the left, pivoting away from the swooping attackers. The mount lurched forward, shooting back across the ridge as one of the dragons cried out, a shriek that sent shivers down my back. Our attackers pumped their wings to pull up and spin in magnificent form through the air to come after us. The mount jerking to the right drew my eyes forward to see a third dragon diving down at us from the left. The three creatures spread out, one above, two from the sides, and dropped down before our mount. My Seeker yanked back hard on his control handles as he eased off the accelerator, and our nose shot straight up. I gripped him as a sudden burst of energy shot the mount up into the air.

Below us, one of the dragons twisted in the air to crash into the ground. It dawned on me what the Seeker had done. Using the gravity beams that kept the mount afloat, he had locked on to a dragon, and used it to pull and push the mount up this high. Before he could bring the nose down, the dragons streaking below us executed sharp turns away from him, and he lost his anchors. He realized the danger and spun the mount around, so now we faced straight down at the ground. What was left of my stomach felt like it tried to exit the back of my body as we plummeted straight toward the shell below. At what seemed the last moment, the Seeker yanked hard on the controls, and power surged inside the mount, repelling us from the ground. We slowed our descent just above the ridge peak and hung there for an instant. The Seeker shifted the directional gravity beams in front of and behind us and the mount shot away, back in the direction we'd come from.

Ahead, the other mounts, harried as well, streaked back toward each other. My Seeker tried to turn to the north, only to find a smaller dragon swooping down toward him. He took the hint and fled back to the group. The Seekers brought their mounts into a large circle and kept moving around, never holding still. Without a signal, they all turned inward, crossing each other's paths at close range and resuming formation, circling. They kept doing this as the dragons surrounded us. All of the Seekers left their pulse guns in their holsters.

"Why are you doing this?" I asked as we crossed the circle in another shift.

"Makes it harder for them to single us out," he called, leaning hard to the left into a turn, me leaning close behind him. "So they can't grab us." He shrugged with his right shoulder. "Least, we think it does."

I got a look at Maryn as we crossed one more time, expecting him to be terrified. He laughed with delight, his mouth split open in a smile as he pointed up at the circling predators.

"Kid doesn't know what's happening, does he?" the Seeker asked.

I shook my head, then realized he couldn't see me. "No, he knows they exist, but to him, they're something out of a story." The creatures flew back and forth around us, gliding through the air with little movement from their wings. "He's never seen a raid before."

The Seeker grunted. "Yeah, they've been rare. With one exception." He turned the mount into another crossing move. "That's why we came this way—wanted to avoid their favorite target."

Shrieks echoed down from the dragons as they circled us. I couldn't tell if they were frustrated or just trying to unnerve us. They didn't seem confused by the Seekers' tactic as much as they seemed patient. Their eyes darted back and forth, sizing us up. Once or twice, a smaller one darted out, swooping over the circling mounts and screeching at us. Patient as they might be, this stalemate of sorts would not last, and the Seekers realized that. They started calling out to each other, seeking guidance. Colvinra and the squad leader barked out for silence when they did.

In the next instant, the dragons struck. Half their number swooped down into the circling mounts with such speed the Seekers had no time to react. With terrifying results, the dragons crashed down into the speeding mounts. A dragon collided with the front of our mount, and I found myself soaring through the air, head down, cloak sweeping about me. My body slammed against something squishy and slid to the ground. The wind was knocked from my lungs; I gasped for air as momentum carried my body away from the dragon it had collided with. As I came to a halt, air raced into my lungs, and they gulped it up. I shook my head to clear my vision and looked about.

Nothing except dragons remained airborne; those that had attacked us had taken off again. One dragon dove, and a Seeker struggled in its claws when it took off, his useless pulse gun falling to land near me. I pushed myself up and ran toward the carnage of Seeker mounts, still unable to see either of my brothers. A Seeker leapt over his downed mount and ran toward me, waving his arms and screaming.

"Get back!" he yelled. "Run!"

"No!" I ran right past him, ducking under his arms, searching for my brothers.

I heard the screech an instant later and did the only thing possible: collapsed to the ground and curled into a ball. The Seeker vanished in the grasp of another dragon, a piece of his cloak tearing free and falling to the earth near me.

Just past the falling cloth, a Seeker clung to Maryn, arm around his neck and a pulse gun pointing up at the screeching beasts. Something clicked inside me, an emotion I'd never felt before. "That's my baby brother. Let him go!" I'm not sure if I said it out loud, but I heard it in my head, and it moved me to action. I searched around for something I could use, and my eyes locked on the only thing nearby: the pulse gun dropped by the other Seeker.

I lunged for it as the Seeker moved with Maryn toward me, eyes and pulse gun trained above. I grasped the weapon and pointed it at his exposed back. As I pulled the trigger, unleashing the massive air pulse the gun generated into him, another thought filled my head. *Don't you ever touch my brother again!* The pulse hit him square in the back, knocking him forward. The force of the blast sent Maryn tumbling to one side. With him clear, I took aim and fired again. And again. And again. Pulse after pulse poured into the tumbling form of the Seeker, knocking him farther and farther away. Maryn crawled away toward a large rock, but I didn't relent. He had to pay. They all did. The others were out of my reach, all the ones that took my mother, my sister, and my father, but I had this one, and he would pay. I fired again and sent the limp Seeker crashing over a rock. He fell partially from sight, and all the rage, all the emotion, everything, just poured out of me like air from a balloon. I fell to a knee, one hand gripping the pulse gun. The cool metal calmed me, giving me something to focus on. Dragons. Dragons were the problem now.

Maryn peeked out from behind the rock. I moved toward him, keeping a wary eye on the sky, pulse gun gripped in my hand. I weaved around rocks and found myself in an open stretch leading to Maryn's hiding spot. How had he made it that far out? I pushed the thought down, gripped my body scarf, and sprinted the last few meters to the rock.

Just as I neared it, something flew into my peripheral vision. One of the larger dragons, golden claws extended, dove toward me. It moved with such speed, there was no way to make it to safety. I pushed my feet out farther behind me and dove to the ground.

Right when the claws should have struck, a resounding crash echoed above me. I landed behind the rock and rolled to find Maryn tucked under an outcropping, screaming his lungs out. Pain burst up my side from what I suspected would become a glorious bruise on my hip. I hobbled toward Maryn and looked for the attacking dragon. What greeted me made me stop dead in my tracks.

There, hovering over us, flew the largest dragon yet. The creature was green from head to tail, a bright, emerald green shining in the core-light. What made it stand out even more? It dwarfed every other dragon present, its wingspan easily half again longer than those of the rest. Above and swooping back from its head, it had a reddish-gold bone structure that looked like hair swept in the wind, flowing down its neck to merge with giant ridged scales jutting high from its spine.

It hovered over us and bellowed a cry at the other dragons. After that, it turned its head to look at me. Eyes deep as a pool of gold with vertical slits of black like those of a cat stared back at me. I looked up, mesmerized for a moment as the beast hovered. It lowered itself to the ground, wings beating to keep it in place just over me. The creature's body neared, pushing me backward onto the ground, my eyes still locked on the beast's, my head craning to look at the head beyond mine. A moment later, the dragon flew away. I pushed myself up to watch its flight. As it left, the other green beasts, scattered by the arrival of the larger dragon, vanished into the distance. The beautiful creature held my awestruck gaze until it dove down, out of sight below the shell's edge.

Only then did my eyes fall back on the scene before me. The Seeker's mounts lay in ruins tossed about, and I saw no sign of their owners. My heart began to race as my eyes sought after signs of my other brother. Movement to one side drew my eyes and a sigh of relief as Donovan peeked out from behind another rock. I grinned and looked down at the outcropping where Maryn had hidden.

He was gone.

CHAPTER 9

INTO A TRAP

I panicked as I climbed over the rock face, looking for signs of my brother. I called out his name and heard Donovan doing the same. It did no good. There was no sign of him. I collapsed to my knees and felt a numbness growing inside me, overwhelming the slicing wound laid bare by my mother and sister leaving. It spread, filling me with a sense of nothingness. I hugged my arms tight to me and rocked, a few tears still falling despite my numbness. What lay around me became distant.

Donovan appeared, standing before me, mouth moving. I closed my eyes, trying to block him out. Hands grabbed me and shook me. A voice filled my ears, angry, saying something. I squeezed my eyes closed, placing my hands over my ears, closing myself off.

A stab of pain ripped across my face, jarring me back to reality. My eyes shot open to see Donovan shaking his palm.

"Micaela, don't do this," he whispered.

I touched a hand to my smarting cheek. "Maryn's gone."

He nodded and sighed. "Yes, taken."

"They've all been taken," I whispered, images of my mother, sister, and father joining Maryn's face in my mind.

"Well, good riddance to the Seekers."

I shook my head but kept silent. Donovan didn't notice and kept talking.

"We can't stay here," he said, trying to pull me to a standing position. "They might come back. The mounts are useless, and we don't know how to operate them anyway. We'll have to walk."

I resisted his tugging, though he spoke the truth. "Where do we go? They'll just keep looking for us."

"I don't know, but we can't stay here. Now get up. You're too heavy for me to carry." With that, he let go and moved toward the ruined mounts. "I'll look for some supplies, but we need to get moving."

I turned my head to watch him. "Where are we?"

"Somewhere east of the settlement. I climbed up to that ridge to get a look around." He ducked behind one mount and reemerged holding a water pack. "The water pipe's out of sight, so we're pretty far from home." He paused to look at me. "We're pretty far from everywhere."

His words carried an implication: we were on our own. I pondered them for a moment as he continued his searching. This far out, the only thing we'd find were raiders, those elements of society that had resisted the Dominance's urging to move inland and turned to a lawless life. Some said the Seekers secretly encouraged the raiders because they made the outer provinces unappealing for resettlement. I shook my head and pushed myself up. Whether that was true or not, I did know one thing: raiders wouldn't attack a Seeker convoy. A wave of dizziness struck, forcing me to pause, my eyes closed until it passed. When I opened them, the scene before me reminded me of one crucial fact: this wasn't a Seeker convoy anymore.

I rushed to help Donovan gather what supplies we could carry. We stuffed them into travel sacks, wrapped our long scarves over our heads and bodies, and set off into the desert. At first, we marched south, directly toward the shell's end, the high mountains at our back. The plan was to turn west and make our way along the edge back to our settlement. From what we knew, raiders stayed far from the mountains to avoid Seeker patrols. While we wanted to avoid both, Seeker patrols were more coordinated and prevalent. We could go months and not see hide nor hair of a raider. If we spent one day traveling between the outlying settlements and the mountains, we would see a Seeker patrol.

So, to the edge we went, thinking ourselves clever. Donovan kept a wary eye behind us, convinced more Seekers would come searching. We didn't travel in a straight line, cutting back and forth across the landscape as best we could. At times, Donovan's instincts seemed dead on. There were moments when it felt like unseen eyes stared at our backs, or a glimpse of a shadow on the edge of my vision drew my gaze. When I looked, nothing was there. After a while, the feelings went away. The day grew long. Gel nutrient packs from the Seekers' mounts gave us ample food, but our water supply would become a problem. How long we had, it was hard to tell. Our minds were preoccupied with our possible pursuit as well as our missing brother. At least, mine was. The wound grew larger, more raw. Another part of me ripped away. As we walked, I found myself moving closer to Donovan, drinking up his presence. The only thing left to me. Yes, I was very distracted, and so was my brother.

So much so, we didn't realize we were walking right into a trap.

That night, as we rested near the edge, a slight ridge to our backs, a low running gully cutting down the edge side providing us some shelter from the wind, my mind drifted, lost in quiet thought. The initial shock of losing yet another family member had begun to wear off. It's not that I was okay with it happening. Still, part of me accepted it. This was becoming my lot in life. As I sat there staring at the sky, the realization bloomed that part of me expected it. Glancing at Donovan, I wondered when he would leave. Part of me panicked at the thought, but another part accepted it. It was going to happen. The only questions were how and when.

Donovan put on a good face, but underneath he was angry. He held his tongue, for once, but a storm boiled under the surface. As the night shield fell, he grew restless, pacing back and forth and grabbing rocks and flinging them toward the edge. This close, the night shield added an eerie effect to the air. Emanating from the citadel at the center of our shell, the shield gave us the illusion of night in a world of perpetual core-light. Here, the night screen dimmed the light, but I could still see the brightness from the core reaching up past the rocks that formed the end of our shell.

"Why did you leave Mother's necklace on that pile of rocks?" Donovan asked, his voice cutting through the silent night air.

I looked up, a bit confused. "I don't know. It seemed the right thing to do."

He stood, a rock in hand, eyes on the vast sky before us. "We found it. On one of our little excursions. Maryn thought he'd found some lost treasure. You'd have enjoyed the story he made up to explain how it got there." He dropped the rock and turned to look at me. "He wouldn't let me leave it." Something hung from his other hand, dangling in the night winds. "I made him give it to me for safekeeping. I managed to distract him enough the rest of the day that he didn't tell you." He looked away, shifting back and forth on his feet.

"I miss her," I whispered.

Donovan nodded.

"Keep it."

He looked back at me, eyebrows raised. "I know how important it is to you. That's why I found it odd you'd leave it there."

I shifted, tucking my legs against my chest and staring out into the night sky. "You need it more than I do."

He sighed and tucked the necklace back into his pocket. He grabbed the rock he had dropped and flung it toward the edge. We remained silent after that, memories keeping me company. I didn't want to be silent, but at that moment words felt like they would just make me lose it. I cursed the Seekers, the Central Dominance, and my father for his water project. Myself for continuing it. Why hadn't I just left it alone? They might never have come looking for us. Maryn might still be with us. Had Father just let it be, he might never have been arrested. I buried my face in my arms and began to weep.

Donovan kept grabbing his rocks, flinging them as far as he could. I could hear the anger as he grunted with each throw. It matched the sorrow filling me inside. After several moments, I heard him begin to mutter things.

"What?" I asked when he exclaimed something midthrow.

"We have to do something!" he hissed, rounding on me. "I'm tired of running. I'm tired of being chased or arrested. I'm tired of being lost out here in this forsaken wasteland we call home when our family is in the hands of those mongrels."

"What do you expect us to do?" I asked, waving a hand around me. "Especially out here."

That made him pause. He looked at me, then off into the night. Finally, he waved a hand in the direction of our settlement.

"You should have been helping me look for them. Anything. You're better at finding things on that network than I am," he said, reaching down to grab another rock. "With your help, I might have found something."

"You don't know if you're right, let alone what you're looking for," I replied.

He flung the rock over the edge and grabbed another.

"At least that would have been useful," he said, tossing the rock up in the air and catching it. "Unlike your other little project."

"You mean the one keeping us from running out of water." I glared at him. "You know full well how important that is."

He nodded. "Yeah, important enough it got someone's attention. Now look what happened."

"It could just as easily have been you," I said.

"No, you heard that Seeker. He specifically mentioned your and Father's little project." He flung the rock away and reached for another. "And now here we are. Stuck out here when we should be doing something."

"And what would you do?" I asked.

He nodded off to the west. "Go searching for them in the only place out here we know people get taken to."

My eyes narrowed as I stared at him. "People avoid that place for good reason. What do you hope to accomplish going there?"

"We don't have to go all the way." He pointed back north of us. "Just to a water station near it. We can use a terminal to do some snooping." He shrugged. "We could find out what happened to them. That's at least something more than we know now."

He fell silent, walking around in a big circle and grabbing rocks as he went to send them flying off the edge. I contemplated his words but couldn't see any way to accomplish anything, even if he could be right. Part of me wanted him to be, but I knew better. We were so focused on ourselves—Donovan on his pacing and rock throwing, me on contemplating my life—we never heard the raiders approach.

"Drop the rock," a voice said from right behind us.

Startled, I spun to see who had spoken. A man in clothes one might see anywhere in the Outer Dominances—nondescript colors, flowing body scarf, and a hood—stood there. The only things that stood out were his eye patch and once-broken nose. He held a pulse gun trained on Donovan and nodded at my brother to drop the rock he held.

Donovan looked at the rock, then at me. I started to shake my head, but the next instant he flung it right at the man's head. The rock hit its mark, sending the man tumbling to the ground, one hand going to his head, the other dropping his weapon.

"Donovan!" I yelled as another man rushed down toward us.

My brother dove toward the first man, and when he stood up, he held the man's gun in his hand. The charging raider lunged at him, but Donovan brought the firearm to bear and fired. A burst of electricity exploded in his chest as he fell past Donovan, his body convulsing from the attack.

"What are you doing?" I asked, grabbing at him.

He swung the weapon around and fired another shot behind me. I spun to see another man tumbling down the hill.

"Move!" he yelled, grabbing my arm and shoving me away from the three downed men.

A rock exploded near me as I stumbled forward, and I heard Donovan grunting as he followed. Shot after shot echoed in the night air as more rocks exploded around us. I heard more men fall as I raced away from the gully we'd stopped in.

A man stood up from behind a rock, a gun leveled at me.

"Freeze!" he yelled.

I stumbled to a halt, and Donovan crashed into me. The collision knocked the gun from his hand as he was bringing it around to aim at the man.

"Back away from it," the man ordered, waving his gun at us.

As my brother and I backed away, more raiders appeared in the night as fast as the dragons had earlier that day. I thought it strange that we'd managed to not get shot by so many of them. They were a motley bunch of gashed faces; torn, nondescript clothing; and pulse guns. A few were missing teeth, and one had a hole in his cheek I didn't care to contemplate too much.

They herded us back toward where the raiders had been knocked down by Donovan. The first man was up again, one hand pressed to his head.

"Well, well, ya two do make an odd pair to be getting such attention," the first man said. "First, ya get all tangled up in Seekers. Then ya escape a dragon raid. And now ya manage to elude more Seekers." He leveled a glare at Donovan. "And bold to boot. I've a mind to be done with ya right now, but I like that in a man." He shook a finger at my brother. "But ya try that stunt again"—he jerked a thumb over his shoulder—"I'll toss ya off the shell, got it?"

I glanced at Donovan, arching one eyebrow. He nodded, then just stared at the man.

"Too bad for them we found ya first, eh, Seekers?" he asked, calling over his shoulder.

I looked up to see more men appearing over the top of the ridge. Other raiders came into view, pulse guns out and trained on two men walking among them. I stared in shock at who came into view.

Quentin and Suyef.

"Well, Seeker?" the raider asked. "Are these the two ya're after?"

Quentin nodded. "My thanks for finding them. Now, if you turn them over to our custody, we'll be sure to not mention you in our report."

The raider burst out laughing, joined by most of his crew. "Word of a Seeker is about as good as what ya get from a psychic: means different things to different people." He stopped laughing, his face going hard. "Except when a Seeker threatens ya." He turned to look at Quentin. "Ya wouldn't be threatening us, now would ya?"

Quentin held up both hands. "No one is threatening anyone here. We'll just take these two and be gone."

"And what do Seekers want with a couple of Edgers?"

"That's Seeker business," Quentin replied, stepping forward.

"Seeker business is our business," the man growled at Quentin. "S'why we're out here, ya know."

"I won't argue that with you. I'm just trying to complete a job. A contract. You know something about doing that, don't you?"

I frowned at him, mouthing the word *contract*. Quentin didn't acknowledge me.

"What would ya Seekers be knowing about contracts?" The leader waved a hand at the pair of them. "Ya work for the Dom'nance. Ya're well paid."

"It's not about money. It's about keeping my word." He pointed at us. "They can hardly be of good value to you."

The raider waved a hand at Donovan. "He'll fetch a hefty load of cash, healthy one like him." He gave my brother a glare. "And ya think I'm gonna part with him after what he done to me?" He shook his head, then grinned lasciviously at me. "Her, well, ya can imagine what we'll sell her for."

Donovan growled, moving between the raider and me. I grabbed at his shoulders to calm him but hid myself from the raider's wandering eyes behind my brother.

"What, ya have something to say?" the raider asked, staring at my brother, nostrils flaring.

"Donovan," I whispered, "don't."

My brother's fist clenched, and he stopped moving forward. He didn't take his eyes off the lead raider, however.

"Don't need ya to look pretty for someone to pay." The raider waved a hand about his head. "If ya feel like expressing yaself again, my boys will gladly have a 'talk' with ya."

All the raiders chuckled, several tossing some jibes in. Donovan looked at them all and shook his head, stepping back from the lead raider and looking down. The pair that Donovan had shot had stood up at last, moving behind the leader and glaring at him.

"See, Seeker, provincials know thar place." The leader turned to look at Quentin. "Thanks to you lot for that bit."

"We'll pay you for the pair," Quentin said. "As soon as we get near an outpost, we can have the currency transferred."

The leader barked another laugh. "Yeah, and a squad of Seekers to carry it, no doubt." He spat to the side. "That's what I think of that idea."

Quentin looked over at me, and I could see his mind working even at this distance. I shook my head and shrugged. He frowned and looked at Suyef, who stood ignoring everything and everyone around him.

"The way I see it, Seeker," the leader continued, "not much of a trade here."

"If you won't sell them to us, we'll be on our way, then."

The leader laughed and nodded at his men, who, as one, turned their weapons on the pair.

"Oh, I don't think so."

"You can't possibly think we'll go quietly," Quentin scoffed at the leader, but Suyef laid a hand on his shoulder and shook his head once.

"I don't think even two Seekers'd stand up to this many pulse guns at once." The leader shook his head. "No, see, we can't have ya going back to yar Seeker friends and telling them about us. Leads to problems our employer likes to avoid."

"Your employer?"

"If ya're lucky, ya might meet him. He's a particular distaste for Seekers." The leader chuckled. "S'not a meeting I'd be eager for."

He barked a few orders, and his men hustled the four of us together. The raiders gagged the two Seekers but left my brother and me unmolested. We kept quiet, nevertheless, as we waited. Older, dilapidated speeder mounts appeared from the surrounding area, but I saw no sign of Quentin and Suyef's mounts. Clearly, the leader hoped to find them, as he kept sending his men out to search.

After almost a chron, exasperated as his men set off in a new direction, the leader came over and removed the gag from Quentin's mouth. "Where're they hidden?"

Quentin shrugged. "Somewhere inconvenient for you."

"Mind your tongue, Seeker," the leader growled, nostrils flaring. "Remember, I don't need ya to look pretty for the selling."

"I doubt you'll fetch any price for a Seeker," Quentin replied, shrugging. "No one will take the risk."

The leader knelt down to be eye level with Quentin. "No one said they had to know where ya came from, either." He reached up and grabbed Quentin's cloak below his neck in a fist, pulling him closer. "Now, where're those mounts?"

"I told you already. Somewhere inconvenient."

The leader scowled, shoving Quentin back and standing up as another raider rushed over to replace the gag. The leader moved a short distance away and stopped, staring off into the night. On a whim, I stood up and walked over to him, drawing a disinterested eye.

"I assume you tracked us most of the day?"

He nodded.

"Did you witness what happened earlier?"

Another silent nod.

"Did you happen to track anyone else that got away from the attack?"

The leader gazed at me for a moment, eyes narrowed. Finally, he shook his head. "People don't usually come outta such things," he whispered. "We stayed away in hopes they'd ignore us. We went closer after the beasts left to see if anything was salvageable."

"That's when you saw us," I said.

He nodded. "I'll not lie and say I wasn't stunned. Like I said, no one walks away from such things." He stared at me for a moment.

"Why'd they leave ya? I'd wager that makes ya even more valuable to my employer."

I shrugged and returned to my seat. Donovan and Quentin both shot questioning glances at me, but I ignored them. Huddling close to my brother, knees gathered to my chest, I let my mind get lost in thoughts about my younger brother. Still, part of me couldn't help but ask myself the same question, pondering the possible answers: Why had the dragons left us? Why take everyone else, including Maryn, and leave the two of us behind? No answers came, and a little more of the hope inside me withered and died.

I set my stylus down, massaging my writing hand as Micaela stood and stretched. Even that she managed to do with a grace that filled me with jealousy.

"Why did Donovan attack them?" I inquired.

She shrugged. "He thought he was defending us."

"But attacking the raiders?" I shook my head. "What did he hope that would do?"

"He wanted to get away. Raiders aren't known for their kind ways." She cocked an eyebrow at me. "People do foolish things sometimes."

"So, you contend the Queen left you for a purpose?" I asked, tapping at one of my notes.

She glanced over at me. "I never said it was the Queen."

I frowned at her. "There's only one dragon in the world that fits the size you described. Especially among the greens."

"True, but I never said it was her. You shouldn't jump to conclusions."

I dipped my head. "My apologies."

"That said, it looked like her," Micaela said, a small smirk darting across her lips. "At least, it did to my untrained eye. As to whether or not it was, you'll have to ask her. Regardless, the other dragons acted on her direction, I've no doubt of that. And yes, I suspect she had them leave us on purpose."

"Why?"

She shrugged. "Why does the Queen do what she does?"

"For the good of all her people," I replied without hesitation.

Micaela nodded once. "A very apt description. And has she ever deviated from that pattern? To your knowledge?"

I shook my head.

"So, I stand by the statement: she did it on purpose."

"So, you know where Maryn is, then?"

"We're getting ahead of the story."

I held up a hand. "Come now, High One." Her glare stalled me. "My apologies. Micaela. Come now, you can tell me that much, yes?"

She stared at me for a moment before nodding once. "I do know where he is."

"And?"

She nodded up at the ceiling. "On this shell."

I smiled. "Good, he's alive, then. And you know about it. So, there's hope."

The look that filled her eyes all but drained the good feeling I felt at discovering Maryn's fate. She stared at me, those eyes a deep, sorrowful pool of pain and loss. In that moment, it was very clear that this woman was not to be buoyed by such good news.

As if reading my mind, Micaela said, "Don't let my inability to see the joy in a small thing such as this put out the light you felt." She looked down at the table. "I long for the days when the little things made me happy."

I opened my mouth to ask a question, but it died on my lips. She saved me needing to find another.

"My brother and I have never had quite the same relationship as we once had. To be honest, him being taken at such a young age, we hardly had more than an older-sibling–younger-sibling relationship. After he was rescued, we never saw eye to eye again. Especially on things that are going on right now." She shook her head. "And after recent events—the war, what happened with our family after all this began—I think he blames me for much of what happened. Me and Quentin."

She fell silent. I kept my eyes on her for a few long moments.

She nodded and resumed her seat. "Where were we?"

"Hope withering."

The leader gave up his search for the Seeker mounts after what seemed half the night. With the four of us strapped on behind some of the raiders, the group set off into the darkness, traveling along the shell's edge. The dim light made it impossible to see, but somehow the raider piloting our mount knew where to go, dodging in and out of gullies, over rocky formations, and along ridges that rose up along the way. It was hard to tell our speed, but it felt fast. I saw nothing that could give me even a frame of reference and so gave up, closing my eyes and leaning in tight to the raider's back.

At some point, I fell asleep, as the next thing my mind registered was the ropes being removed and something pulling me forcefully from the mount. I tried to blink my eyes open, but someone shoved a hood over my head, blocking my sight. A rope appeared in my hand, and someone barked instructions not to let go. A tug on the rope pulled me into a walk and a trance of sightless walking and listening for any sign of where we were. Not much light peeked in through the fabric or up from around my neck, so it was still night. Once or twice, my ears caught murmurs from people as we passed them but nothing more. The surface we walked on was smooth, at least, free of rocks or steps. For that, I remember being grateful.

After a blind march that went on for quite a while, I collided with a halted figure and came to a stop. Someone came and took my hands from the rope, guiding me off to one side. With a jerk, the hood yanked clear, and dim light filled my eyes. I blinked away pain in my head and looked around. A room lacking any decor greeted me, the walls a solid gray and a single small window with thick-paned glass set in the wall opposite the door. Two beds stood on either side, more shelves than beds, really, jutting out from the wall with a sleeping pad set atop and a pillow and folded blanket set at each end. To my left stood a door marked "Lavatory," which led to a small cubby. To my right, another was marked "Changing Room." Someone pushed me forward into the quarters, and I looked over my shoulder as one of the raiders led someone else in, head still covered. A jerk of the hood, and the raider left Quentin standing with me. The door slid shut behind him, his hands bound together in front of him, a gag still in his mouth. I stepped close and removed the gag.

"Thanks," he muttered, working his jaw a bit. "Sparse living quarters, I see."

He watched me with those bright-blue eyes as I finished freeing him.

"Why put me with you and not my brother?" I asked, sitting on the bed.

He shrugged. "Keep you separated from a friend." He shook his head. "I'm shocked we're not all in cells or at least separate rooms."

I sighed, lying down on the bed. Exhaustion struck me hard. Something fell over me like a warm cloak, and I cuddled it close, rolling onto my stomach. Only then did I notice Quentin moving away from the bed. A glance over my shoulder revealed a blanket across my back.

"Thanks," I murmured, drifting off to what every ounce of me hoped would be a dreamless sleep.

It wasn't.

CHAPTER 10

THE WARDEN

I ripped myself from a frightful dream, shielding my eyes against the light. Quentin sat on the bed opposite me. My heart raced, and my eyes darted about the room, breath coming in short gasps. I pressed a hand to my face and leaned back onto the pillow, my eyes closed.

"Bad dreams?"

I nodded.

"Must have been. You've been fitful most of the time I've watched."

I peeked an eye open, mild discomfort shooting through my head from the light. "You watched me all night?"

He shook his head. "No, I slept. Just less than you." He nodded at the window. "Woke up after night lifted. I never sleep well if it's not dark." He returned his gaze to me. "You fell asleep fast but started thrashing about soon after that."

I nodded, taking in a deep breath. It felt good, so I did it again, flushing the negative feelings out when my lungs exhaled. My stomach growled a complaint about its current state. Quentin smiled and tossed a nutrient pack at me.

"They dropped those off after the night screen lifted. Base flavor, nothing too tasty." He nodded toward the door. "Cups in the lavatory, if you're thirsty."

I sat up, ripped into the nutrient pack, and consumed it in a rush. The squishy gel filled my stomach, and a sigh of relief escaped my lips as I leaned back against the wall, facing Quentin. He stared out the mottled glass that served as the room's only window while I looked about the quarters, pondering the predicament.

"Kind of nice for a prison."

Quentin grunted. "I don't think this is the prison side of the facility."

"Where are we?"

"Ostensibly, we're at a Colberran trading outpost near the shell's edge," he replied, frowning as he spoke. "In truth, we're in an outpost dominated by raiders and men that resemble warlords more than they do the politicians they pretend at being."

My heart dropped a bit as he spoke. Everyone in the outer provinces knew of this facility. Most went out of their way to avoid the entire province it resided in, and not just because it lay the furthest west one could go in the Outer Dominance sectors before hitting the Wilds.

"Arya," I whispered.

The one place my brother wanted to go, and now we were there. I couldn't decide which gave me more pause: that we were here or that now we were here he might do something even stupider.

Quentin nodded. "An interesting name, that one. I think it's a derivative of an ancient word from before the Splitting." He smiled. "But my bet is you don't care about ancient history."

"Depends on the history."

It was a trite response to make, I knew, but the last thing I wanted to talk about at the time was the single most destructive moment in our world's history. I was already facing the complete disintegration of my family; I didn't want to think about the world being ripped apart by forces I could only dream of, let alone control like the Ancients had. Quentin, as usual, was completely oblivious to this.

"The word is different now, but I think it's a derivative of an ancient word used to describe a certain type of slave before the Splitting. Its origins are—"

"Where is my brother?" I interrupted. "Have you seen him?"

He shifted on his bed, lips pressed together as he looked about the room. After several moments, he spoke.

"The one guard who delivered our breakfast is the only person who's come through that door since that hood was pulled off."

"Sorry, I didn't mean to cut you off. I'm just worried."

"About him? Or about what he'll do?" Quentin asked.

I looked over at him. "You saw what happened?"

"We saw some of it. When the men started rushing ahead and we heard shots going off, we knew something was up." He shrugged. "All things considered, I think that raider was very reasonable." He gave me a look. "Still, it begs the question: What was he doing?"

I didn't answer but looked at the window. It wasn't an answer I wanted to share. After all, I barely knew Quentin and he was wearing a Seeker uniform. Still, he seemed sincere enough and they had done their part to help hide our secrets.

"My brother believes my family might actually be at a facility like this," I said, the words rushing out. "That instead of being dead from an illness, my sister is a prisoner. My mother as well."

"And your father you know is, which would feed this theory of his," Quentin added.

"Exactly," I stated, nodding my head for emphasis.

Quentin's head leaned to one side. "And you don't agree with him?"

I shrugged, shaking my head. "I don't know what to believe, but my father very much acted like they were gone for good. And until I have other evidence . . ." I looked back at the window.

"You don't want to get your hopes up," he said in a quiet voice. "So, how do you know we're in Arya?"

He shrugged. "Easy. It's one of only two places on the shell where people aren't afraid of Seekers." He laughed. "Well, except for the Wilds, but no one lives there. Come to think of it, there are a lot of places that don't care for them. Still, only place I know that would employ raiders bold enough to capture and detain Seekers." He looked at me. "Plus, we weren't traveling that long, and I stayed awake for it. Arya is the only feasible place we could have reached in that time."

An involuntary shiver passed through me. "We hear tales of this place, warnings to keep us from wandering out too far in the desert. They say no one ever comes out of here free."

Quentin grimaced. "They also say they feed the people to the Wilds or toss them over the edge or—"

"Offer them up to dragons," I cut in, my thoughts shifting back to the events of the day before. I closed my eyes, taking deep breaths to push the memory from my mind.

Quentin, maybe sensing my need for a distraction, went on. "I've heard that, too. Nothing substantiated. Rumors, but no hard evidence."

"It's hard to have evidence when all the witnesses are either taken or offering the victims up," I muttered, opening my eyes to glare at him.

"True," he agreed. "I admit that thought occurred to me before I said it. Can't fault a guy for looking for the bright side."

I grimaced and stood, moving toward the lavatory. "The only bright side I see is coming from that window."

Quentin chuckled. "Not a morning person?"

A grunt seemed the best reply as I entered the lavatory. A few moments later, I exited to find him standing near the window, staring out. He turned to look at me, and I looked away, feeling discomfort under his gaze.

"You seemed to be missing a sibling when we arrived last night," he said in a quiet voice, drawing a nod from me. "We found what was left of the speeders. We tried to get closer, sooner. Frankly, I was shocked when Suyef found your trail leaving the scene."

"You expected we'd all been taken." I sat on the bed, staring at the far wall.

"That's usually what happens after such a raid."

"They leave no one behind?"

He nodded. "Not usually, no."

I closed my eyes, pulling my legs up in front of me and hugging my knees to my head. Quentin got the message and stopped talking. It was impossible to hide from it, I know, but I was so tired of facing this. Would it ever end? Each and every one gone, taken from me. My heart screamed for it to stop. All that life had left was Donovan, and even he lay locked away from me.

I heard movement and looked up to see Quentin settling back down opposite me. Noticing my gaze, he nodded at the window.

"No point staring through that glass," he muttered, settling his cloak around his torso and gazing back at me. "Want to talk?"

I shrugged. Words, at that point, seemed like too much effort.

"Shall I talk instead? Occupy your mind?"

A small smile touched my lips. "The thought's appreciated, but I'm not sure it would help."

"Can't hurt to try?"

I shook my head, staring off to one side. "It won't bring them back." I looked down. "Any of them."

Quentin looked confused but said nothing.

"Maryn isn't the first of my family to be taken from us," I explained.

"Yes, your father, mother, and sister, if my memory serves."

I nodded. "It just keeps happening. Whether it's Seekers like you, dragons, or just raiders putting me in a different cell from my brother, something is always taking my family from me."

Quentin shifted, glancing down at his robe. "Look, I may be wearing this thing, but it's not what you think it is."

"Does it matter? Someone wearing that cloak took my parents and sister from me. Someone wearing that cloak tried to take the rest of us. It seems like every time I turn around, you Seekers are meddling in my family's affairs."

Quentin stopped shifting to look back up at me. "Or your family may just be meddling in the wrong kind of things and getting the wrong kind of attention."

I glared at the Seeker. "What's that supposed to mean? You think we brought this on ourselves?"

"Maybe," he said, shrugging and shaking his head. "I don't know. But you came to our attention, and we weren't even looking for you."

"You never did explain that one. What were you looking for that led you to us?"

Quentin glanced toward the door. "Let's leave that for a different conversation. Suffice to say we were conducting our own search and found you."

I settled my chin on my knees and stared off to the side. Had my father's project been the cause of all this? Could he have brought the wrong kind of attention down on us by accident? Or maybe it was Donovan? I looked back at Quentin.

"You followed us when we left the tower."

He shook his head. "No, we went in a different direction. Questioners are not to be trifled with, even under the best of circumstances."

"So, how did you find us?"

"Dragons aren't invisible. We saw them from a long way off and went to investigate."

"You went toward a bunch of raiding dragons?" I asked, not bothering to hide from my face my thoughts on that idea.

He shrugged. "Probably not the smartest move." He looked around the room. "Especially considering its unexpected end. Still, we took precautions, and the dragons never saw us."

"So, what did you do with your speeders?"

"We left them near where we found the other wrecked ones. Suyef prefers tracking on the ground to using Seeker technology when he has the choice. We weren't sure how far ahead of us you were or who you were, but your choice in direction gave us an idea." He spread his hands out before him. "We caught up to you just after the raiders got there. I'd hoped the robes would convince them to let you go."

"How'd that work out for you?" I asked, giving him a small smile that, to be honest, didn't touch me inside.

"Suyef would agree with you and said as much before we tried it. But we were out of ideas and didn't have a way to keep up with you if it turned out they did take you," he replied. "So, in a way, it worked perfectly."

I arched an eyebrow at him.

"From a certain point of view, I mean."

"Do you always insist on looking on the bright side of things?"

He nodded. "Usually. Especially in the face of those who don't."

"You must be quite popular among your friends," I replied, snorting in laughter.

"Friends come and go." He frowned. "I think only Suyef would classify me as a friend, and he finds my perspective to be . . . What was it he said? 'Naive.'"

"Sounds like the voice of reason, if you ask me." I rested my forehead on my knees, pressing my eyes closed. "We might just get along."

Quentin chuckled. "Don't hold your breath on that one. I haven't known him all that long, but he keeps most things to himself."

The conversation died after that. We discussed nothing of importance for nearly half the day, avoiding touchy subjects.

Quentin seemed to be trying to get to know me without asking any questions that might touch on the subject of my family. I let him ask, my mind wandering from subject to subject, welcoming the distraction.

Sometime in the afternoon, the door slid open. We both looked up, eager for our next nutrient pack, but none came. Instead, a guard beckoned us out of the room.

"The warden wishes to see you."

The facility we marched through proved to be as lacking in decor as the quarters we had occupied the night before. Long hallways of white walls, silver carpeting, and dull, white lighting greeted our eyes when we left our room and turned right. We walked in silence past many closed doors down the hall as it curved to our right until we arrived at a circular room that looked like a hub. Another hallway exited off the opposite side from the one we came through, a large window stood to the left, and a single set of double doors were to the right. Donovan and Suyef stood before the doors with another guard. I rushed over and hugged my brother. The doors slid open to reveal a cramped elevator, into which the four of us climbed, the doors closing behind us and leaving the guards there. We rode in silence as the lift rose into the higher reaches of the facility. After a few moments, we felt it stop, and the doors opened.

A large room easily twice the size of the control station my family had lived in stood before us, its walls made of massive windows that overlooked the desert for leagues in all directions. Across from the lift sat a single desk with a large top and nothing on it. Sitting in a high-backed chair facing the lift sat a man I'd never seen before. He had thin, black hair that hung down, framing a gaunt face. A sharply jutting nose swept down between two cold, gray eyes, and his lips pushed out slightly behind his hands, held folded in front of his mouth. He wore a silver robe and a single ring on his left ring finger. His eyes took us each in, stopping on me, holding my gaze. For a moment, I saw some kind of emotion flicker across his face, a twitch of his thin eyebrows, lips parting. His hard gaze returned, and he waved us forward.

"Please, it's rude to loiter on doorsteps," he said by way of greeting, his voice quiet but firm.

We stepped from the lift, and the doors shut behind us. I looked to my left and saw that the windows continued all the way around behind the lift, which stood in a pillar at the room's center. To my right, the Central Mountains rose in the distance, to my left the shell's edge.

"An impressive view, I agree," the room's occupant said, drawing my attention back to find him watching me. "I, too, find myself lost in it at times. It's a fascinating place, this world. Not what I expected to find."

I glanced at my companions, but none looked at me.

"I'd offer you a seat, but we have none," he said. "Please accept my apologies. I trust you found your quarters comfortable?"

He spoke to us all, but his eyes remained on me. I found myself shifting behind my brother and noticed Quentin had positioned himself just off my other side. When none of us answered, he spread his hands before him and smiled.

"I must also apologize for any rudeness my compatriots may have shown toward you. They tend to be simple in mind, if effective in action, for the tasks I give them."

"You expect us to believe you sent them looking for us?" Quentin asked.

The man shook his head, still not taking his eyes from me. "Ah no. As good as my luck would seem to be, I can't claim to have that kind of foresight. No, these raiders, as I believe they are called by the shell's law-abiding residents, simply scour the land looking for any wayward souls that need some help finding their way back to more civilized parts of the shell." A small smile tugged at his lips. "Even when they prove a bit more difficult than expected."

I felt my face warm up. "What are you going to do with my brother?" I asked. "Will he be punished?"

The man frowned at me. "Punished? Why would I do that to him?"

"He attacked your men," Quentin stated.

The warden's eyes moved to look at him. "To call them my men is a stretch," he replied. "They do what they want for the most part, and sometimes that includes helping me."

"Help doing what?" I asked, stepping out from behind Donovan and bumping both him and Quentin. "You call that help? Capturing people and selling them, or worse?"

The man grimaced and looked away from me. "I can see my compatriots also lack any semblance of control over their tongues." He held up a hand to forestall any comment. "I'll not defend the practices these men have set up. They were that way when I came upon them. I've tried to temper their trade, but they prove to be rather persistent in this business they've established."

"You found them this way?" Quentin asked.

The man nodded. "This outpost has been here for centuries under the control of the raiders. To think I've been in control of them, if one can claim to have that kind of power out here, for that long is just a bit absurd."

"That's not what I meant," Quentin replied. "I meant when you came here, you found them doing this?"

"Oh yes, they've been trading in people for centuries. I just stumbled upon their little project recently and saw an opportunity." He returned his gaze to me. "One that seems to have paid off."

Quentin and Donovan both shifted toward each other, shielding me from the man's gaze.

"You got eyes for my sister?" Donovan asked, anger creeping into his voice.

The man behind the desk blinked and looked up at Donovan, quite possibly seeing him for the first time. He looked back and forth between us, and his eyes widened in amazement.

"The resemblance isn't . . . strong, but I could be convinced it exists," he said, more to himself than the rest of us. "Fascinating."

He had completely lost me, and I was about to state that when he shook his head and stood.

"Forgive me, where are my manners?" He stepped out from behind the desk, long robe swaying with the motion as it stretched to the floor. "My name is Mortac. I'm the warden of this facility." He stepped closer and stopped, standing before Quentin and Donovan, gazing down at me. "But, you knew that already, didn't you?"

I tried to pull my gaze from his but couldn't. He stared at me, drinking me up. He acted familiar with me; that's the only way to describe it. Like he knew me from a previous meeting, and knew me well, if his behavior was any indication.

"Excuse me," Donovan said, stepping between us and breaking his gaze. "Would you care to explain yourself?"

Mortac smiled, a soft, tiny thing that barely touched his lips. "Dear boy, the full explanation would probably stagger you into stupidity, a state I suspect you're not far from." He gave my brother a short glance. "And considering your behavior when my compatriots here captured you, I'd say my suspicions are founded."

Donovan bristled, stepping toward the man, fists clenched. "Now see here—"

Quentin grabbed him and pulled him back, Suyef stepping forward to help.

"Settle down, Donovan," Quentin whispered.

"I don't take orders from you, Seeker," my brother hissed, shoving, attempting to extricate himself from Quentin and Suyef's clutches. "For all I know, you're working with him."

"To what end?" Quentin asked.

Donovan stopped dead. "Well, to kidnap us."

"And why would we do that?" Quentin asked, never taking his eyes from Donovan. "To bring you to him? But you're already here. And, in case you didn't notice, he had us locked away with you."

Mortac stood, a small smile creeping onto his face, eyes watching me.

Donovan shuffled a bit, then looked down. "I'm not really sure what you're doing here." He looked at me. "Or what he wants with us."

"Which is precisely what he can tell us." Quentin turned to face the warden. "Unless you care to hit him and see if he'll cooperate." He leaned near my brother. "I'm not sure you can count on everyone being as amicable after you hit them as that raider."

Mortac raised his hands in a placating motion. "I assure you, as long as I am in charge of this facility, you are safe." He looked at me again. "All of you."

He said "all of," but in my mind I heard *especially*, and that made me even more uncomfortable. Who was this man, and why did he act like he knew me? Before I could even ponder the answer to that question, an interruption arrived.

"Then we'll just have to see how long you stay in control of the facility, won't we, Mortac," a familiar voice said from behind us.

We all turned to see Colvinra exiting the lift.

CHAPTER 11

A SEEKER SOLUTION

To say I was shocked to see the Questioner standing there would be an understatement. I'd also be lying if I didn't say seeing him gave me a bit of hope. After all, if he managed to escape, Maryn may have, too.

Colvinra made his way around the four of us to face Mortac. His eyes never left those of the warden, who finally lost interest in me and watched the Questioner. Quentin and Suyef shifted to stand between us and the two men. The entire situation struck me as precarious.

"What do you want here?" Mortac asked, breaking the silence.

"Why, nothing more than to thank you," the Questioner said, smiling and pointing at the lot of us. "You've found our missing prisoners and even brought our two lost Seekers back for us. I'm here to collect them all."

"You lost a pair of Seekers?"

Colvinra chuckled. "They're a bit new and somehow got separated from their speeders. I suspect the dragons may have had a hand in that?" He looked at Suyef, eyebrows raised in question. Suyef nodded. "Ah, see? Pesky creatures, those foul beasts. Have you had many problems out this far?"

Mortac's eyes narrowed. "You know full well what goes on here."

"Yes, yes we do. Which is why I was sent to retrieve your most recent guests before anything questionable happened to them."

Mortac glanced over at us, then back at the Questioner. "And what would this lot have done to be of interest to the Seekers?"

"Tsk-tsk, you know you shouldn't meddle in Seeker affairs," Colvinra chided the warden. "It's bad enough you held two of them in detainment."

"We weren't in detainment," Quentin stated. "They put us in the facility's quarters."

Colvinra turned to look at Quentin.

"And were you free to move about?"

Quentin shook his head.

"Then, regardless of where you were put up for the night, you were detained. At least, that's how I see it, and what I say will suffice for how the Seekers will see this situation." He turned back to face Mortac. "So, the question that remains is how much Seeker involvement do you want in your little operation here?"

"You still didn't answer my question," Mortac said. "What do you want with the other two?"

"You already know, my friend," the Questioner stated.

Mortac glared at the man. "You're still looking for it, aren't you? And you think they have it? A couple of provincials."

The Seeker glanced at me. "Sure, a couple of provincials. We'll go with that for now. We believe they have information crucial to us finding a mole in our network."

"You are still looking for it," the warden said, his voice quiet. "After all this time, you still haven't learned."

Colvinra stepped nearer the warden. "That is Seeker business. Best you forgot you saw them and that we had this discussion."

"They are guests. I'll not have a Seeker, Questioner or no, marching into my facility and absconding with my visitors."

"Do you always lock your visitors up for the night?" Colvinra asked.

Mortac shrugged. "This isn't what I'd call a vacation resort. The doors were secured for their safety."

"Doesn't change the fact that you violated Colberran law by detaining two Seekers, however you spin it," Colvinra replied. "Nor does it change the fact that those two are Seeker property."

"I'm no one's property," Donovan growled.

The two men ignored him, squaring off across the desk from each other.

"It's not that simple." The warden pointed at my brother. "This one assaulted several of my men. Under the terms of operation, he is ours to punish as we see fit."

"I can assure you, he will be suitably chastised," the Seeker replied, his voice low.

"And you would be the one to enforce such a change in the arrangement?" Mortac asked.

Colvinra's head cocked to one side as the men stood there staring each other down. I could tell that, left unbridled, the testosterone in the room might lead to something ugly, so I decided to ask a question.

"Colvinra, where is my brother?" The two turned as one to look at me, the Questioner arching an eyebrow as he glanced at Donovan. "Not this one. Maryn, the younger one."

The Questioner shrugged. "Do I look like your brother's keeper?"

"I just thought if you escaped, you might have seen him," I muttered, holding the Questioner's gaze.

Colvinra nodded. "Ah yes, well, I didn't escape from the dragons." He looked at Mortac. "No one escapes the clutches of those vile beasts, do they, Mortac?"

The warden didn't answer. The little bit of hope that had blossomed when the Questioner had appeared faded away.

"If you didn't escape, how are you here now?" Donovan asked.

"We Seekers have more than one way to fight dragons," he answered, turning to face Mortac. "Now I'll be leaving with my prisoners and Seekers."

"No, you won't," Mortac stated, his voice resolute, jaw set.

"Need I remind you, Mortac, of your precarious situation here?" Colvinra asked as he pointed at Quentin and Suyef.

Quentin glanced at Suyef, who shrugged. "Don't include us in your fight."

Colvinra turned to look at Quentin. "Excuse me?"

"You two seem to have something between you," Quentin said, waving a hand back and forth between the pair. "Whatever it is, it's not Seeker business, in my book. Yours, Suyef?" The Nomad shook his head. "There you have it. He's not threatening these two here, so we'll stay out of your fight."

Colvinra glowered at Quentin. "Do you require a reminder as to who is in charge here?"

"Him," Quentin said, pointing at Mortac. "This isn't a Seeker facility. Seekers ceded control of this place a long time ago, including extradition laws. Technically speaking, the only person here with any legal authority as recognized by the Colberran government is the warden."

Colvinra took a step toward Quentin, a dangerous look on his face. "When we get back to a Seeker outpost, I swear I'll have you scouring a waste-reclamation center for your insubordination before the day is up."

"We won't be going with you, sir," Suyef said, his voice quiet.

"You'd remain his prisoner?" Colvinra turned to glare at Suyef.

Quentin shrugged. "He hasn't made it clear what our status is here yet. You, on the other hand, have made it quite clear where we all stand."

Colvinra bristled at Quentin's words, and Mortac chuckled.

"He always knew how to push your buttons, my old friend, didn't he?" Mortac whispered, so quietly I almost didn't hear him.

I looked at him, confused, and he grinned at me with that familiar, knowing smile. I looked away, but the thought remained. This man seemed to be very familiar with Quentin and me.

"This isn't over, Mortac," Colvinra declared, shoving past Quentin and stepping near the lift. "For any of you."

With those words, the lift opened, and he stormed out.

"That one causes me more problems than I know what to do with," Mortac said, letting out a deep breath as his shoulders sagged.

"You've butted heads with him before?" Quentin asked, turning to face the warden.

Mortac nodded. "More times than I care to recall." He looked at each of us, smiling again at me, then turned to face Suyef. "Of all the faces I'd hoped or expected to see here, yours was not on the list."

Suyef bowed his head but didn't say a word.

"Still on your quest, I see," Mortac said, glancing at Quentin. "This one's been a bad influence on you, I think."

Quentin frowned, looking at Suyef. "Am I missing something here?"

Suyef didn't answer. He just stood there, staring at the warden.

"Didn't he mention me?" Quentin shook his head, so Mortac continued. "I'm his uncle."

All three of us turned to stare at Suyef. "So *this* is your uncle?" Quentin asked as he looked at the Nomad. "The one you entered into the records?"

Suyef nodded. "After a manner."

We waited for him to say more, but he didn't. Mortac chuckled.

"Still a man of few words, I see," the warden said, returning to his seat. "It's good to see this Colberran hasn't worn off on you too much."

Suyef turned to face Mortac. "I'd thank you to stay out of my business, Uncle."

The warden held up his hands. "I'll not stop you from your foolish quest." He looked at me. "Although I'm curious what it has to do with these two."

I had that feeling again, that while he said "these two," he meant me. That small smile danced on his lips, and I shook my head, turning my gaze to Suyef.

"Our involvement with them is unrelated to the quest you speak of. He and I are on a different mission. How they fit into the reason he and I are here remains to be seen," Suyef answered, crossing his arms over his chest.

Mortac spread his hands before him, shaking his head. "I know of your other mission. Will you not tell me how they are connected?"

"We don't know yet," Quentin interjected. "We're still searching, and our search includes them."

Mortac eyed Quentin for a moment, then glanced at Suyef. "You know my opinion of Colberrans."

Suyef shrugged. "I care little for your opinion, Uncle."

It struck me as an odd thing to say to a family member, but I could tell this wasn't a relationship either valued very much. I began to suspect the word had a very different meaning in his culture. The looks they gave each other bordered on distrust mixed with uncertainty, not what you'd find among close family relationships.

Mortac considered his nephew a moment longer, then looked at Quentin. "Share what you have, and we'll see if these two are of any use."

"Yes, please do," I stated. "All this cryptic talk is annoying."

Quentin glanced at Suyef and held his hands out to either side, shrugging. "The thing is, we don't really know what we know yet." He pointed at me. "She, on the other hand, may have the answer."

Mortac followed his hand to me and stared. After a moment of silence that was just beginning to feel uncomfortable, he looked back at Quentin.

"I'll not risk her to you again," he whispered.

I looked at Quentin, who shrugged at me, shaking his head.

"I'm sorry, but have we met before?" he asked the warden.

Mortac shook his head, waving Quentin away. "No, no, I'm referring to what happened to her yesterday. You had her in your guard and let Colvinra get away with her. Look where that led you."

"Other than straight to you?" I asked.

"By way of a near-fatal dragon attack," Mortac retorted, favoring me with a grimace. "Not what I'd call first-class delivery service."

"I'm sorry, I wasn't aware we were delivering her to you or anyone," Quentin said, anger flaring in his voice.

"Watch your tone, young man." The warden's voice was quiet, but firm, eyes locked on Quentin's. "For now, you are a guest at my facility. If you'd like, we can move you to the prisoner area." He nodded toward the window. "Of course, we're a bit overdue for our next visit, so you can imagine it's getting kind of full down there."

Curious, I stepped near the glass, moving around Mortac's desk. Donovan followed me, as did Quentin. Suyef stayed where he was.

In the distance, I spied what had to be the Wilds, an uncontrolled region on the Colberran shell where the weather-control systems didn't work and no human settlement had ever survived. Long in the past, when the shells were still orbiting close together, Colberran history spoke of a collision with another shell that sheared away an entire section of this shell and left a swath of the outer provinces mangled and ruined. That land had resisted all attempts at resettling, and the authorities walled it off to keep the shell's residents from wandering into it.

Swirling clouds of fog, an almost unseen phenomenon on the outer edge of the shell, obscured most of my vision. It clung to the ground and rose up a few hundred feet. The fog ended in an invisible wall a short distance from the edge of the facility, an energy shield holding it in place. Tales of what lay beyond those energy walls were many and varied, each more fantastical than the last. Far off, just in sight above the fog, I spied the tops of jagged rock formations, the only sign visible from the facility of the damage the shell collision had caused.

Tearing my eyes from the awesome sight beyond, I looked down to the facility. The Ancient construct of the main tower jumped out at once, as it was a uniform look throughout the shell. Building with tall, white, swooping lines and elegant curves, the Ancients no doubt meant their structures to be a beautiful sight. It did nothing for me. At the foot of this tall structure, a series of more-modern-looking buildings, each uniform in height with drab brown walls and no windows, encircled the tower. A few guards stood atop towers spaced along the outer edge of the roofs of those structures. Just beyond the taller buildings, rows and rows of concentric circles extended outward to the edge of the facility several hundred feet from the central structures. Upon closer examination, I saw that each row held small cells with people inside them, the rows snug up against one another. Walkways extended out, forming bridges from the central structures to the wall on the exterior of the complex. Every cell held at least two people, some many more.

"As you can see, our prison is full to capacity, hence your cushy quarters last night," Mortac said, moving to stand between Quentin and me. "On top of that, I felt it wouldn't be too wise to keep a pair of Seekers out among the general population."

Quentin chuckled. "I'll bet Colvinra would have a fit if he heard you suggest that."

"Oh, I didn't keep you from there for fear of the likes of him." Mortac's gaze never left the cells below. "I did it to keep the prisoners safe." He looked up at Quentin. "Can't imagine there are very many fans of the Seekers down there. What do you think might happen if one dropped in for an extended visit? Your reputation aside, I'd wager a few would take a shot or two at you before the night was up." He returned his gaze to the cells. "I'd also wager you'd make them pay for that decision. So, as I said, it was for their own good." He glanced over at me, the small smile back. "Mostly."

My gaze returned to the prison. My eyes roamed over all the people gathered there. Beside me, Donovan leaned close to the glass, and I felt one arm bump me. At that moment, I couldn't help but feel just an inkling of hope he might be right about our family's fate.

"Where did they all come from?" I asked the warden.

Mortac sighed. "My colleagues here have been at this for quite some time, but even they are not as efficient as this facility would make them seem."

I looked back up at him, but he didn't continue, eyes locked on me, waiting.

Quentin stepped away from the glass, moving past me to stand near Donovan. As he did, he whispered one sentence to me: "Seeker hospitals don't exist."

Mortac glanced at him, then back at me, keeping silent. As I looked down at the people, realization blossomed in my mind.

"Those are all the people the Seekers take?"

Mortac smiled in answer.

"They all come here?"

He shook his head. "This facility is one of four in the outer provinces. There's another just on the other side of the wild zone to the west, and if you go east the other way around the shell, you'll encounter two more, although those have been shut down." He raised a finger. "This is the one for this district and the abutting interior districts."

"What happens to them here?" I whispered, my mind dreading the possible answers.

At that moment, a chime went off, a single bell ringing three times and echoing in the room. Mortac closed his eyes and sighed.

"I'm afraid you won't like that answer," he whispered, nodding toward the window before turning to sit down.

Confused, I moved closer to the glass, Quentin and Donovan moving to either side. Even Suyef stepped near for a better view. At first, we saw nothing. Below, the guards all began moving, descending from the towers. The walkways retracted from above the prison cells as the guards moved off. Once they cleared, the clear surface forming the roofs of the three outermost circles of cells opened. The floors elevated to form a single solid row where once three rings of cells had been. The opened tops jutting up retracted, giving the occupants, now pushed up onto the roof of the cells, freedom to move. As one, they bolted, fleeing toward the central structure along the tops of the interior cells. Through the glass we could hear nothing, but I could see them screaming, arms held up toward the tower, a look of pleading on their faces. I glanced at Quentin, but he kept his eyes below, his jaw clenched, hands tightened into fists at his side.

A shadow moving across the window caught my eye, and I turned back to the sight below. My heart froze as my gaze shifted to the shell's edge in search of whatever had moved past the window. There, ascending from below, came a flight of dragons. They hovered in the air for a moment, then dove, attacking the fleeing prisoners.

CHAPTER 12

VALUABLE

We watched, helpless, as the dragons swooped in, snatching up victim after victim and streaking off to descend out of sight, prizes in tow. Their claws wrapped around their victims, some grabbing two or three at a time. Here and there, one would miss, knocking a swath of prisoners to the ground. Other dragons dove in to grab as many immobilized prisoners as possible. A couple of victims, held by a foot or arm, didn't make it, plummeting to their deaths on the clear cells. I averted my eyes.

The beasts kept coming, flying low over the facility, until every prisoner was gone, snatched up. After the last prisoner was either captured or dead, one of the beasts flew by the tower, circling it. Long, lithe, with wide wings the same translucent color as its body, the monster had a row of daggerlike protrusions jutting up along its spine. The beast and its companions looked identical to those in the flight that had attacked us the day before, with one key difference: each of them wore red scales. The creature circled the tower once, letting out a cry we could hear through the glass. After that, it zoomed off toward the shell's edge, diving down after the rest.

The entire attack lasted mere moments, but for me it seemed like forever. All those people, just gone, taken, to who knew where.

I spun on Mortac, who sat facing his desk, hands steepled across his mouth.

"I didn't create this system," he whispered.

"You haven't stopped it," I countered.

He nodded. "It's not my place to. Some of us know when not to mess with things that work." He turned to look at me. "Especially things we don't understand." He looked past me into the sky. "I'll not pretend to understand why your people set this system up. I've seen stranger, but hardly anything as heartless as this."

"We didn't set this up," I whispered, shaking my head and blinking tears away. "We didn't know."

"We? Or you?"

"This isn't common knowledge," Quentin said. "We'd only heard rumors."

"Ignorance is not a defense," he said. "As citizens, it's your duty to know what your government, or their military arm, is doing." Mortac looked at Quentin, a frown on his face. "You're from this shell, wearing a Seeker cloak, and you didn't know this was going on?"

Quentin shook his head. "I wasn't born and raised here." He pointed at Suyef. "I've spent most of my life on his shell. The one time I came back here, my family stayed on the islands, off-shell."

Mortac's eyes narrowed. "How did a Colberran come to be on the Nomad shell?"

"My parents were Expeditionary Forces. They met on assignment there." Quentin pointed back out the window. "But we're not discussing me. We're discussing that atrocity."

Mortac waved his hand at the window. "We don't even know what they do with them. I've tried to find out, but no one has any record of where they go or what they do with their victims. Your people don't even know where the dragons come from, save for legends."

"That doesn't mean we should just offer people up to be taken!" Quentin yelled, pointing at Mortac. "You're in charge here. Stop it."

"I stop the offerings, and the Seekers will take over this facility, plain and simple."

Quentin barked a derisive laugh. "So, you keep up the 'offerings' to save your hide."

"At least with the dragons, there's a chance they might live," Mortac whispered. "What do you think Seekers would do with so many prisoners? Keep them happy in some retirement facility somewhere?"

"You think you're offering them a better option by feeding them to the beasts?" Donovan asked.

"No one has ever seen a dragon eat a human," Suyef said. Every head turned to look at the man. "On either shell."

"What, are you some kind of dragon expert in disguise now, Suyef?" Quentin asked, turning his frown on his friend.

Suyef glared at him. "Don't loose your anger at me. I'm just repeating a well-known fact."

"He's right," Mortac said, waving a hand at the Nomad. "I've searched the database, and the one thing I can say beyond a shadow of a doubt is that there isn't a single account of a dragon eating a human. They just take them, and we don't know where."

"And you facilitate it," Quentin declared. "You're as bad as a war sympathizer."

Mortac's frown deepened, his expression darkening, eyes locked on Quentin. "We can't all be heroes. Some of us help in other ways."

"Like how?" I asked.

Mortac shook his head. "Never mind. The point is, we can't save them all."

"I don't see you saving any." Quentin pointed out to the cells. "Looks like you just offer up whatever happens to be in a row and rotate it."

Mortac slammed his hand into the chair next to his leg and bolted up to face Quentin. "I'll not defend myself to a whining, sniveling, meddlesome brat who has a penchant for sticking his head into things that aren't his business and ruining whatever he tries to fix." He stepped close to Quentin, their eyes level. "Suffice it to say, I've worked hard to ensure only those that deserve it are offered to the dragons."

"How do you define *deserve*?" I asked, trying to defuse another potential fight.

The two blinked and looked at me. Mortac shook his head and moved away from Quentin, who glared after the warden as he retreated.

"The actual criminals brought to us by the Seekers are put in the cells next up for offering. We shuffle them around constantly, and I do my best to make it look random so the raiders don't suspect what we're doing. I assure you, I place the most hardened criminals in the offering blocks first and only resort to the rest the raiders and Seekers bring in if the dragons return before we have another offering prepared. Hopefully, we can sell those off before that happens."

"So, you offer up some and sell others into slavery?" Quentin asked, his voice cracking on the last word.

"A life enslaved is a life still alive," Mortac countered. He held up a hand to forestall Quentin. "I've managed to use the threat of the dragon raids to keep slavers from coming here. It's worked well, but every now and then I still have to hold an auction to keep the raiders and slavers from getting suspicious."

"Slavery is illegal in Colberra," Donovan stated. "So, you aren't selling them to anyone on this shell."

Mortac nodded. "Slave buyers all come from other shells, by way of the Nomad shell. This helps with stalling, as it takes time to organize such things." He held a finger up at Donovan. "But don't pretend this is possible without at least tacit government approval. Your leaders look the other way because they don't have time for

Outer Dominance problems. It's been that way as long as I've been here."

The thought that had blossomed in the back of my mind when I'd looked out the window—and with it a bit of hope in my heart—bubbled back to the surface. I tried to pat it down, to squash it before it bloomed. In part, I didn't want to encourage Donovan and his foolish theory regarding our family. More so, my heart was tired of getting its hopes up just to be disappointed. Still, if there was a chance he was right, I had to ask.

"How long have you been doing this?"

Mortac frowned, and his face scrunched in thought. "At least a decade."

"And do you keep records of all your prisoners?"

He nodded. "Seekers require it as a part of the agreement."

Donovan shifted beside me, but I ignored him.

"Might I look at them?"

He stared at me a moment; then understanding crept across his face. "Ah yes, I can assure you, they did not come through this facility."

"Not even a chance?" I asked, not giving thought at the time to the fact that he knew immediately who I was talking about.

"I promise you, they are not here," Mortac said, his voice soft. "I can also tell you they didn't make it to any of the other facilities, either."

"You're talking about what I think you are, aren't you?" Donovan asked, looking between us.

"Yes, your family members, my dear, stupid boy," Mortac said, rolling his eyes and smiling at me. "Is he always like this?"

I didn't answer, my mind contemplating what he'd just revealed. If my mother and sister hadn't come to a facility like this, that meant they were probably being held in the central provinces, like my father. If what Quentin said was true.

"Do you know of any facility they might take ill people to?"

Mortac's head cocked to one side. "What kind of illness are you thinking of?"

I described Jyen's and my mother's symptoms. As he listened, Mortac sighed and his shoulders sagged. When I finished, he sat down in his chair, head hanging.

"After all this time, we still haven't eliminated that disease," he whispered.

"Do you know something about it?" I asked, clinging, despite my best efforts, to a fragment of hope.

He nodded. "It's an ancient one, what your sister had. One I thought this world had moved on from." He looked each of us over, his features twisted in a frown. "It seems the authorities have just perfected how to hide its existence better than they once did."

Quentin and I shared looks, Quentin even shrugging. Mortac noticed and smiled.

"I can't say I understand your confusion. Suffice it to say I've had some experience with this disease." He turned a sad gaze to me. "Barring some unknown, miraculous cure I've yet to discover, and not for lack of trying on my part, I can assure you, if she had it, your sister is gone from us. As to your mother, she didn't come through my facility."

I nodded, and I felt the hope that had bloomed in my heart wither and die. My hand sought out Donovan's, clinging to the one thing in which I had any faith left.

"What if I don't believe you?" my brother said, his voice firm as his hand gripped my own.

"Donovan, no," I whispered.

The warden shook his head. "It doesn't matter to me what you believe. All I can tell you is what I know. And that is she did not come here."

"How often do these dragons come?" Quentin asked, steering the discussion back to the event we'd just witnessed.

"There isn't a pattern save for they rarely ever come back soon after a visit. Sometimes they'll not appear again for close to a cycle. Other times, they'll come back every few days."

"What happens when you don't have enough victims to offer up to them?"

Mortac grimaced. "They go in search of what they want."

"When was the last time you gave an offering to green dragons?" I asked, thinking back to the attack on us.

"Wait, you've seen *green* dragons?" Mortac asked.

I nodded. "Just yesterday, a flight of them attacked Colvinra's Seekers. They took my younger brother."

Mortac covered his mouth with one hand as he thought.

"And they took people? Anyone else, besides your brother?"

"All the Seekers, save for Colvinra, apparently," I answered.

His head cocked to one side as he stared at me. "What game is this?"

I frowned. "Game? This is my family we're talking about."

He nodded once. "This gets more curious the longer it goes. They left you," he whispered, folding his hands behind the small of his back. "What are they up to?"

"Who?" Quentin asked, but Mortac ignored him, pacing away from us around the room, eyes looking out the window toward the shell's edge. "Mortac, who are you talking about?"

The warden stopped and turned back to us, eyes focused elsewhere. "You're sure it was a green flight that attacked you?"

I nodded, as did Donovan.

"And was there anything different about any of them?"

I frowned. "They were all different sizes, but otherwise they all looked the same."

"No, Micaela, remember that one that hovered over you?" Donovan piped up, turning to look at me. "That one was much larger and had all that bone jutting back from its head."

"The Dragon Queen?" Mortac whispered to himself, his eyes focusing on me. A very confused look twisted his features as he stared at me. "She was there? Had you ever seen her before?"

I shook my head.

"So, it could just have been a large dragon." His eyes widened, and he looked around the room. "Still, it left you behind, and those creatures do not do anything without their Queen telling them to do so." He stared at me a moment longer, then shook his head, the confused look replaced with a smile. "Well, I can't explain her activity to anyone, but it does explain our earlier guest's interest in you."

"How does a dragon not taking me make me of interest to Colvinra? I mean, more than anyone else would be interested in why it happened? It doesn't appear to be that common a thing."

Mortac shook his head. "Survivors of dragon raids are virtually nonexistent. When they want you, they take you." He held my gaze. "And this one left you behind. Fascinating."

"That still doesn't explain Colvinra's interest in her relating to the dragon," Quentin pointed out.

Mortac smiled. "It's simple. He has an unhealthy fascination with that particular dragon, a grudge of sorts. If it indeed was the Queen you saw. Goes back a long ways, that grudge, I assure you. If she really was there, and she left you behind," he said, nodding at me, "then you're of value to her."

He smiled that same smile, a small thing darting across his lips and touching at his cheeks, eyes never leaving mine.

"And that makes you valuable to him."

CHAPTER 13

DARKNESS

I contemplated Mortac's words long after we returned to our quarters. He had admitted at my insistence that he felt it safer to keep us separated in case Colvinra tried any tricks. When I declared that didn't matter, he moved us to adjoining quarters that shared a common space. The only entrance into the living area remained locked, of course. We found four rooms off this suite, each with a single bed. Donovan and I spent the rest of that day together, discussing what had happened. Suyef, it turns out, was as quiet as Quentin had described him to be. Donovan hadn't managed to get more than a few words from him. I didn't tell my brother everything Quentin and I had discussed. I'm not sure why. Donovan was all the family I had left, but I felt if he knew Quentin and I had talked, he might get a bit defensive.

Soon after that, we all went to sleep. We saw no one the next day save for a guard delivering nutrient packs. He ignored any attempt to talk. So, we waited, the next day passing as the previous had. On the fifth day since we had arrived, the four of us sat in silence as we consumed the nutrient packs delivered moments before.

"You're quiet," I said to Quentin.

"So are you. I thought you wanted to be. You didn't seek either of us out."

I shrugged. "Maybe. It's a lot to take in."

Quentin nodded, finishing off his nutrient pack with water from his cup. "I'm sorry you didn't find them."

"It was a slim chance anyway." I looked at the only window in the room, a mottled-glass skylight above the table in the center of the open space that let in a bit of core-light were it not nighttime. "Shouldn't have gotten my hopes up. It never ends well." I could feel his eyes on me.

"You've lost a lot," he said. "It's hard to be hopeful, considering."

I sighed, eyes still on the window. "For a moment, back there, when I saw Colvinra and again when I thought of the people kept here, I felt it, just a bit. Like a flower peeking out above the snow." I chuckled. "Stupid flower. Forgot about the spring freeze."

"It's never stupid to have hope," Quentin whispered.

I shifted my head to look at him. "It hasn't helped me any."

Donovan grunted what sounded like agreement. "I had no luck with that terminal in our room, either."

"You need to drop that, or you're going to get us in even more trouble," I said, my voice firm.

He waved a hand at the room. "I don't believe that warden, and I'm going to keep trying. Someone knows what happened to them."

I nodded. "Yes, we do."

Another silence fell on the room. I gave Quentin a smile.

"I appreciate your efforts, but I don't have much hope left to hold on to," I said, shaking my head.

"Granted, you've got reason to have lost most of it." Quentin shrugged. "But there's always reason for a little hope."

"Why? What will I gain except a bit more disappointment?"

"Your father?" Quentin asked.

"Hoping isn't getting me any closer to him."

"Nor any farther away."

I shook my head, looking back at the window. "So, it's doing nothing."

"You'll find him."

"I wish I could believe that," I whispered.

Quentin didn't answer. He leaned his elbows on the table, hands folded in front of his face. Suyef, having finished eating, moved to sit on one of the room's fabric-covered couches. Donovan remained sitting near me, for which I felt quite a bit of gratitude.

"Why do you care, anyway?" I asked.

Quentin looked at the floor a long moment before answering. "Maybe because you don't. Maybe I'm just being stubborn or contrary. Someone's got to have a little faith around here."

I stared at him. "I don't even have that anymore. What's there to believe in if I keep losing the things I had faith in?"

Donovan grunted at me. "I'm still here."

"Yes, and trying hard to get us in more trouble with people that have the ability to separate us," I said, glaring at him.

He smacked his hand down on the table. "I'm tired of doing nothing and being jerked around like this. The answers are on that stupid network."

"I know you're trying to help, Donovan, but what if you make it worse in the process?" I asked.

That made him pause. I kept on, hoping he would finally understand.

"I want them to be somewhere on this shell, too," I said, grabbing his hand. "But I don't want to lose you as well. I'm not saying give up. Just because I don't believe you're right doesn't mean you aren't. But please, be careful, okay?"

He shrugged. "Well, like I said, I'm still here, so you haven't lost everything."

"You know what I mean," I said, smiling and squeezing his arm as I looked back at Quentin. "Well?"

"Family can't be taken from you just because they're gone," he said. "Otherwise, no one would ever leave home."

"There's a difference," I said with a little more heat than I intended, "between going out in the world and having your mother, father, sister, and brother forcefully removed from your life. Forever."

Quentin held up a finger. "You don't know they're all gone forever."

"My sister and mother are."

"You don't even know that much," he stated, folding his hands. "All you have is the word of—"

"Seekers," Donovan finished for him.

"Actually, it was the warden who said it, and he's not a Seeker."

I glared at Quentin. "Fine, but Seekers like you took them, and then they vanished."

"I told you before I'm not a Seeker." He plucked at the robe he wore. "I'm just borrowing the uniform to find something."

"Me?" I asked. "Everyone else seems to be looking for me. You two as well?"

"No, but our search did lead us to you, so if you count that . . ." He shrugged. "We weren't looking for you."

"If I recall, you knew my father was gone."

He nodded. "Once our search brought you to our attention, our Seeker access allowed us to learn more about you. That's when we saw the arrest report ordered for your father and the subsequent report to find and detain you." He pursed his lips in thought. "The odd thing is the reports were written the same day, but they somehow got mixed up so that your father was detained well before you."

"Why is that odd?" I asked, shifting my back into a more comfortable position and rolling my shoulders back to fix my posture.

"The order to detain your father went to the right outpost," he replied. "The one to arrest you—which didn't mention your brothers, by the way, they were only interested in you—anyway, that order went to an outpost on the far side of the shell. It took several days for them to discover their error."

"How did they make a mistake like that?" I asked. "That seems very incompetent."

Quentin nodded. "And very un-Seeker-like. They're the model of efficiency. It's either a rare case of incompetence in their ranks, or someone didn't want you detained too early."

I stared at him. "That's a huge leap of logic."

"We thought the same thing." Quentin nodded at his companion. "Suyef said I was jumping to conclusions when I suggested that a few days before we found you."

"Maybe he's right?" I offered.

"It's possible, but I double-checked the reports." He shifted forward in his chair, leaning across the table. "The destination codes on the original reports are correct, but when they got to the switching node, someone changed the destination code on your detainment order."

A memory bubbled to the surface. My father working on something he wouldn't let me see just a few days before he was taken.

"You know something?" Quentin asked, eyes on mine, eyebrows raised.

A strand of red fell across my eye, and I pushed the hair back behind my ear. "Maybe. It's possible my father had something to do with this. He was working on something around that time. And he hinted we might not be alone. Maybe he was aware you were watching him?"

I squeezed my lips together, blowing air out through them as I dredged the memory up. Across the table, Quentin ducked his head, smothering a smile behind his shirt. I arched one eyebrow at him.

"Care to share what's so funny?" I asked, waving a hand at him to talk, my head shifting slightly to match the motion.

He shook his head, dropping his shirt back down. "Nothing, it's just your thinking face is a bit, well, comical."

I scrunched my nose at him and returned to my thoughts. "Where did you say the switching node was?"

"I didn't, but it's a primary node from the main citadel to your settlement. Your father could have been monitoring it." He spread his hands. "Considering what else you two were up to, that wouldn't surprise me."

My eyes narrowed. "What else were we up to?"

"Stealing water; we discussed this already," he said.

"Yes, I recall you saying you were very good at finding information on the network."

He shrugged. "It's a talent, not one that's been very helpful in finding what we're looking for." He looked up at me. "Then again, you never know what you'll find when you go looking."

I rolled my eyes and waved for him to continue.

"Anyway, I told you already that we found what you were doing with the water quotas. Ingenious solution, that one."

"You said that before."

He nodded. "I meant it. Simplest way to get around a massive amount of coding is to alter just enough to get what you need from it rather than try to change the whole thing." He leaned farther forward, beckoning me closer. "Thing is, all you and your father did was undo what someone else had already done."

I leaned over the table. "What do you mean?"

"Someone else beat you two to the punch. They altered the code to decrease the water flow, leading to your shortage."

"And when we went in to make our change . . ."

"You simply undid their handiwork." He shrugged. "As I said, ingenious solution you two stumbled on, and even more so because it revealed the original alteration to the code."

"And this information helped you?" I asked.

He nodded. "A bit. It showed us the code could be altered just so. Once we saw what you did, we went looking for more and found the original changes." He looked at the floor. "We found that while we waited for your Seeker escort to get enough of a head start before we followed later. It's how we missed the dragon raid."

The thought of the raid brought Maryn back to the surface. A deep sadness welled up inside me, threatening to overwhelm me. I waved a hand at him and took a deep breath.

"You being there would have made no difference."

"Still, I'm sorry we couldn't help save your brother."

I tried to smile at him but failed. I didn't feel it. "I appreciate the thought." My mind returned to the puzzle he'd revealed. "Why would someone want to steal our water?"

"And now you come upon what we've been looking for," Quentin said. "Well, in part."

"There's more?"

He nodded but said nothing.

"You going to tell me?"

He shrugged. "I'm not entirely sure I'm at liberty to say. Part of this is for Suyef to decide."

I nodded, sitting upright and craning my neck to one side, then the other, in a stretch. "I understand that much."

Quentin eyed me for a moment, lips pursed and fingers tapping each other. "Still, I don't think he would have that much issue with you knowing. Else he would speak up, right?"

The last comment he directed at his companion, who made no move to respond.

I held up a hand. "I don't need to know."

Quentin held his gaze on Suyef, eyes narrowing and his lips pursed to one side. After a moment, he nodded.

"If he had a problem, he'd say so." He leaned forward and nodded at my brother. "So, I'll make you a deal. Suyef and I can help your brother find what he's looking for if it exists. In return, you help us do the same, regardless of if we find anything."

I glanced at Donovan. "You know he's probably wrong, don't you? He has no evidence."

Quentin spread his hands. "So, we waste our time looking for information that doesn't exist. But really, we're only guaranteed finding out one of two things: their final fate inside the Seeker system or that they aren't in it anymore."

"That's not much," Donovan said. "And then what do my sister and I get out of helping you?"

"Besides finding out for certain what happened to your family in that system?" he asked, shaking his head. "That alone I thought would be appealing enough. Plus, you'll have something that will help you even more with what you were doing before. If you go back to it."

"What's that?" I asked.

Quentin glanced at Suyef, who shifted but didn't speak.

"A program that you can use to both insert and extract information from the network," he whispered, leaning over the table. "To do with as you please."

My eyes widened. "That's valuable. Much more than anything we could offer."

Quentin shook his head, pointing at me. "I saw the coding you and your father were doing. I'm not sure where you learned it, but it's beyond my skill. I'm better at making use of what's already there. You know, stuff already functioning. Crafting stuff, writing code— that's not my forte yet." He nodded at me. "So, in that you're very valuable to us. And this program we have I think will do exactly what we want it to with a little help from you."

I glanced between him and Suyef. Next to me, Donovan shifted in his seat, leaning toward me. I held up a hand at him.

"First, why are you here?" I asked. "You know what we're looking for. It's only fair we know what you're after before we agree to anything."

"Fair enough," Quentin said. "We're here for two reasons. One, to find out what is wrong with the network. The water problem is one example of it. There are more, none of them good and all with fairly dire implications for many people, especially on this shell, which I'm pretty sure I don't need to remind you of." He leaned toward me, his voice lowering. "Beyond that, we're searching for the only man who may have knowledge of how Suyef's father died, and how mine almost perished twenty cycles ago."

"You think he's here?" I asked, waving my hand around at the outpost.

Quentin shook his head. "Not here at this prison. But on this shell, yes."

"And you want our help to find him," I said.

"That and the water problem, which you were already working on," Quentin said, nodding at me.

"So, how does getting entangled with us help you figure that out?" Donovan interjected.

"It may not," Quentin replied. "But it's worth a shot. And regardless of the result, you get the program."

Donovan looked at me. "Could you use it?"

I shrugged. "I'd need to see it first to know for sure."

"We can't let you see it unless you agree to help us." Quentin held up a hand to forestall a response from my brother. "And we'll help you first. So, you get the information you're after before we get ours. Deal?"

I glanced at Donovan. It seemed to me to be the only way to get him to stop this foolish quest of his. So, I nodded. A few moments later, we stood in front of the only terminal in the suite: a panel beside the door. Quentin held a device up to the screen, and I saw a transfer program activate.

"Aren't you afraid they'll notice?" I asked.

He shook his head. "The Nomads have been using this thing for decades and never been spotted. So, either they can't see it or they don't care." He chuckled. "Maybe after today they will."

He entered a sequence of commands, and a file structure opened on the panel. He stepped back and waved me and Donovan forward.

"That's a prisoner manifest of this facility," he stated. "I'll keep looking to see if I can find the same for the other prisons."

Tapping on the list, I opened a search function and began looking for their names. Donovan leaned close next to me, his lips moving as he read the names. The list scrolled past, once or twice my eyes falling on a name that looked familiar. A closer inspection showed a similar name but not quite one of the names we sought. Sooner than I would have thought possible, I'd reached the end of the list, having searched for every possible variation of their names I could think of.

"Any luck?" Quentin asked from behind me.

I shook my head. "They're not on this list."

"Well, that only means they weren't here," he said, holding the device up to the panel again. "Try this one. I think it's a manifest from the prison directly opposite this one on the other side of the shell."

"Or they were removed from the list," Donovan suggested as he leaned in to look at what Quentin had found.

Soon, we'd finished that list. Quentin scanned his device, shaking his head.

"As far as I can tell, that's it for manifests," he said. "If they have more prisons, they aren't on the books."

Donovan opened his mouth to argue but stopped when I put a hand on his shoulder.

"Or they never came here at all." He looked over at me, but I shook my head at him. "I'm not saying they weren't taken somewhere, but if I'm doing this, I want to know you are open to the possibility that you're wrong and they're gone."

He nodded but said nothing. I stared at him for a moment, then looked at Quentin.

"So, they weren't here or at that other prison, as far as we can tell," I stated. "Can you find any other place they might have been taken?"

"Maybe, given time," he said, pursing his lips as he stared at the device. "Colberra is a huge shell, and that city dominates it. There are a lot of places you can hide a prison." He looked up at me. "Just takes a little time, is all. We'll find an answer."

He went back to sit at the table and work. Donovan and I moved next to him and looked over his shoulder.

"The program I'm using was invented to insert data to be found in a specific facility." He looked up at me. "It took some trial and error, but I found a way to use it to do the same thing elsewhere. So, I'm trying inserting requisition requests for supplies to be sent to Seeker facilities that house a lot of people."

"How will that help?" Donovan asked.

"Because I'm not specifying which ones to send it to," he explained. "I'm wording it in such a way that the supplier will be required to confirm which facilities they send what to and how much."

"And from that you get the names," I said, nodding as I watched him tap at the screen. "Did you include flaggers for receipt locations?"

He snapped a finger at me. "Good idea, so we know where the people are that open the file."

"If you attach a form to the request that they have to fill out with the data you request, you can embed the same thing in that," I suggested. "If it makes it past their firewall unchecked, you could see where the responses go as well."

Donovan stood up and looked at me. "Why wouldn't they detect it?"

"Because Seekers believe the network is theirs and nothing is on it they don't control," Quentin stated, never moving his eyes from the screen. "So, they don't question what comes to them on it. At least, not at the level this will be read at." He tapped the screen. "There, it's done. Now we wait."

"How long until we know it worked?" Donovan asked.

Before Quentin could answer, the lights flickered off, plunging us into darkness.

"Wait, the lights turned off?" I asked, holding up my hand with the stylus and interrupting Micaela's narrative.

"Completely dark."

"Isn't that impossible in an Ancient facility?" I asked.

She nodded. "Which is why even Colberrans, with all their misplaced hate for the Ancients, haven't been able to wean themselves from the Ancients' technology—it's nothing if not dependable."

"Misplaced hate," I repeated her words. "Why do you say that?"

She shrugged. "They are misinformed, as most are in this age beyond the dragon circles. Even the Nomads, for all their knowledge of what goes on down here near the core, have lost much of what was recorded about the distant past."

"I've done my own work in that field of research," I muttered, shaking my head. "The data just isn't there anymore. Even in a computer as powerful as the network."

"Isn't there at all?" she asked, arching an eyebrow at me.

I opened my mouth to retort, then paused. "You know something I don't?"

"Merely that if you look over your notes, you'll remember why Quentin and Suyef were even on Colberra in the first place."

"The network wasn't working right, they claimed," I said without looking. "Or they just thought it wasn't because they couldn't find the data they wanted to."

"I once believed it was that simple," she whispered, eyes moving to stare out the window. "That the data was just gone."

"What changed your mind?"

She chuckled, a slight thing that only just shook her body. "I saw a ghost."

CHAPTER 14

ATTACK

The room went completely black for several seconds before something bright flared up, slicing through the dark and hurting my eyes. After my vision adjusted, I looked around. Suyef held a staff in hand, one end swallowed in fire.

"Do I want to know where you had that hidden?" I nodded at the staff.

He shook his head and shifted around the room, holding out his makeshift torch. "Something's wrong."

"You think?" Donovan muttered, moving to stand next to me. "Is that because of us? Did they find out what we were doing?"

"I doubt a simple search would take out the power," Quentin stated.

He remained where he was at the table. Suyef stepped near the door, the light from his torch casting ominous shadows across the walls. The door remained sealed at his approach.

"So much for a power outage freeing us," Quentin stated.

Suyef moved around, torch moving up and down as he searched all around us.

"What are you looking for?" Donovan whispered.

Suyef held up a finger to silence him. My brother shot me a glare, which I only half saw in the flickering light. The Nomad continued his investigation. As he did, a sound tickled at my hearing. I turned my head toward Quentin.

"Did you say something?"

He shook his head. I turned around to face the door, eyes focused on the entry, head cocked to one side. Donovan moved close to me.

"What is it?"

"Shh," I hissed, waving at him.

He grumbled, then fell silent. I cocked my head the other way and closed my eyes. The sound hung just audible to my ears, flitting past like a soft breeze tugging at my braid. I stepped toward the door and heard a louder burst, a pop that split the air.

"I heard that," Quentin said, shifting behind me.

Everyone froze where they stood, heads turning this way and that. I stepped closer and heard a faint hum.

"Suyef, put out the light," I whispered.

Darkness plunged down around us. With the sound of the flames gone, I heard only breathing, my heartbeat, and a bit of static. I turned my head back toward the entrance and saw a thin glow emitting from the wall panel beside the entry.

"Is that panel on?" Quentin shifted in the dark, but I didn't hear any footsteps.

"I think it might be." I stepped toward the dim source of light.

As I did, another pop of static echoed through the room, accompanied by a faint echo that sounded like a voice.

"Dange . . ." the voice said.

"Something is very not right here," Quentin whispered.

". . . nger . . ." The sound danced past my ears, the last letter dragged out and distorted.

I leaned near the panel and saw a myriad of alternating white and black dots dancing on the screen. Another pop shifted past my ears, and the dots swirled and waved.

"Hello," I called at the screen.

"... help ..."

Donovan jumped behind me. "I heard that. Did that voice say 'help'?"

I nodded. "Who is it?" I asked the screen. "Do you need help?"

The screen swirled once more, the voice bursting past in a rush. "... dan ... r ... help yo ..."

"Do you need our help?" I said to the screen again.

The screen swirled yet again, and an image coalesced from the dizzying lines. I heard a hiss behind me.

"Is that a person?" Quentin asked, stepping near me.

Donovan moved up on the other side. "Looked like it."

I waved at them to be quiet. "Hello? Do you need help?"

"I think she said 'help you,'" Donovan whispered at me. Louder, he said to the screen, "Yes, we need help."

Several pops echoed into the room, along with a deep distorted sound and a high-pitched whistle. Through the cacophony, a voice slipped through.

"You're in danger. I'm trying to help you!"

"What danger?" I asked, my heart pounding in my chest.

Behind us, Suyef hissed, drawing our attention.

"Something is out there," he whispered as his staff reignited. "Beyond the wall. Lots of things."

I turned back to the screen and froze. Next to me, I heard Donovan choke. Quentin whistled.

"What is it?" Suyef asked.

When none of us spoke, the Nomad moved over and shifted Donovan out of the way. I knew when his eyes fell upon the screen, because he froze, his breath cutting off after a sharp intake.

"How is that possible?" Donovan asked from just behind my right shoulder.

I shook my head, leaning close to the screen. A single image of a face lay frozen, a line cutting across the middle, distorting a small section. Every now and then a row of lines slid down the screen, bending the image as they went. The face never changed.

My face.

The image shifted, fading a bit as it began to move. The voice returned, too distorted to identify.

"He's coming. The black . . ." Static overwhelmed the voice for a moment. ". . . shadow assas . . . beware their . . ."

Another pop of warped bass bent the voice to an unintelligible garble. At the same time, the image froze, the face clearly visible again. My face. There was no doubt.

"How is your face talking to us from the panel, Micaela?" Donovan asked.

I moved back, eyes never leaving the panel. "This is a trick," I said, looking at Quentin and Suyef in turn.

The fiery light cast shadows around their features, making it hard to see them. I could feel their eyes, though.

"This is a trick," I insisted. "You were messing around with that panel. Do you have something to do with this?"

Quentin opened his mouth to respond, but never got the chance.

At that instant, the sound of metal bending out of place tore through the air and an echoing boom shook the room, knocking us to the wall. The screen, now unfrozen, let forth with a burst of audio just above my head.

"Beware the shadows! I'll try to help you!"

The lights flickered on, flooding the quarters with a painful brightness. As I blinked to clear my vision, another loud tremor shook the structure and the sound of groaning metal echoed past us. Once my eyes adjusted, I looked over at the far wall and saw nothing but distorted, twisted metal.

"What did that?" Donovan asked.

Suyef growled, shifting to stand between us and the wall. "Something big." He looked at Quentin. "Very big."

"Another dragon?" I guessed.

The room shook, massive blows striking the wall. As I watched, part of the wall buckled inward, then peeled back out toward the sky. Through the gash in the structure, I saw the darkness of core-night. Another blast knocked me to my feet as more of the wall and part of the roof peeled away. The lights flickered, threatening to go dark. Just as I thought they might give up, they flared to their brightest. I shielded my eyes from the glowing light.

Suyef hissed, shifting toward the left wall. "Watch the shadows," he whispered. "Something is in them."

"Shouldn't we worry about what's out there?" Donovan asked as Quentin moved to cover the other side of the room, brandishing a piece of the wall in one hand.

Before Suyef could reply, a shadow leapt out from the darkness over his head and toward me. The black shape melted into an almost-human form, one arm raised over its head to strike me. Where I should have seen some kind of skin, all I saw was a boiling mass of black and a very faint gray. Suyef's flaming staff struck the attacker square in his exposed side, and he burst into flame. Fire engulfed him for a moment before the mass imploded and vanished, taking the fire with it.

"Shadow assassins," Quentin muttered. "That's what you were telling us."

"That wasn't me," I insisted, waving at the screen.

"Sure looked like you," Donovan muttered from my other side.

The room shook once more as another swath of the ceiling ripped away, exposing us to the night. Behind us, the door hissed open as two guards ran in. Before they could so much as speak, a shadow dropped from a beam just overhead. Arms coalesced around their necks and lifted the men off the ground while they grabbed at their throats.

"Down!" Suyef cried out, swinging his flaming staff at the shadow as Donovan and I dropped to the floor.

The two guards crumpled to the ground when the near-human creature imploded under Suyef's strike like the other had. Neither of the men moved.

"Get out the door," Quentin called out, kneeling to grab the men's firearms as he waved us on.

More shadows dropped into the room as another deafening tremor shook the structure, what remained of the outer wall peeling away as the building trembled. Pushing Donovan before me, I bolted from the room just as bright blasts of light began to strike all around us. Donovan dove to the left as we exited, and I tried to go right, but my foot slipped, sending me careening into the far wall across from the door. Quentin stood in the opening, unloading blasts of air pulses into the shadow-figures. Suyef darted around, his staff ablaze, each strike dispatching another shadow.

"Move!" Quentin yelled.

Donovan rushed over and pulled me up. We raced down the hall in the direction I'd tried to dive. Behind me, I heard the sound of more shadows dropping. Flickering firelight behind us told me Suyef was still fighting them off, even as I heard Quentin's pulse guns hiss over and over. More tremors shook the hall as other guards appeared, armed to the teeth. Blasts of light shot past us, taking out a few of the guards. More of the ceiling ripped away just overhead as we dove to the floor and around a corner into another entryway. Prison guards filled the hallway, sidearms drawn and firing shots down the hall. Shadows fell all around them, some taking out guards, others imploding from air pulses. Donovan pushed me up from on top of him, and we rushed down the hall.

"Stay with them!" Suyef called out. "Stay with them!"

I risked a glance back and saw Quentin leaping over a fallen guard, his pulse guns blazing in every direction. Suyef's staff whirled in a dizzying swirl of fire, dispatching shadows with hissing pops.

Suddenly, the hallway jolted to one side, and I fell into a wall. Donovan crumpled down just beyond me, clutching his ankle. Another section of ceiling ripped away in an explosion of tearing metal and electric pops, sending sparks down all around us. I curled into a ball to protect my head and saw Quentin stumbling over another guard, a shadow right behind him.

"Look out!" I screamed just as he rolled to the ground.

Suyef's staff spun into sight, knocking the shadow into oblivion. Quentin finished his roll on his feet, and the pair rushed at us.

"Get up!" the Nomad hissed, rushing past me and grabbing at Donovan.

"I can't move my ankle," my brother said between clenched teeth.

Quentin's hand appeared to pull me upright.

"Get her out of here," Suyef muttered, nodding at us to go on. "I'll get him."

I was reluctant to leave my brother, but Quentin and the sound of more shadows approaching from the way we had come overrode my trepidation. We rushed down the hall as Suyef's staff reignited; a blaze of pops and hisses echoed after us.

"Where do those things come from?" I asked Quentin when we slowed at a junction.

"Not really sure. No one's seen hide nor hair of them for centuries," he said, leaning to look down a hall to his right. "But we know of them. From Ancient times. Something made during a great war some experts theorize led to the Splitting."

"How did they get here? And why?" Another tremor shook the building. "And what is doing that?"

Before Quentin could answer, the ceiling ripped away off the structure right above us. Shards of metal and debris rained down all around. My instinct was to drop and tuck into a ball, but a shove from behind sent me careening on wobbly legs down the left hallway.

"Don't stop!" Quentin yelled. "Keep going."

I heard the sound of shadows dropping to the ground, a soft thump followed by a hiss. Adrenaline pulsed through my body, and I raced down the hall. Behind me, I heard Quentin's pulse guns going off nonstop. More of the ceiling began to peel away, following me down the hall. As it did, more shadows dropped into sight, separating us.

"Quentin!" I yelled, drawing his attention.

He turned his guns forward, unloading everything he could into the new shadows now chasing me, leaving his back exposed. My momentum carried me around a bend in the hall before I saw what happened to him.

Something dropped to the ground in front of me, and I slammed to a halt, colliding full speed with hard metal as a hand wrapped itself around my throat. My head turned forward to see a grotesque, twisted suit of armor, layered pieces of hard metal folding around a giant body. A warped helmet sat atop the shoulders, sharp, jagged edges sweeping out and upward from the crown. A slit of black glass covered the eyes and a smaller slit the mouth.

From that smaller opening, a raspy, male voice hissed down at me, "Well, well, look what we have here."

The hand tightened, and my feet left the floor. I grabbed his arm, trying to claw the hand free as my lungs began to burn. I kicked my feet at him and only succeeded in finding a small foothold in a crevice of the armor to push up and relieve my neck.

"You have one chance to give me what I want, or I'll make you and your little brother suffer more than this entire world has suffered," the creature whispered, pulling my face to within inches of the armored mask.

I coughed, forcing out words as my lungs struggled for air. "I . . . I . . . don't know . . . what . . . you want!"

"I don't want excuses," the creature hissed, his other hand grabbing my torso. He slammed me up against a wall, knocking out what little air remained in my lungs. "Now give it to me."

I shook my head, pushing at his armored glove with my fingers. "I don't know what you want."

"For the last time, girl, give it to me," he bellowed, shaking me. "I know you have it. You've always had it. I know it's the source of your power."

I coughed, sputtering as he shook me and screamed in my face. I struggled to breathe, willing my lungs to pull in air.

Instead, a disconcerting darkness swallowed me.

A shaft of light burst through the darkness, slicing my head open from the inside. I squeezed my eyes shut against the intruding light and rolled over, covering my face with my hands. I coughed, and a shock of pain rocked my body. Only then did it dawn on me I could breathe. Risking a peek, I saw a wall just inches from my nose. Turning my head in the other direction, I spied a pair of armored boots.

"Ah, you're awake," the creature hissed.

His armored hand grasped my braid and jerked me to my feet. Pain ripped through my head like fire, and I cried out.

"That's just a taste of the pain I'll cause if you don't give it to me," he whispered, leaning his armored face down near mine.

"What? Give you what?"

A blast of light hit the wall over his head, and he jerked me down. His other hand pulled out a firearm of his own, and pulses of bright light burst from it down the hall. The creature barked something unintelligible, and shadows dropped to the ground all around. Tremors continued to shake the building as the shadows moved back in the direction the creature had just fired.

"Get up," he hissed, yanking my braid.

I stumbled to my feet and rushed after him, his hand still holding firm to my braid. Behind, the sounds of pulse guns and the strange firearms these attackers carried filled the air. I heard men scream and cry out. I heard hisses and pops. I heard the sounds of death.

The creature seemed undisturbed. He marched along, muttering words I couldn't understand, all the while jerking my hair to keep me off balance and following.

"Please, I don't know what you want," I hissed through clenched teeth. "I don't have anything."

"Oh, you have it. I know you do," he said, a deep throaty laugh bursting from his helmet. "And you will give it to me."

He stopped, pulling me up to stare into his armored face, his hand yanking my braid back to pin my neck in a painful and exposed position. I felt a finger from his other hand brush along my throat and tap just below my chin.

"You've escaped me for too long, you little ketch. Not this time."

An air pulse blasted into his side, sending us sprawling down the hall. I rolled away from the armored behemoth even as strange voices cried out from the direction the pulse shot had come from. I didn't waste any time looking. The creature moved to stand, and I scrambled away, kicking at his hand. As I did, I saw his firearm lying just to my side. His hand latched on to my foot, gripping it like a vise, just as my hand grabbed at the cool sides of the weapon. Without thinking, I yanked it up to aim at the armored monster crawling up along my legs. I squeezed what I hoped was the trigger, and a blast of light shot out, knocking the weapon backward and up over my head. The shot hit him square in the shoulder, and he fell off of me, screaming. I kicked at his wound to push myself free and scrambled to my feet.

Shadows shifted around the bend toward us, and I did the only thing I could think to do. Grabbing the gun off the ground and gripping it with two hands this time, I took aim and unloaded blasts of light at them. They hissed out of existence with satisfying pops. As the last one imploded before me, something hit my legs, knocking me down onto my backside. The weapon clattered out of my hands as the armored creature struggled toward me. I kicked him in the face, pushed myself up, and fled down the hall.

A terrifying scream echoed past me, and the entire hallway shook. Another section of ceiling ripped away as the echo faded, filling the hall with smoke and debris. I dodged pieces of metal as more shadows thumped down behind me. The ripping destruction followed me down the hall. Pulses of air filled the hall, met by blasts of light that cast strange shadows for an instant and startled me. Still I ran. I didn't dare look back for fear of what I'd see. Shadows coming close. The creature on his feet, chasing me. More of the ceiling coming down.

Another rumble shook the floor, sending me sprawling into an entryway. The doors slid open, and I tumbled into another set of living quarters. I spun around to see the doors hiss shut, sealing me off for the moment. I knew it would not last. Casting about for somewhere to hide, I heard something slam into the doors. I rushed across the space past the table and looked back to see the doors buckle and fold back into the room. The armored creature stumbled in from the hall, screaming. As the sound echoed, the floor and walls began to shake. He stepped toward me as the structure shook with a great force. The ceiling trembled and crumpled down before peeling back. I dove beyond the table as it tumbled away from the door. The wall along the far side shuddered and fell away as the roof ripped free. The table shifted up against my back as wind rushed in, grabbing at my cloak and scarf.

An armored hand darted into sight, grabbing my cloak at my chest and pinning me in place. I struggled to get free as he knelt over me.

"Last chance, ketch. Give it to me, or this is the end of your too-long life."

I glared up into his eye slit. Anger filled me, and I spat into his face.

"Even if I did have it, I wouldn't give it to you!" I yelled at the monster's armored helm. "And you'd kill me anyway, so rot in the core!"

A rumble shook his torso, and a rumbling laugh emanated from the mouth slit.

"Fiery to the end. At least you are consistent." His hand raised overhead, a wicked-looking, black dagger held tight in his grasp. "I've waited too long to do this."

His hand plunged downward, and I started to turn my head, when a hiss filled the room. A blast of light struck the creature square in the top of his head. He froze, blade inches from my chest. His hand trembled, and the eye slit flared red. With a great shudder, the armored monster fell to one side, the blade tumbling harmlessly away.

My entire body trembled as I pushed the lifeless form off me. The adrenaline fled my limbs, and my body shook uncontrollably, tears pouring from my face. Pushing myself up, I looked back at the remains of the door.

Filling the entry, the creature's weapon I'd dropped in hand, stood Quentin.

"Who was that monster?" I asked as Micaela stood up from the leather couch.

"Not who. What." She moved near the window.

"All right, what?"

"As far as we can tell, an automaton controlled by someone else."

I frowned. "How do you know that?"

She looked over at me. "When we pulled open the helmet later, there was no body inside."

"So, who do you think was controlling it?" I asked, jotting a note down.

She didn't answer, drawing my eye. Micaela stood looking out the window, arms folded across her torso. I opened my mouth to repeat the question, then thought better of it. She remained there, silent for several moments, staring out the window.

"You're quiet," she whispered, not moving.

"As are you."

"So. Now what?" She turned to look at me.

"What happened next?" I waved a hand at my notes. "You left me hanging."

"At least you know I survived."

I furrowed my brow at her. "I already knew that much. Just not how."

"Now you know."

"But I'm missing so much. How did Quentin get there in time? How did he escape the shadow assassins? What about Suyef? Your brother? The facility? Were you able to find anything using that program? Was that the reason they attacked?" I glanced at my notes. "And what was making all that racket at the prison? How did you end up here? How are you a friend of the Queen?"

"We all survived the attack. How is each of our own story to tell. Be sure to ask the others for the details. As to the facility"—she shrugged—"I left that place soon after and never returned. I don't know what became of it."

"And what was attacking on the outside?"

She shivered just a bit. "A giant black dragon."

I felt a cold chill grip my spine. "There's only been one black dragon ever recorded in history, and he hasn't been seen in centuries. Since the greens and reds came into this world."

"It was him, trust me." Her voice lowered to a whisper. "I'd recognize him anywhere. I didn't know it at the time, of course. But I do now."

"And was this dragon controlling the monster inside?"

She nodded.

Seeing as she was suddenly so willing to answer questions, I jumped to my last one. "You and the Queen are friends. How?"

Micaela didn't answer. She turned and walked toward the exit.

"Can you tell me if Donovan was right?" I asked.

She stopped halfway to the door and looked back over her shoulder. "Yes, he was," she said.

"So, where were they?" I asked. "Did they ever go to a prison?"

"My father did, yes," she said, her voice quiet.

I frowned. "And what about your mother? And your sister?"

"That answer lay elsewhere," she answered, and began moving toward the door again.

"Do you need a break?" I called after her.

She paused in the doorway and looked over her shoulder at me.

"You need answers from someone else now."

I shook my head. "Who? Quentin? Where is he?"

"Ask Suyef," she whispered, and walked out.

CHAPTER 15

UNEXPECTED

When I landed on the Nomad shell, the first thing that struck me was the stark difference the landmass presented compared to lower shells. Most of the shells in lower orbit were smaller, no larger than a couple thousand kilometers. Colberra, the highest orbiting shell, measures nearly five thousand kilometers across its middle and stands as the single largest occupied shell. The result of a collision of two large shells long in our world's past, the shell I found myself on dwarfed Colberra, measuring easily twice the length of Micaela's home. It was the only landmass large enough to be classified as a supershell. Some experts theorized that collision was the reason Colberra orbited at a higher altitude, moved there by some of the last remaining Ancients before they vanished. Whatever the far-reaching effects were, it still left us with one massive shell where once two had been.

We possessed a lot of information in the network of the supershell, but this was my first visit. The first thing I noticed was the air. There was a noticeable thickness to it at this elevation. Far above lay the water shield, obscured by the night shield that was currently up on the shell. From Colberra, it was possible to see many more details. From here, an observer might spy a few clouds dotting the blue mass and nothing more. My companion, who'd carried me to this shell, had left as quietly as we'd arrived. Landing once the night shield had come up had been a strategic choice, providing us with cover from prying eyes.

"Not that you expect to find too many eyes this far out, do you, Logwyn?" I muttered to myself, tucking my hair back into my cloak and pulling it tight.

The costume given me for this trip felt bulky and thick. A tangled mess of tunic, pants, and something called an obi, I'd cinched it with a belt and covered it with a robe. The mottled brown attire favored by the Nomads left a lot to be desired. Still, as a cold breeze whipped at me from beyond the edge of the shell, I appreciated the warmth the clothing offered.

Along with the air and wind, another thing that stood out was the slope of the ground. My companion, who had been offered me by the Queen upon my request, had deposited me on the upper slope of the supershell. Because of the destruction wrought by its formation in the past, most of this end of the shell lay unoccupied, as it was tilted down to the north.

"Putting me here helped with not drawing attention," I said, scanning the lifeless, dimly lit terrain. "Doesn't help me find someone to talk to now that I'm here."

Once I did find someone, my first problem would come to a head, namely that my destination remained unknown. I had no clue at all, actually, about where to go. Just a name. The only Nomad name known to me at that point.

Suyef.

Finding Suyef turned out to be the easier of my problems to solve. His name is, apparently, something of an oddity among his people. I also seemed to have landed, quite fortuitously, in a section of the shell his family dominated. So, once contact was made with my first Nomads, his name proved quite handy, particularly because, as I was an Off-sheller, they seemed less inclined to believe me.

Soon after, I found myself sitting on a pillow in a tent nestled up against a large mountain, sipping a strong tea while watching an older man puff hard on ancient-looking device he called a hookah. I wracked my brain for any knowledge of such a contraption, trying to find a reason the man would choose to subject his lungs to what had to be noxious vapors. My search proved as fruitless as my access to the network on this mission. So, I sat, as patiently and quietly as possible, sipping my tea under the attentive, if slightly glassy-eyed, gaze of the older man.

"Suyef's not to be bothered," the man said after what seemed like chrons had passed.

I arched an eyebrow at him. "So, you do know him?"

"I would think so. He's my nephew."

"Direct nephew?"

The man shook his head. "Couple times removed." He puffed once on the hookah, blowing out a column of smoke before continuing. "Like I said, he doesn't want to be bothered."

"I need his help," I replied, setting my teacup down and holding his gaze.

"With what?"

I shook my head. "That's for his ears only, I'm afraid." The Queen hadn't been helpful in pointing me to my goal, but she had reminded me of one thing before my departure: to tell no one of my work. So, I spread my hands and shrugged. "Sorry."

He frowned, lips jutting out a bit as he traced them with the mouthpiece. "He's gone to the edge. Where he is on the edge is his knowledge alone. We know how to signal him, but only he decides whether to respond."

"So, can we signal him?" I asked.

The man shrugged. "You haven't given me a reason to."

I gritted my teeth, looking around the room. "Suppose I'm not a good enough reason?" The look he gave me served as my answer. I smiled, shrugging slightly. "Fine, I guess you've left me no choice but to tell you." I leaned toward the man, my voice lowering. "I need his help finding someone." The man continued to stare at me. "Someone very important."

"There's only one person important enough to get his attention," the old man muttered, puffing on his hookah. "His father."

"His father's dead," I countered.

"Since when? I spoke to him recently."

Now it was my turn to give him a look. "*Define* recently." When he didn't answer, I pushed on. "If by recent you mean more than twenty cycles, then okay."

The man puffed on his hookah one more time, then gave me a slow nod. "And you say this person you seek is important?"

My turn to nod.

His eyes narrowed; then he clicked his fingers. "We'll see if he responds. What's your name?"

I spent a few more days among the Nomads and learned very little of them. They kept me isolated in a tent and hardly spoke to me. I did learn one thing: they all dressed exactly alike and, to the outside eye, all appeared the same, down to their voices and gaits. The only discernible difference lay in their genders, and then only because of a few items that tend to stand out. My hopes of finding the person who visited me back in my office dwindled quickly. I was convinced it was a Nomad, and not just because the Queen let it slip in our first conversation.

On the fifth day, Suyef finally responded. The Nomad elder summoned me to his tent, puffing on his hookah and handing me a small note before waving me away. As I stepped outside, my hands fumbled to open the note. All I found were a series of numbers that were most likely coordinates. This guy was not making things easy.

Two days later, a guide deposited me on the edge of a sweeping cliff that overlooked the core. My guide left when we approached the precipice. A quick sweep of the area revealed nothing and no one.

I was alone.

Standing on that cliff did give me one thing: an appreciation for the size and scope of our world. Staring over the edge, looking at the core, I couldn't make out any of the numerous shells that orbited deeper in our world. Glancing up to my left, I spied the only shell visible in the atmosphere at this time: Colberra. Still, my quest hadn't left me completely unaware of current events. Things were changing.

Preoccupied with the size and shape of our world, I failed to notice I was no longer alone. I'm still not sure where he came from. One moment found me staring off into the abyss; the next, a Nomad stood there.

"Suyef?"

He didn't answer. He moved to walk away from me along the cliff. I followed, certain it was him.

"I need your help."

No answer.

"I need to find someone."

He kept walking.

"The Queen sent me."

He stopped, allowing me to move closer, but didn't respond.

"Can you help me?"

"It's hard to help someone who doesn't speak openly of what they need," he said, his voice so quiet I had to strain to hear him.

"I think you already know why I'm here."

He turned, his dark eyes locking on mine through the slit in his cowl. "Looking for me, I presume."

"Looking for a particular item or two. Do you know where they are?"

He shook his head.

"Does Quentin?"

No response.

"You know where Quentin is, don't you?"

His eyebrows rose slightly. "And now we come to the point."

"I need to speak to him."

Suyef looked away. "He's not in a talking mood."

I frowned at him. "A talking mood?"

The Nomad returned his gaze to me. "Things are not right with him. Very not right." He turned and walked away. "Don't say I didn't warn you."

The Nomad led me to a cleverly hidden cave entrance nearby. Even from the air, I doubt this would ever have been found. A fold in the terrain created an odd overlap along the edge of the cliff. At the point where the fold joined together lay a small opening that led down into darkness. Into this I found myself descending, following the now-quiet Nomad.

After a long climb, followed by an underground trek guided by a light in the Nomad's hand, we arrived in what amounted to a living room buried under rock. Four walls, a roof, a floor, a couple of fabricated-leather couches, and a metal table with two chairs.

"No network station," I commented, setting my travel sack on the table.

The Nomad grunted. "One doesn't come here if they want to be connected to the world."

Opposite the entrance stood another door. I pointed at it. "Is he through there?"

"As is the matter reforger, our latrine, and our sleeping quarters," he answered.

"How big is this place?"

The Nomad replied, "Neither too big nor too small."

"So . . . just right."

He glared at me. "Or that. It is here, and that's what matters."

"Why here?" I asked, waving a hand at the ceiling. "Under all this? Why all the secrecy?"

Suyef glanced at the aforementioned door. "Something happened to him near here. At least, he thinks it did. So, this place is here."

I pondered those words, my eyes locked on the door. "May I speak with him?"

"You can try."

Beyond the door, I found a hallway with several rooms opening off to each side. A matter reforger, a latrine, and two closed doors I assumed led to sleeping quarters lay down the hall. The passageway continued on for some distance, ending at another sealed door. It slid open at my approach to reveal a ledge and waist-high wall opposite the door. On the far side of the wall lay nothing but sky and the core far below. To either side, the ledge continued along what looked to be the side of the shell. To the right, the ledge ended about ten paces away in a rock face jutting out from the structure. To the left, it continued on much farther, reaching a small outcropping that gave the ledge a lookout point of sorts.

Sitting there, wrapped in a cloak similar to those worn by the Nomads, I found Quentin. He looked awful. His eyes were sunken, his hair a matted mess, and he looked like he'd been missing a few meals. His lips moved but made no discernible sound. I stared for a few moments, uncertain of what to do.

"This is one of his more lucid days," Suyef whispered from behind me.

A shock raced up my spine, sending tingles into my skull as I grabbed at the wall.

"Don't sneak up on someone like that," I hissed at him, pointing at the expanse. "Especially in a place like this."

The Nomad didn't take his eyes from Quentin. I followed his gaze and rubbed at the tingles on my neck.

"As I said, one of his more lucid days."

"What happened?" I asked, looking back at Suyef. "What turned him into this?" When the Nomad frowned at me, I continued, "I've never met him before, but from what my research revealed, this wasn't what I expected."

"People change, especially after a lot of time has passed," the Nomad muttered, beckoning me to follow him back inside.

He led me to one of the closed doors and opened it. Inside lay a room with a single bed in it. Sketches covered every inch of wall and ceiling space. All on actual paper. So much paper—and I'd thought it in short supply just a few weeks before. Only the light fixture jutting out from the roof broke up the drawings. And every one was of the same person.

"Micaela."

"He started doing this shortly after we came here," Suyef commented, eyes roaming over the sketches. "There are more stored elsewhere."

Every image was different. Each was a head shot, but in every one he changed something: here a scar, there a different hairstyle. In some she smiled; in many she looked thoughtful. One she laughed in. Every one captured her eyes perfectly.

"Clearly, she matters to him," I whispered.

"More than she will admit, I think."

I lowered my gaze to the Nomad. "What happened to him?"

"He tried to sacrifice himself."

I frowned at him. "For what?"

"To save us all." He looked over at me. "To save her."

"Did he succeed?"

He shrugged. "Maybe, maybe not. Only time will tell. And your little quest. That requires getting him to cooperate." He took in a long breath and let it out. "First, you'd have to get him to focus long enough to answer." He pointed up at the pictures. "This is the only thing that brings him out of his madness. Her face. Her name. If you want him to talk to you, you have to make him think of her." He stepped near me. "And then you have to tell her what he says."

A thought pricked at my memory. I stared at the Nomad, trying to glimpse him better through the slit in his cowl. "Why did you visit me? Who started all this?"

He cocked his head to one side, shaking it slightly, but he said nothing. Giving him another look over revealed little, as they all looked alike in build to my untrained eyes. His voice, however— that my ears had heard before.

"You brought me into this," I whispered. "You gave me—"

He held up a hand. "Whatever you speak of, this is not the place, I assure you." He glanced back down the hall toward the ledge. "I suggest you keep your memories to yourself. Focus on someone else's."

I nodded once at him, my hand moving away from my travel sack and the mysterious box it held. I could play along. For the moment.

"What about her story?" I asked. "Will he listen if I tell it to him?"

The Nomad cocked his head to one side and nodded this time. "It's probably the only thing he'll listen to."

Getting Quentin to sit still for a conversation was like trying to catch the wind. It proved just as futile and frustrating. Persistence only paid off so much. You would think in a place that small, a person would run out of places to hide. Then again, I still can't tell you where they found quarters for me. The door was simply there where it wasn't before. Scripting probably played a role, but I never caught either of them doing it.

Suyef proved next to useless in helping me with this endeavor. He seemed content simply to keep an eye on Quentin, although why he felt the need, I would be waiting a while to find out. The Nomad would nod once or twice at me upon my attempts to strike up a conversation, shrug occasionally, and move off. My task, it seemed, was mine alone. So, I took to just following Quentin. If he wouldn't stay still for a conversation, walking around wherever he went seemed my best option. My hope that this might give me some insight into what was wrong with him died quickly. That answer proved as elusive as real conversation. Sometimes he would sit and stare at a wall for chrons, fingers drawing almost absentmindedly what looked like intricate script on the floor. Just as I began to wonder if he'd ever move from that spot, he'd be up, running back and forth from room to room. He'd rummage through things, looking under and inside anything that moved, tossing anything that he found easy to lift whichever way he wanted. After that, he'd stumble to a halt and just stare.

Other times, he would mutter incessantly. Nothing easily made out, mind you. Just gibberish. Suyef seemed the most concerned when this was happening. He'd hover much closer to Quentin when he did this, leaning slightly as he watched. I strained my ears to make out anything intelligible but never succeeded.

"Be grateful his temper is cool right now," the Nomad said to me after one of these occasions. "If the rage takes him, my only recommendation is to make yourself scarce. Quickly."

During those first days, thankfully, the rage never came upon Quentin. Instead, a routine of random behavior seemed to be the norm. It went on for several days before something new finally happened. Quentin was mobile, me in hot pursuit. Suddenly, he stumbled to a halt, turned, and stared right at me. Here it was, my chance to talk to him. I opened my mouth to speak, and he cried out, finger pointing at me. The next instant, he lunged at me, grabbing at my cloak and ripping off a piece of it. I jumped back, yelling for Suyef and preparing to run. The Nomad appeared from down the hall.

"What?"

I pointed at Quentin, who'd fallen to his knees and begun examining the strip of cloth. "He tore that from my robe!"

The Nomad shook his head and turned to walk away. "He was bound to do it eventually. He took a chunk of mine, too."

"Why?" I asked, never taking my eyes from Quentin.

"Ask him."

"Is this part of the rage?"

"You'll know when that comes," the Nomad called, his voice moving away.

Frowning, I looked round at Suyef, but he'd vanished back into the living quarters. I returned my gaze to find Quentin holding the cloth up to his shoulder, letting it fall down his chest.

"It's not really your color," I said, kneeling to be on his level. He didn't answer. "Your eyes are a bright blue. That's a gray. You'd look better with some other color."

He batted at it with his hand, and a heavy sense of confusion and pity overwhelmed me. What had happened to this man? To the man Micaela had met? What had gone wrong?

"Color," he whispered.

I looked up, shaken from my thoughts by the sound of his voice. "Pardon?"

"Color," he said again, holding the cloth up in front of his face. "I remember many colors. Lots of them, all together. Draped over . . . over . . ."

He frowned, bunching the cloth into a fist. He flung the offending item from him, and it landed somewhere behind me. I didn't bother looking at it.

"Do you want to hear a story?" I asked.

His bright-blue eyes locked on mine. "Is it a good one?"

I shrugged. "Not as good as yours, I bet. But it entertained me."

"Can you tell me while I work?"

I frowned, looking around. "Work?"

He nodded, a finger coming up to his lips. "And you know nothing."

I smiled and shook my head. "Not a clue what you mean."

"Good." He jumped up and beckoned me to follow. "Now get to your story."

So, I started telling him Micaela's story. Well, not me. I started it, but after a short bit a thought occurred to me. Pulling out the device with Micaela telling her story and letting her speak instead had an instant effect. Quentin's movement slowed, as if struck by something, listening. He wasn't completely still, but his level of movement changed as soon as he heard her voice. Afterward, he took to sketching as she spoke. It was always the same sketch: her face. I watched him work as he listened, mesmerized. If her voice sounded sad, he sketched her sad. If she sounded happy, he sketched that. Suyef kept a ready supply of paper coming from somewhere, probably the matter reforger. Either that, or he scripted. Watching Quentin's reactions, I took my own notes, recording his responses to her words.

When the story finally ended, we sat in his room, him on the floor, me on his bed. The sketch he'd been working on sat unfinished. It held only her eyes, the same thing he always started with. It took me a moment to realize what was so odd about the moment: he wasn't moving. I opened my mouth to ask a question but stopped, as I wasn't sure what to say.

"You want to hear my story, don't you?" he asked, his voice more lucid than ever. "You collect stories, don't you? Like I collect her." He nodded up at the ceiling.

"Do you know who she is?" I asked.

The look that crossed his face nearly broke my heart. Anger mixed with agony and what might be regret. Yes, he knew precisely who she was. And he missed her.

"You recorded her voice," he whispered. "Can you record mine?"

I nodded. "I'd like to take notes, too."

"Where do I start?"

I shrugged and pointed at his incomplete sketch. "How about there?"

He looked down at Micaela's eyes on the paper before him. "Her eyes. They make me think of the sky."

He moved to open a window I hadn't noticed before.

"Was that always there?" I asked as he sat down on the edge of his bed, eyes locked on the sky beyond.

He held the incomplete sketch tight to his chest and didn't answer my question. We sat in silence for a few moments.

Then he began to speak.

CHAPTER 16

HUBRIS

Look out that window and tell me what you see. Empty sky. Out there are other shells with millions of people living on them. You could live an entire lifetime on a single shell and never see another in the sky. With the exception of the current orbits of this shell and Colberra, most shells spend very little time near each other. Thus, traveling from shell to shell is almost unheard of, because you could end up stuck on that shell when its orbit took it beyond our ability to travel to. Well, unless you're a dragon. Then all bets are off.

That was where the Expeditionary Forces came from. People from my shell wanting to explore other shells, knowing they might be gone a long time. They planned on being gone so long that they might never see home again. It took a special kind of person to join that group. So, I guess that makes my parents very special.

My parents joined the Colberran Expeditionary Forces before they even met. It was one of the few ways to get off the shell if you had that desire. My parents both possessed an extreme wanderlust buried at their core. I suppose I inherited it from them. Be that as it may, the only opportunity at the time to get off the shell for the average citizen involved balloon trips around the landmass, and you had to pay through the nose to just orbit your shell. So, when the Expeditionary Forces began exploring other shells, it inevitably drew a younger, bolder crowd. Still, for the first century it existed, those trips didn't involve much. A few exploratory trips to smaller satellite shells almost perpetually visible. Those expeditions grew in nature to match the technological abilities of the Colberran people.

Over time, the Forces' mission settled on two ideas: exploratory settlement of other shells and reaching the water shield above. Both presented unique and, some said, insurmountable challenges. And while it remained the harder of the two to achieve, reaching the water shield soon proved to have the greater support. After all, we didn't lack for land or resources on Colberra. Making the case to a population happy with where it lives, a population that has ample space and supplies to continue exploring other shells, was a hard sell. Especially for a fledgling exploratory force dependent on the public's good grace. So, the Forces latched on to the one thing our world was completely devoid of: a stable, internal water supply.

Now, you know from your geography that the Colberran land-mass is one of the highest orbiting shells in the world and is the highest with such a large population on it. That places the mass tantalizingly close to all the water in the world locked away from us in that shield. It has taunted the people of Colberra for centuries, just there in sight but so far out of reach. You can imagine that the hunt for a way to get to the water and thus free the people of the shell from dependence on the Ancients' water system played a huge development role in the culture and society of Colberra. The people became of two minds regarding the problem: either it was a concern or it wasn't. Most of Colberran society could not care less that they were entirely dependent on a single structure and system for their water. It is, after all, a very reliable system. The Ancients who built it did an amazing job, one we've never been able to reproduce. Still, not everyone in Colberran society trusted the system to work for-ever. They were a smaller segment, still so even today, but they were always well connected. It's an age-old truth: the most powerful ally to a fledgling scientific group supporting a controversial theory is the government, its deep pockets, and its ability to hide where it spends its money in the bureaucratic quagmire known as bookkeeping.

Despite lacking strong public support for their cause, a small, publicly impotent group of scientists was able to funnel financing from other programs to fund their own projects. They wanted to find another way to get water and provide it in a stable fashion. When the Expeditionary Forces came into being about a century and a half ago, these scientists realized the potential for using the organization to achieve some of their goals. Ironic, wouldn't you say, that of the two missions the Forces ended up focusing on, the one with the most support was the same one the public had all but ignored for centuries?

The Forces' primary mission came to be the search for a stable water supply, primarily how to get it from the water shield above. Using private-sector ideas, the Forces helped design several different prototype ships that could fly through the air up to the water. The first attempts proved as disastrous as they were imaginative. Flight is, after all, a difficult concept to grasp. Getting a ship of sufficient size to carry water off the ground is a daunting task. What made matters more difficult was the scientists' insistence on inventing the technology themselves. Instead of relying on the Ancient technology that gave us the speeders, for example, they tried to reinvent the wheel. The results were telling. It's no secret Colberran society has been distrustful of Ancient technology for centuries, owing in part to the views of the Seeker organization. That, however, is another story. Suffice it to say the Seeker-encouraged distrust for Ancient technology persisted even among the scientific elite pushing these projects, and the effect on their works was, as I said, telling. For the first half a century, nothing they designed ever even left the shell. As the death toll from these experimental craft rose, along with public ire over the expenditures, pressure from the government compelled the scientists to rely on the Ancient designs they so despised. Many refused and quit the projects. Had enough done so, it's possible many of the events that came after never would have happened, including my birth.

What-ifs are fun but don't help tell this story. As it is, some did persist, and with a blending of the Ancient technology, the Colberran Expeditionary Forces soon had several prototype ships ready to fly. The first launched about fifteen cycles before my birth, to much fanfare. The ship, named *Voyager* in some homage to our ancient past, was a complete success. It took off, flew as planned, and left this shell, heading for the water. It was heralded as the beginning of a new era of independence, an era free of reliance on Ancient technology that could not be trusted to work forever.

Yes, *Voyager* was a complete success. Until it reached the water. You see, what no one could account for in all our observations of the water shield above was the nature of the shield itself. What possessed them to approach the water without sending some kind of probe or unmanned test device first, we may never know. Hubris, most likely. Whatever the reason, the scientists marched boldly ahead, thinking themselves brilliant for achieving their goal despite more than a century of public ignorance of their cause. If you watch the footage of those men, they are practically gleeful as they watch the ship near its goal. As *Voyager* approached the surface, its crew broadcasting the event for all of Colberran society to see, the ship encountered an unexpected confluence of physics. Gravity reversed direction. The ship, designed to climb close to the surface and skim along the water's edge, gathering the precious substance into its holds, wasn't prepared for the change. As the shell's people watched in horror, the ship was torn apart, every crew member on board lost.

One would think such a disaster would temper the taste of the public and the scientists for any further endeavor of that kind. One would be wrong. Instead, it was taken as a challenge. The program suddenly became a matter of continental pride. Public interest skyrocketed and, as a result, so did scrutiny of each aspect.

Rather than risk more lives on hubris-laden attempts to prove a still-not-widely-accepted theory, the Force were able to compel the scientists designing the ships to do more tests. Private-sector think tanks offered up their own prototypes, much to the chagrin of the scientists, because some of these designs relied on Ancient technology and quickly proved more reliable. And, in a final insult to the scientists, the public demanded a renaming of the project. *Voyager* was tossed out in favor of *Apollo*, yet another homage to our distant past, but not one many nowadays will even recall.

Apollo eventually launched five unmanned prototypes, each progressively designed to get the ships closer to the water. None of those five was expected to return, but simply to send data back about the shift in gravity near the water's edge. This they did with complete success.

Finally, with the seventh and eighth modules, the Forces figured out the complex shift in physics, landed both on the surface of the water, and brought them back. The ninth and tenth succeeded in taking men near the edge of the water. On the eleventh mission, they finally landed on the water but did not return with anything more than a sample to test its potability. A huge celebration was thrown, despite this. Colberra had proven itself greater than the warped physics of our world. What did the lack of water coming back with the ship matter?

The success did not mean the controversy was over. Even with the eleventh's triumph, the Forces had not decided on a final version of their water-hauling craft. The twelfth mission tested the other version of the crafts, proving it could work. It even brought a larger sample for further testing on what would need to be done to make the water, which the eleventh showed was heavy in salt, potable for mass consumption. So, to help the decision process, the Forces prepared the two versions of the craft, each dubbed the thirteenth, for a final mission each to the water. A simple goal was set: to be the first craft back with its holds filled to capacity with water.

Now, at this point, you're probably wondering what any of this has to do with my story. The answer is: everything. You see, had the people who chose to change the name of their program to reach the water shield done their research a little better, they'd have known the history of their program's namesake. Just like that ill-fated thirteenth mission so long ago, these two missions were about to experience their own tragedies.

And my father was on one of those prototypes.

The two ships launched simultaneously from two different locations on Colberra, each with its own fanfare and support. The two companies that had designed them waited with bated breath, hoping for complete and hasty success for their own mission, while desiring less for the other. As the two ships lifted off, heading for the water high above, sensors at the Colberran continental citadel, the hub of the Ancient network on each life-sustaining shell, detected two more ships launched from a lower shell. The race, it would seem, had two new competitors.

You see, the people of the Nomad shell, Suyef's home, were also curious about the water shield, their landmass being the next-highest mass with such a large population. The water shield, while still observable, is far less detailed when viewed from Suyef's home than from Colberra, where an observer can make out waves moving across the surface. With their orbit placing the shell in relatively close proximity to Colberra for the past several decades, they'd observed our endeavors, enhancing their knowledge by using the very same network Colberrans rely on for all their data needs, and learned from our mistakes. Their two ships, identical in make, were their first two launched. Designed completely using Ancient technology, the ships approached the water shield at almost the same time as the two Colberran ships.

All four made successful landings within miles of the others. Two, one Colberran and one Nomad, landed in sight of each other.

The ships exchanged cursory pleasantries, the records show; then communication, for the most part, ceased. The Nomads, it seems, weren't interested in the water. That's understandable, considering the Nomad supershell, largest of all the landmasses orbiting our broken world, possesses the only known sea still in existence. Theirs was purely a scientific interest. Some, mostly Colberrans, argued they were there to keep an eye on the other ships. That's never been proven. Some even accuse the Nomad ships of being responsible for what happened next. This, also, has never been proven.

Whatever their reason, the two ships, one Colberran, the other Nomad, went about their business like the other wasn't there. The ships didn't even communicate with each other after the initial courtesies. That is, until they discovered the object.

No one is really sure what it was they found. Some say another ship. Others say an Ancient relic from centuries in the past. Some circles argue it was an even more ancient artifact from before the cataclysm that sundered our world, something that was in the waters when they were placed there. We don't know for sure. We know they found something, as the other Colberran ship recorded the radio broadcasts of the two ships talking to each other about pulling the object up together. Why not separately? Well, the designs of the ships required them to work together. The Nomad ship had the ability to pull up the object, but not store it. The Colberran ship had a huge bay for holding water, thus ample storage. This we pieced together from the records kept on the other Colberran ship. Beyond that, we don't know what happened.

Why don't we, you ask? Because what's left of the Colberran and Nomad ships that pulled up the object together now lies entombed in the water shield, far above us, locked away from our reach. All hands went down with the ship, according to the Colberran records. All hands but one. A single crew member from the other Colberran ship, responding to the brief distress signal sent out before it cut off mysteriously, rescued. After pulling him from the water, the ship, its hold full of water, needed no further encouragement to leave and return to Colberra.

The official report insisted there was only one survivor, the man the second ship brought back. They were wrong. Another person survived the fateful event.

My father.

One of the first problems I encountered in trying to get Quentin to share his story was his refusal to tell it in order. It's not that he told me things that would have tipped me off to what was coming. He kept the story pretty much in a progression. Still, it wasn't like the story he told me held any semblance to one I could write down. He would start on one thought, then shoot off on some random tangent he believed related, and then jump back to clarify something he said before. Other times, he'd just stop telling me his story entirely and would argue the finer points of calligraphy or needlework or some such nonsense with me or the wall or whatever happened to be in front of him.

"Getting him to talk in something that resembles a narrative is impossible," I vented at Suyef soon after I'd convinced Quentin to start telling me his story.

The Nomad chuckled and tapped his head. "He's not right up here. What do you expect?"

"How am I supposed to make sense of this nonsense?" I asked.

He shrugged. "You're the scribe. You'll figure it out."

So, I kept at it. Needless to say, I became quite good at being able to tell when Quentin got off topic. My notes became a tumble of lines connecting one section to another so my work later in organizing the narrative from his recording would be simpler. Not necessarily easier. Just manageable.

If only *manageable* meant I understood any of where this was going. It went on a lot longer before I came close to that point.

CHAPTER 17

PATHS CROSS

My father enlisted in the Forces just as the *Apollo* missions began. He had no desire to go to the water shield. His one wish: to travel to another shell. As the Colberran people turned their eyes upward to watch their ships get closer and closer to their collective goal, my father wished to travel down. The one thing he would always do was obey orders. When the orders came assigning him to one of the *Apollo 13* missions, he took his place and headed up toward the water shield.

He never talked much with me or anyone save for my mother about what happened while on the surface of the water. I never did figure out why he kept it secret. I suspected he wasn't allowed to talk about it or that he just didn't want to. I think he also wanted to keep me from pushing too deep into certain secrets. Considering what we found out later about those missions, I can appreciate why he wanted to protect me from such knowledge. I was, after all, just a kid when I started asking. This didn't stop me from trying, though. Whenever I'd bring it up, he'd change the subject. As I got older and more versed with the network, I began to do my own research into the events. What is available to the public was even less informative. Colberran records insist only one person survived the event. Those records don't ever mention his name, just that he was an employee of the winning company and a key witness to how the system worked. The disaster has all but been forgotten in the wake of further *Apollo* missions to the water shield.

The reason my father's survival isn't common knowledge is that he is assumed to have gone down with the ship. If you look at death records, his name appears there. So, how did he come to live, when the Colberrans had all but left him for dead?

The other Nomad ship. She picked up the same truncated distress signal. She was farther away but did respond. When she arrived, the second Colberran ship had departed, leaving my father behind, floating on the surface. The Nomads, curious as to what happened, rescued my father and took him back to their shell with them. He spent several months with them as they picked his brain for the information. Frankly, it's a good thing they did, too. It's entirely possible that, had they not picked up the distress signal and come to my father's rescue, they might have ended up on the bottom of the water shield above. You see, the object found by the lost ships was not the only one found that day. The second Nomad ship had found one of their own, and they'd found a way to bring it on board without the help of the Colberrans. You can imagine that the Nomads partially blamed the loss of their ship on cooperation with the Colberrans. That, as well, has never been proven. Still, it did enough to sour relations between the world's two most populous shells. As such, the outpost the Forces had established on the upper edge of the Nomad shell remained isolated. The Nomads were too kind and polite to force the Colberran expedition to leave. They weren't, however, above simply ignoring the expedition, cutting them off from the rest of the Nomad society.

Because of this, it was several months before anyone of Colberran origin knew my father survived. He spent that time in the care of the Nomads as they interrogated him. I say interrogated, but it appears it was more like intensive questioning. My father suffered no harm from his stay with them, actually coming out on the other end healthier and more fit than when he enlisted. They did not cut him off from the outside world, and he learned much about the Nomads while he stayed with them. Their only reason for keeping him appears to be that they genuinely wanted to know what happened. Can you blame them? They spent a lot of time and resources, not to mention lives, sending those ships to the water. Losing one of them was an extremely costly accident, if it was such as the Colberrans insist in their public records of the event. So, ever attentive to details, the Nomads did a thorough job questioning my father before finally doing the only thing they could do: they sent him to the expedition's landing base on the topmost end of their shell.

Now, I said the Nomads invested a lot of time and resources in the endeavor to explore the water shield. It wasn't just that. You see, the Nomads are a patriarchal society, tribal in the arrangement of their culture. I won't go into too much detail here. Suffice it to say the society took great care of their people, considering them their greatest resource over even water, possibly the most valuable resource in the world now. To send their people so far away just to explore was a great undertaking. To ensure their greatest resource was protected, they chose men from the finest families to lead their crews. One such family, the closest you will find to a royal family, is the Bilal tribe. It is a vast family that loosely controlled the central portion of the habitable part of their continent around the lone working citadel on their supershell. That family was not exempt from the responsibility to man the water-shield expedition and sent one of their finest men to command one of the ships—the ship that was lost, with all hands on board. You can imagine what a national tragedy this was for the people of that shell.

Who was that man who led that ship? The man so many insist, without any proof, was so capable that the only way he would have lost his ship was through some Colberran treachery? That man was the son of the Bilal tribe's patriarch.

Suyef's father.

The loss of such a prominent member of their society was devastating to the Bilal tribe. It led to a power shift on the shell, with his tribe losing control of the citadel region. They moved to a region that bordered the Colberran settlement, a post seen fit for the lowest family among the clans. The only honor given the tribe was the job of returning my father to his people, more of an insult, really.

Suyef, still unborn when all this happened, came into that world a few months later. His father became a martyr in a national tragedy and the icon of his family's great fall from grace. You can imagine the effect this had on him growing up, prince of an outcast family. Despite all that, they carried out their duty with honor. Just as Suyef was born, his tribe delivered my father, now finished with his months of questioning, to the gates of the Colberran settlement. He was left there with no explanation to the Forces commander.

To say the Colberrans were shocked to find one of their own deposited outside their gates when no Colberran had been allowed to leave the settlement is putting it mildly. The settlement, an Ancient outpost from long in the past, lay on a finger of a peninsula that juts out from the uppermost corner of the supershell. Surrounded by high peaks, it stood on the nearest point on the mass to the water shield with, coincidentally, the Colberran shell viewable still in the distance. The records don't show why the Nomads left it uninhabited, but that was what the Forces found when they landed several months before. They took up residence inside the facility and immediately sent out scouts to make contact with their new neighbors. All of the scouting parties returned with word that they found no one. The residents had vanished, they claimed, moved on farther into the landmass.

Soon, however, the Forces found the shell was much more inhabited than they had previously believed. The third day they sent out scouts, the parties found their way blocked, a massive

Nomad army having materialized out of the desert to lay siege to the fortress. It took several days of tense negotiations for the Nomad army to authorize the occupation of the fortress by the Colberrans. That agreement came with a price: no Colberran could travel after core-set, and none could travel beyond the sight of the walls surrounding the facility. The Colberran commander chafed at the restrictions but had no choice beyond accepting.

So, when my father appeared outside their gates, the Colberrans were confused and suspicious. He was brought inside and interrogated, of course. They couldn't let anyone that had seen so much of the Nomad shell get away without doing at least that. Unfortunately for them, the Nomads had done a very good job of concealing from my father where he had been and what it was like, outside of cultural stuff. All he could confirm was what they could see from the settlement's control tower. That's not to say they took him at his word. They challenged everything he said, questioned it more so, and pretty much made it clear to him what they thought of his story.

It took a chance meeting with an intelligence analyst to finally break the ice surrounding my father and his presence in the settlement. And who was that analyst?

My mother.

My mother was raised in a strict environment on Colberra. Very traditional, a no-nonsense kind of family. She was the eldest of eight and expected to set an example for her siblings in Colberran society. Her decision to enlist in the Expeditionary Forces was met with, well, let's just call it less-than-stellar reviews at home. That her siblings followed suit, several of them serving on later expeditions to the water shield, only made matters worse. The strife this caused between her and her father nearly ruined their relationship, and when the chance arose to volunteer for the expedition to the Nomad shell, she jumped at it.

Her job on the mission was simple: decipher the network on the Nomad shell, thus giving the Colberrans information as well as a direct line back to Colberra should the need arise. The network is, after all, the only known way to send information from shell to shell. She and her counterparts spent the first month there cooped up inside a secure section of the settlement, cracking network codes. You know the network systems on each shell will talk to each other, but it takes the citadel control tower of each shell to serve as the translation point between the various systems. With the Nomads in command of that facility, they could keep the Colberrans, who they distrusted for many reasons—not the least of which being the water-mission disaster—completely isolated. You can see the importance of finding some way to get into the network.

During a night shift, she stumbled across a back door into the network. To this day, she insists she found it herself, searching through stacks of what seemed like unimportant data before she spotted an access point. There's no evidence to the contrary, but I've always found coincidences to be highly suspect. How she would happen to stumble upon the one and only entry point available to the Colberrans buried deep in a mountain of useless data I can't imagine. Still, she did it. With that success, the Colberrans had their exploit. They still had to be careful, keeping their usage to minor peaks and shifts of data that would seem natural. My mother's area of expertise lay in shifting data around in clusters to find patterns and break through them. She could spend chrons doing it and did so before stumbling across what at first seemed like another useless bit of data.

What was it she found that finally solved the mystery surrounding my father's arrival at the settlement? Again, the coincidence is striking. She managed to piece together one of the crew manifests of the two ships the Nomads sent up to the water shield. As they all knew of the launches, this information seemed useless, until she found the return manifest a few days later. At first, she saw nothing out of the ordinary. Still, she persisted, shuffling the data around like a puzzle, looking for matches and patterns. Finally, several days later, she found the inconsistency she was looking for.

There were two names buried in the return manifest that she could prove weren't on the ship when it launched. The first belonged to my father. The second? A man named Mortac.

Quentin leapt from the bed, flinging the unfinished sketch in anger.

"That name!" he hissed and ran from the room.

I grabbed the recording padd and raced after him, colliding with Suyef, who stepped across my path.

"Leave him be," he whispered.

"The rage?" I asked, peeking around him to see where Quentin had gone.

He nodded. "And it's best he be alone." He sighed, a deep, long thing that carried a massive weight. "Trust me. When he's like this, he's of use to no one but himself."

"That name, Mortac," I said, watching the Nomad carefully for any reaction. "That set him off."

Suyef nodded. "I'm shocked you made it this long without him running off. He must like you."

"Why would that name send him into the rage?"

"What sends him into a rage varies," the Nomad said, moving toward the living area and beckoning me to follow. "Sometimes her name will do it. Other times that one. Usually neither of those will draw as strong a reaction as some other things."

"What are they?" I asked, seating myself at the table.

He shook his head. "In time, you'll figure that out. Certain names, like Mortac. Colvinra. Other times, it's his family. There isn't a pattern. The madness just strikes when it pleases."

Silence fell on the room. Suyef and I both shifted as it did.

"The box?" I nodded at my travel sack sitting nearby. "Can we discuss that now?"

"I don't—"

"No," I interrupted him. "It was you who delivered it to me. It was you who made me show it to the Queen."

"No one forced you to do anything," he whispered.

I smiled. "Still, you planned the odds."

"I was right to do so."

"But what of this—"

"I warned you not to speak of it here."

"What's in it?"

The Nomad shook his head. "Now is not the time."

"Well, why would the Queen be afraid of it?" I asked.

He frowned. "Fear has nothing to do with it."

It was my turn to frown. "Well, she obviously feels something about it. Else, why force me to show it to her?"

"No one forced you to do anything."

"You insisted I had to show it to her."

He nodded. "And left the choice to you. As with the choice to not look in the box."

"I believed you."

"Another choice."

I frowned again. "Why the focus on my choices?"

"We are what we choose," he whispered, and walked away. "You, more than anyone else, should understand that."

He left me there with those words.

"I should understand," I muttered, looking around the living area. "What does that mean?"

I pondered what knowledge I had of him to decipher his meaning. Beyond his connection to Micaela and Quentin and what Micaela had revealed to me up to that point, there wasn't much to go on. Other than that, he seemed to have a connection to the Queen. That gave me pause. Could his connection to the Queen have some connection to his statement? I couldn't see how. Maybe this was digging too deep. He had said that I should understand. So, I contemplated what he knew of me, but couldn't pinpoint much beyond our few conversations here and the initial time we met. I pored over my memory of that discussion, trying to pick out anything about me he might be referring to. A full chron later, I sat there, contemplating the one thing about me he may have meant. The moment I failed the test for the blessing and lost the most coveted of places among my people. The one thing that all of us strived to achieve, but I had failed to attain. The ascension.

And it filled me with sadness.

Quentin's return saved me from diving down into that pit. He strolled in, a serious look on his face and the now retrieved incomplete sketch in his hand. Seating himself across from me, he stared at me, eyes narrowing and widening a few times. His lips moved to speak, but he never did.

"Are you ready to continue?" I asked.

He took in a deep breath and nodded as he let it out.

I must preface this next part of the story with a caution: I've barely been able to get Suyef to discuss these matters. *Internal family issues you wouldn't understand,* I believe is how he put it. Suffice it to say that what I know I've managed to glean from him, my parents, and a few other sources. That leaves a lot to be learned.

I never met the man my mother said came back with my father from the water shield. The Nomads don't even state in their public records of the event that anyone else returned with them besides my father. They wrapped the mission in as much secrecy as the Colberrans did. Still, my mother's evidence showed someone else came back when they did. The only logical answer is that they dragged him from the water like my father. But where did he come from? No man with that name served aboard the Colberran ships. The name itself is an ancient one. Records show it went out of use soon after the world was split, although the reason for that is a bit fuzzy. Still, a name's a name, and it gave me something to search for. I added it to a list of questions. Who was the man the Colberrans brought back? Who was Mortac? At the time, I hadn't met Suyef or the warden yet. What did the ships find in the water? The list was growing.

The knowledge my mother brought to the Colberrans did serve one good purpose: it relieved my father of any suspicion. Using her access, coupled with that information, they were able to confirm his story. To a point. Colberran officials refused to acknowledge he still lived, insisting he went down with the ship. The commander of the Forces on the Nomad shell found this odd. For some reason, he kept it secret that my father was alive and with him. I'm not sure what sparked that moment of clairvoyance on his part, but it served me well.

My father, you see, soon found out who his savior of sorts was. They met and married almost immediately, my mother needing but a moment to extract herself from what she insists to this day was the worst mistake she'd made after core-set in her life. She never told me more, and I didn't ask. My parents married less than two weeks after meeting and are still married today. I was born just over a cycle later, one of the first Colberrans born off-shell.

That birth, unfortunately, made it harder for them to keep their presence hidden from the authorities. In order to make my citizenship official, they needed to return to Colberra, which meant finally revealing to the Seekers that my father had survived. You can imagine the stress that put on him when they returned. My mother said she'd never seen him so worried, and he lost most of his hair during those few cycles we lived on the orbiting Northern Isles.

He spent several months spread over a few cycles being interrogated by the Seekers. He never told us that was what was going on, but we knew. Still, they must not have found anything suspicious, because he always returned. It would seem the Nomads were very good in keeping information from him they didn't want him to let slip to others. With that source of potential information dried up, the Seekers soon grew bored and let him return to the Forces. When I was a young lad, nearly ten cycles, we returned to the Nomad shell, with one extra passenger: my younger sister, born a few short cycles after me.

It was during that stay with the Nomads that I finally began to piece together some of what had happened. It all started with a gift my father gave me for my tenth birthday. I still remember him coming to my room and handing me a package.

"Happy birthday, son," he said. "I've had this in storage here since before we went to live on the isles. It's something I picked up. I think it's got some technology to it, but I can't make it work. Enjoy."

I opened the package to find a belt in it. It had small circular panels inlaid around its outer edge and a magnetic clasp.

"This looks old," I whispered.

He nodded. "Very. It's about the only souvenir I brought back from my mission to the water."

My eyes darted up to his. He never talked about the mission.

He shrugged. "It's just a belt, probably broken."

I looked back down, running my fingers around the panels. "Anyway, enjoy."

I looked up to ask him another question, but he'd left the room. It was one of the strangest gifts he'd ever given me. I think he may have regretted it after the fact. It prompted me to try to figure out what occurred on the water.

History has always fascinated me, and you can imagine how appealing it was to me to study history that I was a part of. There were answers to be found, mysteries to solve, and I wanted to be the one who found and solved them. Unfortunately, my parents found my interest in such pursuits troublesome and did their best to ignore them. My father became more secretive about his past, and my mother rarely would discuss any part of it. I soon found the dearth of information available to the general public on the matters to be equally frustrating. The world, it would seem, wanted to keep its secrets from me.

Unfortunately for the world, I'm a very persistent man. The difficulties enhanced my desire to know more. Roadblocks diverted my focus; they never squelched it. I consumed everything I could find about the missions to the water. I searched through ancient texts about the previous missions that shared the *Apollo* name, which were very scarce, mind you. To keep myself freshly motivated, I studied the crew manifests in the public records and browsed conspiracy forums to keep track of the kooky theories bubbling up constantly.

For the most part, all I gained was a vast knowledge of the data-storage capabilities of the network. It's nearly infinite, the beauty of quantum computing. There is no end to the information stored there. It's equal parts fascinating and frustrating to have all that knowledge at my fingertips, yet be unable to use it.

Little did I know that knowledge was about to take an unexpected twist, leading me straight to Micaela.

CHAPTER 18

THE NOMAD COUNCIL

My research, you see, didn't go unnoticed. The Nomads kept tight reins on their network. They knew everything I looked at on their version of the network, and I swear they knew all along that the Colberrans had hacked into the system. It's possible they saw it as just a minor inconvenience that served them well: it kept the Colberrans isolated to an unimportant sector of the network. Only when we strayed out of that zone did they step in. In part, they did it for our own safety. You see, the Nomads believe something is guarding the network. They won't say what, but they are mostly distrustful of the entire thing, using it because they must. They do much of their work away from any network access points for fear someone or something might be watching. Their paranoia serves them well, as it does mean most of what they do must be recorded for their histories later. I stumbled across this practice almost by accident, although you know my opinion of coincidences.

One night, as I found myself lost in genealogical research on the great families of the Nomad world, I found a recording made recently that updated the genealogical record of the Bilal family. How this is done is quite simple: any event of import to the Nomads is committed to memory by a chosen member of each family. That person then goes to a network hub and repeats, word for word, what he memorized to the network, allowing it to be saved. In this way, they control everything that is recorded on the machine, even down to who has access to do such a thing. The recording I found, which brought me to the attention of the Bilal family, was of Suyef reading off an addition to his family's record. In it, he listed an uncle they'd just found that had been lost to them. His name: Mortac. He gave no description of the man, just a name and a brief mention of his being returned to the family. I'm not even sure how they knew he was an uncle to the Bilal family. Probably a genetic test of some kind. The Nomads are far from primitive. Still, the addition sparked an interest in me. Who was this uncle? Where had he come from? And why that name? At the time, I hadn't stumbled across any information on this man. The only thing I had was that the name was the same one my mother had discovered on the crew manifest, and I'd just found that. Additionally, I found no image of the man, or any other mention of him after that entry.

As I pondered my discovery, the Nomads came and took me in for questioning. One of the standing agreements, you see, with the Colberrans is that, if the Nomads wished to take us for questioning, we had to obey. A single witness is allowed to attend the proceedings. Up to that point, they'd never enforced it. My father, as a known quantity to them, was allowed to accompany us.

We traveled far into the shell, and, oddly, they didn't blindfold us. We were seeing, as far as I knew, the Nomad shell for the first time with true Colberran eyes. What I saw left me speechless. It's hard to describe the destruction that molded the landscape of that shell after the collision long ago. It's one of the wonders of this modern world. I'll not bore you with grandiose descriptions now. Suffice it to say, it was one of the most alien landscapes I've ever seen, probably the most alien in this world.

When we arrived at our destination, I found myself before the gathered elders of the Bilal tribe. My father was greeted, then summarily ignored for the rest of the proceedings. To this day, the look and feel of that room remain lodged in my memory. The ceilings hung low, smoke clouded the air, and the lighting was dim and foreboding. It would not surprise me to learn the entire arrangement was designed to intimidate. If so, it worked. I felt completely alone. My father was forbidden to speak, either for or to me, here. All that mattered in this place was my voice and theirs.

So, I spoke. Well, actually, I asked a question. Of all the questions available to me in that moment, I'm not sure what compelled me to ask the one I did. Maybe it's because it was the one they'd be the least likely to answer. Maybe part of me thought this was my one shot to get an answer like that, so why not take it? With that thought in mind, I jumped.

"What did you find in the water?"

Quentin stood upright quickly, and I reached for the recording device, preparing to follow him if he became mobile again.

"It was such a stupid move," he whispered. "Why open with that question?"

"I was thinking the same thing."

He glared at me. "Foresight's prophetic, eh?"

"Um, excuse me?" I asked, frowning at his phrase.

"You know, when you look back, reflect on things. Everything's clear then."

I cocked my head to one side, staring at him. "I think you mean hindsight."

"Isn't that what I said?" When I shook my head, he frowned and scratched at his cheek. "I swear I thought I said it right." He waved his hands, shrugging. "Bah, it's not important. You get the point."

Smiling at him, I nodded. "Now I do, yes. Looking back, you wish you'd said something else."

He leaned over the table, his bright-blue eyes wide and focused on my own. "I could have asked so many things. So many other options." His shoulders sagged and his eyes lowered. "Wouldn't have mattered, most likely. They probably would have gone on just how they did."

"Which is?"

Quentin took off from the room. I grabbed the padd and hurried after him. He ran into his room, grabbed his pencil, and tumbled down across his bed. I stumbled to a halt just inside the doorway and watched him begin sketching. Rather, he continued. Moving around the side of the bed, I spied the same incomplete sketch of Micaela's eyes lying under his hand. The pencil lines flew across the page as her face came into fruition before me. I moved closer as slowly as possible, not wishing to disturb him. He didn't seem to notice me, his attention focused solely on his work.

After a few moments, her face was mostly done. This one she smiled in, a rare sight among the myriad faces staring down at us. He paused, looking intently at the image he'd created.

"She's important," I whispered.

He nodded.

"To you," I added.

A look crossed his face, twisting and distorting his features. A look of pain. He closed his eyes, and one hand clenched into a fist. The other crept near the sketch, and I feared he might ruin it. My hand darted out and grabbed it away before he could get hold of it.

"May I have this?" I asked, making a show of examining it. "For my collection on her? It would go well with the story."

His head bowed, fist unclenching, forehead resting on the bed.

"I've ruined so much," he whispered. "Wasted so much. Been so stupid."

A cough drew my attention, and I looked up to find Suyef standing in the doorway. He shook his head and beckoned me to follow. I glanced once more at Quentin before moving to leave, taking the sketch with me. Quentin made no move to stop or come after.

"What's wrong with him?" I asked the Nomad once I entered the living area. "What is he talking about?"

"Regret," Suyef replied.

"For?"

The Nomad looked at my hand and the sketch.

"This? Her?"

He nodded. "It's more complicated than that, but in a simple word, yes."

"Did he do something to her?"

The Nomad shook his head. "You're trying to fly before you've even sprouted wings."

I frowned at his phrase. "What's that supposed to mean?"

"It means you've only just begun to hear the story and already you're jumping to the end." He pointed down the hall to the sleeping quarters. "He makes no sense to you as he is now. You keep asking why. He's telling you why, but you're impatient, wanting to turn to the end of the book and read the final page." He stepped near me. "And we're not even near the end of this story." His voice lowered to a whisper. "We've only come partway, and look what it's done to the two of them."

I looked down at the sketch in my hand. "He clearly feels deeply for her. Does she reciprocate it?"

Suyef sagged a little before answering. "What she feels is deeper than I think even she understands. Deeper even than this rift between them."

"Why is this so important to you?" I asked, locking gazes with the Nomad. "Why are you trying so hard to fix this?"

"Because I've seen the wonders they can achieve together," he answered, his voice barely above a whisper. "I've seen what they are as one. Separate, each is powerful beyond most that have ever walked this shattered world. Together, they are a force unstoppable." He paused and stepped closer to me. "A force that can achieve something even the strongest doubters among us believe is impossible."

"Which is?"

He smiled, a small smile. "You're trying to fly again." He held up a finger. "And even that is not impossible."

With that, he left me standing there, the sketch in hand and more questions in my mind. That phrase he'd used. It stuck with me. He'd done that on purpose, I know. The memory rose again, the memory he'd previously dredged up from the dark pit that I had buried it in so long ago. The failure that defined me.

Yes, he'd chosen those words on purpose. I looked down at the sketch and felt something I hadn't for a long time. The feeling one gets most often as a child, when the world is new and everything is possible if only the child believes and acts on that belief.

Hope.

The elder's answer, predictably, was less than what I'd hoped for. The person in charge, a particularly leathery-looking man with a few dangles of hair gripping for dear life to the top of his head and a nose so pockmarked I thought he'd been poked by someone with a stick, chuckled breathily and nodded at my father.

"Him, you idiot." He shook his head and stated the only bit of the conversation that would be directed to my father. "Not very bright, this one."

My father spread his hands and shrugged, but said nothing. I, on the other hand, bristled at the insult.

"I object. It's a perfectly valid question, and you've dodged the answer."

The man laughed again. "No, it's a question with more than one answer; you just don't like the answer I've chosen to give you."

My mouth snapped shut at that. He was correct. They had found my father in the water. He could have said water, too, and been correct. I kicked myself internally for giving him such an easy dodge.

"We aren't here to discuss the events of that tragic day, however," the old man continued. "We're here to inquire into your actions on our network."

"Your network?"

His eyes flashed with some kind of emotion, either anger or impatience, I couldn't tell which. "You'd best learn when to speak and, more importantly, when not to speak. You have no enemies in this room." He glared at me. "Yet."

I shuffled under his gaze, using the excuse of looking around the room to avoid his eyes. Every person there sat straddling a pillow. Even my father had been offered one, though he'd politely refused. I stood alone in the center, no pillow offered. All the occupants were of an age with my father or older, the man speaking to me being the eldest of the bunch and clearly the patriarch of this clan. I spied several women sitting among the elders, something that stood out to me as a bit odd in what history claims has always been a predominately patriarchal society.

"That's better," he went on, no doubt taking my silence as agreement with his words. "As I was saying, you've been doing some snooping on our network. We feel you're wasting your time, but we can see the value in the questions clearly guiding your search."

"What questions are those?" I asked before I thought about it.

His nostrils flared once; then he shook his head. "We've brought you here because you are not the first to do such research." His eyes locked on to me. "Nor are you the first to chafe under this council's questions on these matters."

For a moment, his eyes flickered over each of my shoulders before settling on me again. Frowning, I turned. My father stood still. To his left, across the entrance, stood another figure cloaked in shadows. I squinted to try and get a better view but failed. I looked back at the elder.

"Yes, your father once stood where you do now. Just before we returned him to your people, we brought him here to question him." The old man let a small smile toy at the side of his mouth. "He had much more decorum bred into him, a virtue of his career choice, I think."

Behind me, my father chuckled but said nothing. I kept my eyes on the elder, trying to hold myself in a respectful manner. It made me feel uncomfortable and scrutinized.

"As I was saying, you're not the first to do this research. You aren't the first to ask these questions, to wonder what happened on that tragic day." He pointed behind me, at the figure cloaked in shadows. "To wonder what happened to his father that day." The figure stepped forward to reveal a man of my age, perhaps a bit older. He wore a loose cloak, billowing off his broad shoulders, massive, thick arms folded across his chest. His face was as dark as the hair in his beard. He looked all of a brute.

"This is Suyef," the elder continued. "He, too, asks your questions. The reason is his story to tell, when he chooses." The elder chuckled. "I think you'll find him a hard nut to crack." He looked at the man. "I pity you, Suyef. I suspect this one talks incessantly."

Suyef looked down, clearly uncomfortable at the elder's words.

"You both seek answers to questions about what happened on those water missions, and we cannot answer you, not because we don't want to, but because we are unable. The network fights us, and all of our attempts to fix the problem have failed." I looked back at the elder, who held up a hand to forestall me. "The answers you seek we believe are elsewhere. We want them as much as you. So, we'll send you where you can find them." He nodded at Suyef. "Together, maybe you can find what alone you cannot."

"Where are we going?" I asked, turning to look at the elder.

"To the place that caused all this: Colberra."

CHAPTER 19

TRUTH OR VENGEANCE

I contemplated the elder's words while resting later in a tent prepared especially for me. No one had spoken to me since the council's dismissal; most of the Nomads simply ignored me altogether. My mind toyed with thoughts on what had happened. At first, I felt I'd come out ahead. The council hadn't reprimanded me much; they'd all but said they wanted the same answers as me and had even been so kind as to give me help. Still, part of me wondered how much they truly wanted to know. This kind of research would be much easier if they'd just give me unfettered access to their network, but they'd balked at even the idea of that. It would seem that, in their eyes, my answers lay elsewhere. Whether that was because the answers truly did lay elsewhere or the Nomads simply wanted to keep me from discovering what they knew, I was unsure.

My hopes that Suyef would be of help initially proved wrong as well. He'd said nothing to me after the council ended, ignoring me as all the rest. He'd been given a nearby tent, as I'd seen him enter it and stay there, ignoring any attempts to meet with him. Setting aside my curiosity on his part in this, I wondered if he was being given this assignment against his will. He clearly didn't trust me and didn't want anything to do with me. I didn't want to push myself on him, but what choice remained? Leaving my tent wasn't an option except to see him, and he refused to see me. So, I sat in my tent, alone, contemplating the situation, wondering how long we'd be kept there before the Nomads tired of this and sent me packing.

I looked up from my reverie to find Suyef standing in the entrance to my tent. He crossed his arms over his broad chest and glared down at me.

"Why do you ask these questions, Colberran?"

I shrugged. "Someone needs to."

He frowned. "What if there is nothing more to know?"

"Governments do not classify missions if there's nothing to know."

"But why do you care to know?" he persisted. "What do you hope to find?"

I shrugged again. "The truth."

He fell silent, eyes contemplating me.

"The truth is a fickle thing," he finally whispered. "And it depends greatly on your point of view."

"No, that's opinion," I countered. "Truth is truth. The perception of truth and opinion of what is found depend on your point of view."

"And what will you do if you find there's nothing to be found?"

"Then we've wasted our time asking a silly question," I retorted, waving a hand at him. "I don't know what you're looking for, but I know what I am."

"And that is?"

"I told you already, the truth of what happened up there. There's more to it than just two ships sinking. Something else is going on here, and the loss of those two ships, I think, is just another step in something much bigger."

Suyef stood silent for a moment, then sighed and shook his head. "Truth is not what I seek."

I gazed at him. "Answers?"

"Vengeance." His eyes flared, locking on mine. "Pure, simple vengeance."

We left that night, escorted across the landscape to another Nomad outpost near the shell's topmost edge. Before we left, the elder and my father visited us one last time. Suyef received a padd from the elder, who bid us farewell. My companion tucked the device away and moved off so I could say good-bye to my father.

"I'm not sure what you hope to find, doing this," he said, shaking his head. "Trouble. That's all I got from this whole mess." He shifted inside his cloak. "That and your belt. Do you still have it on you?"

I pulled the belt off.

"I never told you where I got it," he continued. "I took that from someone on that ship."

"Who?"

He shook his head again. "I don't know. But I can tell you this: if you're so set on figuring out what happened, figure out what that thing is and where it came from." He put a hand on my shoulder. "I know you've tried before to find out about the belt. Do it again. Maybe on Colberra you'll have better luck. I suspect the guy I took it from was from there. That's all I can tell you. The rest is classified."

I frowned at him. "That's just to protect the Seekers."

"Maybe," he stated, shrugging. "It's not my place to decide that." He pointed at the belt with his other hand. "But this, no one knows about. The Nomads I think suspect it, but as I had it when they found me, the belt belonged to me."

I held the belt up. "It looks Ancient."

My father nodded. "And that's all I know about it." He paused and looked around. "Oh, and I think the guy who had it on him was a Seeker." He shrugged. "But that's just my guess."

He bid me farewell and left. I joined Suyef, and we made our way to the shell's edge, the belt now wrapped securely around my waist. There we were secreted aboard a Nomad transport ship lifting off and heading for Colberra that core-night. With the shells this close to each other, ships were able to travel more freely between the landmasses, using their gravity tethers to push and pull their way from one shell to the other. These vessels differed greatly from the variants sent to the water shield so long ago, as these depended greatly on the relative proximity to landmasses, whereas the ships sent to the water had been propelled with Ancient technology that allowed free travel into the atmosphere. Much like Seeker speeders, the ship we traveled on needed something to latch on to with gravity beams and push or pull on to move.

The ship departed that evening with us locked away in our quarters far below deck, only the captain aware of our presence. Despite their fall from grace, which I began to learn about that very evening, the family name still carried a lot of sway among the Nomads, and Suyef used that to his advantage. We had a spacious cargo room all to ourselves, complete with hammocks, washing basin, food, and, most importantly, a door lockable from the inside. The elder's words had proven true: Suyef was a hard nut to crack, making me feel like a chatterbox trying to get him to speak. Eventually, he relented and started sharing some of his people's history and culture with me. He taught me in short order how many cultural blunders I'd made during my visit to the council. Suyef expressed in blunt terms that he'd been shocked they'd even granted me permission to accompany him, considering how rudely I'd behaved before the council.

"Here I thought that was being polite," I muttered after his describing how my quiet shuffling looked.

"Never take your eyes from an elder when he is speaking," he said, holding a finger up. "To do such a thing is to tell them what they say matters as much to you as the air shifting around the room."

"Elders put far too much importance on younger people listening to them with undivided attention," I replied. "Maybe if they said things that interested me, it'd be easier to pay attention."

Suyef chuckled. "That's why I'm surprised we are here. Colberrans, in general, are considered among the rudest people we Nomads have ever encountered. None of you can maintain eye contact for more than a few heartbeats. Is it any wonder you are all so argumentative and distrustful of each other?" He jabbed a finger at me. "Even now, knowing what you know, you've avoided looking directly at me."

"Hey, you said that was for elders," I countered.

He shook his head. "No, I said among elders it's required. Among Nomads as a whole, it's highly encouraged to the point of being required."

I snorted. "Yeah, well, in Colberra, I suggest you break that habit. People there think you're getting too pushy or in their face if you look them in the eye too much."

We spent the better part of the first leg of the flight discussing the many cultural nuances of Colberran society. On the whole, Suyef left me with the impression he found the entire experience discomfiting. The two cultures, Nomad and Colberran, are as different as one will find. Where Colberrans tend not to ask questions about things, the Nomad will never cease questioning. Where Colberrans will never go against the choices of those leading them, Nomads will if they see dishonor or treacherous ways. This doesn't mean the Nomads are anti–central leadership. But they believe in a decentralized version, where each clan leads itself and all the clans join together for leadership in things that either affect all of the Nomads or deal with off-shell peoples, like Colberrans. According to Suyef, the Nomad love for decentralized control is a holdover from their ancient past. A time when they were a transient people who served the Ancients and helped build the citadels. This is what their lore teaches them, although they have no direct evidence to support this. Seeing as Colberrans love letting other people make their choices for them, it's no doubt the two peoples often don't see eye to eye.

To this day, it stuns me how well he did at figuring out how to blend. A master of disguise, that's the only explanation. That, and he was highly motivated. He sat through many questions once I got him talking about his father and his family's fall from grace after the tragedy on the water. For the most part, Suyef answered my questions with as few words as possible, carefully guarding what remained of his family's honor. He walked a fine line with me on that trip, between giving me just enough information that I wasn't blind and keeping me far enough in the dark that the discussion didn't encroach on things that were none of my business.

"I'm still puzzled," Suyef said chrons later, "what it is you are looking for that you couldn't find just by asking your father."

I shook my head. "My father refused to discuss the incident with me. Partly because he doesn't know some of the answers. Partly because of how Colberra views the entire incident. They classified it all, sealing off the information on the network. What's public knowledge is as basic as it comes, and my father refused to confirm or deny anything I ventured to guess beyond that record. It's possible he hoped it would stay my curiosity a bit." I chuckled. "It had the opposite effect."

"But what do you hope to gain from this?" Suyef asked. "Even if you find there is more to the official record, what do you gain by finding it?"

I shook my head again. "Don't know. It's not a secret that I'm just curious about it. Plus, it's my opinion there's more to that event than we're being told."

Suyef pulled out the padd the elder had given him. He keyed it on and held it up to me.

"This seems to confirm that statement."

The padd held a simple message from the elder. It instructed Suyef to do what he could to discover why the network was beginning to degrade and see if the Colberrans, specifically the Seekers, had anything to do with it.

"The network is degrading?" I asked, looking up at my companion.

He nodded. "In parts. It's becoming less accessible, slower to respond." He looked up at me. "Water supplies are dwindling along the outer edges."

"In regions not destroyed?"

He shrugged. "The system still sends water to the broken pipes. How else do you think your outpost gets water?"

"Isn't the station being fed by the one line that wasn't broken?"

"The water still has to traverse a myriad of broken piping networks to get to your outpost," he stated. "Anyway, your theory seems to be correct. So, what will you do with the information you do find?"

"I don't know, share it?" I shrugged. "Hadn't thought that far ahead. For now, it's sufficient we have something to look for. If the answers are there, we'll cross that expanse then."

Suyef sighed. "It's very clear why the elders thought it best someone go with you. A ship without a direction is just lost."

"Apparently, they think there might be something to this whole thing."

"That, or they think you're wasting your time and are just trying to get rid of you," Suyef retorted, tossing me a nutrient pack.

"If that's the case, why send you along?"

The look that crossed his face would have stopped anyone's heart. I didn't need him to answer to know his thought.

"To get you out of the way, too," I whispered.

Suyef nodded and swallowed part of his nutrient pack. "I'm a constant reminder to them of my father's failure, of the loss of all those lives on his watch."

"Sending you on this quest gets you out of sight."

"And out of mind," Suyef added. "Now they've sent me off babysitting some foolish Colberran on his quest for knowledge. And on a different shell. The perfect excuse to remove me from the picture."

"That's why you came anyway, though, isn't it?" I asked. "You knew they were getting rid of you. You came just to spite them?"

"No, I came because my father is still dead and we don't know who killed him," Suyef whispered, his voice icy and quiet. "And you're going to help me find whoever did this."

Being privy to that information put a damper on conversation for several chrons. Suyef, for one, seemed content to let it lie, and the topic had left me in no mood to talk. My feelings on helping him with his quest for vengeance were mixed. On one hand, he deserved what justice he could find. On the other, something felt wrong about a blind quest for revenge. Add that to the fact that we had no clue what we were looking for, and it left me feeling very morose when the ship deposited us on the uppermost edge of the Colberran shell.

I did manage to show the belt to Suyef before we settled down that night. He was able to confirm its origins in Ancient technology, but nothing more. He was very curious why the Nomads had returned it to my father, considering that information.

"Our laws on possession are clear, so in that they simply followed the rule," he explained as he examined it. "Still, most things of Ancient origin are exempt because of their power. A device such as this, as unknown as it is, the elders would have wanted to keep secure."

"Tied in knots by their own rules?" I asked.

Suyef nodded. "That must be it." He handed the belt back to me. "Whatever it is, it seems dead. Or at least inactive." He warily eyed the belt in my hand. "Still, be mindful of it. Even an inactive Ancient device can be dangerous."

That conversation dominated my thoughts for the rest of our trip to Colberra.

While most of the shell is flat, surrounding a large, mountainous center, one peninsula off the far edge of Colberra opposite where Micaela calls home has a mountain range all to itself. Reaching out like an appendage toward the water, the peninsula juts up closer to the water shield than any other place on the shell save for the central citadel. As such, it is much colder and harsher. Just beyond the edge, you can glimpse several satellite shells floating in sight, remnants of a longer peninsula that had broken off some time in the past and formed the Northern Isles, the only part of Colberra I'd been to prior to that. No one knows where that name came from, as they aren't in the north the way the Colberrans see north and they aren't really islands. Still, the name stuck, and the people that clung to life there were of the most stubborn type one could find. One would have to be to live in a place where the only source of water—the precious lifeblood of the shell—was a ship sent out once a month from the mainland. While not numerous, they are a hardy folk, big, thickheaded, and brash. They like to be left alone, and for the most part Colberra is content to leave them be. The Nomads took a liking to them almost immediately, thus allowing us a drop-off point when our ship made its way to the isle nearest to the mainland.

Some time into core-night on the second night out from the Nomad shell, the ship's captain signaled us that he'd be making a pit stop just before swinging out toward the isles. He suggested we disembark then, if we were so inclined. We took his offer, and, in the dead of core-night, I found myself ducking over the side of the ship and leaping onto mainland Colberra for the first time in my life. The air was brisk and the wind strong. Far overhead, the water shield rippled in detail for the first time that I could recall. Waves swept across the expanse as the water felt the draw of the world's now-invisible moon pulling on it. Just ahead lay the shell's edge and, just barely visible through the artificial shield the citadel provided to create the illusion we called core-night, the closest isle and destination for our captain. He waved once, Suyef returning the wave; then we moved away into the night.

"If you'd asked me how my first trip to the mainland would go, a slightly different arrival would have been on the report," I whispered as we slunk our way into the settlement on the shell's edge.

"Expected a bit of fanfare, maybe? The welcoming greetings of your fellow citizens?" Suyef asked.

"More like a bit more clothing, a bed—you know, the simple stuff."

Suyef chuckled. "That can be arranged."

He led us through the night to the settlement's only inn, a small two-story building with bunk beds in each room and a small hearth that I found myself gratefully hovering over while chewing on a bit of bread and slurping a mug of cocoa.

"Better?" Suyef asked, joining me.

"Welcome home to me." I grinned, finishing off the bread and washing it down with a swig of cocoa. "Well, sort of home." I waved my mug at the wall facing south. "Home's out there on those isles. Still, it feels like home."

"Tomorrow we head inland," Suyef muttered, holding his hands out to the fire. "We need to find a point for you to access the network uninterrupted."

"Had a thought on that," I said. "You know these water towers all have control stations in them. We could find an unoccupied one of those to start."

The Nomad nodded, eyes on the fire. "It'll do, for a start. Let's rest. Shops open early tomorrow, and we have some supplies to purchase."

I slept fairly well that night, all things considered. Suyef is many things, but a restful sleeper is not one of them. He tossed and turned enough on the bunk below me to give me the feeling of being back aboard the ship. We both managed to conk out some time later. I came to as the core-night lifted, and found Suyef already up and gone. I hurried out, grabbed a quick bite in the inn's kitchen, and found him outside waiting for me. He tossed me a sack and waved for me to follow.

"You'll find most of what you need in there: nutrient and hydration packs. Warm blanket. A change of underclothing." He shrugged at me. "I guessed on your size for that part."

I nodded my thanks, donning the sack and moving closer. "Have you thought about how we'll travel? Seekers tend to roam these parts, as do bandits."

Suyef grinned and waved me into an alley near the settlement's edge. "That won't be an issue. Go ahead and pull out your cloak."

I did so, curiosity building. The pack's contents left me stunned. "You stole Seekers' cloaks?"

"How else did you think we'd keep them off our backs?"

I blinked at him. "You know it's a capital offense on Colberra to impersonate a Seeker, right?"

"It's a capital offense to think on Colberra." Suyef pulled his cloak on and shrugged, using the motion to shift the cloak over his broad torso. "I'm not from Colberra, so it doesn't matter to me."

"I'm Colberran, so it matters to me," I hissed. "And the first time you meet a Seeker squad, it will matter to you, too."

He chuckled. "Seeker squads don't scare me. And they won't you, either. We'll avoid them as best we can and only use these where necessary."

"And you think it's necessary right now?"

He nodded. "How else do you intend to get some Seeker speeder bikes? Borrow them?"

With that, he strolled out from the alley and marched toward a Seeker outpost. If I'd been one to use curse words, a few might have slipped out right then as I hurriedly donned the cloak and raced after him.

CHAPTER 20

COMPLICATIONS

Not every interruption to Quentin's story was dramatic. Several times, he would just stop talking. Other times, he'd state he was done and leave. I tried following him on those occasions. It amazed me how easily he could hide in an area that seemed to not have that many places to go. As I said before, a lot of higher-level scripting seemed to be going on under my nose. How else do you explain places that weren't there before suddenly appearing? The only explanation I could fathom was that at least one of them was altering the fabric of reality around me using the script, forming new rooms and other objects from the matter around us.

On one such occasion, Quentin left me sitting alone in his room. The ever-present eyes of Micaela stared at me. I tried to concentrate and find the telltale markers left behind when someone altered reality by scripting, but I was at a loss. The symbols eluded me, and my failure to find the clues left my mind wandering back to Suyef's words. The meaning he'd implied hung heavily on my mind. As I sat there, ignoring the sketches and trying to make sense of the Nomad's curious words, I realized my hand rested on something smooth and solid. Looking down revealed the unopened box jutting out from my travel sack. I pulled it out and held the full length of it before me. The magnetic clasp lay closed, and my eyes locked on it. What lay hidden behind that clasp? What secret lay hidden in my hands? What secret would so affect the Queen that she would send me off on this quest? And, ultimately, what secret role did this object play in this whole story?

My thumb brushed the edge of the clasp, my curiosity driving me to peek inside. Just as my fingertip hooked the lower edge of the seal, lifting it slightly, Suyef's words echoed in my memory: *Show no one . . . not even yourself. Only reveal you have it at your direst need.*

Whatever this was, it must be powerful. And dangerous. So, why give it to me? Why entrust such an item to a lowly scribe?

"To hide it," I whispered, my thumb letting go of the clasp. It clicked back into place. "To protect us from something that wants it." I laid the box across my lap, pushing down on it with my hands. "Or from whatever is inside. And what better place to hide something powerful than in the one place no one will suspect?"

I considered at that moment finding some deep, dark place no one knew of and secreting it away there. I banished that thought. If hiding it like that would have worked, Suyef wouldn't have given it to me.

"Unless he only needed me to use it to compel the Queen into action," I murmured, shaking my head at the possibilities. "Maybe now it's safe to hide it."

The possibility of what might lay inside tumbled around in my head like dust in the wind. History is replete with objects of power, items of lore that legends claim could do magical things. Chalices, swords, spears. Looking at the size of the box, another possibility came to mind: a dagger. I searched my mind for any knowledge of such an item but found nothing. At that moment, a network terminal would have been nice. A few moments of research and my answer could be found.

Do not trust any computer terminal you happen upon.

Suyef's final words in his cryptic note. I shook my head. Researching the item was out of the question, if he was to be believed. He had given me no reason so far to doubt his words. As mysterious as he may be, up to this point all his actions had led me to find an amazing story. Several of them. As a scribe, this was a dream come true. Perusing my notes revealed what a golden opportunity they had given me. A story that had all the trappings of something much grander than any of us could imagine.

And one of the sources was currently hiding from me. It was infuriating.

"Patience, Logwyn, patience," I whispered.

Suyef's words from the other day came back to me: *You're trying to fly before you've even sprouted wings.*

He had to know. There was no other way. That comment hit too close to the mark. I closed my eyes, the day of my failure filling my mind. I'd thought it was done with, behind me. That I'd accepted it.

At that moment, I didn't know anymore. Looking down at the box in my lap, pondering the words of a Nomad I hardly knew, my mind filled with what I was convinced was going to become a tragic story of two friends driven from away from each other, and I just didn't know if I had accepted it anymore.

Most of me wanted to, though. That compelled me to leave the room, the still-closed box safely tucked away in my sack.

"It's time we continue, Quentin," I said to no one, going to find where he was hiding and coax him into continuing.

There's an old saying, or at least I think there is. I tend to avoid using them, as I tend to mess them up. Anyway, the saying goes, "If you want to get something done, march into a place like you own it and start barking orders like you belong there." I'd never seen this in action until Suyef marched into that Seeker outpost. Less than a quarter of a chron later, we rode away fully outfitted with Seeker travel gear, the Seekers we'd left behind convinced we'd just returned from a top-secret mission to the Nomad continent and needed supplies and mounts to get our information to our superiors. Only after we left did I realize none of them had asked why we didn't just transmit our data from their secure stations. To be honest, the entire incident was a blur. Suyef strolled in, demanded we be resupplied and given speeders, and, before I realized it, we were on our way and gone. He'd even thought to leave orders for the entire requisition to be left off the books. Just to be sure, we stopped a short distance out of the settlement and watched for pursuit. None came, so we went on. Not wanting to draw attention to ourselves, we left, moving northward along the water pipe that dominated the skyline overhead. Suyef kept us moving most of the day and well into core-night before we reached our destination: a fork in the pipe. We followed the other fork away from the pipe we'd been following, passing the first of several control stations before finally stopping at a station midway down the pipeline. Suyef surveyed the structure for nearly half a chron before we finally entered, confident it was abandoned.

Like most outlying water control stations, it had one control room on the main level, living quarters above, with sleeping quarters one level above that. This particular station looked to be low on supplies, meaning a resupply team would be by soon to restock the various medical items and foodstuffs Seekers and other Colberran government workers would make use of while about their duties. We helped ourselves to several nutrient and hydration packs, saving our own supply, as I started in on the network.

There I encountered the first of many problems we would face as we searched. You see, even though the networks on each shell had the ability to work together, this did not mean they all used the same base language. The network all ran on the same primary coding language. The Ancients invented the language to better grasp the intricacies of the code they'd discovered below the building-block level of existence. Still, variations did exist in how it was displayed. As with any language, until you find a key, or primer, these variations can render a language as an entirely different one. When I first keyed on the display at that workstation, it felt very much like I was looking at a tongue I didn't know. I felt I should, as it all looked familiar. I pored over the coding, looking for anything that would help me. Finally, I resorted to a desperate course of action: I started writing out my alphabets. It seemed so frustrating, to be hampered so when I could make the Nomad system virtually dance at my fingertips within the confines they'd allowed me. Suyef found the entire experience entertaining. Not in an outward, obvious way. Still, I could tell he was amused at my plight.

After a few days of work, I finally began to grasp how this version of the coding language worked. Right about then, Suyef decided we'd overstayed our welcome. We packed up and left the control station behind, heading westward out into the desert. We stuck to traveling during core-night using instrumentation. For a man that distrusts Seeker technology as much as he does, he wasn't shy about taking advantage of it when he needed to, and the dashboard displays on the Seeker mounts were designed for travel at night. You could see the entire landscape painted out before you in shifting lines of terrain and altitude the computer could analyze in a flash and project the safest course through. This had the added advantage of freeing me to continue pondering the language. When we made our next destination—another control station along the water pipeline stretching out from the citadel at the heart of the continent—I was able to get right to work.

Now that I had what seemed like the entire alphabet for this system laid out, experimenting with sentence structure was my next action. Thankfully, the confines of the Ancients' language compelled all variations to form their sentences the same way: vertically, bottom left upward, the central column holding all the nouns present in that part of the sentence, and branches off to either side containing all descriptors or clauses. Between each column sentence, you hung any verb that connected the various column parts of your sentence together.

It took me several more days and many more location changes to get a good enough grasp on the differences in symbology and sentence structure before I began to make progress. Suyef kept us moving around the shell's outer edge, backtracking sometimes. This would have been much more frustrating had I not discovered at our third stop a small padd that someone had left behind. It gave me portable access to the network, allowing me to take my work along. Suyef found this to be a great boon, insisting we rough it out on the cold, windy edge of the shell to lessen our footprint and decrease the odds we'd run into someone or get noticed. My aching back was not much of an argument against this. I only tried bringing it up one time and regretted it almost at once.

Suyef got me out of bed early the next morning. He'd won the battle over our sleeping arrangements the night before, when he just shook his head and rolled over to go to sleep. This indicated that the first watch belonged to me, and I'm convinced to this day that what he did next was his sadistic way of getting back at me for dragging him along to this shell. A slap across my head ripped me from fitful sleep riddled with dreams of uncomfortable things poking me in the back. I blinked my eyes open to see the Nomad standing over me, a staff in each hand. I opened my mouth to complain, and he dropped one of the staves right at my head. Desperation alone awoke my reflexes to catch the long, smooth rod inches before it hit my face.

"If your back hurts, it's because you're soft." He grunted. "That we can fix while you figure out your pretty symbols."

"They're not just pretty symbols," I croaked at his retreating back, sitting up and blinking in the dim core-light shining through the night shield. "What time is it?"

"You've slept enough," he called over his shoulder. "Now get up and follow me."

I grumbled a few incoherent sounds as I pulled myself up, hand gripping the staff, and moved after Suyef. He stood in a flat, smooth area clear of rocks and the only brush plant that still managed to grow. He nodded for me to stand before him, his staff held parallel to the ground at his waist.

"Before we left, I obtained permission to train you as a Nomad warrior," he said, hefting the staff to chest level. "This is my preferred weapon."

"A Seeker's pulse gun isn't going to care about a stick," I said, holding mine up to match his.

"It will when I hit it out of the Seeker's hand," he replied.

Sharp pain exploded in my hand a split second later as he struck. His staff had whipped out, sending my staff flying up over my head. I cried out in pain, grabbing my hand, my eyes watering.

"What the . . . ," I whispered, eyes and jaw clenched shut. "What was that for?"

"Your first lesson." He pointed at my staff with his own. "Never lose your weapon. Now try to pick it up."

I frowned at him, blinking away tears, shaking my hand and wriggling my fingers. Nothing seemed broken, but it was going to be sore for days. I turned to look for my staff and felt something crash into my back. The ground rushed up to meet my torso, and all the air in my lungs rushed out as my chest and the ground became acquainted. I rolled to my back, gasping for air, and looked up. Suyef stood over me, staff in both hands across his body.

"Again, try to get your weapon!"

The next chron went much like the beginning, with me tumbling and sprawling around on the ground a lot and various parts of my body stinging from staff hits. I never once got near my staff, although once it's possible my finger brushed the tip. Suyef didn't say another word beyond his cry of "Again!" every time I failed.

He never smiled, never frowned. His face was a blank slate, eyes focused in concentration on what must have been an easy task for him. Clearly this wasn't a challenge to him.

Finally, he called a halt and collected my staff. He held the two up, eyes on me.

"You can try again this afternoon," he whispered, walking toward his mount and stuffing the staffs into a slot I hadn't noticed. Once inside, they blended into the machine.

"Something tells me those aren't standard Seeker issue," I muttered, nodding at the staffs.

Suyef shook his head. "They're mine. Now mount up."

The next several days, this pattern repeated. A lot. He'd toss my staff out on the ground, and I'd try to get it. Complaining about the fairness of such a tactic would earn me nothing more than a strike from his staff. I'd like to think as the days went by I became a bit quicker at getting out of the way, but my body still felt sharp, tingling spots all over.

On the fifth day of training, Suyef finally said something other than his incessant "Again!" at my failure to get the weapon off the ground. After another sequence of me flailing around like a baby unable to hold itself upright, Suyef shoved me to the ground and stepped across my body. The Nomad placed his foot on my chest and pointed the staff right at my eyes.

"You see, but you don't learn," he whispered, tapping my forehead. "See"—he tapped beside my eyes—"then learn." He tapped my head and heart each once, then moved away.

I pushed myself up, spit out a bit of dirt, and stared at him. He stood a few paces away, my staff lying just beyond him.

"See?"

He nodded.

"See what?"

No response.

"See you?"

He nodded.

"You're standing there."

He shook his head.

"You're standing ready."

He nodded.

"You're standing ready to keep me from my weapon."

No response.

"You're standing ready for whatever I do?"

He nodded.

I saw his weight shift, his body focusing on mine as it moved. I lunged forward, feinting a bit and stepping back. He didn't move.

"How did you know I was faking?"

He shrugged. "You told me."

I frowned. "I didn't say anything."

Suyef chuckled at me, shaking his head. "You know a lot about languages, yet you know nothing." He held his hands apart, staff in one hand. "Do I only speak with my mouth?"

I cocked my head at him, pondering his words.

He pointed his staff at my face. "You're curious, forming a question, thinking."

I furrowed my brow.

"Deeper thought," he went on, smiling.

"And you're amused," I responded, nodding. "Nonverbal cues. But you aren't saying much with your face when you spar."

He raised his eyebrows, a smirk touching at his lips. "So, just your mouth and face can speak?"

I shrugged and shook my head, then paused. Suyef eyed me. I squinted and shifted my weight, preparing to send a kick with my right foot at his left hand, which was now holding the staff. As my body shifted, his eyes darted up and down and he moved in response, staff lowering to both hands, torso and legs turning to move his left side away from me. I reacted, preparing to strike with my left foot. He countered and I saw it, pointing at his waist.

"Your hips."

He arched one eyebrow.

"Your hips tell the tale." I pointed at his waist. "Watch the hips and they tell you where the weight is, giving you an idea of what I intend." I pointed at his shoulders. "Then watch those, see how they move."

He remained still, eyebrow arched.

"Ignore the head. It's the fake."

Suyef nodded once at me, then again at my staff behind him. "Now pick it up."

I didn't. Not with that first attempt. Or the next. The next day, I realized Suyef was playing a trick on me. He may have been doing so all along and keeping me too busy to notice. Something strange seemed to be happening as my skill at reading Suyef's nonverbal cues improved. I never came close to even touching my staff, but I was making progress. One morning, midway through a vigorous session of cat and mouse, I found myself flipping through the air. The world tumbled around me as my body spun over Suyef's arm and hip to what would be an uncomfortable reunion with terra firma. My eyes happened to glance behind Suyef. My staff, which had been lying a mere meter behind him near a rock jutting from the ground, had vanished. Then the aforementioned reunion occurred, and all thought of what I'd been looking at exited in a thud and a whoosh of breath escaping from my lungs.

CHAPTER 21

CHEATING

Once my lungs had reacquainted themselves with normal breathing, I rolled over and sat there, staring at him.

"What game are you on?"

He frowned, staff in hand. A quick glance behind him revealed my staff lying on the ground, a good ten paces from where it had fallen before we began. I pointed at it.

"My staff was not over there." I pointed off to my right. "It was over there. And you haven't had a chance to move it until just now, when you flipped me. But it was already moved." I grimaced. "It was about the only thing I noticed before I landed."

The sides of his mouth twitched. "I don't know what you mean."

I pushed myself up, crossed my arms over my chest, and glared at him. "You're not playing fair."

"Most people don't in a fight."

I shrugged. "In a classroom, they do."

He looked around. "We aren't in one."

"You're teaching me, remember?" I pointed around us. "*Classroom* is a relative term, and you know it." I pointed right at his face. "You're cheating."

He cocked his head to one side, eyebrows raised. "And how am I doing that?"

"It's impossible to catch something that you keep moving!"

He shook his head. "Not impossible."

I grimaced, shaking my head. "Fine, improbable."

"No, not that, either," he replied. "I was going to say difficult."

"It's hard enough already without you changing the rules on me!"

"How am I changing the rules?" he asked, placing one end of his staff on the ground and leaning on it.

"You're scripting!" I exclaimed, jabbing a finger at him. "Plain and simple scripting."

Suyef frowned. "Scripting?"

I looked around, lost for words for a moment. "You know, altering script."

His face remained blank.

"Coding?"

No change.

"Look, I don't know what word you Nomads have for it, but we call it scripting or coding here. You're changing the code around us to move my staff!"

Suyef's eyebrows shot up as his eyes opened wide. "You know of this?"

I nodded.

"I thought such things were lost on this shell."

It was my turn to frown. "What do you mean, lost? Forgotten?"

He nodded.

"Oh, they're not forgotten. Just illegal."

"Seekers?" he asked.

I nodded. "Who else? But they're just enforcing the laws. Colberrans passed those laws centuries ago, distrustful of anyone who codes or scripts or whatever you call it."

"We call it altering."

"That's as appropriate as the other two," I muttered, refocusing my attention on him. "Regardless, you're cheating if you're using that."

"You don't sound so sure of yourself now," he said, pulling the staff up and pointing it at me. "Either stick with your conviction or don't speak up."

I glared at him and batted at the end of the staff near my face—missing it, needless to say.

"You're scripting," I whispered.

He shrugged. "So what?"

"Altering the rules of reality makes it an unfair fight," I muttered, frowning and crossing my arms across my chest.

"Stop pouting like a spoiled brat," he hissed. "Fights aren't fair." He stepped toward me, staff held in both hands before him. "They're never fair. They're often hopelessly unfair." He stopped a pace from me, his eyes—steely black orbs—holding mine hostage. "Get used to it."

With that, he attacked, his staff spinning out before him. I don't recall much of the next chron or so. My staff never moved that day. The next day, however, the training changed. Now scripting became a part of the training. He didn't ask how I'd learned. That would come later. For now, he seemed content just to make me practice it. I think he was testing my limits. There were many. Through trial and error, I found that my largest challenge lay in making things happen when nothing was going on. At first, when Suyef gave me an instruction to follow, concentrating solely on doing just that made my mind waver, leading to failure. If, on the other hand, I allowed my mind to wander a bit, to engage in other activities, success followed more often. Suyef seemed to notice this as well. He incorporated it into my training. Defending yourself while trying to script has its own challenges, but it did help me by moving me into something that was clearly a strength: multitasking. The challenge remained the same: get to my staff. I tried every trick possible to make that thing appear in my hand. He countered every move. It was annoying, frustrating, and embarrassing. I'm not at all sure what he hoped I would learn. The only thing that was certain was that I never got close to picking up that blasted staff.

"I take it, then, this wasn't the first time you ever scripted?" I asked, raising a hand to stop Quentin.

We sat in the living area, a couple of nutrient and hydration packs between us on the table.

"Of course not," Quentin retorted, a chuckle shaking his body. "I thought that was clear in my story."

"So, when did you learn?"

He held up a finger, shifting it back and forth at me. "Nah, uh-uh. You mustn't look before you've leapt."

I arched an eyebrow at him. He raised his in return, smiling in that goofy way he did when he thought he'd said something clever.

"You do realize, Quentin, you've got it backward," I pointed out.

He shrugged. "Whatever. Either way, you're getting ahead of yourself. We'll get to that soon enough."

I rolled my eyes and returned to my notes. Quentin burst out laughing and jumped up.

"I'm tired of sitting here. Onward and upward!"

With that, we climbed up out of the crevice and seated ourselves just under the fold of land that concealed this place. Quentin never moved far from the structure and crept out like a small child stepping foot outside for the first time. The world was a dangerous place, he told me in hushed tones. All kinds of dangers.

I pondered again the depths this man had fallen to. As he sat there, eyes darting around, hands grabbing at stones, dropping them, and grabbing more, I couldn't help but wonder where the man had gone that had stood toe to toe with a Questioner to defend a complete stranger. Seeing the timid, broken, hurting man sitting before me, I began to wonder if he would ever return.

This training continued for multiple sessions every day. At the time, I argued against the need for such work. Considering the predicaments we found ourselves in later, I should have kept my mouth shut. We would spend at least a chron every morning training. If I wanted any time to work on learning the Colberran coding language, it had to be done at other times, either by waking up earlier or sneaking in bits of work along the way. I became very adept at riding a Seeker mount one-handed while using my padd in the other hand.

Finally, after several days of moving like this, Suyef brought us to a control station near the edge of the shell. The water pipe ended at that station, but, unlike most endpoints, this station had no settlement. Well, it had no settlement with people living in it. All we found was an abandoned one, the buildings clearly vacated long ago. Most had fallen apart, save for the Ancient control station. The Ancient structures hadn't aged a bit and looked exactly how they looked according to the historical records available. Everything else around them had fallen apart.

Suyef approached the settlement with caution, leaving me alone in the desert to guard the mounts. I stole a few blessed moments undistracted to pull out my padd and do some more drills with the language. My confidence was growing at that point; I could manage my way around the Colberran network, but the padd was as limited in its functionality as it was mobile. I'd quickly grown frustrated with it when trying to do searches of the network files. It had been this limitation that convinced Suyef we needed to get to an actual control station. He'd been quite convinced the process could be muddled through on the device, until I let him try to use the interface to find anything. I'm not sure if he grew impatient with the device or my inept way of explaining the coding to him. Either way, it worked. Thus, I found myself sitting watch over our speeder mounts as he snuck into the abandoned settlement ahead to reconnoiter. I did my best to keep watch, if for no other reason than to catch him coming back. I'm not sure why I bothered. Boredom took over soon after he left, leading me to pull out my padd to do some drills. Before long, he was standing there in front of me, arms across his chest and a frown on his face. I shrugged, and we went to the control station.

As all signs had indicated, the settlement and control station had long been abandoned. Making quick use of my newly learned language, I made my way to the main floor's access station. The Ancients lacked for creative design when they built these things, as a quick scan upward indicated the same floor plan as every other control station. I took to the panel, but Suyef stopped me.

"Are you certain you'll remain undetected?" he asked.

I shrugged. "As best as I can. I'll only be accessing information pertinent to this station. Staying local. It should go undetected."

He nodded and disappeared above. He'd already checked the place out, so my guess is he wanted to leave me be.

I got straight to work and found my labor over the coding had paid off. Soon, records in the control station flowed across the screen. I tried to stay local so as to avoid alerting someone to our intrusion before we had an idea of what we were doing. Still, I needed to start making some progress, or Suyef might call this whole thing off. He was a bit antsy to get to the point of our trip there or go home and be done with me. So, I opened a search program and began to set some parameters.

There the next problem surfaced. What to look for. I tried basic data pulls, compiling lists of information on the water project and the events of a few decades ago during the water race. Most of that data, however, was useless. Public knowledge that revealed very little. I browsed various data nodes, looking for other people's work on the subject, but found little original thought on the incident. I pondered the problem for a moment and was staring at the screen when a thought occurred to me.

"Suyef!"

"Is someone coming?" he hissed, and I heard him shift to come back down.

"No, no. Nothing like that," I assured him. "You said this place has no food supplies, yes?"

"They haven't been restocked in several months at the least. Did your records say this, too?"

I shrugged, despite the fact he couldn't see me. "Didn't check that." I brought up the station records. "I don't see anything recording a visit for several cycles, at least. In fact, there aren't any records of a patrol even checking on this station in over a decade." I shook my head and looked up to the ceiling. "Did you check the water supply?" Silence greeted me. "That's a no."

I toggled over to check the water system, sliding my seat to the left as the system appeared on screen. It took mere moments to find what I was looking for. To be sure, I moved to another window and accessed information on the settlement. The data confirmed my suspicions.

"Suyef, you'd better come see this."

The Nomad made his way down the ramp and came to stand over my shoulder. He took in the system information at my indication.

"According to this, the settlement was abandoned over fifteen cycles ago. The reason? The Ancient-made water system stopped sending them water."

Suyef looked down at me. "I thought that wasn't possible."

I nodded. "Me, too. This system does one thing and never stops doing it. For some reason, fifteen cycles ago the system stopped sending water."

"Meaning the people here had no choice. Do we know why it stopped working?" the Nomad asked.

I shook my head and got to work, pulling everything possible on the settlement. I combed through personnel files and any available records. Suyef vanished at some point, leaving the station muttering something about checking out the settlement. Time blazed past amid all the information popping up. Late into core-night, something very odd surfaced. As I searched through the data, some of it altered. The files' data showed it was being accessed. Someone else was looking at the same information. It was impossible to tell if it was a monitor or just someone else curious about the same thing. What was clear was that someone had accessed the same files open on my screen. After double-checking that the files were local ones only, I closed them out. Something caught my eye. I opened a station log and began reading. There, buried among all the data, lay the answer.

I pushed myself up and called for Suyef, forgetting he'd left. I rushed out the door and called to him. The settlement looked very strange in the core-night. Shadows played off the angled walls of fallen buildings, casting gloom over everything they touched. I stepped away from the station to yell again, but my call was interrupted by someone grabbing my hand. Suyef spun me around, finger over his mouth, nodding back toward the control station. Once there, he waited until the door slid shut, then glared at me.

"Do you always go barging out into the night calling out for all the world like you are alone?" he hissed.

I looked around at the empty facility. "We are alone. This place hasn't been used or lived in for over a decade."

He leaned close to me. "That doesn't mean we are alone."

I glanced back at the door, expecting someone to come in that very instant. "Who's out there?"

He shrugged. "I'm not sure. I'd only just discovered them when you came out." He nodded toward the far wall of the control station. "Whoever they are, they're approaching from the east."

I stared at him.

"That's where we just came from," he explained.

I nodded. "Sorry, I'm kind of turned around with all the back-tracking we've been doing."

He glared at me. "The mountains to the north should have told you all you need."

"I couldn't remember which way we were facing when we came in," I said, shrugging.

"What did you find out that had you all up and yelling?"

I leaned close to him, my voice dropping to a whisper. "Whatever it was that happened, the water stopped coming because someone made it stop."

He cocked his head to one side, eyebrows furrowed. "Sabotage?"

I shrugged. "Maybe. But it was intentional, and someone here figured it out. Come look." I pointed him to the screen and read off the pertinent parts.

He stared at the screen, reading. "So, someone altered the flow of water into this station? Why?"

"That isn't clear. But someone here found the change worthy enough to report it, and he was told to stay silent about it. He didn't like that but didn't say anything. Just recorded this log for someone to find."

"Someone like you?"

I shrugged, shaking my head. "Or anyone who was looking." Another file jumped to the forefront at a finger tap. "There's more. Look at the date on the first log entry made referencing a drop in the water."

"I thought you said fifteen cycles ago."

I shook my head. "That's when the water cut off completely. Look at the date." I pointed to the column containing the data. "It's the cycle after the missions to the water shield."

"So, within a cycle of their failed attempt to get to the water," he began.

"They didn't fail. The ships made it, and one came back with water in its holds," I corrected him, then motioned for him to continue.

"One cycle later, the water system here began to malfunction," he finished, glaring at me. "Is this connected to the network problems the elder mentioned?"

"Could be. It's too early to tell. All we know is that this settlement began running out of water within a cycle of the water-shield missions. Someone here noticed and began making a record of it. About seven cycles after my birth, this settlement completely ran out of water and was abandoned." I paused, wondering if I should tell him the next part. "There's one more thing worth mentioning. Someone else is looking."

Suyef's head spun to stare at me. "What do you mean?"

"I'm not entirely sure what it means, but someone accessed the same files I was looking at. Not all of them, just some." I pointed at the log. "Including that one."

CHAPTER 22

CONSPIRACIES

"You said they were only accessing local files?"

I nodded at Suyef. "They were local, but you know that anything saved on the network is fully accessible by any access point." I pointed at the panel dominating the room before us. "There isn't a local storage drive of any kind. It's not how this computer works."

"I'm well aware of how this thing is designed," he said. "But you assured me what you were doing wouldn't catch anyone's attention."

I shook my head. "No, I said I was fairly certain it would be undetected. Seeing as this place has been abandoned, it's safe to assume no one is paying attention to it anymore."

Suyef closed his eyes, and his head dropped. "Or, because it's abandoned, they're watching it."

I nodded. "That's a possibility. They could have any of the information from this station flagged." His head shot up, eyes and mouth opening, but I held up a hand. "It's a possibility, but that's not what happened here." I pointed at the screen. "Whoever was snooping around here appears just to have accessed a temporary copy of the file. See"—I tapped a specific data point on the screen—"that's the main file I was looking at. A local version appeared here temporarily when it was opened. What happened was another temporary version appeared, then vanished." I stepped back and spread my hands out to either side. "That could just be the system backing up the file . . ."

"Or someone else requesting the same file," he finished. His eyebrows furrowed. "The odds are not good, you realize?"

I chuckled at him. "About as good as the odds that your incoming somebody is the one accessing the files."

He stood silent for a moment, then nodded at the panel. "Can you hide what you've done here?"

My eyebrows went up while I pondered his question. "Mostly. Anyone who knows what they're looking for can find the—"

"Can you hide your tracks well enough?"

I nodded.

"Do it. We need to leave before whoever it is gets here."

I reached out to the panel, tapped a few places, pulled out my padd, and held it near the panel, watching the files transfer. Suyef eyed the device warily.

"Just want to have the files on hand. Don't worry," I assured him. "They can't trace it that well."

Those words reassured me about as much as they did him. Regardless, he said nothing, and soon we left. Operating the mounts in stealth mode meant turning off all piloting aids for fear they could be tracked, and moving a lot slower as a result. We made our way south toward the shell's edge, then cut to the west and moved ever so carefully the rest of the night. Suyef never told me how he was tracking whoever had appeared on the horizon and who had come to the settlement, but I didn't feel like asking him about it. The day had dragged on, and the buzz from my discovery had long since worn off. By the time he called a halt halfway through the next day, I fell asleep almost as soon as I hit the ground. I'm not sure how long I slept, but when I awoke, core-night had fallen. Suyef grimaced as he woke me.

"No practice," he whispered. "We move."

We mounted, scarfing nutrient and water packs as we went. I figured we'd at least lost whoever had come to the abandoned settlement, as Suyef permitted piloting aids. My sensors showed nothing within range of us as we went. Suyef led us on a much more direct route than normal, and soon we came to a halt on a long ridge. To the left, the ridge ended abruptly in the south in a sharp drop-off at the edge. To the right, the Central Mountains dominated the north. Before us lay another settlement, and a different pipeline filled the skyline leading to it.

"Abandoned," Suyef said, his sharp eyes taking it in.

We piloted our mounts down to the edge of the buildings. Dust blew up in the air behind us as we slowed to a halt. The wind, for once, settled. Suyef stopped, pointing at the structures ahead.

"All the doors," he whispered.

They all lay on the ground, ripped from their hinges. Shutters lay strewn on the ground, but all the buildings stood, their cement walls holding them up. The buildings looked old, their corners rounded with erosion. A quick peek inside one building showed the entire place had been ransacked at some point, the furniture removed. We made our way through the silent settlement, every building missing doors and shutters.

"It's odd they're all knocked off," I commented as we approached the Ancient control station overshadowing the buildings.

Suyef stopped his mount near the entrance to the station and pointed inside. "Find what you need. We stay only a chron."

A chron was more than enough. Now that I knew what to look for, the evidence soon lay spread out before me. I downloaded all of it to the padd and checked the upper levels to ascertain their disappointing supply situation; then we left. Suyef led us out of sight to the west, then brought us to a halt in a gully open to the south. There I perused the new information and brought him up to date.

"Well, here's a problem. These files. They're exactly the same as the previous settlement's. The only difference is the dates. All the pertinent details are the same. Water levels began dropping, the people left, but I can't figure out when." I tapped through the data, eyes scanning it. "Not a mention of a date anywhere. All scrubbed clean."

"Intentional?" Suyef asked.

I shrugged. "It would have to be, right? I mean, other than the dates, the wording is the same as the other settlement's."

"What about personal logs or records?"

"The people in this settlement weren't as diligent in record keeping," I answered, shaking my head. "That or all of their logs were deleted. It's odd that no one ever kept a video journal of any kind. Unless we've found a settlement of paper lovers, and there wasn't any evidence of paper or writing utensils around, was there?"

Suyef shook his head.

"And that stuff is expensive, so, I don't know. I can only guess, but it's possible someone wiped the actual logs of this settlement. They replaced them with the other settlement's, only scrubbing any mention of the dates. Why the dates are important enough to leave out is beyond me."

"To conceal when it happened," the Nomad whispered, snapping his fingers and pointing at me. "That explains all the doors. If you had to guess, how long did that settlement look to have been abandoned?"

I shrugged. "Much longer than fifteen cycles, if the last settlement is anything to go by."

"Precisely. Someone wanted to make that place look much older."

"But the buildings," I protested. "They've all been eroded from the wind."

Suyef nodded. "All to the same level of erosion. Every corner rounded to exactly the same degree. The doors knocked off to look fallen, time's long hand pulling them down. Every shutter dislodged to fall, but all buried in exactly the same level of debris around them."

I frowned at him. "You measured the level of debris around the shutters and the curves of the corners?"

"I had time while you got what you needed from the computer," he muttered, waving his hand at me. "The point is that it was intentional. Someone wanted anyone who came to that settlement to think that place was much older than it was."

"Why would someone want to trick anyone into believing that?" I asked, arching my eyebrows.

He pointed at my padd. "The answer is in there somewhere."

I glanced down at the device and shook my head, holding it up. "If they wanted to hide the age of that settlement, don't you think someone would have thought to scrub any record of it? I mean, there isn't even a mention of a journal or diary. Nothing, all gone, hidden so they can't be found, buried among mountains of data so they will take forever to find, or they never existed."

"People don't just vanish from history," Suyef whispered. "Well, most people don't."

"The Ancients did."

He shook his head. "No, they just abandoned your lot. Remember, there's more to history than what Colberra records."

"Fine, then what about Rawyn?" I asked.

At the mention of that name, Suyef's entire visage changed. "If you value your pretty face, I'd suggest you not mention that traitor's name."

"He was an Ancient, not a Nomad. How can that be offensive to you?"

Suyef shook his head. "We don't discuss him or his treacherous ways. It's enough we know he led the revolution that brought down the Ancient civilization." He leveled a finger at me. "You know the Nomadic tradition claims we're directly descended from the most powerful sect of Ancients?"

I nodded. "The ones who built the citadels."

"So, I think you can put two and two together to see why that man is anathema to our society."

"The point is," I stated, "we know he vanished from history before even the Ancients did, along with his mentor."

"Yet we knew they existed, him and his mentor, as you call him," Suyef pointed out.

"What was his name?" I asked, earning a frown from Suyef. "His mentor?"

"He wasn't his mentor. At least not according to our stories. The two were associates at best."

"Whatever . . . Do you remember his name?" I asked, waving my hand at him.

Suyef shrugged. "Rawyn was the one who led that revolution. He's the one that mattered. The point is, even those notorious few who do manage to disappear, we know why and at least have some record they existed prior to vanishing. Else how would we know they vanished?" He pointed back in the general direction of the second settlement. "There stand buildings and dwellings that once belonged to those people." He pointed in a different direction, slightly to the north of the settlement. "A water pipeline stands as testament to the Ancients' existence, but they all abandoned this shell within a hundred cycles of the Shattering. Still, we know they were once here. Someone lived in that settlement, and someone else wanted the world to think they stopped living there a lot longer than fifteen cycles ago."

I stared at the Nomad a moment; then a thought slipped through my mind. "The water?"

Suyef cocked his head and arched an eyebrow but said nothing.

"What if the water is the reason?" I continued. "We know the water levels went down; the remaining records of two settlements prove that. We suspect it was intentional. Maybe this problem is a lot older than we think."

"Or it's not, but someone wants us to think it is," Suyef suggested.

I nodded. "Not just us, though. The people who lived in the settlements and anyone living to the north in Colberra City. I mean, unless they slaughtered all the citizens wholesale, they had to go somewhere." I pulled up the padd and accessed the network. "I wonder if there's a record of refugees."

"That search could take a while," Suyef muttered, pushing himself up. "I'll take first watch. Don't stay up too long; else you'll be tired come morning."

I muttered something that sounded appropriate and tapped through my search. The Nomad was correct in one thing: the search proved to be daunting. There's an old saying that a bureaucratic society can only survive until it's swallowed whole by the paper it produces to track everything. Computers eventually proved that saying untrue but multiplied the problem. The one thing you could count on was that bureaucrats loved their records, and Colberra was so dominated by them it's a shock they ever managed to get anything done. I cross-referenced everything available on the outer settlements with news articles on anything connected to the water supply running out and people moving inland, but found very little. My eyes became heavy and dry, my back aching from hunching over the tiny device while sifting through mountains of data.

Just as I was about to give up, the answer jumped out at me. After rereading it several times to make certain my thought was correct, I stood up, stretching my back out and waving at Suyef to come closer. He caught the device when I tossed it at him, and looked at it. He stared for a moment, not moving save to arch one eyebrow at me. Then I remembered he couldn't read it.

"Sorry, I guess I'm pretty tired," I muttered, taking the device back. "It's not clear if it's the people of that settlement specifically, but a group of refugees was transferred from an edge settlement for relocation into Colberra City. According to the news agency,

the refugees never arrived at Colberra City, as they were transferred to a Seeker hospital and quarantined."

Suyef shrugged. "So, they got sick. How does that help us?"

I lowered the padd, eyes locked on his. "The Seekers don't run
any hospitals. It's one of many things my parents taught me: stay
away from anything named a hospital run by Seekers."

"So, where did they go?"

I shook my head. "Who knows? But I can tell you what is suspected of Seeker 'hospitals.'" I sighed and looked away from him.
"People don't come back from them, not as the same people they
were, at least. There was a guy at the outpost I grew up in; he wasn't
right in the head. Older guy, off-his-rocker bonkers. Had a particular fondness for robes, a multicolored, striped cloak, and a stick
he loved to talk to. Couldn't recall anything of his past if you asked
him. I'm not sure where he lived or how he survived. No one knew,
actually. My parents used to point him out to me and whisper,
'That's what happens to people who end up in Seeker hospitals,
kid. Behave, or that'll be you someday.'"

Suyef grimaced. "Do we know where these facilities are?"

I shook my head, trying to forget the images from my child-
hood. "Some say in the citadel itself. Others in outposts along
the edge of the mountains. One rumor that circulates more than
others is that it's all one place and it's buried under a mountain.
I recall my father discussing it with another Northern Isles man
assigned to the outpost. Paranoia is common among that lot, trust
me. Anyway, he claimed that if the Nomad shell ever orbited close
enough to Colberra, we might be able to look up at the underside
of the shell from the Expeditionary Forces outpost and see where
the Seeker 'hospitals' were all ingeniously hidden on the bottom of
the landmass."

"So, you don't know," Suyef stated, and pointed at the padd in
my hand. "What about on that thing?"

I shook my head. "I already tried that. They weren't that dumb."

Suyef sighed, eyes on me. "Your parents don't sound like they're big fans of the Seekers."

"That's an understatement," I said, laughing and shaking my head. "Set aside that they're Northern Isle in origin. No one in the Expeditionary Forces is fond of Seekers. Ever since its founding, the Forces have been mistreated by them. It's bred some bad blood. On Colberra itself, the Forces were virtually powerless against them." I pointed at Suyef. "On your shell, it's a different matter."

"Seekers don't come to your outpost?"

I shook my head. "Not openly. Oh, it's a certainty a Seeker or two has infiltrated the place, all in the name of keeping an eye on our citizens' interests. But they keep themselves hidden. That far from their power base, there's no telling what might happen." I leaned closer, waving Suyef over, my voice dropping to a whisper. "One Seeker did try to assert his authority once, I'm told. It was when I was a baby. No one talks about it now, but there's evidence he never made it back to Colberra."

"Your people killed him?" Suyef asked, one eyebrow elevating.

"Not us," I said, shaking my head and leveling a finger at Suyef. "According to the records, the Seeker tried to force a squad of Forces members out to capture some Nomads for interrogation. No one would go with him, so he did it alone." I dropped my hand. "No one ever heard from him again."

Suyef frowned. "I'd have heard if one of your Seekers tried to attack or waylay any Nomads."

I shrugged, spreading my hands out to either side. "Whatever happened to him, that Seeker never came back to us."

"Or someone altered your records to make it look like that happened," Suyef suggested, pointing at the padd. "You've already found evidence Seekers do that stuff."

I nodded. "Just as strong a possibility. But nowhere near as good a story," I said, laughing. "And whatever happened, Seekers have stepped lightly around that outpost ever since."

"That can't have gone over well back here."

"It didn't," I agreed, "and the Forces have faced many hearings about it, concerning the need for such an outpost. All brought by the Seekers' allies in the ruling councils. Honestly, I think the only reason it's still populated is because of the cost of bringing them back. At this point, it's far less expensive to keep them minimally supplied and in contact with Colberra than it would be to bring them all back."

Suyef shook his head. "We've gone a bit afield here."

"The point is, set the bad blood aside, Seekers don't operate hospital facilities," I said, refocusing on the issue at hand. "They never have or, at the very least, have kept them a secret."

"Why hide such a facility?"

I grimaced. "To keep your citizens from discovering what you're actually doing there."

CHAPTER 23

TENSIONS

Needless to say, I didn't sleep much that night. Suyef returned to his watch, and when he came back a few chrons later, I hadn't slept a wink. The sensor on the mount worked well in scanning for any life forms besides our own, freeing me to work on my research. When core-night lifted and Suyef rose from his slumber, about as much progress had been achieved on that as on sleeping. I tucked it away and resigned myself to another fruitless practice session.

Suyef had other ideas.

"We move," he said, pausing to scarf down a nutrient pack before mounting up.

We made good time that day, probably because Suyef didn't keep cutting back and forth across the terrain. Instead, we raced west along the edge of the shell, Colberra's high mountains to our right. By midday, we came to a halt at the next water pipe extending from the citadel. There lay another settlement, as abandoned as the previous two. We stood for a moment, staring down at the empty buildings, before Suyef waved and we raced down. I made my quick check of the station as he checked the settlement, and we went on, having found the same thing. We did this for several days, finding settlement after abandoned settlement along the shell's edge. Each had the same story, but none carried the artificially aged look of that second outpost. On top of that, none of the records had been scrubbed of their dates. Each had been abandoned in the past two decades, most between ten and fifteen cycles ago. And, as with the first two we'd encountered, no record of where the citizens had gone existed.

We found ourselves sitting huddled together in a hollowed-out building on the edge of one such settlement. Suyef had taken to mapping out the locations of all the places we'd found like this. Using the padd, we projected a map of the shell into the air before us and began dropping pins along our route. The outpost from which we'd stolen the mounts stood just to the west of the Wilds, at the end of the closest arm of the pipeline network to the uncontrolled region. A trail of pins proceeded in a westward direction from there, extending a quarter of the way around the shell heading away from the Wilds, a region that dominated a third of the shell's outer edge and the abutting mountains in the Central Dominance. The Seekers and government had spent centuries trying to repair the Wilds after the collision of shells destroyed that region, but nothing they'd done had worked. In the end, they contained it and kept everyone away from it. As such, it meant anyone wanting to traverse the shell had to do one of two things: cross the Central Mountains and thus Colberra City, built around the citadel at the shell's center, or travel around the far edge, as we were doing.

"Looking at this—it looks like they've managed to empty all the outposts and settlements on this half of the outer edge," Suyef muttered.

I pulled up another map and overlaid it on that one. "This is a grid of the water pipes," I said, pointing at the Wilds. "Obviously, those aren't right anymore, as no one outside of Seeker circles knows what happened to that region." I tapped at some near us. "If you watch this," I commented, pulling another overlay up and depositing it over the other two, "this shows you which of these water lines is still active."

The result was telling. Whereas before all the lines had been lit blue, now most of the lines reaching out to the outer edge were red. Almost three quarters of the pipes had been turned off or disabled for some reason. None of the water pipes on this side of the shell worked beyond the edge of the Central Mountains. Only two still remained on: the one extending to the outpost we'd started at and one coming up, which also led to a Seeker outpost right at the edge.

Suyef pointed at one green line reaching out halfway between the outpost we'd started at and the Seeker outpost just ahead of us to the west. "What's that going to?"

I squinted at the text and sighed. "That's a raider settlement. You'd think when they turned off the water and forced the settlements to move inland, they'd have closed that off," I muttered.

"So, they raid . . . who?"

I shrugged. "Anyone foolish enough to be on the outer edge," I replied, nodding toward the Central Mountains. "There are reports they also raid the outskirts of the Central Mountains and certain offshoots of Colberra City, but those are rare." I shook my head. "Rumor is that they once were Seekers or at least Seeker trainees and that they washed out. The original ones, at least. Now they seem to be the landing spot for anyone disgruntled with Colberran society. So, they raid the outer edges of the Central Dominance and anyone foolish enough to challenge them in the Outer Dominances. And yes, they consider crossing their territory a challenge. It's beyond me why the Seekers tolerate them."

"You'd think with all these settlements unpopulated they'd have stopped raiding." Suyef stared at the screen a moment, then muttered, "Unless the Seekers are using them for some purpose."

I looked at him. "Like what?"

The Nomad moved, looking away from me, eyes shifting around and shaking his head. "Nothing, just thinking out loud."

He knew more, but if pushed he'd just dig his heels in and say nothing at all, so I moved on.

"Regardless, this overlay tells us a lot about what's ahead," I said, pointing back at the image floating before us. "There are only six major pipelines still functioning that lead out beyond the edge of the mountains: those lines leading out from the center of the map along this lower side of the shell to the edge. We've passed two"—I pointed at the raider pipeline and the one leading to the outpost we landed at—"and are approaching the third. That leaves three more. That one there," I said, pointing at the farthest one around the shell, standing just east of the other side of the Wilds, "leads to the other major raider outpost, a place named Arya. This one here leads to another Seeker outpost on the shell's edge, like the one we are approaching. This one between those two, however, seems to be going to the only remaining settlement on the outer edge still occupied by people. It's also one of the oldest settlements in the Outer Dominance districts."

Suyef looked at the settlement in question. "What do we know about it?"

"Nothing beyond the standard information. Population, water usage, Seeker reports on the relative law-abiding nature of the citizens, although you'll note there's not a standing Seeker presence in the settlement." I shrugged and shook my head. "Or it's just not mentioned. Seeker units aren't assigned to places like that in secret. Waving the flag and all that jazz."

"Maybe the Seekers don't consider the citizens a problem?" Suyef asked.

I nodded. "That's possible. It looks like they send patrols out there on regular intervals, but the records don't show them doing more than bringing a few citizens in for questioning, sometimes settling some kind of dispute, or every now and then quarantining people with some unspecified illness."

Suyef arched an eyebrow at that last point. "Unspecified illness?"

I frowned, grabbing the floating display and twisting my hand, making it vanish to bring up another report. "It's not described in detail. This news report mentions a slight uptick in the number of people being taken into isolation because of 'unspecified symptoms,' which, according to the Seekers, prove that those people were dabbling in things they shouldn't be." I looked at Suyef. "The kinds of things most Colberrans avoid."

Suyef's eyes narrowed. "I thought you said altering was illegal on this shell."

"It is, but if this report is to be believed, there are people practicing it in secret again." I shook my head as the report vanished. "Colberrans don't joke around with that stuff. They may have mixed feelings about the Seekers, but one thing they all agree on is that scripting, or altering, as you call it, is illegal and for good reason."

"You don't believe the reports?"

I stared at him for a moment before answering. "It's a good excuse to make people you don't like or trust disappear, don't you think?"

"Can you track the occurrences of these events?" Suyef asked. "You know, compile all the occurrences to see if there is a pattern?"

"That'll take some time, but yes," I answered, holding the padd up. "But there's something else you should know." I loaded the map, bringing the water line overlays back up. "This green line leading to that settlement? It's not functioning properly."

"What do you mean?"

I tapped the line and brought up statistical reports on water usage, flow, historical data, and more. I manipulated the information and found what I was looking for. I replaced the map and overlay with a chart showing water usage of that line.

"Look, this shows all the usage since the founding of that line," I said, pointing at the sloping chart. "What do you see?"

The answer was obvious even to him. The oldest data stood the highest, as the numbers began to lower in increments as time passed. About ten cycles ago, the numbers began decreasing exponentially.

"Their water flow is dropping," he whispered.

I nodded. "It was dropping. Fast, too. For some reason, about a decade ago, the water just began to decrease its flow to the settlement. That rate of decrease kept climbing over the last ten cycles until, quite suddenly, it halted and began increasing. I don't know why it did that, but something changed." I pointed at the last point of decrease. "Had this trend continued, that settlement would have run out of water within a few months."

Suyef stared at the data point, then looked up at me, his dark eyes locking with mine. "I think we need to go visit that settlement."

"Quentin, I'm starting to wonder about the original reason you guys wanted to go there," I interrupted. "You seem to have forgotten about the water-shield missions."

My interviewee shook his head. "No, remember, we'd found that the water-shortage problems began to occur around the same time as the water-shield missions."

"But why weren't you looking for more information? The two problems might not be connected, merely correlative in terms of occurrence."

He frowned. "Did you strain yourself to construct that sentence?"

I smiled at him and didn't say a word.

"Anyway, we're getting to that. They are related, trust me, but I can't fly without wings, can I?"

My eyes shot up from my notes to stare at him. Quentin was looking out into the distance, fingering a rock in his hand. Had that been intentional? Did he somehow know of my past as well?

"You ready to continue, or do you have any more complaints about my storytelling?" he asked, glancing up at me as he flung the rock toward the edge.

I eyed him a moment longer before nodding.

Of course, we didn't just go straight there. A lot of ground lay between us and the occupied settlement. A direct line would have had us traveling through at least one stretch of Colberra City, and that wasn't an option. Impersonating a Seeker is a lot easier in a mostly uninhabited region. Doing so in a populated city, one that held a mighty Seeker presence, was a different matter. Suyef wanted to stick to the outer edge, thus decreasing the odds of us running into anyone. I favored a more direct route, one that circumvented the mountains and the city but allowed us to shave a lot of time off our trip. At first, Suyef won.

This did give me time to research the matter further. I still had no luck whatsoever in finding any information on the doomed mission to the water shield. The truth of that matter, it seemed, was going to take a lot more work. Facing a dead end there, my focus shifted to solving the mystery of the water shortage, specifically why the outlying regions were losing it. As the records on the events were clearly doctored, a different tactic seemed in order. At the next abandoned settlement we came upon, I insisted we stop to examine the water station itself. Suyef didn't feel it was necessary and would have moved on if not for me parking my mount and going into the station without him. I could feel his icy stare when he followed me in, despite my best efforts to ignore him.

"What do you hope to find?" he asked, settling in near the entrance. In his hand, he held the padd the elder had given him. Once I'd mastered the coding language here, he'd immediately made me link control of his mount to his padd so he could access and view its sensors from nearby. "You already downloaded the files on this settlement and found they're identical."

"I'm not here to look at historical data," I muttered, concentrating on my work. "I'm here to look at coding."

Suyef huffed, "And what could you possibly find in that?"

I shrugged. "Maybe nothing. Doesn't hurt to look."

The look on his face, just visible through the near-translucent panel of my workstation, stated with certainty that he didn't agree with that justification. Regardless, I pushed on, examining the coding that controlled the station. Close to a chron later, Suyef insisted we leave despite my having not finished my search. I quickly downloaded a snapshot of the coding and took it with me on the padd. That evening found me poring through line after line of the complex language, virtually lost.

"You look about as happy as I felt when the elders ordered me to go on this mission with you," Suyef joked, sitting across from me and staring at his padd.

I frowned. "Shouldn't you be standing watch or something?"

He waved the device at me. "I can see fine with these sensors," he said, smiling at me. "They're hardly perfect, but they suffice for you and get the job done."

I glared at him, and he chuckled.

"Yes, I've known for a while how you've been using the sensors while manning your watch." He arched an eyebrow. "The question is how you didn't figure out I knew before now."

"You're adept at keeping secrets," I muttered, staring at my padd. "How else would I not know?"

"Come now, you can't think of a single clue that might tell you?"

I closed my eyes and sighed. "You're not going to leave off, are you?"

"Nope." He grinned again. "You're stuck. You need a new problem to solve. That'll get you unstuck."

"You could be right," I said, fingers working my shoulder muscles, "but what makes you think it's possible for me to guess when you figured me out?"

"If you gave me a task and found out I'd been cheating to accomplish it, what would you do?"

I stopped massaging my neck and looked up at him. "First, using the technology we have to improve our senses is not cheating. Not all of us have supereyes like you Nomads."

He shrugged at that statement.

"Second, I'd punish you."

He arched an eyebrow, causing me to have a strong urge to throw something at him. "And you can't think of anything I've done that could be construed as such?"

I opened my mouth to respond, then stopped. My head turned to the side, eyes never leaving him. "No, you wouldn't have . . . ," I whispered.

He just smiled at me.

"I thought you were training me!"

He clapped and cheered. "Ah, good, I was wondering if your mind had become addled by all this coding you've been staring at," he said, voice jovial, eyes twinkling. "And I was. But not at first."

I grabbed a rock and flung it at his chest. "You twit!" I hissed.

"What?" he asked, jerking his hand up to catch the projectile. "You needed the training, and I needed an excuse to do so."

Reaching for another rock to throw, I stopped short and looked at him. "An excuse?"

"You think we teach just any outsider our ways?" he asked, frowning at me. He held up the rock. "You really are thick sometimes, even for a Colberran."

I grabbed the second rock and flung it at his torso. This time, he caught the rock and flung it back at me. I barely dodged a shot to the head.

"Hey, I wasn't aiming for your head!" I yelled, jumping to my feet and knocking the padd to the ground.

Suyef followed suit. "You should always aim for what will cause the most harm, idiot. Why else throw it?"

I lunged at him, intent on shoving him backward. He grabbed my arms and flipped me over his shoulder. I locked my grip around his arm and pulled him with me as my body fell past his. We rolled around on the ground for a few moments, grappling with each other until I landed on my chest, arms pinned behind me.

"You fight like a Colberran, Off-sheller!" the Nomad hissed in my ear.

I pushed hard, trying to pull my arms free, and only found pain. Kicking, trying to throw him off balance, only earned me a mouthful of dirt for my effort. As hard as I pushed, he had more strength to hold me back, and leverage to boot. If I twisted, he shifted and compensated. If I kicked, he absorbed it and gripped me tighter. Desperate for an option, my eyes spied my staff lying where Suyef had deposited it when we stopped. He must have noticed me looking.

"If you can't get free from a simple hold, Off-sheller, how do you think you'll get your weapon?" he said, his tone quiet but serious.

I twisted my body one more time and felt pain as an answer. There just weren't any other options. A rock sat next to the staff, giving me the only option I could think of. I scripted.

It was just a simple change. My intent was only to surprise Suyef, if nothing else. Instead, the rock launched itself into the air and smacked him hard on the shoulder. Crying out, he dropped me and spun away, coming to a halt over me in a defensive crouch. With the opportunity in my hands, I scripted again and felt my staff appear in my outstretched hand. Without pausing to think twice, I swung for his legs, but he spotted the move at the last second. He jumped away, dropping low and catching my staff squarely between his arm and his torso.

"So," he whispered, black eyes locked on mine, sweat glistening on his dark-skinned face, "you can teach a Colberran new tricks."

We each grimaced as we tried to pull my staff free from the other's grip.

"What do we have here?" a new voice said from our right.

Suyef let go of my staff and jumped upright. I pulled my staff back and pushed myself up with shaky arms. Surrounding us was a squad of Seekers.

CHAPTER 24

QUESTIONS

The squad moved in closer, three Seekers taking up positions behind and to the sides. Two others remained standing where they were, on a slight rise, looking down. They all wore their hoods up, masking their faces. Suyef stepped toward the two above us, eyes never leaving them. I remained still, right behind him. The Seeker robes we'd grown accustomed to wearing seemed a very bad idea in retrospect. Standing there, waiting for someone to do something, I contemplated the various outcomes. How much had they seen? If any of them saw me script, we were done for. I glanced at the Nomad and hoped he had a better explanation than the few occurring to me. When Suyef did speak, what he said stunned me, although I should have been used to his tricks by now.

"Training, sir," he said, pointing at me. "Tyro, here. He's been slacking off on his duties and needed a reminder or two."

I'd like to say my shock remained hidden, but my mouth dropped open and I snapped it shut. My heart began to race as my eyes peeked at the nearest Seeker. Surely he could hear it, too, as the throbbing in my ears seemed deafening. Above, the Seeker that had spoken glared at me with eyes solid black and hard as stone, then glanced back at Suyef.

"Training mission?" he asked.

Suyef shook his head. "First mission out of academy." He shrugged and frowned at me. "He's a bit green, but he's got promise."

I glared at the Nomad but composed myself when the Seeker looked back at me.

"When did you return to Colberra, Off-sheller?" he asked, eyes on me.

Confused, I started to reply when Suyef spoke up. "Several weeks back. The festival was over, so my duties called."

"I don't recognize you. New replacement?" the Seeker asked.

"Yes, sir, I took over after the festival," the Nomad replied.

The Seeker nodded, never taking his eyes from me. "You, where did you train?"

Suyef glanced at me as I searched for some answer. There was only one thing I could think of.

"My parents sent me to the academy from the isles, sir," I replied, holding my breath.

The man's cold, black eyes narrowed as he watched me. "That's a rare one," he finally said. "Didn't think the islanders fancied Seekers much."

I nodded. "They don't, sir, but my parents felt the discipline would do me some good," I went on. "Too much trouble to deal with, they said."

The other Seeker standing next to the first laughed. "See, even on those cursed floating islands good sense can be found."

The first glanced at his companion and gave him a tiny nod. He looked back at Suyef.

"What's your mission?"

Suyef shook his head. "Classified, sir. I have orders stating as much, if you care to check."

The man nodded, and Suyef leaned over to pick up both our padds. He pocketed mine as he keyed his on and looked for the supposed orders. Once he found them, he handed the device to the Seeker standing to his left and waited while the man perused the file. Only then did it occur to me that Suyef hadn't needed my help to translate the code. My mind spun a little as it tried to take in all this new information.

The Seeker nodded and took the device to the two men standing on the rise. He handed it to the first man and returned to his position. The first Seeker perused the orders, scowled, and flung the device at Suyef.

"Bah," he hissed, "I demand to know what you're after. Questioner's prerogative."

Suyef spread his hands, the padd he'd just caught gone, no doubt pocketed with mine. "Orders specifically exempt us from that prerogative. Questioner's seal is attached, if you care to see it."

The man shook his head. "You're crossing our territory. I am allowed to know your destination."

"Only if that destination falls inside your jurisdiction. It does not, as we are headed west. I assure you, we are passing through, as the orders you just read state," Suyef responded, clasping his hands behind his back.

The Seeker glared at Suyef, then nodded once at his men. They retreated behind him, joined by the other man, as the first Seeker approached us.

"Make sure you are quick in your transit, Off-sheller," he said in a low voice, his eyes never leaving me as he spoke. "I'm not a huge fan of having you among our number. Give me a reason, and you'll be off this shell permanently."

To this day, I'm still not sure which of us he was speaking to. Judging by the way Suyef shifted, my thoughts leaned toward him, but there were definitely a few questions on how much this Questioner knew about us.

The man stared at me for a moment, his eyes never blinking, his lips pursed; then he turned and glided away. Suyef followed him up to the rise and watched them leave. I remained below, eyes never leaving Suyef. After a few moments, the Nomad nodded and came back to face me.

"Well, that went better than expected," he said, a small smile dancing across his lips.

I stared at the Nomad, leveling a finger at him. "You mind explaining to me what just happened?"

"Isn't it obvious?" he asked, frowning at me. "We've been given free passage through this territory. Seeker patrols won't bother us now."

I shook my head. "Not that. The entire thing. You, them, this whole thing."

He furrowed his brow and cocked his head to the side slightly. "I'm confused. What part?"

"How did we not just get arrested for impersonating Seekers?" I cried out, my voice rising with frustration. "How did they find us without you knowing? How do they know who you are?"

Suyef crossed his arms over his chest and leveled a steady gaze back at me, one that had become all too familiar. No answers would come from him. I'd have to figure them out myself.

"Fine, you want to play that game, let's play," I said, shoving past him and seating myself on my rock, staff still clutched in my hand.

I pondered what had happened, mulling over what was said, searching for clues. Suyef seated himself opposite me and watched, a bemused look twisting his features in an annoying manner.

"No need to scoff at me," I whispered.

He affected an innocent expression and looked away. "I'm doing no such thing."

"They know you."

He didn't answer.

"They've known you for some time. You're a Seeker."

He nodded. "Correct, in part."

"Which part?"

He smiled. "Fair enough," he said, chuckling. "They do know of me, although not me personally. And yes, I am a Seeker."

"How long?"

He frowned, furrowing his forehead in thought. "We've carried on this farce for . . . oh, I don't know, two centuries, I think."

My confusion must have leaked on to my face, because Suyef let loose with a short laugh, the first I could recall.

"No, I'm not that old," he said, shaking his head. "My people have been doing this for that long. I'm just the latest to be assigned to it." He looked over at me. "You think it was an accident the elders chose me to go with you?"

"So, you've been here before?"

He nodded. "Several times, in fact. But only on training missions. This is my first time here alone, per se."

"And you know how to read their system?" I said, pointing at his padd.

He chuckled again. "Don't get angry. I was under orders not to let you find out about this until absolutely necessary. "

"What purpose does that serve?" I asked.

He shrugged. "We're a distrusting people when it comes to you Colberrans."

I stared at him. "This entire time, you were just pretending to learn because you already knew how."

"What does it matter? So, we've been sneaking up to your realm and passing ourselves off as Seekers. No, not even that," he corrected himself. "We're actually Seekers."

"Do you each keep coming and joining their academy?"

Suyef shook his head. "Water above, no. After the first of us managed to forge documents and plant them on the network establishing us here, we started just doing that." He waved his padd at me. "As you've found out, it's easy to do. As far as the Seekers are concerned, we've all completed the academy." He grinned at me, his eyes twinkling a bit as he hunched toward me in a conspiratorial manner. "Why would we waste our time on such inane training, anyway? It's just indoctrination and reprogramming designed to fabricate the perfect robots for their system." He shook his head and sat upright. "Besides, the lifestyle of the Nomad makes their 'training' look like games children play." He held up the padd. "The fact that we've pulled off this charade for as long as we have is proof enough of that."

I sat quietly for a moment, pondering his words. Finally, I looked over at him. "Why do this? Why send your people up here for this? Just to keep an eye on us?"

He nodded.

"So, why would you personally do this?"

He raised his eyebrows and smiled. "Now, that's a better question, indeed. But you know the answer already."

"Your father."

He nodded once.

"So, that part at least is true."

He nodded again.

"Why would they let you come here if they knew what you'd be doing?"

He shrugged. "They believe it will motivate me to find what they're looking for." He gave me a sharp look. "You didn't think we'd be going back before we found what they were after, did you?"

I shook my head. "We don't know it was murder. It could very well have been an accident."

"You don't believe that any more than I do," Suyef replied.

Silence fell over us. The wind, for once much softer that night, still whipped at our cloaks. The fire danced in the core-night, sending strange shadows shifting over everything.

Suyef finally asked the question I was dreading he'd ask since our training began. To be honest, I was shocked he hadn't asked it sooner.

"So, where did you learn to alter?"

CHAPTER 25

PARTICULAR SKILLS

"So, where did you learn?" he repeated.

"On your shell," I replied. "My parents aren't what you would call run-of-the-mill Colberrans. You've spent enough time here to know the typical Colberran view of scripting."

Suyef nodded. "Only shell in the whole shattered world that bans the practice."

I looked over at the Nomad. "You've been to other shells?"

"No," he said, shaking his head. "But my people have."

I nodded. "I was about to be very jealous. My parents were heading off to another shell as we left, and the curiosity about what they are seeing there keeps me awake sometimes."

"You're changing the subject," Suyef commented, nodding at the staff. "Your little stunt almost ruined our cover. Lucky for you, they didn't see you alter and throw that rock at me, then grab your staff." He grimaced and massaged his shoulder. "Speaking of which, that hurt."

I rubbed at my neck. "So did that." I suddenly felt sheepish and looked away. "That was kind of stupid."

"Which part?"

I glared at him. "What we did."

The Nomad let out a bark of a laugh. "What you did was stupid. Attacking a Nomad without a weapon, then altering right in front of a Seeker squad."

I shrugged. "It was my only option."

Suyef reached out and gripped my shoulder. "There are always options," he said, his voice quiet and serious again. "You just finally let yourself see more."

I stared back at him for a moment. "We've been scripting this whole time during our practices," I stated, watching him for a reaction. "Why do you suddenly have an issue?"

Suyef let a small smile brush his lips. "It isn't that you did it; it's when you did it."

"I didn't know they were there."

He frowned at me. "You should always be able to tell someone is around if you can alter."

I stared at him, momentarily speechless. A thought bubbled to the surface. "That's how you're so good at tracking!" I exclaimed. "You've been scripting."

He frowned at me. "I don't need to alter to do that."

"But you've been doing it?"

He didn't move or react in any way. Finally, he held up a finger. "I'll trade my secret for yours," he said, and held out a hand for me to shake. "But you first. Altering, out with it."

"I told you, I learned it on your shell," I answered, gesturing toward the shell's edge. "It's one of the things the Expeditionary Forces picked up soon after they took that base. That you Nomads don't view scripting the same way Colberrans do."

"We have long considered your people backward in such things."

"Well, my mother developed a knack for it once she got to your shell and could study it without fear of Seekers," I continued. "She split our time between attending the school and learning at home. It was there that I first began studying the code language. Didn't realize it was that at first." I chuckled and patted at my pocket. "The same language we read to use the network. It's all based on the same system. The Ancient language."

I reached into my pocket and pulled my padd out. I thumbed the edges, staring at it.

"Of course, most Colberrans don't know that," I went on. "They think it's just the programming language that makes the system work. Their entire world is built on a lie, and they're happy not knowing it."

Suyef nodded. "People often are blissfully ignorant of most truth in their world," he said. "And they fight tooth and nail to stay that way."

Not knowing what to say to that, I continued my story: "My mother made a point of teaching us the code language. I didn't think anything of it at first. Simple stuff to help us use the network. I took to it right off, and once I had a good grasp of the system, my mother brought other teachers into it. People in the Forces, others who had a similar view of the system as her." I held up a finger. "Nothing bad, mind you. These were law-abiding people. They just didn't agree with the traditional Colberran belief system on education, society, and whatnot."

Suyef nodded. "Not traditional people, then."

"You could say that," I replied, pursing my lips and furrowing my brow in thought. "That word's changed meanings since our world changed. At least on Colberra. Here *traditional* means you adhere to the system, the government. You don't question except in school, when you're learning, and even then there are rules about it." I grimaced. "Needless to say, I didn't like the schooling they offered. It was worse when we lived on the isles, all those cycles the Seekers were interrogating my father. Most of our studies had to happen in private there." I smiled at the Nomad. "We were quite happy to get away from here and be transferred back to your shell. Not only did it put some distance between us and the

Seekers' meddling in my father's past; it freed our education up. After a while, my mother just gave up on the system and taught us at home. You can imagine, had she tried that here on Colberra proper, the Seekers would have had something to say about it." I shrugged. "On the isles, maybe not. The authorities tend to give the people of the isles a bit of leeway. They're mostly harmless. Just want to be left alone. Their population is very low, so I guess the system tolerates them."

"So, why did your mother join the Forces if she's so nontraditional?" Suyef asked. "Seems a bit counterintuitive."

I shook my head. "I don't know, really. Wanderlust, maybe? People of the isles move around a lot to survive. You don't really have a place you call home there. The isles shift their orbits, and the government won't always bring water to the isles that move farther out. A few have fallen out of Colberra's gravity well in the past, so the people just got used to the idea of moving to another isle if one shifted too far." I looked over at the Nomad. "Kind of like your people, from what I know of them."

He nodded. "We don't stay in one place very long either. Only our elderly, sickly, or the very young and the caretakers of that lot stay put in what you call settlements. Even then, one must be very old, very sick, extremely young, or some combination of those."

"Not exactly the same, but close enough," I commented, shifting on my rock. "There's no pattern to the orbits, so on the isles you live your life prepared to move at a moment's notice. You could have two cycles; you could have ten. Most are smart and choose an isle moving inward in its orbit, where they'll have longer to stay. That doesn't always work, as an isle could shift; for the most part, it does. From what I remember, my mother's family was on one of those."

The fire caught my attention. The stuff mesmerized me at times and often gave me an urge to reach in and touch it. Remembering Suyef sitting there, I refrained.

"So, that could be where she got the motivation to go off and join the Forces. Maybe she just wanted to see something other than the isles and Colberra. She doesn't talk about it much. To be honest, it was a very short period of her life, and once she met my father, she got out of the Forces as soon as she could. We didn't discuss that part of their lives." I stretched, reaching a hand over my shoulder and working at a sore spot. "Maybe she just disliked Colberra enough to be willing to do most anything to get away from it. My father has little reason to love it. Even now, my father is finishing up his tour with the Forces but is still employed by them as a craftsman. That's why they're on that other shell."

"So, altering?" Suyef prompted me back to the subject at hand.

"Getting there," I muttered, hanging my head and shaking it. "My mother had a knack for the coding language, but she wasn't alone. My father also had a skill for it. It's the reason he was accepted into the Forces. And his skills are particularly important to this story." I looked at Suyef, my eyebrows elevated in as questioning a look as I could affect.

The Nomad chuckled and shook his head. "So, what skills does your father have?"

"Glad you asked," I said, smiling. "It's not necessarily the skills he has, but rather what he does with them. Most everyone can read the coding language if they've used any part of the network, and everyone does that. What he does is help build bridge programming language between stuff we created and the Ancient coding language."

Suyef whistled, nodding as he did. "That is quite the skill," he stated. "And the Seekers let him do this?"

"How do you think they've designed all their technology?" I asked, pointing at the speeder bikes. "Those things aren't Ancient design, and neither is this." I held up the padd. "No, this is craftily designed modern technology forged to make you think it was of Ancient design. People like my father helped design the coding language that allows the computers on these systems to talk to the Ancient network." I frowned as I eyed the padd. "It's far from perfect. That's why it's been so hard doing research on this thing. Still, it's effective."

Suyef pulled his own padd out and activated it. He turned it around, peering at the device from all angles.

"That is masterful work," he whispered. "I mean, now that you mention it, the minor design differences stand out." He looked up at me through the translucent display hovering above his padd. "So, is all Seeker technology of modern design like this?"

"That's not Seeker technology," I answered, shaking my head. "The speeders are, but these are commercial devices built just to access the network. Nothing too fancy."

"So, I'm guessing your father designs programming code for more important stuff?"

I shook my head. "Pretty run of the mill. Control programs for water systems and matter-reclamation devices. Your standard equipment present in most settlements." I held up a finger. "But there's the kicker to this story. No one notices what a man's doing when he spends his days perfecting and troubleshooting programming code for interfacing water-storage devices and control sensors for matter reclamators. As long as the water gets into the holding tanks and people get their food and other material from the reclamator, no one is asking any questions about the guy making it work." I grinned at Suyef. "And no one's thinking to ask questions about why his kids aren't in the system schools and why his wife is teaching them coding language in secret."

"So, your mother taught you to alter?" Suyef asked.

I shook my head. "Nope, I stumbled onto that all by myself."

Suyef frowned. "By accident?"

"Yeah, and, as you can imagine, it didn't go too well," I said, shuddering at the memory.

"What happened?"

I shrugged. "I nearly burned down the entire settlement."

CHAPTER 26

SECRETS NEVER TOLD

Suyef's arched eyebrow told me all I needed to know of what he thought of that claim.

"Well, okay, maybe not the entire settlement," I said, amending my statement. "Ancient fire-suppression systems are state of the art, you know that. Still, it took them a decent time to put it out."

"Explain," he said.

I shifted, that fateful day coming back into my memory. "I should explain that it was actually my third attempt that caused all the ruckus. My first two attempts ended as bad, just not in as amazing a fashion and without any proof I'd done anything. That was the problem. I could claim it was scripting all I wanted, but if no one saw it, I was just some silly teenage boy who was pretending just to get attention." I shrugged. "Call it a foolish-pride moment. I just wanted someone to see me do it. Not even really sure why. It was going to cause a lot of trouble. Maybe part of me just wanted someone to notice I could do it. Recognition. It's a powerful draw for a young mind." I almost whispered the last part. "Heck, not even just for the young."

I stared off into the core-night, my words having run out for the moment. Suyef let me sit in peace for the time being. To be honest, how to explain what had happened was difficult, and for

a reason beyond my ability to understand at the time, an extreme
sense of shame filled me whenever this story came up. The part
most people knew was in large part a fabrication, a lie told to cover
up what really happened. Now, confronted, my instinct was to lie
again, to keep telling the same old story. I fully intended to; I had
the words formed in my mind and even opened my mouth to speak
them.

What I said was the exact opposite.

"There was this guy who lived on the settlement. A bit older
than me. Mostly harmless." I took a deep breath. "Mostly." I looked
down as the wind kicked up some dust and whipped at our fire,
trying to put out the endless flame emanating from the Seeker
device below it. "I won't go into detail, but you need to know this
much: things were done." I looked over at the Nomad. "To me." I
looked back at the fire. "By him. Repeatedly."

Suyef nodded but said nothing. He joined me in staring at
the fire.

"I tried to pretend nothing happened," I went on. "Tried to act
like nothing was wrong. I didn't know what to feel. I needed something to latch on to. Something to . . ."

"To protect yourself," Suyef said.

"Maybe that, too. I was thinking more that I needed people
to notice me." I ran a hand over my short-cropped hair. "If people noticed me, he'd stay away. But at first, it was just desperation,
something to make him fear me. Something to make him stop. If I
could script, he would be scared of me. That was my thought process, when alone, at least." I slumped down, the memories weighing heavy on me. "Then he'd come and I couldn't do anything. I
couldn't think, didn't know what to say or do. I could smell his
sweat, feel the roughness of the cloak he would wear. I'd go numb
inside, do whatever he said, hoping he'd stop and go away. Wanting
the light to go out. I remember the light hanging from the ceiling.
I would stare at it, willing it to go out. Longing for it to go out and

take me away with it. Then it would go out and I'd be alone, wanting for nothing more than the light to come back."

I pushed myself to my feet, stepped away from the fire, and stared off into the distance. Suyef remained sitting, and I could feel his eyes on me. What must he have thought of that revelation? In part, he was uncomfortable, no doubt, and not because of the subject. Nomads tend to keep problems like this inside their close family circles. To have what amounted to a complete stranger sharing such secrets must have crossed so many cultural taboos. It's a knack of mine, despite my best efforts to the contrary. This moment was no different.

Whatever he thought, Suyef stood and joined me. Silence remained our companion for a time as we watched the low-growing bushes shift in the wind, dust clouds dancing up among them as core-night passed. High overhead, the moon, hidden from sight behind the water shield, passed by. The telltale tug of her gravitational force bent the water upward toward her. The ingenious design of the core-night shield the Ancients crafted never ceased to amaze. It blocked out almost all light from what remained of the planet's core yet let you see beyond the shield to the world around and above. Colberra orbited so close to the water shield, it was perpetually visible. I stared up at the shifting water, imagining what it must look like up close. I'd seen pictures of it in news articles and even some ancient imagery of what history called oceans. Whitecapped waves danced across those images, and sometimes I imagined they still did up there.

I stared down at the fire, watching its rhythmic dance, longing to touch it. A cough from the Nomad drew my attention.

"You seem overly fascinated by fire," he commented, nodding at the flames.

I smiled and took a chance. Reaching into the fire, I grasped a handful and muttered the words, breathing life into a new script. The fire danced onto and around my hand but did not burn. I held the fire out to Suyef, letting him feel the heat. The stoic Nomad face cracked into a look of astonishment.

"Now, that's an impressive bit of altering," he whispered. "Do you shield your hand?"

"In a manner," I said, shifting the fire to my other hand. "The coding of the fire's been changed to not burn me or anything touching me."

"Save your clothing," he commented, nodding. "Smart."

I laughed. "Yeah, wish that thought had come sooner," I muttered, half of my mouth splitting into a grin. "Incident number two." I held my hand out over the fire and mimicked dropping, scripting the necessary code in my mind and seeing it act. In response, the flames fell in a ball to rejoin their mates below. "I'm not sure why it's fire that drew me in. It may have chosen me. Who knows. I just needed something to feed my feelings into, and fire fit."

Suyef pointed at the fire. "No words, not even mouthing." He eyed me, one arm tucked across his torso, his other hand brushing a finger across the opposite cheek. "Have you always been able to do it that way?"

I shook my head. "That took a lot of practice. All those cycles studying coding." I spread my hands and grinned. "My mother's handiwork paid off. Still, I have issues when it's simple or singular tasks. Except with fire."

"Can you make fire without some around?"

"It's harder, but yes," I answered. "Not that I go around lighting things on fire like that for show." I grimaced, looking down at the ground again. "Well, not anymore."

Suyef moved past the fire and took his seat again. I squatted across from him, staring into the dancing flames.

"So, what happened to the . . . guy?"

I looked up at Suyef. "I didn't light him on fire, if that's what you're thinking."

He shrugged. "I'm not thinking anything, although that thought does amuse me."

"It did me as well. For cycles." I shifted to rest my weight on my left foot, arms wrapped around the other leg. "But I never could bring myself to show this side of me to him."

"Fear?"

I shook my head. "Pride. I didn't want him to know about it."

"You were afraid he'd make you do things for him?"

I shrugged. "Maybe, but I never thought that consciously. It was more that part of me was special, different. He didn't deserve to have any part of it."

"But you told your parents?"

I looked at the ground and shook my head, the shame returning in my gut. "No, I didn't even show it to them. Not at first," I said. "Part of me blamed them. They should have kept me safe, after all. Should have made sure it didn't happen." I looked up at Suyef. "That's what parents are for, right? And they failed, so when I figured this out, keeping it secret from them seemed okay."

Suyef held up a hand to stop me. "Wait, you kept both secrets from them?" he asked. "Your altering and what that guy did to you?"

"I was afraid to tell them," I confessed, looking back at the ground and fiddling with a rock. "In my mind, it was my fault, I had done something to get his attention, to make him think I wanted that . . . stuff to happen. Part of me believed him when he said it was natural for kids to do that sort of thing for adults. The other part of me just went dead when it happened, and when it was over I rushed to bury it. Hide it."

"Pretend it never happened," Suyef stated, his voice quiet.

"Why bring it up to someone else? I've never done that." I looked over at him. "Until now."

Suyef bowed his head. "I'm not sure what has earned me your trust, but thank you."

I shrugged and threw the rock off into the distance. "I'm not sure what made me tell you."

We fell silent for a few moments; then Suyef asked, "So, what did you first try to alter?"

I remained silent for a long time, pondering how best to answer his question. Several possibilities came to mind. I chose the most direct.

"I tried to change my memory."

"You can understand my motivation," I went on. "I didn't want to remember what had happened; I wanted to pretend it hadn't happened. So, one night, resting alone in my room, unable to sleep for fear of my dreams, I snuck out of the house. I made my way to a secluded area near the shell's edge. It was a popular place for kids our age to sneak off to. Inside the settlement lines, but a bit isolated by a rock outcropping jutting up near the edge. That time of night, it was almost always abandoned, most decent people asleep.

"I sat there, staring off over the edge for what seemed like chrons. The idea of finding out what was below did occur to me at least once, but I just laughed it off. Even in my depressed state, my mind was able to grasp that ending my own life was just a punishment for me and my family, not the real guilty party."

I stopped for a moment, finding another rock to fiddle with while composing my thoughts. Suyef waited, quiet, eyes on me.

"Still, no part of me wanted to think about it," I continued. "That memory needed to be gone. The feelings, too, and the more time my mind dwelt on it, the angrier I got. One reason we found that place such a good one was because we thought no one could see us beyond the outcropping. What happened next ended that illusion."

I held up the rock for Suyef to examine. "It's a simple thing, this rock. Most people just ignore them until they trip on them or turn an ankle on them or throw them. If you look closely enough, you can see that even this simple rock is a complex piece of geological coding."

Suyef nodded, looking at the rock. "It has to be. The code is paired with the elements of existence."

"You mean the elemental table, yes?" I asked, and he nodded. "So, a complex piece of coding.

"That night, I wasn't looking closely enough. My instinct pushed me to just grab rocks and throw them as hard as possible at the outcropping. When that didn't satisfy my anger, flinging them off the edge became my next course of action, seeing how far they would soar before dropping out of sight. I threw rocks until my arm hurt, then started kicking at them. I did that until my foot struck one rock that wasn't a rock. When my foot collided with it, the piece of ground didn't move."

Suyef smirked at the thought, earning a chuckle from me.

"Yes, after the pain subsided, I laughed, too," I said. "But what happened next, while I was lying there on the ground—that's what's important. My head was mere inches from the rock that wasn't a rock, and I saw the coding for the first time. The multi-colored swirls forming columns that lined up with the elemental table. My eyes finally looked closely enough, and I could see it. To this day it's unclear to me if it was the anger or the laughter, but something clicked."

Suyef nodded. "It was neither, actually," he interjected. "According to our teachers, it's the release you feel after a strong emotional moment that brings you to that point. A letting go of something that allows you to grasp the coding and see the code language in everything. If you know what you're looking for, that is."

"And all that knowledge was in my head because of my mother and her insistence we learn the computer code." I arched my eyebrows at Suyef. "Even then, it was just a bit of a shocker. To suddenly see a rock break down into its base coding language right before my eyes. To see the mottled, brown edges of the rock suddenly painted in the swirls of coding stacked around each other.

"And, just as I was beginning to recognize and read the coding, it all vanished," I said, mimicking something disappearing with my hands. "At first, my mind was convinced it had imagined it. So, I looked again, concentrating, but nothing happened. Still, something had happened, and I wanted to find out what. This new mystery gave me something to distract myself with."

Suyef picked up his own rock and tossed it into the air, catching it when it came back down. "Did you tell your mother?"

I shook my head. "I wanted to be sure before saying anything," I replied. "The next several weeks were spent trying to see the coding again, with no luck. Getting angry again didn't work for me, and neither did working myself into fits of laughter. I'm quite sure my mother feared for my sanity or something. She must have spent many nights lying awake worried something was wrong with me, but not knowing what. Since the answer about what happened continued to elude me, I wasn't about to tell her. Seems silly, considering she'd taught me to read the coding, but no one ever accused teenagers of being intelligent. We think we are, think we know everything or at least can figure it out without any help. I was no different." I sighed, resting my hands on my lap, rock still grasped between them. "Maybe that's why I messed it up.

"About two months after that night near the edge, I'd begun to give up hope of duplicating the event," I continued. "You see, it hadn't occurred to me yet that I hadn't actually seen coding in the rock. It would take me several months of studying before figuring that out. Still, I trudged on, struggling to find something that would help me break through.

"So, I had to figure it out on my own. I went back to the basics of working with the network code, like I did to learn to read Colberra's network."

Suyef raised a hand. "You say your parents came back to Colberra for a time before you returned to my shell. Did you not learn the Colberran code then?"

I shook my head. "We lived on the isles. The network doesn't exist out there. They have devices and stuff, but they're all of Seeker design, or they just built what they needed on their own. Plus, I was very young. I barely remember the code until much later, when we went back to your shell."

Suyef waved for me to continue.

"So, I stumbled my way around, trying to create the code language of the network outside of the network," I said, shifting to get some feeling to return to my posterior. "Most of my time was spent wandering the settlement alone, wearing a headpiece to convince people to leave me alone. I pumped a lot of music into my head, trying to coax the creative juices from my brain.

"Then, one afternoon almost a cycle after that night with the rock, I figured it out." I held up the rock, grinning at him. "It isn't the actual coding that makes the rock into a rock. The coding is superimposed over it. Teenage pride took over, and soon the coding was appearing to me everywhere, so much so that I wasn't really paying attention to anything else. And then it would vanish."

"The coding?" he asked.

I nodded. "Concentrating too hard on it made it vanish for me. It took a lot of trial and error before it dawned on me to passively pay attention to it." I tapped my ears. "Music provided the key. It would distract part of my brain, allowing me to focus just enough on the code and try to change it."

I sighed, long and deep. "If only I'd known what I was messing with, maybe my first attempts would have been different."

Suyef shifted a bit, propping a leg up on the rock he was sitting on. "So, what did you do?"

I hung my head. "Being full of teenage hubris, nothing short of amazing would suffice. Something that would get everyone's attention."

I paused, suppressing memories. "Then he returned."

Quentin stumbled to a halt, the last words he spoke hanging heavy in the air.

"How old were you?" I asked.

"Thirteen cycles, maybe fourteen." He shrugged. "I think I was twelve when it started."

I motioned for Quentin to stop. A raging storm of emotions crested inside me. Anger and disgust for the man who had done this. Thoughts of what would happen if I ever met him boiled to the surface. Pity and sadness for Quentin rose up, and part of me wanted to reach out and take his hand, to squeeze it, to let him know someone cared. I saw a sketch in his hand.

"Does she know?" I asked before giving the question a second thought.

He held it up and nodded. A tear crept down his face.

"She blames it for what I've become," he whispered, more tears pouring down. "Oh God, what have I become?"

He curled into a ball, arms wrapped around his head, and silent cries crept out. Suyef entered the room and beckoned me to leave. We left Quentin, still crying, on his bed. The sketch of Micaela remained gripped between two fingers, his clenching fist not having damaged it.

"He blames himself for what that man did to him?" I asked, stepping into the living area. "Worse, she does?"

Suyef shook his head. "I can't speak for her. I can only surmise." He pointed at the room. "What I do know is what he thinks she thinks of him. He can only base that on how she reacts to him." He lowered his hand and looked away. "Rather, how she reacts to what he's become."

"A broken man? Insane? Heartbroken?"

The Nomad's eyes flashed, and his features twisted, brow furrowing, jaw setting.

"He's also become a rage-induced maniac who lashes out with powers that are out of his control," he whispered. "Once angered, he wrecks everything and everyone that comes near him."

I opened my mouth to reply, only to shut it again abruptly. "Everyone? So, why are you still here?"

"Because what he needs is at least one person in this world to stand by him. Since she's too damaged emotionally by what he did to her the last time they saw each other, it falls to me."

I watched the Nomad for several heartbeats before asking my next question. "What has he done to earn such devotion?"

Suyef shook his head. "No wings yet." He held up a hand to forestall my response. "Give him some time. What you two are discussing is still, after all that has happened, a very raw subject for him. He never dealt with it, not properly. He's discussed it with me and her. But never to a point of truly understanding what it did to him." He looked me square in the eyes. "Until maybe now. He may just finally be coming to a point of realization."

I looked down at my notes and the padd, both gripped in my hands. "That's what this is about, isn't it? This entire quest. It's not just to find these missing pieces. It's to help him and her find the missing piece."

He didn't answer. That response was wearing on me, so I returned to the previous topic.

"Suyef, surely you can give me something these two did to earn this kind of loyalty from you?" I asked. "Even a hint, without telling me what happened?"

He contemplated my words, lips pursed. "They taught me that justice isn't found in retribution, but in forgiveness."

CHAPTER 27

FIERY EMOTIONS

"It wasn't like he'd left the settlement or anything." I continued telling my story to Suyef. "He'd just not been around my everyday life. Then he came back, and it all started again. I so wanted to stop it, but..."

I looked at the ground. Suyef shifted as the wind whipped around us.

"You said you tried to change your memory?" the Nomad asked, prompting me.

I nodded. "Soon after that last time, he left. Rumors abounded as to why. He apparently had a reputation as a troublemaker, and the Forces finally had enough of him and shipped him back to Colberra." I paused and looked over at Suyef. "But something did happen that might have instigated their decision.

"You see, the memories wore on me. Just as I'd begun to bury them, he rehashed them all again and added new ones. That part of me, screaming inside, needed them to go away." I held up the rock. "I wanted to fling them away like those rocks that one night." I let my hand fall back to my lap. "So, I started envisioning that very thing. Balling my memories up, wadding them tightly together and ridding myself of them. Throwing them into the abyss that is our world."

Suyef eyed me, head cocked to one side. "That's a . . . complicated bit of altering," he whispered, lowering his eyes to the fire. "Even more so than what you did with that earlier."

"You're not kidding," I said, nodding. "It was impossible to figure out. I had no clue how to do it. Imagining them all in a ball and throwing it." I shook my head. "Didn't work. I could form air into a ball and fling it, but how do you grab a memory out of here"—I pointed at my head—"and make it into something tangible you can throw?

"In my frustration, what was actually happening had completely eluded me. Here I thought flinging a ball of air was safe. It didn't dawn on me that that ball of air kept going in the direction it was sent. The thing nearly leveled a building along the edge of the settlement." I looked at Suyef. "That was incident number one. The second incident occurred a week later. I sent a rock soaring over the settlement, and it nearly destroyed a Seeker speeder. They weren't able to prove who did it, so everyone without a good alibi was punished." I glared at the Nomad. "They never even used those things, because you Nomads never let anyone leave the settlement, but by the way they reacted, you'd have thought the water control station had been damaged."

Suyef chuckled. "People can be very particular about their stuff."

"That's the truth," I agreed. "Finally, about a week after that incident, in another attempt to ball my memories up and be done with them, my anger pushed me to light a rock on fire and use it to graffiti the side of a building. Seemed pretty cool at the time, flaming letters spelling out the coding that frustrated me." I shrugged, shaking my head and smiling slightly. "Those fires were fueled by my rage, unbeknownst to me, and they just kept burning. I went home and just sat there, raging over my failure, finding anything to keep my mind from drifting places it didn't need to go. Music played a big part in this."

I looked over at Suyef—a cold, hard look. "Someone discovered them chrons later when they burned through the wall. I remember the alarms going off, and my father rushing out of the house. My mother kept us behind, just to stay out of the way. We heard all about it when he returned.

"The entire structure was lost, the fires gutting an entire supply building in a matter of chrons. The suppression systems prevented the flames from spreading to any other building, but my father insisted that they couldn't put the flames out. They just wouldn't die." I leaned toward Suyef, my voice lowering. "Until shortly after my father arrived. He said that when he got there, the flames had started to die down, and only then were the suppression systems able to extinguish them."

I eyed the Nomad, waiting for him to put it together. For his part, Suyef shrugged and waved me on.

"No guesses?" I asked, eyebrows raised.

He nodded. "The fires were connected to your anger. They lost the connection."

"Exactly," I exclaimed, raising a finger to the skies. "Right when we found out about them, and my father ran off. Up until then, I'd been fuming and raging alone in my room. When we heard the alarms, I stopped doing that." I dropped my hand to my lap. "I was thinking of other things, and I lost the rage. The instant that happened, the flames died down and were put out."

"So, what happened to you?"

I shook my head. "Nothing. They never connected me to the fire." I cocked my head to one side, a sly grin breaking out on my lips. "He did."

"Your father knew you were connected to it?"

I shook my head. "No, my father never put that together. The guy who did all that to me. He took the fall for what happened."

Suyef frowned. "They blamed him?"

I nodded. "They weren't able to pin it on anyone, but everyone except him had an alibi. So, the Forces used the incident as an excuse to get rid of him."

Suyef frowned. "Not exactly what you call justice for his actions, but I can't say I feel sorry for him." He looked at me. "So, did you try again? With your memories?"

"Didn't need to," I replied, holding the rock up, then chucking it into the distance. "The Forces did it for me."

"The Forces didn't take your memories away," he retorted.

"No, but they took my tormentor away, and they helped me push my memories down and not focus on them. That's as good as what I was trying, and a whole lot safer."

"So, do you specialize in anything else?" the Nomad asked, his head turning to look out into the desert. "Besides failed attempts at memory wipes, tossing rocks, and lighting things on perpetual fire?"

I made a sour face at him before answering. "I've become quite adept at moving things, as our practices have shown you. Pushing them and pulling them around, tossing them up. And fire has sort of become my servant." I held up a hand, and the entire fire leapt from where it was to float in a giant ball above my hand.

Suyef reacted like he'd been shot, jumping toward me and waving at the fire. "Stop that!" he hissed, eyes darting around. "Put it back!"

Frowning, I turned my palm to face the Seeker device, and the fire fell back to where it had been. "What's your problem?"

The Nomad stood there, eyes roaming the horizon. "We need to move."

And so we did. We packed up, mounted our speeders, and took off into the dimly lit desert. We traveled for several chrons before coming to another pipeline, one of the many we now knew were empty. Suyef followed it north toward the shell center until we came to a control station. He stopped on a hill overlooking the tower.

"Is it just me, or do they always build these stations in small valleys?" I asked, staring down at the facility.

"Maybe," he replied, nodding as he shifted. "Let's go."

We moved our mounts down and parked them near the tall, cylindrical building. Soon after, I found myself sitting before yet another control panel, using the sensors on the mounts to scan for anyone approaching. Suyef stood near the door, as usual, watching me.

"You mind telling me what that was about?" I asked, tapping open another panel on the screen and continuing my study of the water station control coding.

"Do you have any idea what those Seekers might do to us if they see you altering like that?" he hissed, pointing at the door. "Especially with a Questioner around?"

"You didn't seem to mind the first time."

"They were gone then."

I focused on him through the translucent panel. "So, all that time later, there was a better chance they'd be back?"

Suyef frowned. "You shared your secret. My turn." He waved a hand at the panel. "It's all well and good, using the sensors like that. Especially with us inside. Outside, however, I've got other ways of tracking."

I focused on him through the panel. "You script to track?"

"Passively. It's second nature to me," he explained. "Remember, altering isn't taboo among Nomads, as it is among your people. I've had many cycles of training in it." He nodded at the panel. "As a result, I learned a long time ago I have a sixth sense about what's moving about near me. I can feel the changes in the code when someone approaches."

"So, were the Seekers coming back?"

"I sensed someone approaching, and it was safer to assume it was them than take the chance you'd again do something foolhardy," he stated, walking over to stand just beyond the panel. "You're from this shell. I shouldn't have to explain this to you."

I pushed myself up, somewhat emboldened by being taller than the Nomad. "If you let them come to us, then what is your issue?"

"My issue is with you showing off your altering ability for every Seeker this side of the mountains to see," he said, his voice dropping to forceful whisper. "My issue is with your blatant stupidity in nearly blowing our cover."

I moved away from the panel, Suyef following me. "All I did was play with a little fire. At your request!"

The Nomad stepped close to me, finger pointing at my face. "I didn't request a thing. I simply asked what else you'd been working on with your altering. I said nothing of a demonstration."

I knocked his hand away from my face. "My apologies if I felt the need to show you," I stated, stepping closer to the Nomad. "It's not often someone asks me to show off my abilities with fire."

Suyef looked up at me, eyes going back and forth on mine. The next moment, he chuckled and looked away.

"What are we doing?" he asked.

Tension I hadn't noticed creeping into my back relaxed, and a breath I'd been holding without realizing escaped my lips.

"Being asinine?"

The Nomad barked an even louder laugh, smacking me hard on the shoulder. "You have a knack for being blunt, Off-sheller. I'll give you that." He rested a hand on my now-smarting shoulder, his face serious. "Don't get me wrong, Quentin. I am impressed by what you do with fire. I've known other alterers whom you would learn a lot from. Just be smart with it."

I nodded. "I wasn't thinking they might come back," I replied.

Suyef pointed at the panel. "Your search. Any luck?"

I shrugged as I turned back to the panel. "I need some time to study this station's coding and compare it to others."

He nodded and waved me back to work. "I'll check the supply situation," he said, stepping near the panel and tapping a program open. "This will tell you if anyone comes close. I've tied our speeder sensors into this station and sent them up to the top of the tower to give them better reach." He stepped around the panel and made his way toward the walkway leading above. "If anyone does come, just call out."

That said, he disappeared to the upper levels and left me to work. I stood for a moment, staring at the opening to the second floor before shaking my head. Nomads, I decided, were a bit too crafty for their own good. Focusing on my work, I examined the coding for that station, going through line by line, reading each symbol. I pulled my padd out and tapped open a program to help me with translating the symbols. Suyef would probably have called that cheating, too. I shook my head and focused on the coding. It took me all of about ten minutes to find my answers.

"Suyef!" I called to the Nomad, who was still out of sight above. "Suyef!"

Apparently, my tone indicated trouble, as the Nomad bolted into sight, sliding down the ramp to face the door. I raised my hands, making a placating motion with them.

"Whoa, easy there, man," I said.

Suyef looked at his panel through the translucent screen, then nodded once. "You found something?" he asked, stepping around the terminal.

I pointed at the file. "Just look at that, right there," I said, tapping a particular column.

He leaned in close, and I watched his eyes move around, reading each column of coding. Finally, he shook his head and looked at me.

"I understand it, but loosely."

"No worries," I replied, waving a hand to indicate the entire construct. "This is the base program coding for how much water moves through this station." I looked pointedly at him. "Rather, how much water used to run through it."

"So, this water line is dead as well?" he asked.

I nodded. "Been so for a decade." I pointed at the coding. "And this column is the reason why. It took a bit to notice it, as it's blended in so well with all the rest."

Suyef read the column. "It's just a quota coding, yes?"

"Correct," I answered. "A limiting quota. It's establishing an ever-increasing limit on the water flow." I held up my thumb and forefinger and looked at him through the gap. "It's a tiny one, multiplying over time." I reached over to another panel and brought up a system layout of that particular water pipeline. A tap of a few symbols, and each control station blinked red on the line. "I'll bet you several nutrient packs that we'll find the same coding change at each of those." I tapped the panel again, and the display changed to an overview of all the pipelines reaching out to the shell. "You know what I'm going to say next."

Suyef nodded. "That's not a bet I'll take," he said, then looked at me. "Can you verify your finding at those other stations from here?"

I shook my head. "That coding is internal to each station. It probably can be done, but not by me." I pointed at the column. "Someone with citadel access might be able to."

"You don't know they did that from somewhere else," the Nomad stated, nodding at the station door. "They could just as easily have come here to do it."

I held up three fingers. "Three possibilities. One, they did this from a distance, say from the citadel. Two, whoever did this physically came to each station to add that piece of coding. Three, they had help, someone no one would question coming to each station and altering the coding."

"Seekers," Suyef whispered.

"Seekers," I said, nodding. "The question is, why would Seekers want people to leave the Outer Dominances?"

Suyef held up a hand. "We still don't know it was them," he insisted. "All we know is they might have done it, either on orders from within or from the government."

I shrugged. "Seekers are the government on Colberra," I retorted. "The Central Dominance founded them, and the two have been wedded at the hip for centuries."

"That still doesn't answer who did this and why," the Nomad replied, pointing at the screen. "All we know is that someone altered the coding at this station and the few we've visited to decrease the water flow to the outer shell. We suspect the Seekers because they have the ability and the freedom to move around to do this." He held up a cautionary finger. "But ability does not equal motive."

I shrugged, shaking my head. "Power is their motivation," I stated, pointing at the panel. "Regardless, that is a complex bit of coding, hidden in a simple addition to the control code. To do that, you need to know this system forward, backward, inside out. Only the Seekers and the Dominance have that kind of knowledge."

Suyef looked over at me. "Yet you found it."

I pointed at my chest. "I had a mother who bucked the system to teach me coding." I pointed off in the general direction of north. "Most of the people on this shell don't get that kind of education." I plucked at the cloak I wore. "Except Seekers."

Suyef nodded and pointed at the panel. "I'm not disagreeing that this was most likely done by Seekers. It still begs the question: Why?"

I shrugged yet again, waving a hand at the access terminal's giant screen. "Why else? To stop the water and make the people living in the Outer Dominances move into the Central Dominance."

"Why do that?"

I paused, contemplating the answer. "I'm not sure," I finally said. "Could be any number of reasons. Water shortages, system failures, politics." I held up a finger. "One thing you can count on in Colberra is politics. That and Seekers."

Suyef pointed at the panel I'd brought up. "What about that last active line, the one out to the west?"

I looked over at the screen, reaching over and tapping the indicated line to bring it to the forefront. "I can't tell from here, but I wouldn't be surprised to find the same bit of coding going on there."

"Yet the line is still active."

I nodded, looking at the Nomad. "The lines we've encountered show a progression of sorts." I brought the shell map back up and pointed at a settlement we'd passed. "That's the one where they changed all the timing so we couldn't tell when it happened." I pointed at the water lines next in both directions. "The records we have show these all had their own problems in a progression forward in time heading out from this line."

"Meaning that one was first and whatever happened moved east and west around the shell from there," Suyef said, continuing my thought.

"With a few exceptions," I replied, nodding. "They skipped these lines leading to Seeker outposts on the shell's edge."

"And stopped short of the raider outpost to our east."

I pointed at the last line that was still active. "According to all the records we've found so far, most of this started nearly two decades ago, most of these settlements emptying around ten cycles ago." I tapped the active line. "I can't say for sure until we get to it, but this problem must have hit that line long before now."

"So, for some reason we don't know yet, something or someone is keeping that line active," the Nomad said, holding a hand toward the screen.

"Or what they did to that line is just moving a lot slower," I said, never taking my eyes from the map on the screen. "Either way, the answer lies on that line."

Suyef shifted toward the door, then stopped. "You said before someone was accessing files you were looking at?" he asked, looking over his shoulder at me.

"Haven't noticed it in a while, but initially, yes," I answered.

Suyef frowned, looking at the panel.

"What are you thinking, Nomad?"

He shrugged. "I'm not sure, but if someone out there has figured out what you've figured out, maybe they're the ones trying to find the same answers as you?"

"That's a long leap of logic right there." I nodded at the panel. "And that's an impressive bit of coding skill. I can't tell if this alteration is on that line from here. If they can, I'd like to meet them."

He nodded. "You may get your chance. It's just a theory. It could just as well be our Seeker tails or a Colberran censor monitoring the files," he said, pointing at the panel. "Get what you need, and get some rest. We have a water pipeline to visit."

CHAPTER 28

NOMAD SECRETS

If we'd known then how much trouble those Seeker tails would end up being, Suyef might have reconsidered his original plan to just involve them and be done with it. We first noticed them when we left that control station; Suyef indicated them on our sensors. Over the next week, they remained at a distance, following us. They stayed just far enough away that our sensors couldn't discern how many there were. Someone among them had a healthy understanding of Nomad senses as well. They never strayed close enough for Suyef to sight them, even with his altering sixth sense. Still, we knew who they were, and, for the time being, they left us alone.

"You know we can't go to that settlement with them on our tail," I said one night as we rested in yet another control station. The translucent panel filled the room before me, and I pointed at the two marks on the map indicating our nightly watchers, the rest having retreated to another control station farther up this line. "And if that Questioner is as good at coding as rumors say he is, he'll figure out what I've been looking at eventually."

Suyef nodded. "Good, I hope he does."

I stared at him, eyebrows cocked upward, head shaking slightly. "You mind sharing your plan with me?"

He pointed at the screen. "If he figures out all we're doing is looking into water-coding programs, he may deduce all we're doing is checking on the levels. Making sure the system's working the way it's supposed to be."

"But it's not," I pointed out. "And we're only checking one station along each line."

"This time," he said, smiling. "And it just has to give him pause. Get him thinking."

"About what?" I asked, nodding at the screen. "That we're just looking for information?"

"We're checking the status of the system." He held up a finger. "As a guise for what we're really doing."

I stared at the Nomad, my head shaking slightly side to side. "Which is?"

"Figuring out why that one line is still functioning," he finally answered.

I frowned. "That's a bit too close to the truth for my comfort."

"The best lie is one that is made from truth," the Nomad said. "See religion."

I barked a laugh. "On Colberra, that's almost a dead joke."

"There is a state religion, yes?" he asked. "Funded by the Central Dominance?"

I nodded. "Just to keep the citizens happily placated. Preaches government doctrine more than anything else, and attendance isn't required. Oh, they'll give motivational speeches and whatnot, keep the people looking forward and smiling. But nothing like what you have on your shell."

The Nomad sighed. "As much as we think we know of you Colberrans, there's still much missing."

"That, my friend, is what you get when all information is controlled by one central authority," I quipped, playfully punching him in the shoulder. "You know, like on your shell."

"There's a difference between keeping Off-shellers from accessing information and keeping our own people from doing so."

I shrugged. "Probably." My eyes wandered back to the blinking lights on the screen. "You're going to meet them again, aren't you?"

The Nomad nodded. "Seems simpler to just confront them. Let the Questioner know we're noticing his presence. At the very least, it will make him send for word from his superiors."

"If he gets a response, your story is going to fall apart," I pointed out.

Suyef turned to look at me. "And that's where you come in." He reached into his cloak pocket and pulled his padd out. "I've got something to share with you." He held his out for me to hold mine near, swiping a finger across the screen and sending the data to my device. "That's a very particular bit of coding, and attached are instructions on what to do with it."

I perused the lines. The magnitude of what he'd just given me slowly washed over me. I looked up at Suyef to find him staring at me.

"Is this how you Nomads snuck your way into Seeker ranks?"

He nodded.

"That's some serious coding going on." I read through the lines, finger tracing up and down the columns of symbols. "This isn't a new program. This is just how to access one that already exists?"

The Nomad nodded at the padd. "How else do you think we keep them confused about us? Seekers are nothing if not persistent." He pointed at the coding on my screen. "That little program has allowed us to keep Seekers from ever really getting a good foothold on our shell." He looked meaningfully at me. "And they have tried. Many times. It's part of the reason we kept your Forces so isolated. We suspected they might be another Seeker attempt to get onto our shell and into our network."

"But doesn't having this create a window into your network?" I asked.

"No," he answered, pointing at the large screen over my right shoulder. "You have to be at one of these for this to work. Actually on this shell. That program just grants you access to a very specific location on the network. One that lets you insert information to be found."

"Like fake mission files," I whispered, finally putting two and two together.

"Precisely. I've never had to do this, but you should be able to get it working. Once you do, I have the file ready," he said, holding up and shaking his padd. "I just need you to figure out how to make that work."

I frowned at the Nomad. "They didn't teach you that before you left?"

"They didn't think it was important yet. My information was added to the file by my predecessor. I haven't needed the skill until this mission." He pointed his device at me. "That's not important. What is important is that you need to wrap your brain around it and get it to work. We need to give that Questioner something to find when he goes asking questions."

"If he hasn't already," I muttered, turning to the workstation and setting the padd on the surface before me.

"That's possible. He may still be looking, which is why he's just tailing us." Suyef pointed to the north. "If he knew we had no orders on file, he'd have arrested us already. But he hasn't, so I suspect he either hasn't thought to look or—"

"He's still looking."

"Exactly," Suyef said, moving toward the door. "I'm going to make a show of checking on them. You get to work."

I nodded, and turned my focus to the program. It wasn't complicated. The instructions were extremely simple to follow. What proved difficult was coming up with some mission. Creating a reasonable-looking facsimile was part of what this program did, but it did not provide content. I had to do that. With Suyef outside, it meant waiting for him, going to get him, or just doing it myself. As I stared at the screen, pondering my options, my eyes saw a file flash once on the local drive displayed before me. I quickly tapped the folder open and looked at the file: water-control coding. Someone was accessing this station's data, possibly to see what the coding looked like. Who was doing it, though, and why? Maybe someone needed to know what we did, how the coding had been altered. Maybe they were looking for comparison files, examples to hold up to theirs. Or it could just be a censor. Still, a censor would probably check other things. What would the odds be of a censor just happening to check the one file Suyef and I kept checking just after we'd done so? If the file contained a trigger embedded in it, the odds would be pretty high. Still, that was a pretty large leap of logic, but no more so than wondering if whoever was accessing that file was simply looking for something to compare to. I couldn't help but be impressed. That coding skill had to have taken cycles to learn.

My eyes wandered back to the map and came to rest on the one remaining functioning water line not leading to a raider or Seeker outpost. I glanced at the file Suyef's people had created and made my choice.

It was time to go find some information.

"You have a theory on who it was, don't you?" I asked Quentin, interrupting his story.

He held up the sketch in his hand.

"So, while you were stumbling upon one of the problems in the network, she was doing the same thing," I muttered, jotting a note down to make a parenthetical reference later.

"What she was looking for isn't important." He held up the sketch. "What's important is that she was doing it. Specifically, how she was doing it. I told you, that's an impressive bit of coding. I could do it now. But not then."

"She says her father was even better."

He shrugged. "Maybe. I've only ever seen her do it."

I arched an eyebrow. "Meaning you've seen him otherwise?"

He grinned and winked at me. "Up to your tricks again?" He waved a finger at me. "You'll not fool me into revealing anything before its time."

I shook my head, bowing it in defeat and motioning for him to continue.

When Suyef returned, he found me sitting, legs extended out before me, crossed at the feet, and arms folded over my chest. I wore a smile on my face.

"You succeeded, then?" he asked, coming to stand next to me.

"Not just at that," I said, nodding toward the screen. "Look."

Suyef stepped close and perused a series of files open on the screen, all laid next to each other.

"What is all this?"

"Those, my Nomad friend, are the control files for water flow from every control station still functioning properly in the Outer Dominances," I boasted, a big grin splitting my face.

His head turned to look at me. "I thought you couldn't access these from anywhere except for the stations themselves."

"I couldn't," I admitted, lacing my fingers behind my head, arms jutting out to either side. "Until you gave me that file."

His eyebrows rose as he looked from the padd to me and, finally, to the screen. "That is impressive," he stated. "And saves us some time." He held up a finger. "But it doesn't fix our immediate problem."

"Oh, I did that already," I commented, waving a hand at a file open off to the left. "There's our orders. We're to check, in an unobtrusive manner, mind you, on all the water lines to make sure they are 'functioning within acceptable parameters' as a guise to inspect the stations all along that one line and discover why this bit of malicious programming isn't functioning the way it was intended to."

"Malicious programming?"

I nodded. "I didn't say that in the report, of course. It's intentionally vague enough not to give away what we're really doing, while giving us access to the right locations to do so." I nodded at the map. "Those poor people in the settlement will be as convinced as anyone else we're legit and there on official business."

"Giving us access to carry out our secret mission to sabotage their water supply," Suyef stated, nodding and smiling. "That should keep the Questioner off our backs." He indicated the other files. "That's this station's control coding, isn't it?" I nodded, and he glanced over it and another file. "This file is missing the—how'd you put it?—malicious programming."

"Yes and no." I highlighted a column of symbols in the local file and on one of the other files. "It's there, just a bit different. It's all in the symbols. Whoever did this wanted the malicious coding to blend in. To an untrained eye, which on this shell means virtually everyone outside of Seeker and Dominance upper circles, this coding would look identical. Even more so when you consider that most people wouldn't have access to the local control files of other stations." I pointed at one symbol, halfway up the column. "Look closely at that one."

Suyef leaned over and peered at the indicated symbol. He moved to look at the corresponding symbol in the other files. Finally, he stood up and nodded.

"It's amazing that one symbol can change so much," he said.

I held up a finger. "One stroke, not just one symbol. Those two symbols are the same one. But that upward tick there versus the downward tick there changes the meaning to the exact opposite."

"And everyone in the Outer Dominances runs out of water because of it," Suyef whispered.

"Everyone except the chosen few allowed to remain," I stated, waving my hand at the functional stations' files. "All of the water lines are identical." I tapped the changed column, resting my finger on the crucial symbol. "What this little fancy bit of coding did was convince the primary system there are more control stations farther down the line. Which makes you wonder where all that water is going."

"And why they needed that fix," the Nomad murmured. "That makes it seem like this problem hit the entire line, or even the entire system, all at once."

"That, or when it was implemented it took out the entire line and the only way to prevent it was . . . No, that doesn't even make sense." I tapped a finger on my lips while thinking, eyes locked on the voluminous files spread out before me. "If they planned this, they could have just exempted the lines they didn't want turned off."

"Precisely," Suyef said, putting a hand on my shoulder and waving his other hand at the screen. "But this shows every line was affected, and the only fix we've found was to trick the system into thinking some lines were longer than they really were." He pointed at each active water line. "All of these end in Seeker-controlled settlements on the edge, save for three, and two of those are near the edge also. All the points the Seekers control have one thing in common besides being on the edge: they're ports."

I looked over at him. "Everyone knows that, but they don't get used. We're too far from any other shells to trade currently, besides yours, and you won't trade with Colberra."

"We used to," he said, stepping away and moving behind the screen. "Do you recall what we used to trade with your shell?"

I frowned at Suyef through the panel. "If I remember my history correctly, water. The records aren't very detailed once you get back that far."

He snapped his fingers. "Exactly. To be precise, you sent water to our shell centuries in the past when our shell collided with another and our water system broke."

"What's your point?" I muttered, eyes roaming away from his just-visible face through the panel to the data.

"The point is," he continued, glaring at me, "if the system existed back then for your people to off-load water . . ."

I pondered his words. Then it hit me. "You're saying they're dumping the water off the shell?"

"Can you think of a better way to create a water shortage?" he asked.

"You slow down the production at the citadel?"

He shook his head, pointing at the map. "You have to keep the majority of your population in the dark about this, right? You can't have their primary source of water suddenly start malfunctioning."

"You're assuming most of the population doesn't know already," I said, arching my eyebrows at him.

"If they did, we wouldn't have had this hard a time finding information on it, would we?"

"That was satirical," I muttered, waving a hand at him.

"You mean sarcastic."

That warranted a glare from me. "Moving on. Your hypothesis is they're dumping the water off the edge to manufacture a water shortage?" I tapped on another panel, bringing up a search. "The problem is, I don't recall there being any major water shortage in recent cycles. Not even historically." I scanned through my search, looking for anything that might fit. "Nothing in the media or historical archives. Water supply has never really been an issue on this shell, because we're so close to the water shield. That's probably why it was so easy to convince us to send water to help you."

Suyef looked around for a moment, shaking his head, lips moving as he talked to himself. He looked at me. "Try the opposite."

I focused on him through the panel. "Too much water?"

"Too much water *use*," he said, his eyebrows going up, one hand raised next to him. "You could spin that to convince your population you need to exercise some controls."

I shrugged and altered my search. It took a few moments, but soon we had a few hits.

"Here we go, a news article from about fifteen cycles ago. And here's another from close to twenty," I said, pointing at the list as it populated. "Another from ten. Seems there was a big kerfuffle about water usage." I tapped open a few of the documents and started skimming them, Suyef moving around to join me. "Look, here's some Central Dominance bigwig giving a speech." I tapped the link, and another window opened, revealing a man standing at a podium before a large crowd. "Clearly a politician."

I keyed on the audio, and his voice filled the room.

"There are times in the history of our nation when our very way of life depends upon dispelling illusions and awakening to the challenge of a present danger. In such moments, we are called upon to move quickly and boldly to shake off complacency, throw aside old habits, and rise, clear-eyed and alert, to the necessity of big changes. Those who, for whatever reason, refuse to do their part must either be persuaded to join the effort or asked to step aside."

The man in the video paused to look up from his speech. "Those are the words of another man facing another problem long ago. But they still ring true. As do these, also his: 'And even more—if more should be required—the future of human civilization is at stake.' Well, what we are facing is as paramount as the challenges humanity once faced, and, yet again, the future of our way of life is at stake."

I rolled my eyes and paused the feed, tapping open a transcript. "He goes on like that for a full chron."

"What is he talking about?"

I skimmed his speech and tapped on a section halfway through. "Here it is, buried deep. His audience must have already known what he was talking about." I grimaced at the text. "This guy needed a better speechwriter."

"Or a word limit," Suyef stated, smirking at me.

I chuckled and nodded. "Anyway, it is the water. He's going on about the Outer Dominances wasting water." I highlighted a column. "Ironically, he accuses them of doing the same thing you're suggesting: pouring it over the side just to spite the Central Dominance."

"So, now we know how they did it," Suyef said, moving away from the panel. "Decrease the water flow to the outer settlements while massively increasing the flow to your few controlled ports on the shell's edge. You create the illusion of an uptick in water usage."

"And convince your population the people in the Outer Dominances have it in for your way of life. Enter this politician and more like him," I added, nodding at the man standing frozen on the screen.

He held one hand up, pointing at the audience, and, in that moment, his face suddenly looked very familiar to me. I stepped near the screen, opening up another search and loading an image of the man. When his face filled the screen, I heard a sharp intake of air behind me. I looked over to see Suyef standing there, eyes locked on the image.

"You know him?"

Suyef nodded.

"He seems familiar to me as well, but I can't quite place him."

Suyef stepped near the panel and covered the lower half of his face and his hair with his hands. Once he did, I knew immediately.

"The Questioner from the other day?"

The Nomad nodded. "The Questioner," he whispered. "His name is Colvinra."

CHAPTER 29

FACING A QUESTIONER

"Wait, you recognized him even though you had only seen his eyes?" I asked, interrupting Quentin.

He glared at me, head cocking to one side. "No, I recognized his voice. Then his face started to look familiar. And those eyes. You don't forget solid-black eyes like that."

"I'm assuming this is the same Colvinra whom Micaela encountered?"

He frowned. "Do you want to tell this story?"

I held up two hands. "No, no, I'm just clarifying. It's a lot to keep track of."

"If you have a hard time keeping track of a familiar name in this, just wait until you meet Nidfar," Quentin muttered, settling down on the floor next to the table.

My ears perked up at the name, one the Queen had mentioned.

"Do you know where I can find him?" I asked.

He nodded. "He's dead."

I ground my teeth, eyes narrowing at him. He must have heard the grinding, because he looked up at me, eyebrows raised.

"I was told you died, too."

He shrugged. "I did."

He fell silent, and no amount of prodding on my part would get him to tell me more. After several minutes of me trying, he finally lost his cool and fled the room. I let out a long breath and shook my head.

"You can't push him like that," Suyef said, walking into the room.

"What do you do? Stand outside the room all day and wait for him to stop talking? How do you always know when to show up? It's creepy. And you aren't exactly giving me much to go on here," I muttered, grabbing my things and making to leave the room.

He held an arm across the doorway. "I've told you, he's unbalanced. He's not right in the mind. You've done well to get this much out of him. Be patient." He lowered his arm but held my gaze. "Trust me, you'll get all your answers."

I shrugged and moved past him, making my way to my room. I noticed Quentin's door stood open, so I stopped and peeked inside.

There in the corner, I found him. He lay huddled up into a ball, his knees gripped to his chest, his eyes squeezed shut. Over his head, he wore a listening device, a set of silver implements that filled his ear canal and wrapped around his ears. I couldn't hear what he was listening to, but I could hear one thing: him humming. The melody filled me with competing emotions: dread warring with joy, agony with peace. Over and over, he hummed the notes, occasionally taking a breath. As he did, he slowly uncurled, his body relaxing. Within a few moments, he fell asleep, the hum falling to a murmur and eventually a grunt as he dozed.

When he awoke nearly a full chron later, I sat on his bed. He stretched and shifted to sit against the wall.

"What were you listening to?" I asked when he removed the device.

He shrugged. "Something I found in the network. It's ancient. As in very old. I think it used to have someone singing to it."

"Does it help?"

He shook his head. "Nothing does."

"So, why listen?"

"Because it's better than listening to my own thoughts."

"If this Colvinra is as interested in the water usage as he claims to be in this speech, or at least in using it to control people, he shouldn't have an issue with our mission at all," I pointed out, nodding at the face of the Questioner on the panel.

"As you'll soon discover, I'm sure, Colvinra has a way of making things as complicated as possible," Suyef muttered, moving away from the panel. "My predecessor left a lengthy report on his encounters with the man. It seems that since he came on the scene he's taken a particular interest in the few Nomad brethren in the Seeker ranks." He turned to look at me. "You can imagine I wasn't too surprised to find him in charge of the squad trailing us."

"But you'd never met him before?"

He shook his head, eyeing the image from the other side of the room. "Just seen images and read the reports of my two predecessors."

"Wait, only two?"

Suyef looked at me. "Yes, we tend to complete two rotations up here on this mission. Roughly ten-cycle rotations."

"So, your predecessors didn't report on him prior to the water 'crisis' starting on Colberra?" I asked.

"No, he first appears in our records a little over twenty cycles ago," Suyef answered.

I stared off at nothing, trying to wrap my brain around something that couldn't quite be seen, like a memory of a dream.

"What are you thinking?" Suyef asked.

I shrugged. "Which means he didn't appear on the scene until just after the water missions. That seems a bit convenient as well."

"All things concerning him seem a bit convenient."

"I'd say contrived. The entire situation seems fabricated," I stated, waving at the panel. "All of this—the water, the network, him. All of it."

Suyef stared at me, not saying a word. I shrugged and nodded at the image on the screen.

"Your reports say anything else about him?" I asked.

Suyef shook his head. "Just to step carefully and avoid his questions. He's quite good at them, you can imagine."

"I don't suppose you get that title without that skill," I stated, stepping near the panel and tapping open another search. "I'm going to see if there's anything else to be found about him."

A few moments later I'd found next to nothing.

"This man hasn't done much that's worthy of public record, it seems," I said, stepping away and staring at the small amount of information available to me. "Name, rank, a brief reference to his work in the Dominance governance prior to his appointment as a Questioner, and nothing more."

"He was appointed?"

I tapped open a file. "Here's the memorandum." I skimmed the document. "Pretty straightforward. Lauds him for services to the Central Dominance but doesn't state what they are. Appoints him to Questioner, and that's it."

"Look at the date," Suyef said, nodding at the screen.

I peered closer. "That's the same cycle as the speech he gave."

"And you can find nothing on him besides this speech?"

I shook my head.

"They must do a purge of records when you become a Questioner."

"When you become a Seeker," I pointed out. "No one really knows who the Seekers are individually. Seeker records aren't exactly public knowledge, and if I was running that organization and had the power to do so, I'd make my employees' history disappear."

"Organizations like this are dangerous," Suyef muttered. "No accountability when no one knows who you are."

I looked over at the Nomad. "The Central Dominance doesn't care about accountability. Who's going to stop them on this shell? And they leave you pretty well alone on your shell, so what does it matter to you?"

"People should not be ruled like this. It's not natural."

"It's what they wanted. It's their own fault," I retorted.

"So, we should just let them continue to wallow in their misery because they chose it?"

I shrugged. "Talk is cheap. The Central Dominance controls the citadel. As long as they control that, and the Seekers protect them from anyone that might wrestle that control away, the people are stuck with it."

"That's not very Isler of you," the Nomad whispered.

I glared at him. "I've only been there once and then as a young kid. I've spent more time on your shell than this one, and the world the Forces live in is a whole different one compared to the rest."

Suyef nodded. "Very isolating, that life is."

I shrugged. "It's what we had, so we made do with it."

"I'm not judging you for it," the Nomad said, resting a hand on my shoulder. "Merely commenting."

"This is neither here nor there," I said, nodding at the screen. "We don't know any more about him than we did before."

Suyef removed his hand and nodded. "We may not ever," he said, looking at me. "Can you use our file to find anything?"

I shook my head. "I tried that. As nice as it is, there is still something limiting its access," I muttered, frowning at the panel. "It's weird, I always thought the restrictions on the network we had on your shell were the Nomads' doing. You even said they were."

"They are," Suyef stated. "We couldn't have you tapping into our network. We knew where your loyalties lay."

"Sensible approach. One problem," I said, pointing at the panel. "I've found the same restrictions here. The same blocks. Same access limitations. It's different information, and it's guarding less, but it's there."

"What are you saying?" Suyef asked.

I looked at the Nomad for a moment, then shrugged. "I don't know what it means. I just know that whatever your people used to limit our access to your network is on this system as well. Protecting a much smaller amount of information, as far as I can tell."

Suyef frowned. "How our people managed to block your access is still a bit of a mystery to me. I've asked them before, when I went through my initial training. They never answered, just dodged the question."

"You suspect them?" I asked.

"No," he replied emphatically, looking back at me with hard eyes. "They have their reasons and chose not to share them with me."

I held up my hands. "Easy, I wasn't accusing them of anything," I said.

Suyef sighed and looked away. "I know. It's just frustrating."

"That they'd send you on this mission without trusting you with all the information?"

"Yes, but how could they know what I would need to know?" the Nomad asked, waving at the panel. "We had no idea what we would find doing this. You know my opinion of this 'mission,' as you call it. It's their way to get you and your meddlesome questions off our shell and somewhere you might, at best, find something beneficial to them and, at worst, land in Seeker hands."

I chuckled, shaking my head. "Not very nice of your elders."

He barked a laugh. "They'd just as soon peel off their skin as be nice to an Off-sheller."

The conversation ground to a halt. Suyef murmured something to himself, then nodded at the screen.

"Could this have something to do with the problems the elders mentioned?" he said.

I shrugged. "It could be. It's possible a problem on the system might cause this." I held up a finger. "But remember, it looks exactly like the blocks your people put up."

"So, something is protecting the network," Suyef said. "And potentially causing problems because of it."

I stared at the screen for a moment before remembering something.

"Whoever is peeking at files did it again," I said. "And I pinpointed the information they're looking for."

Suyef arched an eyebrow.

"The water control program for this station."

"A monitor?" he asked.

I shrugged. "Maybe, or someone else interested in the system."

The panel Suyef had set up to monitor the tailing Seekers flashed to the front. We both looked over to see the five markers moving toward our position.

"What are the odds?" I asked.

We remained at the panel, closing out my work and awaiting the approaching Seekers. The sensors showed them surrounding the tower and taking up positions. A single blip moved nearer, and soon the door slid open, revealing the Questioner. He wore his cloak, head wrap covering most of his face, save for his black eyes, which remained hard as stone. He stood tall, filling the door as he entered, shoulders broad. His hair, a strand just visible under his hood, matched his black eyes. He stepped into the room, and the door slid shut behind him.

"You're heading for the settlement," he said.

I glanced at Suyef but held my tongue. The Nomad spread his hands to either side and shook his head.

"Our orders state we speak to no one," Suyef said. "Not even Questioners."

"I've seen your orders, Off-sheller," Colvinra hissed, slicing a hand through the air. "Including the original directives your orders stem from. My sources just found them. So, let's cease these stupidities and move on." He jabbed a finger at me. "Remove your hood."

I frowned and looked to Suyef, who nodded. I took the hood off. Colvinra's eyes widened slightly as he watched.

"Is there a problem with my trainee?" Suyef inquired, eyes still on Colvinra.

"Do you know who I am?" the Questioner asked, ignoring the Nomad.

I shook my head.

"You don't recognize me at all?"

I shrugged, head still shaking. "Can't say that I do," I replied, uncertain of how much to reveal of the little we did know.

"Very strange," he whispered, glancing at Suyef. "I assume your predecessors informed you of me?"

The Nomad remained motionless.

"Yes, we know they've been keeping tabs on us, sending reports back to your people. We've known for some time. You've sent mostly harmless information back, so we allowed it."

"Why let a potential leak remain in your system?"

Colvinra shrugged. "That's a question for the politicians. Seems they like the idea of having you here. I think they believe if they let you keep coming up here to join our most secretive organization, you'll be inclined to return the favor someday." Colvinra barked a short laugh. "You can guess my thoughts on the likelihood of that happening."

Suyef nodded. "Slim to none, if our elders have anything to say about it."

Silence fell as Colvinra shifted his gaze back to me. "You are a puzzle I'll admit I did not expect to find. You say he's a trainee?"

Suyef nodded.

"When did you graduate the academy?"

"Last cycle, sir," I answered, latching on to the first thing I could think of.

He frowned. "Strange, as your orders don't mention your name, just his." He nodded toward the Nomad. "Mentions an accompanying trainee, but even that is a mystery." He turned to look at Suyef. "It's not often they send a trainee on such an important mission."

Suyef shrugged, shaking his head. "It wasn't my call. In fact, he was sent on this mission over my vehement objections," he muttered, glancing at me. "I was overruled and not told the reason. So, I've been tolerating him and attempting to fill in the gaps in his academy work."

Colvinra nodded, eyebrows arched. "Yes, we've been less than pleased with the academy's products the last few cycles ourselves." He waved a hand before him. "That's another discussion. Last word of you, Nomad, placed you on your own shell tending to . . . What was it? Family business. When did you return?"

"Just recently, sir, as I indicated before," Suyef replied, nodding at me. "Just before I was assigned him for this mission."

"Normal port of entry?"

Suyef nodded once.

"And the trainee was waiting for you?"

Suyef glared at the Questioner with more fire than I could muster. "The particulars of how and where I acquired the trainee aren't of interest to this mission. His existence was revealed to me a few moments before they gave me this assignment."

The Questioner's eyes narrowed as he watched the Nomad. Finally, he shrugged. "You're heading for the settlement now, I assume?"

Suyef's head cocked slightly to one side, eyes on Colvinra. "We've visited a lot of settlements. You'll need to be more specific."

"The only one that matters," he retorted. "The only one with people still living at it."

Suyef nodded. "Eventually, yes, we are meant to go there."

Colvinra pulled out a padd of his own and tossed it to Suyef. "Here's an update to your orders."

Suyef keyed the device on as I moved to look over his shoulder. The Nomad scanned the document, then handed it to me. It was an almost-exact duplicate of the document I'd just created a short while before and secretly planted, with a simple amendment column tacked on to the end.

"So, we go there directly," Suyef said, looking back up at Colvinra.

The Questioner nodded, clasping his hands behind his back. "We're on our way there. It seems a local administrator's been messing with the water system and been detained. He's being held at a Questioner facility now, and we're being sent to take his daughter into custody." He nodded at the padd. "You'll find the details there. Only other document." He looked around the station. "I'll leave you to your chosen abode. We depart in the morning."

"You don't need our help to detain a citizen," Suyef pointed out, nodding at the padd in my hand.

Colvinra nodded. "True, but us going on a detainment mission gives you better cover to accomplish what you need to do without raising any suspicion."

Suyef and Colvinra remained locked in a stare for a few breaths before the Nomad nodded. The Seeker turned his gaze to me, eyes narrowing. He shook his head and left without another word.

"I don't buy that for a second," I whispered once the door was closed.

Suyef held up a hand, eyes on the panel. We waited in silence until Colvinra's blip on the map had joined one of the others. After a few moments, all five blips retreated to where they'd been. Only then did Suyef speak.

"I'll admit it is suspicious, but it gets us to the settlement a lot faster," the Nomad said.

"Gets us there faster?" I retorted, snorting. "And puts us under the watchful gaze of a Questioner."

Suyef spread his hands, this time at me. "I'm not sure how to avoid it."

"We disappear now. Make Colvinra think we've left already. Maybe he'll go on without us."

Suyef frowned. "You don't seriously believe he's going to let a couple of Seekers suddenly go rogue, do you?"

"We can plant alternate orders showing we contacted our superiors and they altered our directions so as to avoid associating with him."

Suyef laughed, shaking his head. "There's no way to word that without raising suspicion," he said, holding up a hand to forestall my response. "I'm more interested right now in this daughter he's going after. Did you open the report?"

I held the padd up, tapping the orders document closed and opening the only other file stored on the device. "It's a standard arrest warrant. Well, not an arrest warrant. Simple detainment for questioning in relation to possible illegal network activity."

"That doesn't sound simple," Suyef said, his voice soft and low.

I nodded. "Sounds the exact opposite. Look here in the justification clause. This girl who is being detained? The Seekers already have the father. This also says she has two male siblings. Why wouldn't they have taken them all into custody when they detained the father?"

Suyef shrugged. "I haven't a clue. Maybe the father wasn't taken in under suspicion but later came under it." He looked down at the document. "Any mention of a mother?"

I scanned it and shook my head. "Just mentions the three." I looked up at him. "Why?"

"No reason," he said, shrugging. "I wonder what that means, 'illegal network activity.'"

I looked up at the panel, then at Suyef. "You don't suppose they're the ones we've been noticing, do you? Accessing the network files?"

"That, or they attempted to but didn't succeed and then the father got arrested because someone noticed their attempts."

I felt my breath quicken. "You don't suppose we got them arrested, do you? I mean, they were just looking for information. We found it. What if the censors couldn't tell them apart from our meddling?"

"How long ago was the father detained?" Suyef asked.

I scanned the document one more time. "It doesn't say. It has his name, Allyn. We could look him up."

Suyef jerked his head at the panel. "Get to it. I'm going to replenish our supplies."

He returned a short while later to find me staring at the panel.

"You find anything?" he asked, breaking me from a momentary reverie.

"Not much," I answered, shaking my head.

"Where were you?"

I frowned. "Honestly, who knows? Mind spaced." I pointed at the panel. "Managed to find his detainment date. It predates our arrival, but not by much."

"So, he wasn't arrested because of our snooping."

I nodded at the report. "Look at the issue date for her father's detainment order. Now look at hers."

Suyef read the data. "These were sent on the same date."

"I tracked the delivery. Her father's went to the right station. Hers went to the other side of the shell."

The Nomad cocked his head to one side. "That seems . . . inconvenient."

"I'd say suspicious. Like someone was trying to prevent her from being detained sooner."

Suyef nodded. "Keep that tidbit for later. It might come in handy."

"How?" I asked.

"I don't know," he replied. "There's a lot we don't know. At least we know the father wasn't detained because of our work."

"If he's been in Seeker control since before we arrived, who do you suppose has been accessing the files?"

Suyef turned a silent gaze to me, one eyebrow elevated. I stared back at him. His eyes darted down to the padd in my hand.

"The daughter?" I asked, holding up the padd.

"It docs say she's being detained for illegal network activity."

I shook my head. "Possible illegal activity."

"In the Seeker world, possible is probable, and you know that," Suyef retorted, moving behind the panel. "If they're taking her in, she's either guilty in their eyes, or at least they can make her look guilty."

"It might not be her," I said, looking down at the document. "It could be her father is the guilty party and she's being brought in to be a witness."

"Then who's been messing with your files?"

I shook my head and stated with a bit more force than intended, "Anyone. We don't know it's them."

Suyef raised a hand to calm me. "I know, but one way or the other, she, the Seekers, and we are all connected, even if only by circumstance." He looked up at the panel. "Close out what you've been doing here and mask it. We need to rest." He turned to go up the walkway to the living quarters and paused. "By the way, what's this girl's name?"

I looked up at him, blinking away some random thought. "What?"

"Her name? What's her name?"

I frowned. "Who?"

"The daughter, nitwit," Suyef hissed, shaking his head and frowning. "You okay?"

I nodded. "Yes, I'm just distracted," I replied, tapping the padd back on. "Her name is Micaela." I looked back up at him. "That mean anything?"

"Yes. Now we know what to call her when we find her first," Suyef stated, smiling as he disappeared upstairs.

I sighed, muttering to myself while hiding our work on the control terminal. "Great, so now we're going to go find a girl a Questioner is after before he can get to her." I glanced up at the ceiling and yelled, "You're crazy, you know that?"

"And you're stuck with me," came the answer.

"Don't I know it," I whispered. "Don't I know it."

My eyes drifted back to the padd. I read it three times over, but it revealed nothing more. I stared at the daughter's name a moment more before shaking my head to focus and finish my work.

"Guess we'll find out soon enough if you're the guilty party or not, Micaela."

CHAPTER 30

SHADOWS

After that, we went straight for the settlement, only now under the watchful eye of the Questioner. Needless to say, our staff practices were a lot different and we hardly ever talked about the same stuff. I didn't even touch my padd to research for fear Colvinra would intercept my work and figure us out. Suyef, for his part, played the perfect Seeker and kept me on my toes as a freshly graduated rookie.

The odd thing is, the Questioner enjoyed watching that part. I couldn't say how many times we caught him watching us, particularly me. That gaze of his sent shivers up and down my spine, even when I wasn't aware he was looking. Once, on the occasion of an embarrassing training session, I found him shaking his head as he turned away.

His eyes never changed. Cold, hard as steel, and black as a room absent all light. When he watched, I swear it felt like ice touched me. It wasn't clear if he hated us or me in particular, but something was up with that man. He never spoke to us on our way to the settlement. He left that to his squad leader, who would let us know when we were leaving and stopping. Beyond that, all five of them ignored us, and we were all happier for it.

It took a few days to reach our destination. Once we got close, Colvinra finally spoke to us. Well, to me, really. We were just preparing to leave a control station we'd stopped at. It lay near the mountains in the north along the same water line that led to the settlement. Suyef, being his normal distrustful self, had moved on ahead to look at what was coming to the south. Colvinra used that moment to come see me.

He loomed over me and said words I would never forget. "I don't know what game you're playing at, but I'll figure it out. Mark my words, I'll stop you, if it's the last thing I do."

There was no doubt after that he knew we were fake. Why he didn't detain us, I'm not sure. I got the feeling he was using us, playing along to see what we would turn up, in addition to detaining Micaela and her brothers. First chance presented to me, I told Suyef, and his feeling was the same as mine. The time to part ways with the Questioner had come.

That proved far simpler than I thought it would be. We volunteered to scout the outer control stations. As he was convinced his targets were inside the settlement and this kept us out of the way, Colvinra readily agreed. This also kept us pursuing our supposed mission, as checking each of those control stations along the line continued the ruse.

And that's how we found them first. Dumb luck, that was, and it didn't help much, as he got to them just after we did. Still, it gave us a few moments, and that little bit of trust would prove to be very important for what followed.

"What happened next?" I asked.

Quentin shook, his body twitching as he pondered what I said. His head turned to one side, and his mouth hung open just a bit. Then he shook his head.

"All of it. The tower, the raiders, and the prison." He waved his hands around his head. "All of that and much more. So much more." He frowned and focused his blue eyes on me. "This is taking so long. We're not even to the good parts! Can't you write any faster?"

I glared at him. "This moves as fast as you talk," I said, pointing at the recording device. "You keep saying we can't move too fast. Can't 'fly without wings,' I think were your words."

He coughed a laugh. "That sounds pretentious. Suyef must have said that."

I nodded. "He did as well."

"Anyway, we're wandering off the shell," he blurted out, slicing a hand through the air. "Focus, we need to focus. There are important parts coming." He pointed at me. "And not just for us, you hear?"

I waved at him. "I'm all ears. What important parts come next?"

He grinned, a wide, toothy thing that reminded me of nothing more than a young child happily regaling a parent with tales of his adventures.

"You get to hear about me being a hero." He leaned forward, his voice dropping to a whisper. "I saved us all."

"At the prison, yes? You don't want to talk about anything else?" When he frowned again, I continued. "Meeting Micaela? Tailing them to the raiders? Going to the prison? Any of that?"

His brow furrowed. "Why? You already know that part. Just go read your notes." He shook his hands at me. "No, no, time for the important part. My shining moment."

I arched an eyebrow and nodded.

"So, when the walls began to buckle . . ."

When the walls began to buckle in around us, I knew we were in for some trouble. As much as I wanted to question Micaela as to how she was talking to us from that panel, there wasn't any time. Pieces of what many believed to be indestructible Ancient wall fell around us, sparks flared out from ruptured power conduits, and the entire room lay swallowed in shadows. Even when the lights came back on, flaring bright against the looming darkness, the shadows remained.

Only now they moved. I thought at first my eyes weren't seeing straight.

"Watch the shadows," Suyef called. "Something is in them."

"Shouldn't we worry about what's out there?" Donovan asked behind me as I shifted to cover our right.

A shadow lowered from part of the fractured roof like a drop of water slowly stretching from a spigot. As it neared the floor in front of me, I heard Suyef grunt and a hiss enveloped the room. I looked to see something implode from sight in a ball of flame.

"Shadow assassins," I growled, my teeth grinding. "That's what you were telling us."

"That wasn't me," Micaela stated, her voice shaking.

"Sure looked like you," Donovan whispered.

I remained wary for the shadow I'd seen drip down even as I held a piece of the former ceiling in my hand, brandishing it. Another tremor shook the room as even more of the ceiling peeled away. Overhead, the night remained dark, making it impossible to see what was attacking the building. I had my suspicions, however.

Behind us, the door hissed open as someone finally entered. I heard footsteps stop behind me and a strained gurgling sound. Spinning, I found two guards caught in the grasp of a shadow, their feet kicking as they dangled in the air. I raised my makeshift weapon, but Suyef was two steps ahead of me.

"Down!" he cried out, swinging his flaming staff at the shadow as Donovan and Micaela dropped to the floor.

The two guards crumpled to the ground as the creature imploded like the first under Suyef's strike. Neither of the men moved.

"Get out the door!" I yelled at Micaela and her brother, kneeling to grab the men's firearms as I waved at them.

More shadows dropped into the room as another blast shook the structure, what remained of the outer wall peeling away as the room trembled. I backed toward the entrance, pulse guns up and firing at any shadows that moved. Suyef spun around the room, his staff ablaze, each strike dispatching another shadow.

"Move, move, move!" I yelled at the crouching pair behind me.

Once the siblings were on their feet and running down the hall, I darted out of the room, Suyef right behind me. Shadows fell as fast as my guns and Suyef's staff could dispose of them. I tried to focus on those nearest the fleeing pair. Ahead, I saw guards begin to fill the hall, their own pulse guns out and firing at the assassins. The ceiling ripped away down the hall, in the same direction the siblings fled.

"Stay with them!" Suyef called out behind me. "Stay with them!"

A guard fell across my path. Just beyond, the siblings had paused to look back. I waved at them as I leapt over the guard, taking aim at more shadows as they fell. Suyef's staff whirled behind me, a dizzying swirl of fiery light dispatching shadows with hissing pops.

Suddenly, the hallway jolted to one side, sending my shots askew. The siblings tumbled down another hallway as another section of ceiling ripped in an explosion of tearing metal and electric pops. Sparks fell all around. I rushed toward the fallen pair, leaping over a guard.

"Look out!" Micaela screamed at me as my feet hit the ground.

I tumbled into a roll and heard a hissing pop just behind me. A quick glance showed Suyef standing there, staff outstretched. I jumped to my feet, and we rushed toward the fallen siblings.

"Get up!" the Nomad hissed, rushing past me and grabbing at Donovan.

"I can't move my ankle," Donovan said between clenched teeth.

I held out a hand to Micaela and pulled her upright.

"Get her out of here," Suyef whispered, nodding at us to go on. "I'll get him."

I tugged at her reluctant arm and moved down the hall as more shadows moved behind us. Suyef's staff reignited, and a blaze of pops and hisses echoed after us.

"Where do those things come from?" Micaela asked me when we slowed in a hallway junction.

"Not really sure. No one's seen hide nor hair of them for centuries," I whispered, leaning to look down a hall to the right and trying to get my bearings. "But we know of them. From ancient times. Something made during a great war some experts theorize led to the Splitting."

"How did they get here? And why?" Another tremor shook the building. "And what is doing that?"

Before I could voice my suspicions, the ceiling ripped away. Shards of metal and debris rained down in every direction. Acting on instinct, I shoved at Micaela's back, pushing her down the other hall.

"Don't stop!" I yelled. "Keep going."

The sound of shadows dropping to the ground, a soft thump followed by a hiss, echoed in every direction. Micaela bolted down the hall with more speed than I would have given her credit for. Shadows coalesced before me, and I unloaded my pulse guns into them the instant they formed. As fast as I could dispatch them, more appeared. The hall behind us swarmed with shifting shadows, their dangerous hands reaching toward me. My guns hissed, filling every shadow with a pulse of air. As they imploded, more came.

"Quentin!"

I turned my guns forward and unloaded everything they had into the new shadows that had formed between us as the ceiling ripped away. Micaela rushed out of sight as I fired. As she ran, the shadows chased her.

Including the ones behind me. I froze as the assassins rushed past, ignoring me. Slowly, my guns lowered as they moved on, not one stopping to touch me.

"What the . . . ," I whispered.

After a moment's pause, I raced after them, my guns ready. Whenever a shadow showed even the slightest inclination toward looking at me, I shot it. Most ignored me. The hallway continued in a bend of massing shadows and twisted metal. Soon, the shadows filled the passage, making any further progress impossible. I tried pulsing them out of my way, but more filled the gaps as fast as I could shoot. Worse, they started to take notice of me. A pair of shadows lunged at me, making it to within inches of my neck before I downed them. Something clattered to the ground as they did, and I dropped down to spy one of their weapons. On a whim, I grabbed it, took aim, and fired.

A blast of light shot out, careening down the hall. The shadows melted away from it, and it struck the wall several meters away. In the gap the shadows had left, I spied a grotesque, twisted suit of armor, layered pieces of hard metal folding around a giant body, standing over the prone figure of Micaela. A warped helmet sat atop the shoulders, sharp, jagged edges sweeping out and upward from the crown. A slit of black glass covered the eyes and a smaller slit the mouth. The shadows shifted again, covering the monstrosity from my sight. I took aim and fired. This time, they didn't move.

They screamed instead. As the pulse of light tumbled into them, they peeled away in boiling agony, a terrifying screech filling the air. I fired repeatedly, tearing the shadows away from me as I progressed. Finally, my path lay clear. The monster stood over a now-kneeling Micaela, his hand holding tightly to her braid. I took aim to fire, but a shadow lunged at me. I jerked to dodge the assassin, and my shot went wide, striking the wall near the monstrosity.

The monster pulled out a firearm of his own, and pulses of bright light burst from it down the hall at me. The creature barked something unintelligible, and shadows dropped to the ground all around. Tremors still shook the building as the shadows moved back in the direction the creature had just fired. Directly at me. I took aim and ripped through the assassins. Still they came, wave after wave perishing at the discharges of their own weapon. Behind me, I heard air-pulse guns going off. Mortac's guards had found me, lending their own weapons to my assault. The shadows unleashed their own fire at us, and men fell around me.

The battle raged on as we made our way down the hall. Shadows and guards fell left and right. Still we pushed on until the monstrosity came into sight again, holding Micaela's head back, a finger tracing down her exposed jugular. A guard next to me took aim and fired. The air pulse blasted into the beast's side, sending the pair sprawling down the hall. Micaela rolled away from the armored behemoth even as the guards around me cried out, cheering. The shadows poured out from the ceiling and floor, filling the space between Micaela and me. The guards and I unleashed a salvo of air and light at them as they fired back at us. A cacophony of pops and grunts filled the air as men and shadows perished together.

A terrifying scream echoed past me, and the entire hallway shook. Another section of ceiling ripped away as the echo faded, filling the room with smoke and debris. I dodged pieces of metal as more shadows thumped down behind me. Shielding my eyes from the dust, I rushed out across the open room and saw the monstrosity rushing away. Micaela was nowhere in sight. The ceiling ripped away in the opposite direction as the creature ran. The guards and I took aim and fired at the monstrosity, our shots missing and careening wildly down the hall. The weapon in my hand overheated, and I tossed it aside, spying another, larger one lying in the hall as I moved forward. Air pulses filled the space, shooting down the hall at shadows and the monster alike.

Fearing we'd hit Micaela, I waved the guards off and rushed down the hall myself. I could no longer see the beast, but I could see the path he'd left. Rather, the path whatever was outside had left as it ripped the roof to pieces. Another tremor shook the floor, and I fell against the wall to my left. Just around the bend, the monstrosity ripped a door away, disappearing inside. Not wasting a moment, I rushed after, the ground shaking horribly under me and knocking me flat on my stomach as I neared the entry. The wind rushed out of me as my eyes filled with tears. Shaking my head, I gasped for air, forcing my lungs to work as I pulled myself up.

What remained of the double doors lay in the entryway. Beyond, a room similar to the one we'd been in lay in ruins, the ceiling torn asunder and the table in the center knocked toward the door. Just beyond, I saw the head of the monster, its eyes trained down at something behind the table. An armored hand appeared over his head, a wicked blade held tightly in his fist.

My eyes still filled with water, I took aim, blinked once, and fired.

The creature's hand plunged when the blast of light struck him square in the top of his head. He froze, blade and hand just barely visible above the table. His hand trembled, and the eye slit flared red. With a great shudder, the armored monster fell to one side, out of sight.

The tremors stopped, and the building finally stood still. The room lay quiet. I stayed in the door, gun trained on the table.

Just as I opened my mouth to speak, a flash of red hair appeared over the table, and Micaela looked back at me.

CHAPTER 31

CHALLENGES

Micaela sat in the Queen's room as she always did: on the sofa, staring out the window. She wore a different, yet equally beautiful, gown of an identical turquoise to the previous one, this one lacking the embroidery around the neckline and down the dress. This time, I found her crying.

"What is it you find so saddening out that window, High One?" I asked by way of announcing my presence.

She turned her head, wiping at her tears. "Nothing out the window, Logwyn," she whispered. "Let's just say it's a lonely world for people like me."

I pondered her words, moving toward the table for another session.

"If you please, Logwyn, I'd rather do it here," she said, not moving. "My back is still recovering from yesterday on those benches."

I nodded and made my way over. Just beyond the sofa, previously concealed from my view by Micaela's head, stood a desk and chair.

"The Queen brought them to make your work over here easier," Micaela commented as I sat on the new seat.

"How thoughtful of her," I whispered. "She's monitoring our work here?"

"You think she's unaware of what you do simply because you aren't aware she's around?"

My eyes shifted from her to the recording device. Micaela smiled as realization made it to my face.

"Never underestimate anyone bearing that title," I said more to myself. "So, shall we continue?"

Micaela's smile faded as she sighed. "Must we?" she whispered, her face altering, a sorrowful look shifting in as fast as the night shield did on populated shells.

I frowned and shrugged. "This isn't my wish, High One. It's the Queen's."

"I guess it must be told."

After the attack, Mortac moved us into the main tower. From that room, we had a commanding view of the facility and, when the night shield lifted, the damage done to it. The entire roof of one of the surrounding superstructures lay mangled and gone. Gashes, in what many believed to be indestructible metal, told the tale. Something large and powerful had torn through the Ancient building like a knife through bread. Sparks of power still flared as the four of us stared in silence at the destruction.

I'm not sure how long we waited in that chamber staring at the damage before the warden came to see us. He joined us at the window in silence for a moment.

"We're not sure what it was," he whispered.

"Could the Questioner have some role in this?" I asked.

The warden shrugged. "Maybe. If so, colluding with anything large and powerful enough to do this is a capital offense."

"You mean colluding with a dragon," Donovan muttered. "Stinking Seekers breaking their own laws."

"We don't know this was a dragon," Mortac said, his voice quiet.

The four of us turned to look at him.

"What else could do that?" Quentin asked, pointing at the destruction below. "Those rents aren't carefully made with a cutting torch. Those look like claw marks."

Mortac nodded his head slowly. "I agree. But without proof, it's circumstantial." He looked at each of us in turn. "Anyone want to accuse a Questioner on circumstantial evidence?" When no one answered, he went on. "As I thought. If Colvinra had something to do with this, we'll need more evidence."

"If he can do this, we're not safe here," I said.

"You're not safe anywhere," he whispered, his voice so quiet I almost didn't hear it. His voice got louder. "But he won't try this again." He turned to look at me. "Any idea what he was after? Besides you?"

My eyes narrowed, and I glanced at my companions. I hadn't told them what the creature had demanded of me, so I shook my head. Mortac held my gaze a moment before nodding and moving toward the door.

"I've doubled the guards and deployed aerial sensors. If anything comes to try this again, we'll have more warning. For now, you're as safe as I can make you."

With that, he left, the doors sliding shut behind him.

"I don't trust him for a second," Donovan muttered, turning back to the window.

"No one does," Quentin said, "but he did lose a lot of men trying to help us." He sighed, his shoulders sagging. "A lot of them."

I looked at the floor when he turned to look at me.

"So," he said. "Care to explain to us?"

I looked back at him. "What?"

"Your face? Warning us?"

"That wasn't me," I insisted.

"Sure looked like you," Donovan said from the window.

I glared at him. "I've been with you all this time. It wasn't me."

Quentin shrugged. "I never said it was you. Just your face. Ideas?"

The last he directed at Suyef, who stood silently near the window, watching us all.

"It's a trick," he said. "She's correct in that she's been in our presence almost exclusively since this whole fiasco began. More than that, her brother has been with her longer. That wasn't a simple recording. Whoever did that was actively talking to us and aware of what was going on."

"So, she has a doppelganger out there?" Quentin asked, nodding at me.

"It's the only logical choice left," he said, eyes moving to watch me. "Anything else you want to tell us?"

I shifted, looking between them. "That . . . thing was after something."

"You?" Quentin asked, to which I shook my head.

"No, something it thought I had. Something it insisted I had."

"Did it say what?"

I shook my head again. "Just that I had it, that I've always had it, and that if I didn't give it to him, we'd all suffer."

The silence that fell lay heavy with questions. Thankfully, we stopped talking for the moment and rested. When we awoke, our meals had been delivered. Quentin and I passed the time getting acquainted, including him explaining how he and Suyef stumbled upon us. It still wasn't clear how much we could trust him, but the story did fit the circumstances. Despite that, it left me with more questions than answers. Just as I set in to asking some of them, the door opened. A guard indicated that only Quentin and I should follow him. He escorted us back to Mortac's office, where we found the warden sitting behind his desk, reading a report. He waved us forward to two chairs placed across from him.

"I have something to show you," he stated after we'd sat. "You'll recall my last words to you regarding our friend Colvinra, yes?" When we didn't respond, he added, "Regarding how persistent he is?"

We both nodded.

"This was just transmitted to me from the regional Seeker headquarters."

He slid a padd across the broad, smooth desk. Quentin picked it up first, read it, and frowned. He handed the device to me to read.

> To Warden, Prison Facility #2: You are hereby ordered to hand over any and all guests you have staying in your facility to be escorted out of the area. Your facility is not a secure location, and their presence there places them in danger. Please make use of the squad of Seekers we have currently dispatched to your location to ensure their safe return to the Central Dominance.

I glanced up at Mortac, his gray eyes locked on me again. "Didn't you say that because we are guests, the Seekers couldn't take us?"

"It would seem our Questioner is more resourceful than we imagined," the warden stated, nodding once at the padd. "He's convinced the higher-ups that our facility is unsafe for unauthorized personnel." He spread his hands to either side. "Considering last night's events, he may be right. Regardless, he's tied my hands. If I refuse the order, he has grounds to take over the entire facility. I'm not so concerned about the location, but it would make keeping you out of his hands complicated."

"Why do you care so much about keeping me away from him?" I asked.

Something distorted his face, a look of momentary anger and anguish. As quick as it appeared, it vanished, replaced by his customary steely gaze.

"Let's just say," he answered, voice cold and hard, "I have my reasons for wanting to thwart this particular Questioner."

"He's taken someone close to you for questioning?" Quentin asked.

Mortac's gaze darted over to Quentin. "For someone who is generally clueless, sometimes you hit too close to the mark."

"Clueless?" Quentin frowned. "You've just met me."

Mortac's eyebrows raised and lowered, head nodding. "Indeed."

I cleared my throat. Mortac glared at Quentin a moment longer; then his gaze softened as he looked back at me.

"Your companion is correct in his guess," the warden said. "This particular Seeker has caused me trouble in the past. Great trouble."

"Still doesn't explain why you'd be willing to lose your facility for me."

"I won't lose this facility," he stated. "Not until I'm ready to leave it. Mark my word on that."

Quentin cleared his throat. "It won't take the Seekers long to bring in more squads. You resist this one, more will follow."

Mortac nodded. "You see my dilemma. How to foil this one Seeker without bringing the wrath of all of them down on me."

"I don't suppose we could sneak away," I suggested, shrugging as I said it.

Mortac shook his head.

"Didn't think so."

"For the short term, the only option to keep you completely in my control is to detain you," Mortac stated, his voice lowering in volume.

Quentin shifted, standing up. "So, you'd have us turn ourselves over to you to keep us from Seeker hands?"

"Not you, my hotheaded friend," Mortac said, eyes never leaving me. "Her and her brother."

"How does that help us?" I asked.

"Colvinra may be crafty, but he must abide by the laws," the warden explained. "Seeker laws regarding this facility are very specific. If you're a prisoner here, you're under this facility's complete control. To take you from it would involve the kind of review I don't think even Questioners are willing to undergo."

"Bureaucrats foiling bureaucrats," Quentin muttered, chuckling. "I like it."

"You would," Mortac whispered, almost to himself.

I eyed him warily, still uncertain how much we could trust him. "I'm with Quentin on this one. Regardless of who has us, I'm not too keen on being detained."

Mortac nodded. "A wise precaution," he said, pointing at Quentin. "I can't arrest him or my nephew, though. Detaining Seekers will only make the situation worse." He looked pointedly at Quentin and shifted his head to emphasize the next thing he said. "Even fake ones."

I glanced at Quentin, then at the warden. Although surprised, I had to admit part of me expected the warden had known.

Quentin's eyes narrowed. "Why do you say that?" he asked.

"Come, now, you didn't think the room was that secure, did you?"

Quentin nodded. "Well, that does give you an out, if you want to take it."

The warden shook his head. "No, impersonating a Seeker is a crime punishable only by Seekers. I arrest you for that one, and Colvinra can seize all of you."

"Why me?" I asked. "I didn't know he was a fake."

"You did long enough to hide it from Colvinra, and that's all he'll need," Mortac pointed out. "No, I make that arrest and I might as well just hand you all over to him directly." He glared at Quentin. "I'm compelled, at least for the moment, to conceal your stupidity."

For a split second, I thought I heard him say the word *again* at the end of that sentence, but I must have imagined it. Still, the longer I was around this warden, the more I began to wonder how much he was hiding. Glancing at Quentin, I pondered the possibility that the warden could know him and that the two of them could be hiding that fact from me. Try as I might, I couldn't think of why they would. Still, it bore thinking on. Quentin, I noticed, looked confused but said nothing.

"The thing I don't get is why his orders to detain us before don't supersede your authority here," I said, trying to wrap my brain around the situation. "Shouldn't that make your attempts null?"

Mortac shot a glare at me. "Not if I haven't seen such an order."

My face flushed. I should have thought of that one. "Ah, well, forget I mentioned that part."

Mortac nodded. "I think I will."

"Still, regarding that thing she didn't mention," Quentin continued, pointing at me, "why hasn't Colvinra made a point of bringing that up?"

The warden shrugged. "He has his reasons. Could be he's holding that as a last resort, although why is beyond me." Mortac shook his head, stringy hair shifting on either side of his face. "I gave up ever understanding that fool long ago."

"Could the orders be faked?" my pseudocompanion asked the warden. Mortac frowned at him, so he continued. "Could Colvinra have faked the detainment orders? It would explain why he doesn't want to use them just yet. You might request confirmation."

"That's standard procedure anyway," the warden stated. "It would buy us a little time for the bureaucrats in charge to verify them."

"Right, which means he would want to start that process right away," Quentin went on, sitting up and picking up speed. "He would've brought those up at the outset so he'd have his answer by now." He paused, lips pursed, eyes narrowed. "Something doesn't add up here."

Mortac nodded. "That's the first intelligent thing you've said," he said, smiling.

Quentin frowned and shook his head. "You're not helping."

"I'm not sure how I *can* help you," the warden stated, spreading his hands out before him.

A thought bubbled up through the turmoil inside my head. "What if they tried to take us from you?" I asked, nodding at Quentin.

Mortac looked at him. "You mean as in breaking them out?"

Quentin nodded.

"We're allowed to detain you."

"And then?" Quentin asked.

"An inquiry board is sent to ascertain what happens. Colvinra would have to recuse himself from a seat on that board because he is here."

"So, all we need to do is try to kidnap her and her brother from you, and you retain control of us," Quentin said.

"For now," Mortac pointed out. "Until the inquiry board comes and investigates. How long do you think your guise will hold up then?"

"I'm just trying to buy us some time here," Quentin stated, shrugging. "You made it sound like that's what you needed."

"Yes, but to what end?" Mortac asked. "All you're doing is delaying her and her brother from falling under his control."

Quentin sat for a moment, mind pondering the situation.

As he sat there, another thought bubbled to the surface. "Well, what if you did actually take or kidnap us?" I asked, looking at Quentin. "Where would we go?"

Quentin looked out the window. "There," he said pointing.

Mortac and I looked out the window. All that greeted my gaze was the Wilds.

Mortac turned to look at him. "Are you insane as well as stupid?" he asked, standing up. "You can't take her into the Wilds. No one goes in there—"

"Exactly. No one will follow us," Quentin said.

"Except Seekers," Mortac said, closing his eyes for a second. "You didn't let me finish. Seekers go into the Wilds. Colvinra won't be shy about following you in there." He glanced at me. "Besides, I'm not letting you just *take* her in there. That place is dangerous."

I shifted, discomfort regarding the warden's particular interest in me returning. I had never met him before, but those looks he gave me left me with the strong impression he thought I had.

Quentin shrugged, shaking his head. "I'm not a big fan of it myself, but what other option do we have?"

"Anything is better than the Wilds," Mortac hissed, waving a hand at the window, his calm demeanor suddenly gone. "There's a reason it has that name and a shield around it. Between broken weather controls and shifts in the code, the place is very unstable. And that's not discussing the creatures in there."

"We don't have to stay in there long. I trust Suyef to find us a safe way in and back out."

"I don't doubt he could," the warden said, running a hand through his hair. "But even his prowess in the wilderness isn't going to help you out there." He leaned over the desk, pointing at Quentin. "That place doesn't want you there. I know you're stupid, but you're not that clueless, are you? The environmental controls were destroyed long ago, and what wildlife there still is on this shell is out there."

Quentin stood up, bringing himself to stand right before Mortac. "I'm getting a little tired of you calling me stupid," he whispered. "I've never met you in my life. Where do you get off judging me?"

"Stupid ideas like that one, for starters," Mortac said, standing up to match Quentin's height.

I got up, sensing another intervention might be needed.

"I haven't heard a single idea come from you here," Quentin said.

The warden smiled. "When one occurs to me, I can promise you it will be better than anything you've said so far."

"I won't hold my breath," Quentin retorted.

"Boys, if you're done thumping your chests and seeing who can grunt the loudest," I said, drawing both of their eyes to me, "you're not getting anywhere with this."

"It's our only option, Mortac," Quentin continued, looking back at the warden.

Another thought. "Unless you can find a way to trick Colvinra into kidnapping them," I suggested.

Quentin glared at me. "What good would that do?"

I pointed at the warden. "Then Mortac could detain him and his Seekers until an inquiry board arrives."

"That's as unlikely as either of your escape plans to happen," Mortac retorted, slapping a hand down on a light shining up from his desk as a signal chimed. "What?"

"Questioner Colvinra to see you, sir," a voice stated, echoing through the room.

Mortac looked at each of us in turn. "Send him up."

"Yes, sir," the voice answered, and Mortac tapped the same place on his smooth desk, the light turning off.

"Coincidence?" I asked, turning to look at the entrance to the room.

"If there's one thing I've learned, there's no such thing," Mortac muttered, sitting down in his chair, one hand brushing his hair back behind his ear. "Especially where this Questioner is involved."

The lift slid open behind me, and Quentin tensed. I motioned at him to sit down, but he didn't see me.

"Ah, Warden, I see you're occupied," the Questioner said from the lift, his usual cowl hanging down his back, his entire face revealed. "And with just the person I'm interested in seeing." The doors slid shut. "How fortuitous."

"Yes," Mortac whispered. "Fortuitous." He glared at the Questioner and said in a louder voice, "Can I help you, Colvinra?"

"Tsk-tsk, Warden. Don't forget your place," the man hissed, stepping into view and ignoring the glower Quentin leveled toward him. His cold, black eyes remained locked on the warden. "Titles, after all, are the only decorum we will find out here."

"I care little for your usurped titles, Colvinra," Mortac replied, returning the Questioner's steely gaze with his own.

Colvinra smiled, a small thing that hardly touched his face. "Yet you call me that name."

Mortac shrugged. "Until you provide me with a reason not to, I will."

"Ah, my dear friend, when did we come to this?" Colvinra sighed, shaking his head and finally glancing at Quentin and me. "It's these two, isn't it? They've come between us again."

Quentin mouthed the word *again* at me. I shrugged and looked at Mortac. The look he gave to Colvinra nearly froze my heart.

"You know full well why we've come to this, you fool," Mortac whispered. "You took my wife from me."

Silence followed as the warden and Questioner traded glares. Quentin shifted past the Questioner to stand just over my right shoulder. Colvinra ignored him, keeping his eyes on Mortac.

"What happened to her was your choice."

"Not to sacrifice her," Mortac hissed. "I wanted to save her. And you promised to help me. Instead you took your chance to prove yourself right, and I lost her in the process."

"You know why I did what I did," the Seeker said to the warden. "What happened, how it ended. That's not my fault. The calculations were too much."

"I don't want to hear your excuses, Colvinra," Mortac stated, his jaw tight. "You've taken enough from me. You'll not have her."

The Questioner spared a glance for me, then looked up at Quentin. "You'll forgive my boldness, Mortac, but I took the liberty of sending for your other 'guests,'" he said, not taking his eyes from Quentin. "I have questions regarding this one's training, which I'll ask while awaiting the release of your guests for their safe return to the Central Dominance."

"We're not from the city," I retorted, drawing the Questioner's black eyes to me. "If anything, we're going back to our settlement."

The Questioner smiled, again a small thing that didn't much alter his face. "You forget our orders to detain you, my dear," he said, his voice quiet. "Those will need attended to before you are allowed to go home."

"Allowed to go home?" Quentin asked. "I saw your orders, Questioner. They said questioning only. I saw no charges leveled against either her or her brother."

"You will remember your place, Seeker," Colvinra hissed, his black eyes locking on to Quentin. "Speaking of which, where is your supervisor?"

"We were invited up here at the warden's request," Quentin said, pointing at me. "Actually, she was. I volunteered to accompany her."

The door hissed open, and I turned to see Suyef and my brother walking into the room with one of Mortac's guards and a pair of Colvinra's Seekers.

"Your men will leave my office at once," Mortac stated, standing up.

Colvinra turned his head to stare at Mortac. "Excuse me?"

"My facility, my rules," the warden said. "You two, get out and wait for your leader downstairs. Now!"

The Seekers looked to Colvinra, who took a moment before nodding at them to leave. They retreated with Mortac's guard, leaving the six of us. I got up and ran over to Donovan, hugging him tight. He glared at the Questioner, but remained silent, for which I was grateful. The last thing this room needed was a bit more hotheaded testosterone. Suyef moved to stand near Quentin.

"Is there a reason my trainee is here without me, Questioner?" the Nomad asked.

"The warden can answer that one," Colvinra said, pointing at Mortac.

"You know why they are here," Mortac answered Suyef's look, pointing at Quentin and me.

Suyef nodded. "That I didn't mind," he said. "What I mind is the Questioner being here with my trainee. It's highly inappropriate."

"I sent for you, didn't I?" the Questioner asked. "I was here but a few moments before you."

Suyef glanced at Quentin, who nodded.

"I assure you," Mortac added, "your trainee provided escort only, and the Questioner has not been interfering with your training."

"As you are here now," Colvinra continued, "I have some questions regarding this one's training. His respect for rank is lacking, and from what I saw of your work with him before, his combat training is all but nonexistent."

"He is progressing in the latter," Suyef stated, looking at Quentin. "His attitude is a problem, but nothing I've had a problem with." He looked at the Questioner. "Maybe you're just a bit too sensitive."

Colvinra glared at the Nomad. "Don't let your position embolden you too much, Off-sheller," he said, his eyes widening as he spoke. He even took a step toward the Nomad, who held his ground. "I can have you escorted off this shell easily enough, and your trainee reassigned."

"That would require an inquiry board," Suyef replied, clasping his hands behind his back. "A board that will dig into your mission out here as much as mine. Do your orders carry a protection against such an inquiry, as mine do?"

From the way Colvinra shifted, I gathered they did not.

Suyef smiled. "I thought not. We'll be released long before you will be, so maybe we should avoid the matter entirely."

Colvinra looked at Quentin, then back at the Nomad. "As a Questioner, I can inspect your training to make sure you're conducting it in accordance with Seeker laws." He turned to look at Mortac. "We'll need your arena."

Mortac shrugged. "An arena I can provide, but that doesn't answer the other issues."

Colvinra grinned genuinely for the first time since he had entered the room. "My friend, I think what we are about to do will solve all of that."

If only he knew how correct he was.

CHAPTER 32

THE ARENA

The arena in question lay on the far side of the outpost from the Wilds. It stood connected to the holding circles by a large tunnel, which allowed the prison population to migrate out of and into what amounted to viewing stands. Row upon secure row filled upward from the base of the arena, with thick, clear walls keeping the prisoners isolated in the row they chose to enter. Along the base of the stands stood a length of seating left unsecure. The arena field, as it was, stood bare and empty, with a single entrance along the same side as the tunnel. A walkway extended out above the concentric prison circles and along the tunnel, allowing the prison guards and, in this case, us to walk out. We entered a small door just above the tunnel and followed a narrow hallway to the unsecured row of seating.

There I found myself sitting with my brother on my right, Mortac to my left with several of his guards on either side, and two of Colvinra's Seekers standing in either direction. More of the warden's guards and a ragtag bunch of raiders filled in the rest of the seating in that row. I noticed the Seeker squad and their squad leader were positioned among the raiders around the arena. Above us, all around, thousands of prisoners filed in and began pounding on the glass, filling the space with a cacophony of anticipation.

"The people do enjoy a good fight," Mortac muttered, noticing my gaze. "It distracts them from their predicament."

I pressed my lips tightly together and didn't acknowledge him. The man made me feel uncomfortable, more so than the Questioner. The way he looked at me, as one would look at someone dear to him, made my skin crawl and filled me with an urge to run away.

"So, what's going on?" Donovan asked.

I shrugged and leaned closer to my brother, putting an arm around his shoulder. "You know about as much as I do."

"I doubt that," my brother joked. "I get the feeling you and Quentin have been talking a lot more than Suyef and I."

"Quiet, that one," I whispered.

"A stone is quiet. That one makes a stone sound like a gossip," Donovan said, shaking his head and smiling. "I think he said all of three words to me the entire time we were in that room."

"You could have sat with us," I pointed out.

Donovan waved a hand at me. "I don't buy his story for a second."

"Then consider yourself lucky," Mortac said, leaning forward to look at my brother. "Such doubts will serve you well with most people."

"I also doubt that," my brother retorted. "People aren't all as deceitful or untrustworthy as you lot."

Mortac shook his head, smiling. "Youth," he said, sitting back.

"So, what's happening here?" my brother asked the warden.

He shrugged. "Seeker nonsense." When my brother frowned at him, Mortac chuckled and asked, "Have you ever seen a Seeker fight?"

My brother shook his head.

"Well, I gather you're about to."

"Wait, Seekers fighting Seekers?" Donovan asked, eyes shifting to take in the Seekers standing nearby. "That can happen?"

Mortac laughed. "Seekers are no different from the rest of us, boy," the warden said, shifting in his seat, hands forming a steeple before his face. "Crafty, jealous, petty creatures that have all the same weaknesses." He arched an eyebrow as he looked at Donovan. "You don't believe they're immortal, do you?"

Donovan shrugged. "No, but nearly so."

"Seekers are as mortal as the rest of us," the warden stated. "Just better at preventing your knowing so." He nodded at the Seeker to his left. "They all wear that garb to mask what they look like beneath. Notice, most Seekers are relatively identical in size and build. And the area of their face you most often see is free of any telltale markings or scars. That's to make them forgettable."

"What's your point?" Donovan asked, shrugging and shaking his head slightly.

"To keep you in the dark about how many there are and how long they live. To create the illusion of immortality." Mortac pointed at my brother. "Can you recall ever even hearing a story about a Seeker dying?"

My brother shook his head, as did I when Mortac looked at me.

"Precisely. You don't have to be immortal if no one can tell you apart and no one remembers any of your deaths."

"So, why let Suyef and his predecessors join?" I asked.

Mortac shrugged. "Bureaucratic nonsense, that. It's what happens when politicians make military decisions."

"The Seekers aren't military," Donovan protested.

The look Mortac gave my brother spoke volumes. "You go on thinking that, boy. They'll leave you alone after your predicament resolves itself."

My brother opened his mouth to reply but stopped when the entrance to the arena field opened.

Colvinra entered, with Suyef and Quentin following a few paces behind. Each carried a staff in hand. Our former roommates stayed close together, deep in discussion as the Questioner strode to the middle of the arena and turned to face them. They stopped about ten paces from him, still talking.

"Those two had better focus, or this is going to get ugly," Mortac muttered, waving a hand at Quentin and Suyef.

"Two on one—they should have the advantage, yes?" Donovan asked.

Mortac barked a short laugh. "Against a Questioner? Maybe if they had a squad of their own," he said. "Suyef's good; he's a Nomad. But Questioners earn their rank for good reason." Mortac shook his head. "This will be a much greater challenge than anything Suyef's faced before."

Suyef and Quentin finished their discussion and separated, moving around the Questioner. Colvinra kept his eyes on Suyef, ignoring Quentin.

"I'm still not sure why an inspection requires a fight," I commented, then snorted. "Males."

Mortac chuckled. "Will ever be males," he added. He shrugged, shaking his head. "You won't catch me pretending to understand Seekers, but men I get, and Colvinra is as male as they come. Extremely simpleminded for someone as intelligent as he is."

Below us, the Seeker had moved, shifting his back to the tunnel as Suyef continued to circle him. Quentin remained where he was, standing closer to us.

"Why would someone you claim is so smart resort to something like this?" I asked.

"Seeker laws require it," Mortac said. "Apparently, this is a part of their training, and Colvinra thinks Quentin is suffering under Suyef's training." He smiled and waved a hand at the arena. "Hence the spectacle."

"Will you two pipe down?" Donovan hissed. "I'm trying to watch."

"They're not doing anything yet," I pointed out, smacking his shoulder before turning to glare at Mortac. "This spectacle is as much your fault as theirs." I waved a hand at the prisoners above us, all banging against the glass for the fight to begin. "You didn't need to let them come watch."

"Why deny them some entertainment?" the warden asked.

"Distract them from their impending doom?" I shot back.

Mortac grimaced. "As explained already, I have no control over that. If that stops, the raiders and the Seekers will remove me."

"An excuse for doing nothing," I stated, crossing my arms and sitting back in my seat.

Mortac moved next to me, and I heard him take a breath to respond, but he never got the chance. At that moment, Colvinra struck.

The Questioner lunged across the field, staff swinging in his right hand to strike at Suyef. The Nomad parried the strike, spinning and directing a kick at the Questioner. Colvinra blocked the kick with his arm and shoved into the Nomad's back. Suyef rolled away, swinging his staff back in the direction of his attacker. The Questioner dodged backward, head darting to check on Quentin, as he avoided Suyef's staff. Quentin remained where he was, staff held at the ready, eyes watching the fight.

Suyef didn't wait long. He jumped and attacked the Questioner, staff spinning to strike first at the head, then the feet. Colvinra whipped his staff up, then spun a tip down to catch both strikes. Suyef persisted, his staff darting around in a blur, Colvinra's spinning as quickly on the defensive. The crack of each strike echoed in the arena, and the silence caught my attention. I glanced up at the prisoners to find them pressed to the glass, mesmerized by the fight. I looked back down to see Suyef backflip over Colvinra's swipe to his legs. He landed and drove his staff down at his opponent, who brought his up in both hands to catch the staff. The resulting crack resounded off the glass walls, and a groan rolled down from the prisoners. Colvinra shoved against the Nomad, driving him backward and separating. The two men came to a halt, five paces between them, staffs at the ready. Neither was winded or sweating.

"This could take a while," Mortac muttered. At my arched eyebrow, he said, "Colvinra won't stop this until he's won, and Suyef is as much a match for him in a staff fight as he's seen in a long time."

"I thought you said a Questioner was more than a match for a Nomad?" Donovan asked, never taking his eyes from the combatants.

"The Questioner hasn't started fighting yet," Mortac answered. "Only the Seeker has."

Donovan frowned and shook his head. "You make no sense, Warden."

"Just keep watching." Mortac nodded at the arena floor.

Suyef and Colvinra resumed their fight. Staffs spun, striking here and there, kicks and punches in between. The two were clearly a match in staffs, and both ignored Quentin, who remained where he'd been the whole time. *What could he be thinking?* I wondered. Why wasn't he helping Suyef? I noticed him watching the stands and followed his gaze.

"You see their strategy," Mortac said, his voice barely audible as the audience above began to grow loud.

I frowned. "He's watching the other Seekers?"

Mortac nodded. "You think their placement is an accident? On all sides of the arena floor?"

I shook my head.

Mortac smiled. "Always a thinker."

I ignored the comment, but the feeling returned, the itch of discomfort along my spine at this man's air of familiarity. I focused on Quentin to distract myself.

"Seems like a waste to me," Donovan muttered. "Go get the Questioner. Knock him out of the fight."

"You think they'll let that happen?" Mortac asked.

My brother nodded.

"You're more a fool than you look."

Donovan glared at the warden. "You talk a lot for someone just sitting here."

Mortac shrugged. "Words are easy," he said, laughing. "And this isn't my fight."

Donovan sniffed at the warden and went back to watching the trio in the arena. Suyef had been forced back against the wall by the Questioner, but neither seemed to have the advantage. Indeed, in the next instant, the Nomad caught a strike by Colvinra's staff, pivoted, and flung the Questioner to the side. He rolled and came up facing Suyef, now with his back to the wall. Neither looked even remotely tired. Quentin remained on watch for the other Seekers to do something. He didn't have to wait long.

As Colvinra launched another series of attacks, he waved at one of the Seekers opposite from me. He vaulted over the railing and landed on the far side of the arena floor, facing Quentin. Suyef barked something, and Quentin launched himself, not at the new Seeker, but at Colvinra. This tactic caught the pair of Seekers off guard as Suyef and his companion brought both of their staffs to bear on the Questioner. Colvinra spun, his staff a blur deflecting the assault from both sides. The new Seeker wasted only a moment before leaping after Quentin. Suyef launched himself into a roll, coming up before the new Seeker and cracking him across the chest with his staff. The Nomad turned, bringing his attack back to bear on Colvinra as Quentin, who'd held the Questioner's attention as Suyef struck the other Seeker, lunged to strike a blow at the new Seeker's head. The man ducked, but Quentin was ready. As his staff shot past the man's head, he spun into a sweeping kick. The Seeker tumbled to the ground as Quentin finished his attack with a crack of his staff to the fallen man's head and returned to fight with Colvinra.

At that moment, the other three Seekers vaulted the wall and landed on the arena floor. Donovan jumped to his feet, calling out to warn Quentin and Suyef, but he needn't have bothered. Even as the new attackers landed, the pair had shifted around, placing Colvinra between them and the new attackers, the arena wall at their back.

"Nice strategy," Mortac stated. When I glanced at him, he continued. "Now only three of them at a time can attack." When I opened my mouth to ask how this was an advantage, he said, "The fourth must either commit and compel one of the others to shift, or stay back."

"They're still outnumbered," I muttered.

"But they have weapons," he said, nodding at the staffs. "Among the Seekers, only Colvinra has one."

"It's not fair!" Donovan yelled, shaking a fist at the Seekers. "Cowards!"

"Battle is never fair," Mortac whispered to my brother, who didn't hear. "Ever."

Suyef and Quentin held their own, the pair fending off attacks from Colvinra and two of the Seekers. Their staffs made it difficult for the Seekers to press their numbers, and even as Quentin and Suyef appeared to be flagging, so was Colvinra. The Questioner dodged a strike from Suyef and then Quentin as the pair spun back and forth, keeping the other two Seekers at bay. Colvinra lunged toward Quentin's legs, but he shifted away, spinning his staff to deflect the strike and turning to block a kick from his other attacker. Suyef knocked the other Seeker to the ground and vaulted toward the Questioner's back, screaming. Colvinra, his back exposed, dropped and rolled to his left, away from the fray and toward the fourth Seeker. He came to his feet and ordered the other Seeker to attack. As that Seeker moved in, Suyef and Quentin each struck a blow at Quentin's remaining attacker, knocking him to the ground. He fell there, motionless; Suyef shifted toward his previously fallen foe, who was now on his feet, and Quentin turned to face the last Seeker.

"And now the odds are relatively even," Mortac stated.

"You said a Questioner breaks a tie," Donovan reminded him.

Mortac nodded. "Usually it does," he said, eyeing Colvinra as he fell back from the fight. Overhead, the prisoners were in a frenzy, pounding the glass and screaming. "Our Questioner seems to be holding back a little."

"Why would he do that?" I asked, my eyes moving around the arena, watching the prisoners. "And why are they getting so frantic?"

"There's no love for Seekers among that lot, I assure you," Mortac replied, waving a dismissive hand at the lot of them. "Had you been paying more attention to them, you'd have noticed they only got really worked up when the first Seeker fell, and that second one going down for good sent them over the edge." He pointed at Colvinra. "No, he's up to something, and I'm not sure what."

I tried to pull my eyes back down to the fight, but something about the prisoners bothered me. Something with how they were frantically pounding against the walls, as if they were trying to get away from something.

At that moment, a shadow shifted overhead, darting across the heads of the prisoners. I turned to follow it and felt my heart freeze.

Dragons.

My heart raced as the Seeker shifted away from me. To my right lay the prone figure of the Seeker we'd managed to knock out. Suyef remained at my left. Beyond him, one Seeker stood, favoring a leg. Before us, the third Seeker stood at the ready, having just escaped a strike from my staff. Colvinra remained behind him, watching us, his staff in hand. Overhead, the prisoners were nearly rioting, pounding against the walls. When the last Seeker had fallen, the noise had grown thunderous, and part of me wondered if the glass would hold.

I shook my head and focused on the Seeker before me. I gripped the staff and again whispered a silent thanks to Suyef and his blasted lessons. With his help, this fight hadn't gone nearly as badly as it might have. Having the weapons gave us an advantage, and it still baffled me why Colvinra had fled with his instead of giving it to one of his Seekers. Still, two down, and only three to go. Our chances looked pretty good at that point.

Then the shadow fell over the arena. At first, I ignored it, thinking it a possible distraction. When the Seeker looked up and began to retreat, that was my clue something was wrong. I craned my head around but saw nothing.

"Quentin," Suyef hissed, pointing his staff toward the sky.

I spun and saw something just disappear from sight beyond the top of the arena. Enough had been visible to fill me with dread.

"Dragons!" I yelled, to be heard over the crowd, and glanced at the Seekers, who'd moved back and left their fallen behind. "We're exposed out here."

Suyef nodded. "Colvinra, we need to get out of here!" the Nomad bellowed over to the Questioner.

The man didn't answer, just stared up at the sky, a hungry look on his face.

"That man is obsessed with those beasts," Suyef said, grabbing my shoulder and pulling me along. "Let's go."

As we stepped forward, something in the air behind us changed. The wind picked up, howling past us. I turned to find the arena disappearing into the ground as an alert sounded from the outpost to the west. All around us, the protective shelter the arena walls had offered us vanished, the concentric rows of glass prisons folding away as we'd seen before, pushing the prisoners out into the open. With the walls gone, the sight beyond came into full view, and I stopped dead in my tracks.

Overhead soared nearly a hundred dragons, each one in vary-
ing shades of dark red. They ranged in size and length, with grotesque hornlike structures jutting from the tops of their skulls and
protruding from their spines. Some had massive wings, spreading
as wide as two or three of the smaller ones. All were enormous
compared to us.

And every one bore down on the unprotected mass of terrified
people fleeing toward the outpost.

"Quentin!" Suyef yelled. "The Questioner!"

I spun around, eyes scanning for Colvinra. With his silvery
robes, he stood out among the rags the panicking prisoners wore.
Colvinra looked to be making his way through the fleeing mass, not
toward the outpost, but toward where Mortac's guards were fending off crowds of prisoners trying to attack the warden. I could just
make out Micaela huddled beyond the man, clinging to her brother.

"Come on!" I yelled, and we charged after the Questioner.

When the alert sounded, Mortac's men jumped up around us. The
warden cursed and barked orders to them.

"Form a circle! Keep them away from us!" he yelled.

I looked around in bewilderment as the arena began to vanish. As with the prison, the walls folded away and shifted down
into the ground. In a few seconds, where an arena had once stood,
we found ourselves standing in the open desert, the shell's edge in
the distance, the towering outpost behind. All around, the mass of
prisoners, now loose, began fleeing for the safety of the structure.

"Keep tight!" a guard bellowed, the men forming a shield
around us as the prisoners fled the dragons.

I tried to look up to the beasts and saw too many to count. The
color stood out: all red, the color of blood. It sent a chill down my

spine. We began to move, so I grabbed Donovan's arm and pulled him along.

The prisoners ignored us for the most part, more worried about fleeing the threat circling overhead. Still, when the outpost failed to let them in, they'd no doubt turn on us. Mortac seemed to have the same idea. He directed his circle of guards to move, not toward the outpost, but north, around the side of the structure. With the panicking prisoners clamoring against the one entrance on this side, there was no way we could get in. As we cut across the flow of bodies, a few raiders in their worn-down cloaks that looked like Seeker robes came into view here and there, defending themselves. They never stood a chance alone or in pairs like that. A few prisoners flung themselves at the phalanx of men encircling us, but those that did fell to the ground, unconscious, stunned by the pulse guns Mortac's men carried. I tried to get a glimpse of Quentin and Suyef but only saw the flowing cloak of some Seeker moving through the crowd after us.

Overhead, the dragons bellowed as one, an earsplitting cry that sent the prisoners into an apoplectic frenzy. Those nearest the wall were soon crushed as men and women alike climbed atop those nearest the wall, trying to reach its apex. As the echoes of the dragons' cries fell around us, they struck, diving down into the mass of bodies nearest the wall. Entire swaths of people vanished. The beasts soared high into the sky, their prizes clenched tightly in their claws.

"Keep moving!" Mortac yelled, his head constantly turning to look behind us. "Keep moving!"

I followed his gaze and felt a new chill tickle my spine. Colvinra, eyes on me, was coming through the chaos. I turned to pick up my pace, and the bodies began to fall from the sky.

CHAPTER 33

TAKEN

I tried in vain to keep Micaela and Donovan in my sight, and watched in horror as the dragons began bombing the chaotic mass of people with the bodies of those they'd grabbed. Wave after wave they came, swooping down to scoop up as many of the prisoners as they could and flying high over the chaos to drop their prizes to the ground. It was impossible to tell where they were dropping them, but I could guess.

"Suyef!" I called to the Nomad, who was using his staff to keep the panicking prisoners at bay. "The dragons!"

He looked in the direction where we'd last seen Micaela and her brother. He nodded and swung his staff in a sweeping arc before him. The prisoners fell away, and we pushed forward, trying to get through the throng. A body fell near me, landing on two of the prisoners. I turned away to avoid seeing the carnage.

"Ghastly beasts!" Suyef yelled, waving a fist at a dragon as it flew by.

"Don't they just take prisoners?" I asked, shifting closer to the Nomad as we dodged another falling body.

"Green ones do," he said, looking up at the red monsters flying over us. "Red ones," he grunted, and knocked aside a prisoner that had launched himself at us. "I'd say no."

I swung my staff, striking the leg of another prisoner as he tried to flank Suyef. "Where's Colvinra?"

Suyef pointed to his left, toward the outpost. I stepped over another fallen prisoner and risked a glance. The Questioner was bogged down, he and his two remaining Seekers fending off even more prisoners.

"They're all fleeing right at him!" I yelled, jumping to Suyef's aid as a big, burly prisoner tried to pick up a smaller one and throw him at the Nomad.

Suyef twisted under the screaming prisoner as he flew through the air, striking at the knee of the burly man. I hit him across the head to finish the job, and he fell with a crash between us.

"Move!" Suyef yelled.

We bolted through a gap in the crowd and heard a scream behind us. I glanced over my shoulder to see a dragon swooping past, grabbing the fallen burly man and another fleeing prisoner and taking to the sky. As I watched the dragon fly away, my eyes caught sight of the Questioner. A dragon had flown right past him, clearing away a large swath, the remaining prisoners scattering to get away. He now had a clear path to Mortac's circle of guards.

"Suyef!" I cried out, charging toward the Questioner and his Seekers, hoping the Nomad was close behind.

Mortac's men were falling around us now. Fending off disorganized, panicky prisoners was one thing; the dragon onslaught from above they could do nothing about. As the bodies fell all around us, one by one his men fell with them. I shielded my eyes from it, clinging to my brother as we fled. We couldn't help but see the bodies fall to the ground, exploding with the force of the impact, and hear the terrified screams of the prisoners suddenly cut off as they landed.

Mortac had taken to helping his men now. As prisoners would break through the line, he'd level his own sidearm at them and pulse them into unconsciousness. He spun about us, shooting in all directions as needed. A shot here or there, and a prisoner would fall. Try as he might, the warden could only do so much to help his beleaguered guards. More and more prisoners came. We had no choice. Donovan and I took up weapons from some of the fallen guards and helped fend the prisoners off. I had to keep reminding myself it was only air we were shooting at them. Well, air moving with enough force to blast them backward a short distance and usually knock them unconscious. Still, it made me feel bad. I saw no other choice. The crazed men and women had no way of telling us apart from anyone else: between the dragons above and the guards and Seekers below, the crowd had descended into a boiling mob of anger and fear.

Another guard fell to the ground near me. I moved to cover him and check his injury. My father had taught me only the rough basics of injury and treatment, but the man had fallen trying to protect us. Something needed to be done for him. He lay unconscious, and no obvious injury stood out. I had to leave him be. I looked up, and no one was coming at me for the moment. To my left, Donovan had his pulse gun trained on an approaching man. Mortac, seeing my brother's hesitation, leveled his gun over Donovan's shoulder and downed him.

"Pity is only going to get you killed out here," the warden hissed, whirling to take down a man charging from the other direction.

Donovan moved up to stand next to the guards and began firing at anyone that moved near. I turned my gaze back to the carnage around us and tried again to catch sight of Quentin. The sight that greeted me scared me to the core.

Colvinra had broken free of the crowd, his arm waving at a dragon as it swept low, scaring most of the crowd fleeing in its path. He made his way toward us, his two remaining Seekers following behind. I cried out to Mortac, pointing at the approaching Questioner. The warden downed another charging prisoner and spun around to face the new threat.

At that moment, Quentin and Suyef broke into sight, charging at the Questioner and his men. Their attack emboldened some of the prisoners, who took advantage of the distraction to swarm over Colvinra's Seekers. The Questioner spun around to fend off Suyef's attack, as Quentin helped the prisoners dispatch a Seeker before turning to help the Nomad.

Staffs spun through the air as the mass of bodies shifted all around. The crack of weapons striking each other echoed over the chaos, the Questioner's staff whirling around to block every attack Quentin and Suyef brought against him. Hope had just begun to blossom that the pair could overwhelm him. It died when the Questioner finally struck. Quentin, turning to bring his staff around to strike Colvinra's head, found himself facing a body flying through the air. Then another lifted off the ground. He ducked the first and dodged the second; too many came. As Suyef pressed his attack, Quentin dodged body after body. Finally, one struck him, knocking him to the ground and pinning him down. Colvinra tried to level an overhead strike at Quentin's head, but Suyef knocked him off balance and shoved at the body on top of Quentin with his leg. The Nomad continued past the rising Quentin to press another attack at the Questioner. More bodies lifted from the ground and soared at Suyef's back.

Quentin, back on his feet, held out a hand, and the bodies halted in midair, wavering. His body shook, the bodies shuddering toward him as he stumbled, but his hand held firm. With an obvious effort, he threw his hand to the side, and the bodies flew off in that direction.

"That's going to make things difficult," Mortac said to me as I rose from my protective position over the unconscious guard.

"Did he . . . Did he just . . . ," my brother stammered.

"Yes, he scripted," the warden hissed. "In front of a Questioner. If Colvinra and Quentin survive this, that will cause problems."

"But the Seeker scripted, too," Donovan cried out, downing another prisoner that charged at him. My side of the circle appeared calm for the moment.

"The laws don't apply to them, idiot!" Mortac yelled, shoving us away from the fight. "Now move!"

I craned my head to watch the battle. Colvinra had lost his cowl and face mask in the fight and now stood facing Suyef, his face twisted in rage. He continued to fling bodies at Quentin, who deflected them and sent them off to either side. Suyef kept his staff on the attack, forcing Colvinra to defend himself. As he did, his attention toward the bodies flagged and Quentin faced fewer. The mass of the crowd shifted around them, swallowing them from my view. I turned to run with my brother and ran headlong into him. We fell to the ground, and I rolled instinctively to keep from being trampled. Once I was back on my feet, Mortac stood there, not moving, eyes locked on something above and behind me. Donovan pointed as well, mouth agape in horror. I turned, looked up, and my mouth fell open.

A flight of green dragons, as large as the red already there and led by the giant creature we assumed was the Dragon Queen we'd seen before, flew into sight. As we stared in awe at their beauty, glimmering in the core-light shining up from below, the green dragons attacked.

As a mass of bodies soared through the air at Suyef, I had no choice. Bringing the symbols to mind and crafting the column sentences to feed them into reality, I erected a wall of air before us. When the bodies struck that wall, my body trembled. The wall leaned back against the force of Colvinra's pull. I wanted to lower my hand, to let the wall fall, but I could not let that happen. I pushed back against the wall, leaning my weight and will into it, compelling it to exist in this reality. With the wall stabilized, it was possible to alter the code, allowing me to fling the structure to the side, dragging the bodies with it. As they fell out of the way, my legs nearly collapsed in exhaustion, but more bodies lifted off the ground. Behind me, Suyef's and Colvinra's staffs struck with alarming speed. The Nomad must have pressed his attack, trying to overwhelm the Questioner to prevent him from being able to script like that again.

Still the bodies came at us, forcing me to change my strategy. Instead of a single wall of air before us, I erected two at an angle, the tips just before me, reaching past us. As the bodies struck the new walls, they deflected to either side, bouncing off like balls hitting a solid surface. Colvinra grunted with each effort. I spared a glance and saw the Nomad's staff was almost invisible with the speed of his attack on the Questioner. Colvinra's hood had fallen, a sheen of sweat glistened on his pate, and the look of concentration on his face told the tale. Fewer bodies lifted off the ground to fly at us.

Something green flashed past me overhead, and I looked up to see the last thing we needed. More dragons.

A green flight as massive as the red one already attacking us swarmed into the air above the entire battle. They dove, and I prepared myself for an even-greater onslaught on the ground. Another body hit my wall of air, pulling my attention back on keeping those walls as real as possible. Ahead, a red dragon dove low, sweeping along the ground toward us. As the beast reached out to grab at a mass of fleeing prisoners, a green dragon crashed down into the red monster, knocking it to the side. All around us, the green dragons attacked the reds, driving them away from the prisoners. The red dragons cried out angry bellows, unleashing fireballs at their green brethren, who came back with cries and fireballs of their own.

Just as another body flung by the Questioner bounced off the air wall to my left, two smaller green dragons dove low, heading right at us.

"Suyef!" I called out, pointing at the approaching monsters.

Colvinra and the Nomad halted, their staffs held across their bodies and pressed against each other's weapons, their heads turning to me. When they saw me point, their eyes shifted to see the diving greens.

"Run!" I yelled, and tried to do so myself, but I never got the chance.

As I turned to move, one of the monsters grabbed me and the ground fell away.

CHAPTER 34

WEEPING

The green dragons, sweeping in above the entire battle, dove and struck at the reds, driving them away from the mass of people. A red dragon flew low to grab at a fleeing man, only to have a green crash into its side, sending it careening off to the right. The fleeing man dove to the ground, the grasping claws just missing his legs. All around us, the greens interfered with the reds, forcing them away from the panicked crowds.

"They're helping us!" Donovan cried out, cheering. "Get 'em, greens! Get 'em!"

I smiled slightly but remained wary. This had happened before, and the possibility of the result repeating itself filled me with dread. Donovan huddled close to me, each of our pulse guns aimed at the sky even though we knew they were useless. The massive dragon flew back and forth above the fray, her cries bellowing through the air. The smaller greens, small only when compared to her, dove when she cried, following her commands. Dive after dive, the greens thwarted the reds from lifting off with any more people. My spirits rose, just a bit, thinking we'd been saved.

A second later, that thought died. Two of the green dragons dove toward the ground. People scattered in all directions, and, for an instant, Quentin, Suyef, and Colvinra came into view. The

Nomad and Questioner stood facing each other, staffs pressed together, eyes locked on the diving dragons. Quentin, nearer the beasts, turned and yelled something at them, making to run. He didn't move a single step. One of the beasts snatched him clean off the ground, soaring up and over us. The other struck the combatants, knocking Colvinra to the ground and grabbing Suyef, climbing to join the other.

"Quentin!" I screamed after the ascending beasts. "Suyef!"

Something tugged on my arm. I wrenched my eyes from the sky to see Donovan, one hand pulling my sleeve, the other pointing behind me. The look on his face sent a chill down my back. I turned to see another green dragon flying down over the battlefield, heading straight for us.

The thought to run, to dive away, to do something, never came. I just stood there, watching, a numb feeling falling over me as the claws grasped me firmly. My body twisted in their grip, facing down. The receding forms of Mortac and his guards fell away. And I saw my brother crying out to me. The next moment, something struck at my core; a tearing seared my insides like something ripping itself free from my heart. I held out a hand to my brother and watched, tears filling my vision as a green dragon swept down toward him.

The beast never made it. A pair of reds knocked it to the ground, sending it crashing into the fleeing masses. As one red landed atop the green, blasting fire in its face, the other flew past and scooped my brother up in its claws.

I screamed as my brother's face slipped from my sight in a flash of red.

Micaela stumbled to a stop, a haunted look filling her face. I glanced down at the recording device, thinking of pausing it.

"Do you need a moment?" I asked, motioning at the device. "We can take a break."

Micaela stared at the padd, her mouth moving. She stood from the sofa and moved to the window. There she stood, back to me, her body shaking as she wept. Her long, red hair flowed down her back and the silver belt given her by her family still adorned her waist. I reached to turn the device off.

"Leave it," she hissed between sobs. "Just a moment."

I leaned back down, leaving the device on, unsure of what to do. My heart felt for her, and part of me wanted to go comfort her, but I didn't know how. This seemed like a private moment, a memory she'd been forced to dredge up, and my going to her at that moment would probably make it worse. It was my fault she'd had to bring it up, to relive that fateful day.

"I'm sorry," she said from the window, back still turned to me. "I thought I'd be fine."

"Don't apologize. Losing someone is hard enough . . . ," I whispered.

Her head lowered as her hands fell to her side.

"So, your brother . . ."

She turned to look at me, a quizzical look on her face.

"The reds took him?"

Her face hardened. "The reds took him, and, as you know, the reds and greens don't get along at all."

"That's putting it mildly."

Micaela turned to look back out the window. "We're not even sure which shell they claim as their primary nest," she said. "They've spread over all the minor shells in the inner core system, like vermin. The Queen and her flight have tried for cycles but have never discovered where they take their captives." She looked over at me. "You know all that."

"Hence the code to protect," I stated, nodding at her. "To keep them from controlling the core."

Micaela shrugged. "Not that keeping them from taking that has helped me."

"You know we don't know what happens to them, right?" I asked.

She shook her head. "We know what happened to him."

"Wait, he's alive?" I asked, my eyebrows rising, feeling hope swell inside me.

Her eyes moved to look at me, and that feeling slipped away like a breeze.

"The brother I knew died that day," she whispered. "That day, my world ended."

"But that's not the end of your story."

She looked out the window, not speaking for several moments. "No, that's just the beginning. How my world ended." She looked back at me. "Just because mine ended, however, doesn't mean everyone else's did."

I glanced at my notes. "Both of your siblings were taken by dragons, yes?"

She nodded. "That's the theory, at least, regarding Maryn. The Queen insists she knows nothing, but I have my doubts regarding that creature."

I frowned at her. "And here I thought you were friends."

"That's a loose term for what we are," she replied, turning to face the window. "Let's just say we're allies by circumstance, and not enemies, not yet."

"You blame her for what happened?"

Micaela remained facing the window. "She and those her size are large enough beasts to carry ten people in their claws, yet that creature chose to leave the task of carrying us to smaller dragons. Why? Why make that choice? Why leave my brother below? In all these cycles, I still can't answer that. Someday, I hope to understand." Micaela sniffed and shrugged. "Same answer as always." Her shoulders slumped.

"Should I return later?" I asked, hoping the offer of a rest might help her.

She sighed and turned away from the window. "Food, then we continue." She nodded at my notes. "This part isn't over."

The dragon flew from the battle, taking from me any hope of seeing my brother. As I craned to see what happened to him, the greens continued to push the reds away from the outpost, driving them back out over the shell's edge. The dragon turned, pulling away from the outpost and taking the battle out of my sight. It dawned on me a moment later where we were going. Turning my head to the front, despondence beginning to take hold of my soul, I spied the energy shield closing fast. I braced myself, and a moment later we crossed into the Wilds.

A blast of wetness hit me square in the face and blinded me. While I'd never seen rain before, my studies had covered weather and its various forms. Most of the shell enjoyed a steady weather pattern, owing to the citadel and its weather-control machinery. It hardly ever rained, and then only in controlled places in the Central Dominance. Clouds were virtually nonexistent, as were sleet, fog, and any other kind of precipitation. Most people had never seen what they look like, outside of the network images and videos.

When we crashed through that energy shield, what greeted us seemed like every kind of weather possible. Fog flowed over us, a billowy, moist substance that left me drenched in seconds. After that, we dove toward the ground and left the fog behind. As soon as we did, rain began to pour around us. My hair stuck to the side of my face, and water streamed over my eyes. Wind whipped the falling moisture up into my face, making it hard to see. Blinking the water from my sight, I saw the ground zooming up to meet us. The claws let go, dropping me a few feet into the mud, a cold, mushy substance that swallowed my limbs and nearly my face. The retreating form of the dragon vanished into the storm raging over me.

My body began to shiver as I struggled to crawl toward what looked like solid ground. Tall stalks of some green substance whipped at my face, one sharp enough to slice my cheek. My hand grasped something solid and round, and I pulled myself toward it. Upon closer examination, it turned out to be about the width of my arm, dark brown, very knobby, and reaching up from the ground. It led to a more solid version of the same, and realized I was leaning against a tree. Above me, the branches of the giant plant waved around in the wind and rain. I clung to the tree, the only solid thing available to me, and squeezed my eyes shut. Rain flowed down the trunk and onto my head. Every inch of me was soaked, covered in mud and grime. My insides felt hollow and empty.

"Micaela!"

I turned my head, forcing my eyes open. With rain in my eyes, and my hand in my face to shield myself from the storm, it was a struggle to even look around. In every direction, plants of various sizes and shapes danced in the wind and rain, a chaotic mess that made the madness of the fleeing prisoners seem mild. Shadows shifted in random patterns, giving the illusion of things moving toward and away from me all at once. I squinted, trying to find the source of the voice.

"Micaela!" the voice called again.

I jerked my head to the left, trying to focus on the source. The sounds of the storm made locating anything almost impossible. I pulled myself up, leaning my back against the tree, one hand still shielding my eyes from the driving rain. No wonder the Ancients had built the citadels. At that moment, I never wanted to see another storm again, and those machines had all but eliminated this kind of weather.

Something shifted through the dancing shadows just ahead of me, something solid and large. I shrank back against the tree, hoping whatever it was wouldn't notice me. The reports detailed which beings called the Wilds home, all manner of nasty creatures, the only true wildlife to exist on Colberra. Wild beasts that had probably never seen a human before. Suddenly, I found myself wishing for that pulse gun lost to me when the dragon scooped me up.

The figure moved closer, clearly walking on two feet. I pushed myself to the right, trying to blend into the roots of the tree at my back. The figure stopped and lifted something to its head.

"Micaela!" the figure called out.

It was Quentin. "Over here!" I screamed into the storm, lunging from the tree toward him.

We collided and clung to each other. I pressed my face into his chest as he pulled me back in the direction he'd come from. We shuffled along, me glad to be led, my eyes closed tight, arms clinging frantically to his torso for fear of getting separated.

After a very long hike, water pouring into every crevice of my clothing, wind lashing my hair and plants my face, it all faded away. The sounds, the feelings, everything. I dared to peek, and I saw Suyef standing over me, smiling. We were in a small cave lit by a fire device. Quentin leaned down to sit against the rock face, and I clung to his chest. Part of me felt I should move to let him up, but, at that moment, it all hit me. The arena, the dragons, Donovan. All of it.

I buried my face in his chest and wept.

CHAPTER 35

THE WILDS

I woke up some time later, still clinging to Quentin. We hadn't moved from where he'd sat. I pushed myself up, head still groggy, and felt the cave spin.

"Are you okay?" Quentin asked from beside me as I closed my eyes and took a deep breath.

"Fine, just sat up too fast."

I opened my eyes a moment later, and the cave remained where it belonged. A small device sat on a set of rocks, flames emanating from it, providing illumination and filling the cavern with a soft heat. Suyef was nowhere in sight. Quentin, finally free of me, stood and stretched.

"Oh, man," he said, massaging a spot on his lower back with one hand and his neck with the other. "You weren't out long, but, ouch."

"Sorry about that," I whispered, looking down and trying not to think about what had happened for fear the tears would start again. It didn't work. I closed my eyes, willing the images to go away. Donovan falling to the red. Maryn hiding behind the rock. My sister, head lolling as she's carried away. My heart started to ache as the feelings overwhelmed me.

Quentin placed a hand on my shoulder. His touch brought me back to the moment, giving me something to latch on to. I looked up at him.

"Don't apologize for that," he said. "If that's what you needed, then that's what you needed."

"I meant for the backache."

He shrugged. "It was worth it," he said, smiling and walking over to the fire device.

I eyed him for a moment, pondering his words, then shook my head. "Where's Suyef?"

"Scouting the area," Quentin answered, nodding at the cave entrance.

My eyes roamed around the small space. The cave had only one entrance, to my right, and some rocks piled all around the wall, forming makeshift benches. Beyond the fire device and two travel sacks on the opposite side of the cave, the place was empty.

"Where'd the packs come from?"

Quentin shrugged. "We found them here," he said, looking around the cave. "They'd been here a while. Suyef thinks this might be a Seeker cave, a haven to go to when storms hit." He nodded out the entrance, where the storm seemed to be dying down. "He says he found another one a short distance from here, along the shield wall. He surmises he'll find more beyond that and in the other direction."

"Havens?" I asked, feeling a chill take hold of me. I shivered. "Do they really need to come in here that much?"

Quentin nodded. "In search of escaped prisoners or anyone foolish enough to try to cross the shield border," he said, shrugging. "If I were sending people into this mess, places like this for them to go to would be at the top of my list."

"If this is a Seeker safe spot, should we stay here?"

"Hence Suyef's scouting. As soon as he finds a better option or this storm dies down, we're moving," he said, rubbing his hands as he stared at the flames flickering above the device. "I'd offer you a change of clothing so you can dry out, but there's nothing here."

My hair remained very damp. "I feel terrible."

Quentin chuckled and shook his head. He held up his hands and smiled at my glare. "Considering the day we've had, give yourself a break."

I tried to smile, but it died before it started, my eyes dropping down to look at the ground. It felt wrong to smile about anything. Quentin shuffled and took a step toward me.

"What happened to Donovan?" he asked, stepping nearer.

I shrugged.

"He didn't . . ."

I shrugged again.

"So, he was still okay when you last saw him?"

Looking down at the fire seemed the best answer. There wasn't anything to give him. My insides felt empty, painfully so. They were all gone from me now. Taken. I put my head in my hands and looked at the ground.

"Do you want to talk about it?" he asked.

I sniffed, shaking my head. "There's nothing to talk about. My family is gone. All of them."

"You don't know that," he stated.

"Don't I?" I asked, holding his gaze. "What's happened to prove me wrong?"

"Yes, it looks bad, but you don't know what happened to him, do you?"

I shook my head. "The dragon turned away with him in its claws, taking him from view."

"So, he might still be okay, back with the warden."

My face heated up, my anger at his insinuation rising. "Do you trust that man?" When Quentin didn't respond, I went on. "Exactly, and what makes you think my brother is safe with him? What might have stopped those monsters from taking him? From dropping him like the rest? Or running off with him like they do the prisoners?"

Quentin held out his hands to either side. "You don't have to get mad at me," he said.

"This isn't about you, Quentin," I blurted out. How could anyone be as callous as he seemed to be at that point? "It never was. It's about me and my family. About how they've all been taken from me."

"I just wanted to help," he whispered, lowering his hands and looking down at the fire.

My next statement was selfish, but I didn't care. Getting my family back was the only thing that mattered to me.

"Unless you can make them appear right now, how can you help?" I asked, sitting down on a nearby rock and folding my arms across my chest.

"I didn't mean it like that," he said, settling himself down near the entrance. "Just to talk about it."

A twinge of guilt surfaced over the roiling emotional stew pot inside me. "Quentin, I know what you're trying to do, but not yet." I looked down at the fire. "Not yet."

The fire calmed me a bit, eating away at some of my anger as it flickered. Unfortunately, it left me feeling very much alone. Alone and lost in the Wilds with what amounted to two strangers. True, two strangers who had just fought a battle to rescue us, but strangers just the same.

Quentin stood up, interrupting my thoughts and stepping near the entrance. "Okay. Whenever."

He moved toward the exit, drawing my gaze.

"What is it?" I asked.

"Suyef's back," he said, stopping short of the entrance to let the man enter.

"Ah, you're awake," the Nomad said, shaking water from his cloak before coming in to stand near the fire device. "We'll need to move quickly now that you are."

"Something wrong?"

He shrugged. "It's hard to tell, but I think we're being stalked."

"Seekers?" Quentin asked.

He shook his head. "Whatever it is, it smells off. Dirty. And it moves too quietly to be Seekers." He glared at Quentin. "Whatever it is, it's not human."

To say the next couple of days were uncomfortable is an understatement. The storm let up only a bit, shifting around us from a torrential downpour to a howling, face-shielding windstorm to a soft, misty rain that soaked through everything in a matter of moments. The only thing it didn't do was stop.

"This can't be normal," I called out to Quentin as we rested a bit under a massive tree root. Suyef had gone ahead to scout.

"It's not," he said, looking up into the gloomy sky. "The system is broken here, so whatever happens is random. You're just as likely to get a drought as this."

"So, why all this rain?"

He shrugged. "It doesn't like you?"

I stuck my tongue out at him, and he laughed. "Feeling better?" he said.

"No, not at all." I shook my hair to one side, wrapping it and squeezing it with my hands. "But you earned that one."

Quentin watched my hands. "I don't see why you bother. It's just going to get soaked."

"It's soothing."

It was the truth. Squeezing the water out felt good. It felt like taking my feelings and choking them. Like the storm, they had been raging and shifting. Whenever we'd stop to rest, what sleep the storm granted me was fraught with nightmares of things being taken away. In a particularly bad one, the ground pulled at my skin, ripping at my hair. When I awoke, the pain persisted, leaving an empty, aching feeling over every inch of me.

"Well, by all means, squeeze away," he said, waving at me.

As he spoke, the rain stopped completely. We both looked around, peeking out from under our makeshift shelter at the skies. The clouds, ever present since we'd been dumped in this broken region, were gone, and core-light shone through. I could just make out the water shield high above.

"Moon's moving past," Quentin said, pointing at a depression where the orbiting satellite's gravity pulled at the water.

"Where'd the storm go?" I asked, stepping out from under the tree, one hand still wrapped around my braid.

Quentin shrugged, pulling his hood down and shaking his cloak, remnants of the rain flowing off him as he did. "Broken system, remember?" He nodded up at the now-clear skies. "Be ready for it to come back without warning."

With the newly gained light, I took a moment to peek at my surroundings. Endless vegetation met my sweeping eyes. Green, brown, and other colors all jumbled together in a mixture of sights accompanied by smells all new to my senses. A pungent, old smell hung in the air, filling my nostrils with the scent of something like death. I scrunched my nose and covered it.

"Something wrong?" Quentin asked as he examined a rather large, leafy plant nearby.

"Can't you smell that?"

He sniffed and nodded. "Odd. I wouldn't expect that a place so alive with vegetation would smell like it's dying."

"Some of it must be rotting," I suggested, covering my mouth and nose with my very damp red scarf.

"That can't be much better," he said, pointing at the covering.

I shrugged, eyes still taking in all the plants. "It's better than nothing."

Suyef came into sight a moment later from over a rise twenty paces off. He nodded at us and waved.

"Best chance we'll have to put some distance between us and the shield," he said, turning and heading off.

"Where are we going?" Quentin asked as he made to follow, glancing once at me as he did.

Suyef pointed beyond him. "West, as before."

"How can you tell which way is west in all this?" I pointed up at the forest around us.

"Never question a Nomad's sense of direction, Micaela," Quentin cautioned, smiling his half smile at me. "It's an insult to his honor, and he might have to duel you."

Suyef shot a glare over his shoulder. "I just know." He looked off to his right and chuckled before moving on. "Keep up."

"What's he laughing about?" I whispered to Quentin.

"Probably that," he answered, pointing in the direction Suyef had looked.

Through a gap in the trees, I could just make out mountains, tall ones that looked very familiar.

"The Central Mountains?"

Quentin nodded. "Lucky that happened to be there, I'm sure. Probably why he laughed."

"Is it me, or do Nomads have a strange sense of humor?"

"I know, right?" Quentin agreed, helping me over a tree root. "But don't tell him that. I think he's convinced humor is a waste of time."

"Are you two going to talk all day, or get moving?" the Nomad called back to us from beyond some large, menacing-looking plants hanging over the path he'd chosen. "I mean, we could sit down and have a chat or take advantage of this lull in the weather."

Quentin eyed me, and I smothered a laugh as we hurried to catch up with the Nomad. The banter had distracted me from my thoughts for a moment, but the sadness surged back the instant we stopped talking. I missed my brothers. It hadn't dawned on me how attached I'd become to them, like a familiar blanket used each night to curl up and sleep in. The two of them had been there as our family was torn apart one by one. Now they all were gone. Even my brothers. A swelling feeling took root in the back of my throat, that feeling one gets just before crossing the threshold into crying. It became as persistent a companion as my recent protectors.

We continued that way for another chron before Suyef called a rest in a clearing on an elevated bit of ground. I took the moment to pull out my brush and whip my hair into a decent braid so it would stop annoying me. Quentin offered me a food pack, and we all wolfed down our sustenance as politely as possible. Being able to eat the pack without also taking in a mouthful of rainwater with each bite was glorious.

After the meal, Suyef let us rest for a moment, and my mind wandered back to the events at the outpost. As Quentin stretched his cloak over a rock to let it dry out, the image of him standing on that field jumped to the forefront, hand held out, deflecting the bodies Colvinra had scripted to fly through the air at him.

Quentin noticed my stare and looked around. "Did I do something?" he asked.

I shook my head. "Just remembering something you did," I said, pulling my own cloak off to air it out.

"Um, something I did?"

"During the battle." He watched me lay my cloak out and pull my head scarf free. "Something you did to stop Colvinra."

Quentin darted a look at Suyef, who folded his arms across his chest and shrugged.

"Fought him?" Quentin asked, a half smile molding his lips.

I favored him with a very pointed look, my hands patting and smoothing the scarf out.

"Yeah, didn't think that would work," he stated, pulling at his cloak to work out a fold. "So, you saw what?"

"You hold up your hand and stop several bodies flying through the air," I said, standing up and putting my hands on my hips. "You scripted." The Nomad remained motionless and relaxed. "Clearly, you've done it before, and he knows about it."

Quentin shrugged. "It's not a crime—"

"Yes, it is."

"On his shell," Quentin finished, pointing at the Nomad. "People script there all the time, although they call it altering." When I just stared at him, he went on. "Just explaining why he's not reacting."

"Quentin, you scripted in front of a Seeker!" I hissed. "And made off with us and managed to make it look like you planned it with the dragons."

"Coordinating with dragons?" Quentin asked, looking between the two of us. "Usually it's me making leaps of logic, but that tops anything I've done."

"They're going to spin it that way," I said, leveling a finger at him. "This is going to get messy."

"Like it wasn't already," Quentin muttered, sitting down and pulling a boot off to get at his sock.

"And you made it more so by scripting in front of Colvinra," I said, steering the conversation back to the topic.

"Yes, yes, not my smartest move," Quentin replied, pulling his sock off and wringing water from it. "I didn't have a choice. Colvinra would've buried us. Literally."

"We've discussed this before. You're a bit too rash with it," the Nomad said, standing up and stretching.

"Considering my actions may just have saved your life, a little more gratitude might be in order," Quentin retorted, pulling his boot back on over his sock and foot.

"It's possible to be grateful and wary," the Nomad said, pointing at me. "She's not wrong about your actions."

"Look!" Quentin blurted out, jumping to his feet and glaring at each of us in turn. "I'm not sure why you're ganging up on me."

"Calm down, Quentin," I said, making a calming motion at him. "I actually just wanted to know about what you did."

Quentin sat down and began pulling at his other boot.

"Don't take it off," Suyef whispered, head turned toward the forest. "Get your cloaks."

I looked around, grabbing at my garments. "What is it? Seekers?"

Suyef shook his head. "Same as before." He motioned us to follow him and moved off in the same direction we'd been heading in. "Something's hunting us."

CHAPTER 36

PREY

Whatever it was, the creature didn't relent. Suyef kept us moving at as frenzied a pace as we could manage through the wild landscape. The jungle went on forever, its vegetation—this region of the Wilds having feasted on near constant rainfall—tall and impenetrable. The Nomad did his best to find us a trail through the jungle, but that proved more and more difficult the farther we went. Always, just behind us, came our stalker. Suyef never spied it, though he tried to on several occasions. The creature stayed just out of sight, just out of earshot.

Strangest of all, it never attacked; it only stalked us. I pointed this out to the Nomad, who just shrugged.

"Who knows the mind of a wild beast," he said, indicating we should keep moving.

After almost two days of hiking through more plants than I believed could ever exist in our broken, waterless world, we broke free of the dense jungle. There, sweeping across our path, stood the first evidence of what had once destroyed this region: a massive canyon ripped through the shell. To our right, way off to the north, I could just make out the Central Mountains, the center of the shell. To the south, sweeping away in the other direction, the canyon turned to the west and bent out of sight. Just beyond the tree line, the ground dropped out in a jagged slope of broken stone, rocks pushing out from the ground like teeth knocked from some giant beast's mouth and strewn across the land.

"How in frag's sake do we get down that?" Quentin asked, one hand on his head, the other waving at the canyon.

"How we get down is less worrisome than how we cross what is at the bottom," Suyef whispered, eyes locked downward on the wide, jagged valley far below us.

I leaned a bit farther out, hand resting on Quentin's shoulder as he did the same. There, just visible over the sharp-edged rocks, water rushed past.

"Is that a river?" I asked, my eyes widening.

Suyef stepped up on the far side of Quentin. "Yes, and crossing that will be impossible unless we find a ford. I doubt we'll find any bridges."

"Surely something civilized must have lived out here before this region was closed off," I said. "They must have had bridges."

Quentin and Suyef both turned to look at me, equal looks of confusion on their faces.

"Sorry, did I say something wrong?"

"You do know why this region is how it is, yes?" Quentin asked.

"Vaguely, yes," I answered, nodding. "Collision with another shell messed up the region, breaking the citadel's control over it."

"Not just a head-on collision, side against side," Quentin said, pointing at the canyon. "The other shell landed on top of this region, crushing it and sweeping out to the south. Pieces of the shells broke off and fell into Colberra Citadel's gravity well, giving us the isles my parents later were born on." He looked down at the canyon. "This wasn't here before that collision."

"But no other shells exist higher than Colberra," I retorted, pointing at Suyef. "His shell is the closest to ours, and it's barely close enough to trade with. Wouldn't the collision just have been one up against the other?"

Quentin shook his head. "There are several theories about that. The historical records are a bit spotty prior to the Dominances being established several centuries ago. About the only things recorded in history prior to the Dominances were water being traded to the Nomads and the banning of scripting. Oh, and the Seekers. That's it. As long as the Dominances have existed and tracked it, the shell has been in this orbit and the Wilds has been here, shielded off and out of control." He pointed at the river. "And a drain on the system." He shrugged, continuing, "That's another issue. The fact is, this shell's been in this orbit for as long as Colberran history records, but there's a huge gap wherein our historical records just don't tell us much. Whenever this happened, it predates Colberran Dominances by a long time."

"Ancient times?" I suggested.

"That's another theory. If it happened back then, the Ancients could have built the shielding system to keep people out of the broken area," he said. "It's also possible they moved the shell. Colberra is the only shell to exist this close to the water shield. Almost as close as you can get without being drawn into the water. No other shells orbit this high." He pointed at Suyef. "They all orbit down on a level with his shell or lower." He looked at me, eyebrows raised slightly. "A region of airspace where collisions happen a lot."

I looked at the Nomad. "His shell is . . ."

"Two shells," Quentin said. "A supershell, with two citadels, although both are malfunctioning because of the collision. So, if you were an Ancient living on a shell down in that orbit and your shell had just been struck and severely damaged, what would you do?"

"I'd move the shell to a safer orbit."

"The safest orbit you could find." He waved a hand around him, eyes moving about the landscape. "Colberra."

At that moment, a cawing screech filled the air around us and we looked to see a large creature soar past. It was dark brown, with a swooping orange nose and two equally orange three-toed feet tucked underneath. Its wings swept out to either side, the creature flew past us. It beat them every now and then as it moved down the valley.

"Was that a bird?" I asked, my eyes never leaving the beautiful creature.

Suyef nodded. "One of many we'll see now that we're clear of the jungle, I'm sure."

"I didn't think they still existed in the wild."

"The Wilds is the only place they can exist," Quentin pointed out, face uplifted as he watched the bird move away. "Only place with a steady supply of water outside of zoo facilities and animal nurseries."

"What do they eat?" I asked, straining to keep sight of the bird as it flew north.

"If there are birds, there are other animals, including rodents and reptiles," Suyef said, moving toward the canyon edge and looking up and down the valley's walls.

I looked down at Quentin. "So, what are the theories on where the animals came from?"

He shrugged. "No theories at all. What few animals survived the breaking of our world were in captivity or captured if they survived. When this"—he waved a hand at the canyon—"happened, they broke free of the facilities holding them and made their way to wherever they could find." He tugged at his cloak. "In one of history's little ironies, the first task given to the Seekers when they were organized was to go into the Wilds and recapture the animals."

"How is it we know *that* much, but the rest is theory?"

"Seekers keep different records," Suyef muttered. "While they don't confirm anything Quentin's mentioned about what exactly happened after this did, they do let out enough to keep their reputation squeaky clean and shiny."

A light dawned in my head. "And if your citizenry still buys into the fact that you're just going out and cleaning up the conse-quences of accidents . . ."

"That's one way to describe what they do," Quentin stated. "Suyef, what do we do?"

The Nomad pointed south. "We go that way and hope we find a way to cross."

Quentin looked back into the jungle. "And our tail?"

"Is still there," Suyef answered, already moving in the direction he'd indicated. "Distant, but there."

"What is it?" I asked, walking alongside Quentin, just behind the Nomad.

Suyef shrugged. "It's unclear, but I'm sure the answer will com-plicate things," he said. "If we put off finding out as long as we can, I'll be a lot happier."

To this day, how he felt about the answer is still unclear to me.

If there's one thing I learned about Nomads during those days it's that they don't like not knowing something. They don't need to know everything or even seem like they know everything. However, when there is something they need to know but they can't figure out, it really bugs them.

As we made our way along the top of this side of the canyon, the river far below to the west of us, the jungle tight up to the east, Suyef persisted in trying to figure out what was stalking us. The creature moved as we did, keeping just enough distance so as not to threaten us, but staying close enough to keep an eye on us. The Nomad became so obsessed with discovering what the creature was that for several days we hardly moved as he and the creature played a game of hide-and-seek with each other. Quentin and I kept moving along the canyon, but not as quickly as we wanted to for fear Suyef and this creature would vanish behind us in their stupid game.

"Is this normal Nomad behavior?" I asked one morning, a few days into the hike. We were nearing the turn of the canyon, a sharp cut that was hardly natural. "He seems a bit overfocused, and I'm getting worried."

To be honest, having something to worry about helped distract me from my own sadness. It was always there, bubbling to the surface whenever we stopped. When we moved, the concentration I needed to stay on the trail and interact began to distract me. When a moment arose where my mind could contemplate things, an overwhelming sense of guilt filled me for having been distracted from my feelings. It was, emotionally, a losing situation on all sides for me.

"From what I know, it's not, but we've never been in a situation where he couldn't readily find the answer he needed," Quentin said, pulling me from my thoughts as he helped me over a fallen tree.

Somewhere nearby, we heard something scuttle away through the underbrush, but we'd given up hope of ever seeing what the creatures were. The bird, on the other hand, seemed to live in this region, for we saw it fly past us up and down the canyon several times a day.

"Did you try the search he asked you to do?" I asked.

Quentin frowned, pulling out his padd. "Something, maybe the shield, is messing with the link. I've tried just about every trick, and the connection just won't work."

I held out a hand. "Let me try." When he leveled a questioning glance at me, I added, "It can't hurt."

Shrugging, he handed the padd over, which went into my pocket for later.

"You two act like you've known each other a lot longer than you have," I said, following him past a rock jutting up from the canyon toward the tree branches overhead. "Almost like brothers."

Quentin shrugged. "Considering how it started, that's a good thing."

We moved past a large bush and froze. There, just ahead and in the middle of the makeshift path we'd found along the canyon edge, the ground had cracked open. A fount of water shot forth from the crack, frozen in place. The air felt crisp and cold. Light from the core reflecting off the water shield hit the icy sculpture just so, sending a myriad of multicolored lights reflecting off every surface.

"How is that possible?" I whispered, not taking my eyes from the magnificent sight.

Quentin crept forward, craning his head to look up at the underside of the water spouting outward from the central column. "Not sure, really," he said, head ducking to look at the crack. "It looks like a water pipe burst belowground."

"But why is it frozen?" I asked, moving closer and around to the left of the beautiful sculpture. Some of the light reflected on my hand when I held it out, and a grin came to my face unbidden. "It's amazing!"

At that moment, my heart felt better than it had in days. As my hand moved through the rainbows reflecting off the waterspout, for a moment my spirit lightened.

Quentin stood up, scratching his head. "Environmental controls must have done it. Well, malfunctioning ones. Feel the air?"

I nodded, tucking my head scarf in tight around my neck as my body convulsed with a shiver. "Yeah, very nippy."

"Still, to freeze a waterspout like this. Where is it coming from?" Quentin whispered, kneeling to peer into the crack. "I can't see a source at all."

"What are you two doing?" Suyef asked, coming out of the jungle just beyond the frozen waterspout.

He stopped when he saw the sight. Quentin peeked around the icy column and waved at him.

"Can you see where it's coming from?" he asked.

The Nomad shook his head. "Move away, Quentin. Such things are not to be trusted."

"It's a column of frozen water." Quentin rested back on his feet, which were tucked under him, and stared up at the icy structure. "What harm can it do?"

"Whatever caused it to happen is the source of my fear. Now let's move on," the Nomad insisted.

Quentin glared at Suyef but stood up and moved around with me to where the trail picked up. He asked me for the padd and held it up at the structure, tapping the screen.

"What are you doing?"

He handed the padd back to me, a picture of the column now displayed on the screen. "Odds are that's something we'll never see again. I want to remember it."

As I pocketed the device, I turned to look back at the myriad of lights reflecting on the plants and ground. Part of me envied it, frozen in such a wondrous place, unchanging. Another part pitied it. Captured in an unnatural state, forever trapped. My heart felt very much like that column.

My voice dropped to a whisper. "I don't think I'll ever forget it." I never did.

We moved away from the icy column, and soon the landscape swallowed the beautiful sight. I turned my attention ahead to the canyon. Directly before us, the entire valley ended in a sheer rock face. Low hills, which Quentin said reached all the way to the shell's edge, rose up beyond the cliff. The canyon, however, didn't end there. It turned, slicing through the ground as it cut to the west and moved along a range of mountains that rose up just to the south of the hills beyond the cliff face.

"Not a natural formation, that's for sure," Quentin said, taking in the sheer drop-off our trail led to. "At least the jungle ends at those hills."

Glancing down at the canyon, I smiled. "Won't be too sad not to have that next to me."

Quentin glanced at Suyef. "Is it still there?"

He nodded. "Never left. She just moved farther off." He glared at Quentin. "Even the beasts know better than to go near such things, and there you are with your nose crammed up the thing's skirt."

Quentin raised both hands up in defense. "I was just curious where it was coming from."

"Next time use your imagination," the Nomad hissed, pushing past Quentin and continuing along the canyon edge.

"Something's wrong with him," Quentin muttered.

"Maybe he's just worried."

Quentin shook his head. "It's more than that." He glanced into the jungle. "Did you hear what he called it?"

Frowning, I tried to recall Suyef's words.

"He said 'she,'" Quentin went on, not waiting for me.

I shrugged. "What does that mean?"

"Who knows? But he doesn't act like this. He never acts like this." Quentin moved to follow the Nomad. "If there's one thing you can count on, it's that he'll always be calm and in control."

"Maybe that's just a face he puts on for your benefit."

"It's very Nomad to be calm and in control."

"Less talk, more hiking," Suyef called back to us.

Quentin shot me a look and moved on. The dense jungle drew my gaze. What was out there that could make even a Nomad act out of sorts?

I wasn't sure I wanted to know the answer, but soon enough we found out. As we rested that core-night at the edge of the foothills, the creature finally made its move.

CHAPTER 37

HUNTER

Even in the Wilds, core-night fell. It was one constant you could rely on besides the water above. The night shield would lower, and the light would dim. Suyef, wary of traveling in the dim illumination, always had us encamped and resting before core-set, before the ever-present light of the planet's core far below was dimmed. As that moment neared, Suyef brought us just to the edge of the hills, where the sheer cliff face rose up to meet the chasm we'd been following. To the west, the jungle followed the base of the foothills on toward the south. To the east, we could see down the valley now. The river continued on the bottom of the canyon, the mountains jutting up high on the southern edge, separating the chasm from the expanse to the south.

Suyef made camp with our backs to a large rock outcropping at the base of one foothill. It was a short distance from the cliff's edge, facing the jungle. As Quentin set up the flame device, the Nomad took up watch on a boulder standing just south of us. No one said a word as we consumed our food-and-water nutrient packs. Quentin eased himself down to rest and stared into the flames, holding his hands out to warm them. I had his padd in hand, my mind working through the coding.

"Any luck?" he asked.

I shrugged. "It's still not connected." I frowned as I used my finger to move a column of code around on the flat screen. "It's hard to manipulate on this small panel."

"Project it," Quentin suggest, waving at the air.

The column of coding appeared at a finger tap in a translucent glow right above the device. I set the padd on my lap and perused the columns, ticking off each symbol with a finger.

"Is that the connections strand?" Quentin asked.

I nodded at him through the image hovering between us. "The problem has got to be here." A junction where the column connected to another brightened as my finger graced the edge of it. "Something is breaking the connection here, and it's not clear where the culprit is."

"The shield?"

A twist of my hand spun the column around, allowing me a view from the other side. "Maybe. I doubt the Ancients would have created a shield their own signals couldn't get through."

"Save for that one," Quentin said, pointing up at the water. "That shield is impenetrable."

I looked up with him.

"What is going on outside that shield?" he continued, lowering his hand. "The universe is still out there. What are they doing?"

"You know there's no record anywhere in the history stating our ancestors ever found intelligent life out there, right?" I asked, looking down at the column and resuming my work.

"Didn't mean life forms. I meant all of it. The stars. The galaxies. The other planets that were in our star system. The only thing that we know for sure is still out there is the moon, and that's just because of what it does to the water."

"If that shield is impenetrable," I asked, zooming the projection in to closer examine the break, "how does the moon affect the water?"

"No one's quite sure," he answered. "They theorize the moon is just pulling the shield out a bit, warping it, and that causes the water to ripple as it goes by." He shrugged. "Still, that's one powerful gravity well the moon must be generating to pull on that shield. It would have to be massive." He looked over at me. "One scientist postulated about a hundred cycles ago that what history recorded as the moon is no longer there. He claimed the gravity well generated by the shield captured something larger."

I looked at him through the projection, which lit his face lit up blue. "Like a planet?"

He nodded. "Or a star."

I looked up at the water. "That's a powerful shield if it's true."

"It's just a theory. No one really knows."

I shook my head and turned back to the coding. The symbol looked like it was just sliced in half. Maybe if I put it back, the connection would return. An editing program superimposed over the broken symbol allowed me to manipulate it and complete the coding. Something on the device beeped. The holographic projection dissolved, and the padd restarted. When it came back on, the connection flashed on.

"It worked."

I tossed the padd to him. "Enjoy."

"What did you do?"

"Drew a line."

Quentin frowned, shaking his head as he buried himself in what looked like a search.

"Little to nothing on this region," he said, shaking his head. "The Seekers just don't care that much anymore. There aren't any public records on them doing anything out here for several hundred cycles."

I frowned. "Why not check their own records?"

"For fear of tipping them off we're out here alive," he commented, tapping on his screen. "Or helping them pinpoint our location."

I nodded, leaned back, and closed my eyes. The wind tugged at my cloak.

"You can always tell when you're near the edge," Quentin muttered, rolling onto his back, eyes on the device.

"How's that?"

He waved a hand in the air. "It's windier."

I glanced around, eyeing the nearby jungle foliage. "It doesn't seem windier."

"Maybe not to you. You're used to it."

"How is it not windy on the isles?" I asked.

"Oh, it is. Very windy. A different kind, though." Quentin rolled onto his stomach, one arm folded under his head, eyes still on the padd. "More a howling, cloak-stealing kind of wind. The kind that feels like it wants to grab you and throw you off the edge."

"Thanks for that mental image." The thought sent a shiver through me.

He had the decency to look ashamed. "Sorry, didn't think that sentence through." He stared at the flames, and something in his eyes changed.

I said, "Suyef mentioned you did something with the fire before?" My eyes joined his, looking at the dancing flames.

Quentin looked up in the direction of the Nomad and sat up. "I don't suppose it will do any harm here." He grinned. "No Seekers to worry about."

"That we know of," I pointed out.

Quentin shook his head. "Only thing out there is whatever he's named 'she.'"

"That he's told you about."

"True, but why not tell us the Seekers were there?" he asked, holding a finger up to me. "No good reason I can think of."

Shrugging, I looked out at the forest. "Your trick?"

"Already doing it."

I looked back at him and jumped. His hand was on fire.

"Help!" I cried out, grabbing my scarf and flinging it over Quentin's hand.

"What are you—" Quentin blurted out, catching the scarf in his now-empty hand.

"Where'd the . . . Where'd the fire go?" I asked, pointing at his hand.

"Um, I extinguished it."

At that moment, Suyef bounded into view. "What's going on?"

"He had his hand on fire!"

The Nomad frowned. "I thought we'd discussed you showing off."

"You said to be wary of doing it around Seekers." He waved a hand around. "None here."

"Not technically true," I whispered, pointing at Suyef.

"He doesn't count." Quentin waved a hand at me and looked out at the forest. "No other Seek—"

His voice died, eyes locked on the foliage. Suyef spun, staff unfolding and whirling into sight from wherever he kept it.

"What did you see?" the Nomad whispered.

Quentin pointed into the trees. "That bush moved."

"The bush?" I asked, shifting closer to the fire. "Can the controls make the plants move?"

Suyef shook his head. "Not without natural means."

"Is it your creature?" Quentin asked the obvious question.

Suyef didn't answer. He didn't need to. At that moment, it stepped into the light.

The creature stood on four legs, covered in what looked at first to be silver-colored hair with red tinges around her neck and in her tail.

It didn't look like any kind of hair I'd ever seen, let alone human hair. She stood nearly halfway up Quentin's torso. Her snout was long and thin, her eyes a bright green, and her ears stood up toward us. I'd never seen one before and was at a loss for words.

"A wolf," Quentin whispered. "She's a wolf." He was looking at his padd, a picture of the beast displayed with columns of text flowing over it. "Amazing."

"What's that on her body?" I asked. "It's not hair, is it?"

He shook his head. "Fur." He glanced at Suyef. "They travel in packs, usually."

"Packs?" I asked, eyes darting around. "Meaning there's more?"

Suyef shook his head. "She's alone."

"How do you know?"

"Because if I wasn't alone, Red Tail Two-Legs, you'd know it already," a squeaky female voice said from the direction of the animal.

I shook my head and looked at my companions. "Did that wolf just talk?"

Quentin looked just as puzzled as me. He tapped at his padd, scanning the data.

"I don't see anything about wolves learning to talk."

Suyef waved a hand at Quentin. "Put that blasted device away."

"You do seem quite attached to it, Long Nose Two-Legs," the voice said.

"All right, that definitely came from the animal," Quentin said, pointing at the beast as he put the device away. "And who are you calling Long Nose? Have you seen yours?"

"Quentin," I whispered. "You're arguing with a wolf."

He huffed at me. "She started it."

I arched an eyebrow at him, and he glared at me. An instant later, Quentin burst out laughing, and I smiled. Part of me almost laughed, but the feeling wasn't strong enough yet.

"Are you losing it back there?" Suyef hissed over his shoulder.

"That one does seem a bit out of sorts, Brown Skin Two-Legs," the beast said. "Like a pup just discovering his tail moves."

The animal's words coaxed a semblance of calmness out of Quentin. I stepped next to Suyef.

"Is that a name for us? Two-Legs?" I asked.

"You are Two-Legs. And you are Red Tail."

I glanced at Suyef and mouthed the words *Red Tail*. He moved one end of his staff near my head and lifted my braid.

"Oh, you mean my braid?" I grabbed the bundle of hair in my hand as Suyef let it fall.

"Yes, Red Tail."

"And Quentin's Long Nose?" My eyes shifted over to look at him as he moved up on the other side of Suyef. "Yeah, I can see that."

"Hey," he blurted out. "Don't you start!"

Ignoring him, I nodded at Suyef. "And Brown Skin. Simple."

"Your kind is of a new scent to me, Brown Skin." The wolf's head cocked to one side as she looked at the Nomad. "Were your parents of mixed color? One black, the other pale?"

Quentin covered his mouth with his hand, chuckling. Suyef remained calm and emotionless, eyes never leaving the animal.

"That's not quite how it works," I said, taking a step toward the wolf.

Suyef's staff raised up, catching me across the gut. "What do you think you're doing?"

"Talking to a wolf." I nodded at the animal. "A phrase I didn't think when the day started would come from my mouth."

"From here," he cautioned, pulling me back next to him.

"Your fear is unwarranted, Brown Skin," the wolf stated, tongue lolling out of her mouth.

"Uh, is it okay if we ask the obvious question here?" Quentin raised his hand, looking back and forth among the three of us. "How's the wolf doing this?"

All three of us turned to look at the animal. She turned her head to look to her right. I followed her gaze and saw Quentin's face light up, his hand shooting up to point at the animal.

"Around her neck!" He almost squealed with delight.

I looked at the beast and saw what appeared to be a collar fitted tightly and mostly hidden under her fur. Now that she turned, it became clear that her fur was a wide mixture of silver, black, brown, and red. The darker colors streaked along her back, and the lighter colors poured down her sides to her paws, which were all a light brown.

"What about it?" I asked, leaning to one side to get a better look.

"It's got an Ancient device on it," he whispered. "That's how she's doing it."

A closer look revealed the telltale metallic silver just under her jaw. She turned her head back to us, and her fur swallowed the collar.

"So, that leads to another obvious question," Quentin stated, his fingertips at his mouth.

When he didn't say anything, I asked, "You going to ask it, or just leave us waiting all night?"

The wolf let out a short bark. Her head and body shook with what looked like a coughing fit.

"Red Tail, you will find this one hardly ever gets to the point," the beast said, her computerized voice giving us the impression she was amused.

"I don't recall meeting a wolf," Quentin said, dropping his arms.

"She's not the first one to act like she's met you before," I pointed out.

He looked at me. "Or you, for that matter."

Suyef took his eyes off the wolf to glance at both of us. "Mind filling me in?"

"Mortac and Colvinra," Quentin said.

Suyef nodded. "We'll discuss those two later." He looked back at the wolf. "Her first."

"Staying on the hunt, Brown Skin. As always," the wolf said.

"So, now you've met me?" he asked.

The wolf's head cocked to one side. "We have hunted one another for a few days now."

The Nomad bowed his head at the animal. "My apologies."

"I think Suyef's found himself a kindred spirit," Quentin whispered to me, earning himself Suyef's over-the-shoulder glare.

"You were going to ask another obvious question," Suyef said between clenched teeth.

Quentin pointed at the animal. "Where'd she get that collar from?"

The wolf barked a couple of times, her body shaking with another apparent coughing fit.

"If forced to make one, my guess is she's laughing," I whispered to my companions.

"I am, Red Tail, I am," the wolf said to me.

"Why?"

The wolf's body stilled, her green eyes locked on Quentin. "When you figure out the answer, you'll be laughing, too."

"So, did he laugh?" I asked, interrupting Micaela from my desk.

She frowned. "You ask the strangest questions sometimes."

"I ask what piques my interest," I said, shrugging. "So, did he laugh?"

She shook her head. "He didn't have time to. When he did finally figure it out, there were other things on his mind."

"Such as?"

Micaela paused, and I held my breath, waiting for yet another person to tell me to stop trying to fly without wings.

"Attacking me," she whispered, her voice carrying an iron in it still.

"Why would he do that?" I asked.

"Because he was out of control. You've seen him. You know he's not right up here." She tapped her head.

"But I thought he did that sacrificing himself to save you?"

She nodded. "He thought he was. In truth, he was committing suicide and botched it. It left him the broken man you see him now."

"And did this person the wolf was talking about have anything to do with it?"

She nodded. "He was the reason we were in that situation in the first place."

For the first time since we'd begun, I had no words to say. I opened my mouth to ask more questions, but Micaela held up a hand.

"Not yet," she stated, shifting on the couch. "The time isn't right." Her bright, blue-green eyes, glinting in the core-light from the window, locked on to mine. "I think you, of all people, can appreciate that."

I frowned at her. "Pardon me, High One, but why is it you people keep assuming you know so much about me?" I asked. "I'm beginning to feel like you did when Mortac was looking at you."

"An apt comparison," she whispered, almost quiet enough that my ears didn't catch it.

My eyes narrowed, and my mouth opened to press her for more. Before I could, she shook her head.

"Logwyn, let's just say I've been watching you since before you failed the test," she said. "And have been following you ever since as you fled from pursuing the blessing. I've often wondered why you did so."

"That's not the story we're telling right now," I whispered.

"It's as important," she replied.

"I fail to see how it will help us find the missing pieces to whatever it is I am carrying."

She stared at me for a moment. "Not yet, you don't, my dear woman," she said. "Trust me, you'll understand soon enough."

CHAPTER 38

A DARK PLACE

"So, now what?" Suyef asked.

The wolf's head cocked to one side. "You sleep?"

"With you here?"

The wolf's head cocked even farther. "You have slept the past few nights with me nearby."

The Nomad shook his head. "We'll move off. You can have this place."

I glanced at the sky. "Suyef, the shield's going to go up any minute."

"I'm curious why you revealed yourself," Quentin said, ignoring us and stepping toward the beast. He dodged Suyef's staff, shooting a smile at the Nomad and speaking to the wolf. "You've had plenty of time to do so. Why now?"

"You wander like a beast who's seen water shoot from the ground," the wolf said, looking back down the canyon. "You think you've found water, only it's not real."

I glanced back the way we'd come and thought of the waterspout we'd seen. Had it been an illusion? Or maybe it wasn't water?

Quentin caught my eye and shrugged, turning to face the wolf. "You didn't answer my question."

"Yes, she did," Suyef muttered, glancing at the sky.

As he did, the shield activated and the light dropped, bringing core-night. I blinked my eyes as they adjusted and saw the wolf standing as still as before, eyes glowing from the fire behind us.

"Um, how?" Quentin asked, looking around.

"We're lost, and she's offering her services as a guide, if my guess is right," Suyef stated, pointing at the wolf with his staff. When the beast dipped its head in what I assumed was acknowledgement, Suyef continued, asking, "What do you get from it? And where would you take us?"

"The pleasure of watching you pups traverse this untamed land," she replied. "And to the one place you want to go."

"And where is that?" I asked.

The wolf looked at Quentin. "To the one that gave me my collar."

A bit later, I found myself seated at the fire, a wary Suyef standing over my left shoulder, staff in hand, and a curious-looking Quentin seated to my right. The wolf stood several paces from the fire device, eyeing it, head cocked to one side and sniffing the air.

"You have fire, yet you don't feed it," the wolf whispered, head bobbing around as she looked at the fire.

"It's a machine," Quentin said, pointing at his neck. "Like your collar."

"This word," the wolf replied, looking up at Quentin. "Machine? What is it?"

Quentin pointed at her neck. "Like your collar. It makes you talk."

"It does no such thing," the wolf said, growling as the voice spoke.

Suyef's staff shot out to point at the animal, but the beast didn't move. It held the Nomad's gaze for two heartbeats before he pulled his weapon back.

"Then how are you talking?" Quentin asked.

The wolf's head cocked to other side. "As I always do."

I pointed at her mouth. "It's not moving, Quentin."

"Yeah, I noticed. The device is making the sound."

"How does that work?" I asked. "Is it reading her mind?"

Quentin shrugged. "Maybe. She could be thinking her words, as much as a wolf does, and the device translates them to something we understand."

"So, how does she know what we're saying?" I asked, my eyes wandering back to the wolf's collar.

"Your pictures, your scents, your sounds," the wolf answered.

"So, you don't hear words, you see pictures?" Quentin inquired, shifting down to sit on the ground before the animal, one foot tucked under him.

"I answered you," the wolf replied.

"So, tell us again why you wish to help us," Suyef stated.

"You are lost in a place that is not kind to those not born of it," the creature said. "The one who gave me this collar can help."

Quentin made to speak but paused at my hand on his shoulder.

"What's your name?" I asked.

The wolf turned her eyes, shining like crystals in the firelight, on me. "A very strange question."

"I'm sorry if I offended you," I said, waving a hand at her and bowing my head.

The wolf's head twisted to one side. "And now the Red Tail pup is sad? Are all Two-Legs this confusing? I'd hoped that meeting more would make them less confusing."

"Meeting more?" Quentin asked. When the wolf turned her gaze back to him, he smacked his head and said, "Oh, your collar."

The wolf's head bowed once, clearly a nod.

"So, the person who gave this to you is confusing?" Quentin said. "As much as we are?"

The wolf barked her version of a laugh. "Oh, that Two-Legs is as confusing and single-minded as a male in heat looking for his female to mount."

My eyebrows shot up, and I glanced at Quentin. His mouth hung open as he pointed at that collar.

"That thing's amazing," he whispered, turning to look at me.

I shook my head at him and looked at the wolf. "So, is your name a private thing?"

The wolf looked at me for a moment, head cocking back and forth, tongue hanging out just a bit. "What is this thing, 'private'?"

"Is your name for the ears of your pack only?" Suyef asked.

The wolf looked at him and bowed her head.

"A family-only name. So, what do we call you?" She didn't answer, so I tried a different tack. "This other Two-Legs. Who is it?"

The wolf barked another laugh. "Even when you meet him, you won't know. I doubt even he knows anymore."

"Does he have a name for you?"

She didn't answer right away, just looked at me. After several moments, she said, "You see much, Red Tail, right into my pack, to what is *private*, as you say."

"Do you have a different name for each pack you belong to?" I asked.

"We only belong to one pack," she answered. "Until that pack is no more; then we find another. What we were in one pack is not what we are in another."

"Do you have a name for yourself?"

She bowed her head.

Quentin shifted to look over his shoulder at me and said, "Bet that's even more secret than the other names."

I nodded as the wolf answered him.

"Very secret, Long Nose."

"So, does your new pack give you a name?" I asked.

Another bow of the head. "Sometimes they do, but we earn it. That is a good name, an earned one. No wolf wants a name given them unless they have earned it."

"So, what name has she earned for this pack?" Quentin asked, glancing at us. "I mean, we've got to call her something."

"Can we do that?" I asked, eyes still on the animal.

Again, her head bowed. "If it is has been earned, then yes."

I thought about that, about all she had said.

"Hunter?" Quentin offered up.

I shook my head.

"She's been hunting us for several days," Quentin said.

The wolf kept her eyes on me, ignoring Quentin. I'm not sure why, but at that moment it seemed the animal wanted me to name her, to give her one that suited this pack. Her emerald eyes gazed at me. As she did, the answer rolled off my tongue.

"Dyad."

Quentin looked around, a curious expression furrowing his brow. "What's that mean?"

"Two is one," I answered, shrugging.

Suyef nodded. "Because she's a beast but speaks like a human. She is a Four-Legs, but acts like a Two-Legs."

The wolf bowed her head low, sniffing at the ground near me as she did.

"So, Dyad is acceptable?" I asked.

"Very much so, for it honors me with a compliment. By naming me so, you've given me respect as one of you. As Brown Skin said, a Four-Legs acting as a Two-Legs would."

With that, she stood tall, head extending toward the sky and letting loose with the most beautiful and terrifying sound I ever recall hearing to this very day.

The sound echoed all around, setting my skin tingling with goose bumps and sending shivers up my spine. It filled me with equal parts dread and wonder. When she stopped, the sound reverberated in the air for several moments before fading away.

At that precise moment, the weather controls malfunctioned and unleashed an even-stranger storm than the one that had assaulted us during our first days in the Wilds. As her call finished echoing across the hills and rocks, snow began to fall.

The blizzard buried the landscape in snow, turning the jungle and hills from a mixture of greens and browns to a whitewashed scene I'd only seen in pictures. The cold substance stuck to everything and soaked into my clothing as fast as it fell. Staring around in bewildered ecstasy at the wondrous sight, I felt a childlike joy that pushed the sadness away. Nearby, Quentin stuck his tongue out, catching a flake and swallowing it. I laughed and tried the same, getting a mouthful of snow that froze my tongue and melted into an icy beverage. We both burst out laughing.

Suyef and Dyad, on the other hand, appeared to think we'd both lost our minds.

"Are you pups okay?" the wolf asked, looking back and forth between us.

Quentin responded by grabbing a pile of snow and flinging it at me. The makeshift ball plastered me on the side of my head, and slushy snow dripped under my cloak.

"Gah!" I cried out, wiping at the cold and trying to shake off what was running down my bare skin.

Quentin doubled up laughing, smacking his legs as columns of cloudy breath escaped his lips. I grabbed at my own pile of snow, compacting it with my hands, and flung it right at him. Unfortunately, he saw it coming and ducked, grabbing at more snow. For the next several moments, we leapt around the Nomad and wolf, flinging balls of snow at each other, once or twice tossing one a bit too close to the stoic pair. The snowball fight ended when Quentin, ducking past an errant throw of mine, tackled me around the waist into the snow beginning to pile up around us at a rapid rate. I landed with a thud in the bank, and he fell to my side. There we lay, staring up at the still-falling snow, hearts pounding, clouds of steamy fog emanating from our mouths at a rapid pace.

At that moment, something welled up inside me, something that had been missing. The rush of emotions, held at bay by the newly arrived wolf and the snow, flowed back in. I closed my eyes as images of my lost siblings flitted to the surface, of my mother, my sister. I felt it all start to rise, a water pitcher filled to overflowing. Tears began to pour down my face, freezing on my skin in the cold air. I pushed myself up and covered my face with my red, shaking hands. I felt Quentin move closer and place a hand on my shoulder.

"You miss them," he said.

I nodded, keeping my face buried, tears still flowing.

"You can't give up hope."

I lowered my hands to glare at him. "I don't have any more to give up."

"There's always hope," he said, a faint smile twisting his lips. "Always."

"Not for me, there isn't," I replied, brushing the snow from my hair and pulling my scarf up to cover my head.

"I know it seems like that, but there is, I promise you."

I leveled a stare at him, saying nothing. His words were empty, and we both knew it.

He shrugged, saying, "Yeah, yeah, cheesy phrases."

"You mean clichés," I corrected him.

He nodded. "Yes, that. Cliché. I know. But it's true."

"You mean well, Quentin, but I just don't believe there's hope anymore," I whispered, feeling a growing emptiness deep inside me. A dark, open spot at my core. My newest and closest companion of the assorted bunch I'd picked up.

"I mean it, Micaela," he said, shifting closer to me and drawing me back from staring into that dark space. "And I can prove it."

I arched an eyebrow at him, skeptical.

He grinned. "It's a cute look, that one. Is this your 'I'm about to disagree with what you say next' look?"

I scrunched my nose at him. "Get on with it."

"Why there's always hope?" he asked, to which I nodded, waving a hand for him to get to it. "Because I'm here."

His face, up until that moment smiling, became very serious, his eyes locked on mine.

"And I'm not going anywhere."

Dyad interrupted our conversation, stepping up to us.

"If you pups are done frolicking in the frozen white water, we need to get to some shelter before we can no longer see," the beast said, her tone making clear what she thought of frolicking.

"Shelter?" Quentin asked, pulling himself up and helping me to my feet.

The wolf turned back to face Suyef. "If your alpha male concurs, there is a cave nearby where we can wait out the storm."

"How long will it last?" I asked, brushing the snow from my cloak and backside.

The wolf's head twisted to one side in her version of a shrug. "It is hard to tell. It may end as we get to the cave, or last several dark cycles."

"Dark cycles?" I asked Quentin as we moved to follow the beast back to where Suyef knelt, packing up the fire device.

He shrugged. "Maybe that's what she calls night? When the night shield activates?"

The Nomad and wolf started moving toward the sheer cliff face a hundred paces from us. By that point, snow mounds covered everything and made it almost impossible to hike. Suyef and Dyad seemed not to notice, but I began to struggle. As the snow continued to fall, my body began to shiver and falter. Quentin came alongside me, lending his arm and, blessedly, what body heat he had. The hike became nothing more to me than keeping one foot moving in front of the other, hoping the next step would take me into the shelter the wolf knew of.

When it seemed my body would not make it another step, I found myself sitting down in a dark, enclosed space. A flash of light sent a stab of pain through my head. I squeezed my eyes shut, feeling another shiver convulse through my body. Next to me, Quentin wrapped his arm around my shoulder, leaning close to share his body heat. My head rested on his shoulder, my eyes peeked open.

This cave looked identical to the one we'd found that first night in the Wilds. Small, cramped, with rocks piled like benches around the walls and a fire pit in the middle. The flame device sat in that depression. I stretched a hand to the flames, and Quentin helped me move to sit on the ground cross-legged before the flickering fire. As the heat seeped back into my body, my brain began to move a little more quickly and the details around me came into focus. Dyad lay across the entrance of the cave, her fur damp but free of snow. Quentin's and Suyef's cloaks both lay on rocks nearby, as did my red body scarf. I massaged my fingers as I stared at the flames, feeling sensation just beginning to return to them. Quentin offered me a nutrient pack, and we all sat in silence, consuming our food.

"Has the storm let up at all?" I asked between bites, eyes on the flames.

"It has worsened, Red Tail," the wolf answered, drawing my eyes to her. "It may be several cycles before it lifts."

"Are we safe here?" Quentin asked, looking about the small space.

Dyad bowed her head. "This cave has not seen a Two-Legs in many cycles. It is far from the invisible wall, and the Silver Two-Legs never come this far anymore."

"Silver Two-Legs?" I asked.

Dyad looked at the Seeker cloaks my companions had laid out. "They wear such things."

"You mean Seekers?" Quentin asked. "They come into the Wilds a lot?"

The wolf shook her head. "Only in search of lost Two-Legs, like her." She looked at Quentin and Suyef. "She came with two already, so it is unlikely we will see more."

"Don't hold your breath on that one," Quentin muttered. When Dyad just stared at him, he said, "We're not Seekers. Um, Silver Two-Legs. We aren't them."

"You wear their coats; does this not make you one of their pack?"

Quentin pointed at the Nomad. "He's in their pack, technically, but he's an outsider."

Dyad looked back at Quentin. "An outsider?"

"Not of their pack," Quentin went on, waving at the cave wall. "Not from this shell."

Dyad glanced at Suyef. "You fly across the skies?"

Suyef nodded.

"What wondrous power you possess."

Suyef shook his head at the wolf. "No, I don't fly. There are ships."

When the wolf didn't answer, Suyef looked at the pair of us. "How do you explain flying ships to an animal?"

"Dyad, have you seen the speeders the Silver Two-Legs ride?" Quentin asked the wolf.

The wolf growled, her demeanor changing to something more ominous, hackles on edge, hair just over her shoulders standing on end, teeth bared.

"You speak of the horses that are not horses," she whispered between growls.

"Is that an animal a Two-Legs might ride?" he asked.

The wolf bowed her head. "The wolves sing and dream of such things, so it must be so."

"Never seen one, so I'll take your word for it," he agreed. "These horses that are not horses. We call them speeders. Now picture something like that, only large enough to carry hundreds of Silver Two-Legs standing on top of it."

The wolf glanced at each of us. "Such things exist?"

"In large number, at least on this shell," Quentin muttered, nodding at Suyef. "Not sure about his, but I assume they have the same."

Suyef shrugged. "What my people have is of no consequence here."

"Anyway, there are things like this that carry people and things like food and water between the shells. That's how he flies across the skies. It's how we both have done it."

The wolf stared at Quentin, her hair settling back down. "You travel the skies as well, Long Nose?"

Quentin nodded, grabbing a hydration pack from his belt and popping the tab off. "I've made the trip from his shell to this one and back multiple times, actually." Quentin frowned and looked at Suyef. "We won't be able to do that much longer, will we?"

Suyef shrugged, shaking his head. "What do you mean?"

"The shells are drifting apart. How long until we can't make the trip across?"

The wolf looked at me and asked, "Are these flying machines broken somehow? Can they only travel so far?"

I closed my eyes, rubbing at my forehead. "No, they're not broken. They just don't work over a certain distance. Right, Quentin?"

He nodded. "They work like the speeders do. Gravity beams pushing and pulling to keep them afloat."

"Gravity beams?" the wolf asked.

Quentin's face twisted into a rather perplexed look. Needless to say, it was amusing, making me chuckle. He frowned at me before speaking.

"Um, you know how when you jump, you always come back down? Or when you fall off something, you go down, not up?"

The wolf bowed her head a tiny bit.

"We call that thing that's pulling you down gravity. The speeders have beams that can push or pull like that force pulls you."

"You Two-Legs are as crafty as foxes," Dyad muttered.

"Is that another animal?" I asked.

Dyad bowed her head at me. "A small, annoying one. A pest."

"And you just compared us to them?" Quentin inquired.

She looked away. "Foxes may be pests, but they are intelligent in their own sneaky way."

"Thanks, I guess," he continued. "Anyway, back to the ships. They work the same way. Once airborne, they use that to latch on to whatever's closest to them and drag or push the ship where they want it to go. The intershell ships also deploy massive wings, like what birds use to fly, to take advantage of the winds." He nodded at Suyef. "As his shell is orbiting at a lower altitude than Colberra, most ships traveling that direction can just float their way down once beyond the edge of our shell." He held up a finger at the wolf. "That's assuming they get enough speed. That's what the gravity beams are for. They push the ships high in the sky toward the water shield, then push and pull them toward the shell's edge. When they get to the limit of the beams, the wings and gravity take over, and the ships float to his shell."

"Water shield?" the wolf asked, repeating his words. "What is this?"

I pointed at the top of the cave. "The water far above."

"The upside-down lake?" Dyad asked, looking at Quentin. "Why not use that word?"

"I didn't think of it," he said. "It's more a shield than an upside-down lake. I mean, I guess it's that, too." He shrugged, waving a hand at the wolf. "That works as well as any other word for it."

"What is it shielding us from, if it is that?" the wolf asked, head cocked to one side.

"Space," Quentin whispered. "The deep, dark cold of space."

When the wolf looked at me, it was clear Quentin would have a hard time explaining that one. When he looked at me for help, I held up my hands, shaking my head.

"Oh no, you talked yourself into that one. You get out of it," I replied, leaning back against the rock and closing my eyes, thankful to be resting.

"Let's just say beyond the shield, it's very cold and very deadly. The water shield keeps us safe," I heard him say.

Silence fell as the wolf contemplated his words. I let myself drift, not paying attention to the conversation anymore. My body began to float as the heat from the fire worked its way into the stitching of my muscles, seeping deep into my core and lulling me to sleep. As I drifted off, faces floated above me. My mother, my sister. My father. My brothers. Each hovered just out of my reach. My hand reached up, trying to grasp them. Each face flitted away just as my fingers brushed at their edges. I tried to call after them, but my voice was muffled. The air tightened around me as my body struggled to float higher, trying to chase them. The harder the effort, the farther they got from me. One by one, they each winked out, like candles flickering out in a dark room. Finally, only my brothers' faces remained, each very distant from me, a pinprick of light in a canvas of utter darkness. I tried one last time, calling out to them. They never answered and soon winked out, too. A cry built up in my lungs, reaching from deep within me, from the bottom of my gut. Floating in the darkness, alone, my body curled into a ball and let loose a mighty wail, sending a howl reverberating through the blackness.

CHAPTER 39

BLIND

I jerked awake to find Quentin kneeling over me, a look of concern on his face.

"Are you okay?" he asked, helping me to sit upright.

I shook my head, trying to free my mind from the cobwebs of sleep. "Sorry. Did I . . ."

"Cry out?" He nodded at my glance. "Bad dream?"

I shrugged. "I'd rather not talk about it."

Suyef lay along the far side of the fire, and Dyad hadn't moved from the entry, save to turn her back to the fire. The way she lay there gave me a feeling of a guard watching over something. It wasn't clear to me whether she was keeping us safe or keeping us here.

Quentin settled down next to me, eyes on the flames.

"Why did you say that?" I asked. The blank look on his face compelled me to repeat his words. "That you're not going anywhere."

His eyebrows elevated, and he shrugged. "I'm not. You seem to need me."

"Need you?"

He nodded. "Well, need someone. Someone who will stay with you."

"They didn't leave," I stated, feeling a bit of anger welling up inside. "They were taken."

"Yes, I know, but either way, they're gone, forever if you're to be believed."

He turned his head to look at me. I shrugged and looked at the fire.

"I don't know what to believe anymore," I said. When he didn't immediately respond, I glanced over to see him staring at me. "What?"

He shook his head, a confused look on his face. Finally, he said, "I'm sorry."

"It's not your fault."

"Some of it is," he said, nodding over at Suyef. "That fight didn't go as well as we'd planned, and your brother paid the price."

A sudden, overwhelming sadness gripped my heart, and tears welled up in my eyes. Quentin's hand gripped my shoulder.

"They were in my dream," I whispered, tears pouring down my cheeks. "My family. All of them. Even my sister." I wiped at my face, trying not to cry and failing. "Just their faces, floating there. They wanted me to catch them and . . ."

The tears came with more speed. Quentin kept his hand on my shoulder, a firm grip holding me through the tears. I muffled my cries behind my hands, trying not to wake the others. The sobs kept coming, and a chill began to creep into my body. I wrapped my arms tightly around my torso, rocking back and forth with the tears. Quentin moved closer, slipping his arms around me and just holding me. At first, I held myself in a ball, shielding myself from him. As the cries continued to pour from within, a warmth flowed into me from where his arms touched me. My face turned into his chest, and soon my arms wrapped around him as I sobbed into his chest. Something inside let go with each sob, each cry, into his chest. My hands gripped at his shirt, desperate for the warmth, the comfort, he provided.

I'm not sure how long the tears flowed. It seemed like chrons, but it was most likely only a moment or two. As the cries finally began to fade, my voice hoarse from screaming into his chest, I pushed myself up and covered my face with my hands. Quentin grabbed my hands and pulled them down to hold them between us, his face leaning close to mine.

"Don't hold it in, Micaela," he whispered. "Trust me, I know. If you hold it in, the result won't be fun. And it will hurt more."

"It hurts anyway," I said between sniffles.

"It's going to." He smiled at me. "But less so if you share it."

His hands held mine as I tried to think of a response. As the emotions of the moment faded, a sense of discomfort crept into me at his closeness, at his holding my hands. A strand of hair falling into my eyes gave me an excuse to extricate myself from the contact. Quentin caught my cue and moved away to sit near the fire. My eyes roamed around the room to find the others hadn't moved. In fact, the pair seemed to be hardly breathing.

"Your politeness is appreciated, but you can stop pretending," I said in a loud, clear voice.

The pair at least had the decency to appear ashamed, a look which, on a wolf, seemed as out of place as it did on the Nomad.

"You seemed to need a moment," Suyef said, standing and stretching.

I nodded my thanks while putting myself back into some semblance of order. At least my braid, a utilitarian choice for anyone with long hair living in the windy Outer Dominances, remained intact. The wolf stood up, stretching and shaking her fur.

"It is not shameful to cry, Red Tail," she stated, moving around the fire to stand an arm's length from me, Quentin pulling his legs up to make room for her. "It is shameful to hide that you are in pain from those that care for you."

I glanced at the other two. "I hardly know them."

Her head cocked to one side. "I think you know them better than you realize." That said, she maneuvered her way back to the entrance and stepped outside.

"I thought *human* females were complicated," Quentin muttered, unfolding his legs. I stuck my tongue out at him as he pointed at me. "You know I'm right," he said.

"If you two pups are done talking," the wolf stated as she reentered the cave, "the storm has stopped. It is time we went to see the other Two-Legs."

"Didn't you say it would last several days?" I said, getting up and grabbing my body scarf.

"As is often true in this land regarding the weather, I was wrong." She turned and moved out of the cave. "Prepare yourselves. Now we must cross the gorge."

I glanced at my companions, Quentin shrugging at me as he pulled his cloak on and moved to the entrance. Suyef deactivated and packed up the flame device, and we followed the wolf out of the cave. Busy with wrapping my red scarf around me for warmth, I bumped into Quentin's back. He'd come to a halt just outside the entrance. I pushed past him and stumbled to a stop.

A few feet from us, we could see that the snow was entirely gone, melted away. Beyond a few feet, we could see nothing.

A thick layer of fog now lay over the land, concealing everything.

To say we had a hard time navigating in that fog is an understatement. It rolled in so thick and heavy that seeing my companions walking an arm's length from me became difficult. My argument that we should wait for the fog to lift before we tried to continue fell on deaf wolf ears.

"To live in this land, you must take whatever weather you can walk through and use it," she said, starting off.

"We can't see to walk," I muttered as we hurried to keep up with the vanishing animal.

For the first chron or so, we had no clue where we were. All around us we saw a blinding gray haze that pushed down, wrapping us in a strange, moist blanket that condensed on our cloaks and hair and ran down our faces as we hiked. We were near the canyon, but I had no clue how close. Soon, I began to suspect how close we were, and deep down, I felt glad I couldn't see. As the trail we followed began to hug a smooth rock face slick with moisture from the fog, it became very obvious that we lacked a wall on our right. A quick peek at the trail showed it vanished a pace to that side. After that, my eyes focused on Suyef in front of me and didn't look down except when absolutely necessary.

The trail began to slope downward, and I wondered how much farther we might have to go before coming down below this fog. The thick, soupy substance muffled the air around us, making the slight sounds we made disappear. The faster I wiped the moisture from my face, the more it began to creep down my back under my clothing. The fog pushed down on us, forcing an eerie quiet over everything it touched. We spoke just once during that soupy hike.

"This stuff is nasty," Quentin whispered behind me after several chrons of hiking. "Not even a hint of wind."

"Yeah, that's a good thing," I said over my shoulder, turning my head just enough to talk to him without taking my eyes from Suyef's back. "Imagine how much worse this would be with a strong breeze."

"There's that," Quentin replied.

We walked in silence thereafter, each of us picking our way down into that gorge, following the wolf in the lead. Down and down we went until, after most of the day had passed, a sound tickled my ears. At first, it sounded like my imagination, like an echo of a sound heard once before. After a while the sound began to get louder, and Suyef looked down into the fog, letting me know I wasn't the only one who heard it.

"What is that?" I pointed through the fog. "That bubbly sound?"

Suyef pointed down. "The river. It's moving around the rocks."

I risked a glance into the fog and saw nothing but gray haze. Still, the sound was getting louder, building from a dull bubbling noise to a much larger roar. As the sound increased, it drew more peeks from me into the fog, trying to catch a glimpse of the water. From the roar, the water had to be raging past us down there. My hand never left the rock wall, and I spared as much of my attention from the trail as possible in hope of seeing the mighty flow of water.

"It seems like such a waste of water," I called back to Quentin.

"Maybe, but out here they can't stop it," he said, stepping closer to be heard. "You'd think they could, but obviously they can't."

"Where is it coming from?" Suyef held out his hand to help me across a rock.

Quentin replied, "Broken pipes is my guess."

I paused, glancing back at him. "You mean this water is coming from the citadel system?"

"Where else would it be coming from?" he said, nudging me to keep moving. "There isn't enough rain, even here, to account for that much water."

"So, where do you think it's going?"

"Off the edge," he answered, placing a hand on my shoulder as I wobbled a bit. "Else we're going to run into a massive lake somewhere ahead, I imagine."

My mind spun at the possibilities. A lake full of water, just sitting in the open. The existence of the river, uncontrolled, raging through the Wilds, was strange enough. The settlement had a tightly monitored canal used to help with crop growing for those wary of nutrient packs. A body of water large enough to be called a lake just seemed so far beyond that. As we stumbled our way through that fog, the amazing things this untamed region of our shell might contain filled my imagination. Creatures of so many kinds, plants long thought extinct, and formations of land altered by free-flowing water the likes of which no one could ever recall outside of pictures on the network.

When the wolf stopped and looked back at us, I wondered if she was leading us to see one such thing.

The animal stepped back toward us and looked out into the fog. "We're near our goal," she said, just audible over the roar of water.

I looked into the fog and felt a mounting sense of trepidation rise in my gut. "What's out there?"

In answer, she turned and continued down the trail, the three of us following behind. A spray of moisture hit my hand and face as the noise level rose. The fog still concealed the water, giving rise to worries the wolf intended to take us right down into the teeth of that violent-sounding river.

In a single moment, before which we'd been walking through fog as thick as soup, we stepped into the clear below that blanket of gray covering the land. What I saw there made my heart skip a beat.

The trail ended about fifty paces ahead. The mighty river, foaming white and raging in massive swirls, raced past us over a steep drop. Sharp, daggerlike rocks jutted out from beneath the water, clawing at the sky against the weight of the torrent racing past. On the far side, another sheer cliff reached up to meet the thick fog still hanging heavy overhead.

"Oh, my word," Quentin whispered, his hand pointing down the canyon.

I leaned out to see around Suyef, and my heart nearly stopped. The river swept underneath a small formation of rock reaching out from our side of the canyon to connect to another jutting out from the far side. And our trail led straight to that precarious-looking bridge.

"We have to cross *that*?" I asked the wolf. She bowed her head. "Over *that*?" The raging river echoed as the wolf bowed her head even farther. "Are you insane?"

The wolf's head cocked to one side. "It is the only way to cross. I am uncertain what the state of my mind has to do with this."

"You can't be serious," I said, eyes locked on the narrow rock. "That's impossible!"

Someone took hold of my right hand, drawing my attention away. Quentin, eyes locked on the same bridge, gripped my hand. His face appeared calm, but his jaw was clenched, his neck tight, and his grip a little too firm.

"We'll get across," he said, voice wavering.

The wolf took his words as a cue, turning to head down the trail. Suyef followed, but I held back as Quentin began to move forward.

"Are you okay?" I asked him, leaning close.

He nodded, but his eyes betrayed him. He couldn't look at me, darted glances at the bridge, and shifted around to look at anything but me. He also didn't speak, his jaw was clenched so tight. It dawned on me he needed me more than I needed his show of strength.

"Quentin, look at me," I said, reaching up with my other hand to hold one side of his face and guide his eyes to mine. "Just focus on me, keep your eyes on me, and we'll make it across." Those words didn't convince me, but they did him. His mouth opened, and his neck muscles relaxed. "Good, just stay right behind, and don't look away from me."

I squeezed his hand and turned to face the bridge, guiding his hand to my shoulder. His hand gripped my cloak tightly, his other hand coming up to grasp my other shoulder. I took a deep breath, let it out, and stepped toward the end of the trail. The water raged past us, but my eyes stayed on the trail, my left hand on the rock face. All too soon we reached the point we both were dreading and turned to face the crossing.

The bridge looked to be nothing more than a formation of rock that the water somehow failed to wipe away with its passage. That, or rock had fallen from above to form it. That possibility made me shiver, and Quentin's grip tightened in response. I steadied myself and focused on the narrow walkway before me. The path traversed a series of steps that time and water had formed ascending to the apex of the cross, the entire bridge no more than two paces across at its widest point, where we stood. At the peak, it narrowed to a single pace's width. The bridge seemed to shrink. The water rushed past below, beckoning me and making the entire structure shift in my vision. The effect was very disorienting, and I had to take a moment to close my eyes and take a few breaths before continuing. Quentin's right hand patted my shoulder, as much encouragement as reassurance. I opened my eyes and took my first step.

Much of what came next is a blur. A lot of deep breaths, eyes moving about, water racing past, and an overwhelming sense of dizziness. Keeping my eyes focused on the bridge only helped so much, because that kept the water directly in my vision, making the dizzy feeling even worse. I settled on a point on the far side, a rock jutting out from the cliff that let me keep just enough of the bridge in sight to keep moving without seeing the water below. Quentin's hands kept a firm grip on my shoulders, a strange sense of reassurance in the cacophony of sensory input threatening to overwhelm me.

Before I realized it, we were across. My knees gave out as I collapsed to the ground, extremities shaking, my heart pounding. Quentin fell down to a knee next to me, hand on my back. He leaned in close and whispered thanks in my ear, squeezing my shoulder before standing up.

"Once you've recovered, Red Tail, the hard part begins," the wolf said.

I looked up at her, a feeling of incredulity mounting inside. "The hard part? That wasn't the hard part?"

The creature didn't answer. She just turned and began ascending a trail that followed the wall of the canyon on this side of the river.

"Whoever this person is we are going to see, he had better be able to help," I muttered.

Quentin helped me to my feet, and we started after the beast. The canyon on this side looked identical to the other. The trail began its slow ascent, climbing up to the blanket of fog. A sense of dread filled me at the thought of entering that gray mass again. The wolf didn't have the same trepidation. She climbed at a quick pace, and soon we found ourselves entombed in the moist, sound-dampening fog, ascending out of the canyon over several more chrons. Just when it seemed the trail would never end, the fog would never lift, that we'd be walking up the side of that cliff face, lost forever, the fog began to clear. It was subtle at first, a slight hint that the haze was thinning. Dyad, several paces in front of Suyef and all but invisible to me, became more defined through the fog, where before she'd been a slight silhouette, a shadow shifting in the gray gloom. After that, more of the trail ahead and behind came into view. Eventually, the haze cleared around and above us, revealing the water shield for the first time since the snow began to fall. Below, the fog remained thick and heavy, hiding the river we could still hear rushing over the rocks. Over the top of the gray blanket, the hills on the south side of the canyon had given way to jagged-edged mountains, bursting forth like claws reaching out from the fog. To the north, the land sloped upward away from us to form matching mountain peaks. The valley between, through which we'd just come, lay swallowed in fog.

"That's quite the view," Quentin whispered, moving to stand next to me. "It's like giant teeth breaking through to swallow the fog."

"With us in the middle," I commented, nodding at the peaks to the north.

"There's that," he said, chuckling and moving toward the wolf. "So, where to now?"

The wolf turned and moved along the trail, which continued up this side of the gorge as far as my eyes could see.

"You know, just a hint of where we're going might be nice," I muttered.

"We know where we're going," Quentin stated from behind me as we moved to follow Suyef and the wolf. "We just don't know where 'where' is."

I shot him a look and continued on. We marched in silence for a while, the trail ascending at the same rate the previous one had descended.

"Whoa!" Quentin said from behind me.

He had turned to look back the way we'd come. I stepped closer and peeked around him.

"Look at the fog," he whispered, pointing back up the valley. "That explains how we came out of it so quickly."

"What does?" I asked.

"The fog is lower here," he said.

Up the valley, the fog did indeed rise up to swallow more of the land back that direction. After that, it just dropped off, like the top had been carved off as it came down the gorge.

"There's something very unnatural about that fog," Quentin muttered.

"The entire weather system here is unnatural," I pointed out. "Heck, it's not really natural anywhere, so here it may be more natural than anywhere else."

"Weather still acts the way it's supposed to; we just control where it can do what it's supposed to do," Quentin said, turning and moving up the trail.

"That's a semantic difference," I argued.

"Yes, and you should appreciate the importance in that," he said from behind me. "Change a word here, a symbol there, and you get an entirely different construct. A column that makes sense in one instance suddenly has no context and falls apart."

"You're talking Ancient construct language. It's not the same for what we use today."

"Maybe, but the principle is the same. Think about the computers. The programming language operates under the same premise as the scripting language. It's how they get those machines to do those fantastical things. And if you alter a single bit of coding . . ."

"You get a water shortage where there wasn't one before," I said. "I get it. So, are you saying the coding is broken here? That the machines controlling the weather are messing up the script, and that's why the weather is out of control?"

"Maybe. There's no telling what kind of damage a collision like that one might have inflicted on the citadel. It may even explain why the network on Suyef's shell and this one are out of alignment and won't communicate with each other."

"But isn't his shell the result of an even-worse collision?" I asked.

"It is, and that may just make it all the worse. There are two citadels on his shell, one entombed at the bottom of an inland sea, the other cocked at an angle along the upper slope of his shell."

"Did you ever see that citadel?"

"No," he answered, stumbling and catching himself on the rock face. "My one trip outside of our settlement didn't go that far inland."

"Has he seen it?" I pointed at Suyef.

"I asked him that on our way to Colberra," Quentin answered. "He wouldn't say."

"He refused to answer?"

"Maybe, I don't know. I'm not that good at reading people, but the mention of that citadel brought some kind of emotion to his eyes. Fleeting, mind you; it was only there for a split second."

I eyed the back of Suyef's cloak as we hiked, pondering what secrets he was hiding from us, wondering if it was our place to pry.

"You won't get anything from him, I assure you," Quentin said, coming up beside me as I stopped. "It takes something truly earth-shattering to get him to open up."

I glanced at Quentin and shrugged. "Well, hopefully nothing that traumatic happens."

Little did I know how soon saying those words would fill me with regret.

CHAPTER 40

DREAD

"You seemed to put a lot of trust in people you'd only just met," I said. "Quentin. Suyef." My fingers ticked off each name. "Mortac, to a point. This wolf, Dyad. There's a pattern here."

"I'd hardly call what happened at the prison me trusting Mortac," she replied, shaking her head and looking back out the window. "That was more a matter of circumstance."

"And the others?"

She shrugged. "Same thing? I don't know." She ticked off her own list. "Dyad, what choice did I have? Even had there been a reason to doubt her, which there wasn't, the others would have out-voted me. Suyef is quiet and a bit cryptic, but mostly golden inside. And you can tell that once you meet him. As to Quentin . . ." She tilted her head to one side. "Let me put it this way: Quentin just wouldn't take no for an answer. He's stubborn and rash at times, but fiercely loyal and one of the hardest workers I know." She leveled a gaze at me. "Look at your notes. If you had to choose one word to describe him on that bridge over the river, what would it be?"

"Terrified," I said without looking.

She nodded. "And he trusted me. Someone he barely knew. He trusted me to get him across." Her face changed, the sadness that seemed to be her constant companion creeping into her eyes.

"Trusted me like my brothers did." She looked down. "There's something about that. Being trusted. It makes you want to be worthy of it. I don't know. Maybe I needed that then." She pointed at my notes. "The word you'd probably choose to describe me is *morose*, maybe. Depressing. A downer." She smiled, just slightly. "Him trusting me was like a warm blanket in a cold place. Very welcome."

"So, is this the point where things started to look up? You started to feel better?" I asked.

Micaela had a way of looking at me that just broke my heart, or scared me. This was one of those moments. She appeared tormented as her eyes locked with mine. So much pain; something caught in my throat.

"Better? No. But something did begin to dawn on me then. I didn't know at the time what it was. I figured it out later. But that was the beginning of it."

I watched her in silence, waiting for her to continue.

"Remember how this all started?" she asked.

I nodded. "You lost hope."

"How?"

"You lost your family," I said.

"Precisely. And this was when it occurred to me that family could be something else. It took much more to happen before I got to that point. But it started there."

I nodded. "So, it started to get better?"

"Not at first, no," she whispered. "First, it got much worse."

The hike up the trail was uneventful until we reached the split in the gorge. We hiked along the canyon's edge, climbing far above the fog and the sound of the river. Still the trail went higher, the mountains ahead shielding from view where the canyon went.

Finally, we reached a peak of sorts, an apex in the trail, and took a moment to rest.

From where we stood, we could see all the way down the gorge in both directions. The canyon continued along to the west, cradled between the two ranges of mountains before turning at a sharp angle north in the distance. The fog remained inside the gorge, highlighting where it lay like a marker. The trail followed the edge of the canyon at the base of the mountains rising up to the north.

"Odd," Quentin muttered, pulling me from my gazing.

"What is?" I asked, taking a nutrient pack from him and tearing into it.

He pointed down the direction we were heading. "Look, the fog splits just where the canyon appears to turn northward."

I followed his finger. "Don't see it."

"You can't, but if you look at the motion of the fog, it's moving in that direction, and instead of turning to flow up the canyon to the north, that fog is moving down to join this flow." He waved a hand to the left. "Since this fog isn't coming back or stopping, the two flows must be going somewhere else, and it looks like they're moving to the south, just beyond that outcropping."

"If the fog is doing that, is the water?" I asked, glancing at the wolf.

She bowed her head a bit. "You are perceptive, both of you." She looked down the canyon. "There join two rivers to become one on their way to the Great Abyss."

"The Great Abyss?" I asked.

"Off the shell," Quentin whispered. "That's where the water is going. Straight off the edge."

"From two rivers? So much water being wasted."

"You can't assume it's intentional. It's possible this is the reason the Central Dominance is trying to preserve water. They can't stop this."

The wolf shifted at his words.

"Dyad, do you have something to say?" I asked her.

Her emerald eyes locked on mine. "The rivers were not always as strong as they are now. In my time they have been, but wolves sing of how the rivers were once little streams, calm enough to cross at any point. Once, there were many ways to cross and keep your paws dry. Now there are very few."

"So, the rivers grew larger, higher, at some point," Quentin said, pursing his lips as he tapped his cheek in thought. "Was this during your mother's time?"

The wolf didn't move.

"Her mother's?"

The wolf bowed her head.

"So, within two generations, but as I don't know how long you live, that doesn't help me."

"Most of us do not count the cycles as we once did long ago," she replied. "We count the dark cycles. However, my benefactor, who also knew my mother and her mother, taught us of the old way and measured it for us." She looked up at the water shield. "Using the great wolves of the sky."

"Do you mean the sun and moon?" I asked, following her gaze.

"These words are familiar to me," the wolf said, bowing her head. "The one who tugs at the upside-down lake."

"Yes, the moon," Quentin blurted out, snapping his fingers. "So, how long have you lived?"

"I have lived five cycles according to this method," she answered. "My mother and her mother each lived fifteen."

"Is that normal?" I asked.

She cocked her head at me. "Again, so perceptive. It is not. I am of the opinion that this *machine*, as you called it, on my neck improves my health, extends my time."

"So, you live longer," Quentin said, waving a hand at the thought, dismissing it almost. "When in your grandmother's time did this happen?"

"Near her end," the wolf replied.

Quentin opened his mouth to speak, but I raised a hand to stop him. "But when were you born?" I asked. "And your mother?"

The wolf eyed me. "You see much. I was born when my mother was fourteen cycles old. This is late for our kind."

"Maybe that thing helps with that, too," Quentin suggested.

Dyad bowed her head. "I agree. My mother went on to the Great Hunt four cycles ago. She was born to my grandmother when my grandmother was also fourteen cycles."

"Did she die a cycle later also?" I asked.

Dyad bowed her head.

"So, about twenty cycles ago," I said, doing the math.

"Which is right about the time our shell began having this 'water crisis,'" Quentin muttered.

"So, the two might be related," I said.

Quentin nodded. "I don't see any other conclusion. It's possible it's coincidental, that the water system out here suddenly began to malfunction twenty cycles ago and the Central Dominance did the only thing it could think to do." He frowned as he finished that sentence. "It's oddly convenient for them, though."

"I don't trust that kind of convenience," I said, turning to the wolf. "And my bet is your benefactor knows something about this."

The wolf bowed her head. "You will find he knows much about many things." Her head turned just a bit to one side, and she growled. "The problem is getting him to focus long enough to figure out if any of it matters."

"Take us to him," I said, stepping toward her. "I'm ready for some answers."

"And did you get those answers?" I asked as Micaela stood up from the leather couch and rolled her shoulders back. Even in that, she held herself with a poise that filled me with envy.

"None that would make either you or me happy, I can say that much." She looked down. "I apologize, Logwyn. I'm not trying to be evasive or cryptic. To answer your question, no, we did not get the answers we sought."

I nodded, pulling myself up straighter in my chair to match her posture. "No, I apologize, High One. My questions make your job more difficult."

She frowned and moved to the window. "It's difficult already." She put a hand on the glass, the first time I could recall her even touching it. "Have you ever just stood and pondered the nature of our world?"

I sat there, silent for a moment. Her change of topic confused me. "Pardon?"

"Our world? Have you ever thought about it?" she asked, turning to look at me.

"Our world is as it's always been."

"Always?" Her head tilted to the side, and she pointed out the window. "Like this?"

"No, High One, just as it's always been in our lifetime," I clarified.

"And in your Queen's?"

That stopped me. The Queen was an enigma in our world. The only dragon that lived eternally. No one knew precisely when she was born. Our histories only detailed when she first learned how to become the being we called the Dragon Queen.

"I suppose she might have seen the world as it once was," I allowed. "Pardon, High One, I'm confused as to what this has to do with our topic?"

She looked out the window one more time. "Call it a tangent. Thinking of Dyad again made me ponder it."

"Again? Do you not know what became of her?"

Micaela stared out the window a moment before answering. "The same happened to her as to many in this tale. She vanished."

A sense of urgency fell over us as we made our way past the fork in the canyon. Quentin's guess proved accurate about the river and fog. As we reached the point where the trail turned to follow the new river, we took a moment to look off to the south. The great expanse of our world could be seen just above the fog between the mountains the river flowed through. While I couldn't see it because of the fog, I imagined all that water rushing headlong to fall down toward the planet's core. Wasted.

We made our way up the new canyon in silence. The only conversation that took place involved the necessities: food, rest, and the like. Even the wolf sensed something had changed in our moods and eagerly kept us moving. The fog remained, shrouding the water. I wanted to ask the wolf if that was normal but thought better of it. My questions could wait until we met this mysterious benefactor. I did wonder why the weather suddenly improved, why it remained calm and windless without even a hint of the unpredictability it had shown before the fog arrived.

We rested when the night shield fell, finding an alcove along the way to hunker down in as we slept. As soon as the shield lifted, we moved out, following the canyon as it began to narrow. The peaks on either side didn't seem to reach up as high anymore, and the far side of the gorge edged closer.

Later that day, we found the fog beginning to thin below us. We kept moving, and, as we came around an outcropping, the group came to a halt. The fog finally dissipated enough to reveal our destination: the end of the gorge. Our trail continued down into the valley to meet the river, even as the north face of the gorge swept up to form a giant cliff. The river, visible at last, flowed down toward us around two massive rock formations, plateaus in the middle of the gorge, the farthest of which reached almost as high as the northern cliff face. The south side, dominated by a flat plateau, as the peaks we'd followed were now gone, ended where a giant slice of rock jutted up from the edge of the gorge. The rock structure stretched up farther than any of the peaks we'd passed. It split almost three quarters of the way up into two peaks, one reaching even farther above the other. On the north side, on which we traveled, I could see more structures similar to the rock tower just visible above the cliff's edge, reaching up like fingers to point at the water shield.

"Is that where we're going?" I asked, pointing at the structure.

The wolf bowed her head. "Inside lies the domain of my benefactor." She turned her head to look at us. "No Two-Legs but him has ever entered in my time."

"How many Two-Legs have made it this far into the Wilds?" Quentin asked, stepping up to stand next to Dyad and look down at the river. "Does the water lower enough for us to ford it? Or do we have to go up beyond the structure to get across?"

"The water bursts forth from under the ground just beyond that plateau," Dyad said, pointing with her snout at the rock structure. "The far side of the canyon is all sheer cliff faces. You cannot approach his domain from that way."

"So, we cross the river," Quentin muttered, pointing at the water. "Where? I don't see another makeshift bridge."

"My instructions are to bring you to the river's edge. After that, you are on your own," Dyad said, stepping forward to go down the trail.

"Wait, you aren't going with us?" I asked, hurrying to catch up with the wolf. "Why not?"

"My benefactor made it clear I am not to try to cross the river with you," she said, glancing back at Quentin, who was walking right behind me. "He seems to think there are things better left unknown to me." She turned her head back to the front. "How little he knows of our kind." She walked a bit longer, then asked, "Long Nose, please excuse us. Keep Brown Skin company. I wish to speak with Red Tail about—well, let us just call it feminine things."

Quentin looked at me before shrugging and slowing down to walk a respectable distance behind.

"I cannot tell you much of what is to come, Red Tail," Dyad said in a near whisper. "But I know this much: my benefactor has not been well recently. Not sickly, just not right in the head. He has been dreading something of late and sent me to find you."

"Do you know why he sent you to find us?"

Her head bowed a bit. "He gave no indication of his motivations, but he did say someone would need my help and that my instincts would guide me when I found them." She glanced at me. "It's becoming clear to me he knew I'd be finding you three, and that is what he has been dreading."

"Why?" I asked, glancing back at my two companions.

"What comes next has a fearful scent to it, Red Tail, not so much as it concerns me, but my benefactor." The wolf looked up at the towering rock structure. "Something is about to change."

"In a bad way?"

The wolf bowed her head. "In a very bad way."

CHAPTER 41

CONVENIENT

The wolf was true to her word. As soon as we approached the river's edge, she stopped, refusing to come down with us. When we made it to the bottom, I looked back up and didn't see her.

"She's gone," I whispered.

Even though it had only been a little over a day, I'd very much grown accustomed to having her there. Now that she wasn't, the Wilds suddenly felt a bit more so.

Quentin glanced back up and frowned. "Where did she go?"

"She can't come with us, remember?"

"Yes," he said, nodding and pointing back up the way we'd come, "but there isn't a place to hide anywhere on that trail for a good distance. So, where is she?"

My eyes wandered all the way back up the length of the trail along the cliff face. Finally, I shrugged.

"It's not the first strange thing we've encountered," Suyef said, stepping near the water and squatting. "You're looking for a talking wolf, after all."

I chuckled and looked at the river. Now that we were closer, it was easy to be awed by its majesty and power. It filled the canyon with a pleasant, soothing sound. Still, it did present an obstacle.

"So, I assume we cross."

Quentin stepped near to look down where Suyef was examining the water. "Can we walk through it?"

Suyef shook his head. "There's a drop-off a few paces out. It's difficult to make out how deep it is, but I'll wager the flow is really strong under there."

"How would you know that?" I asked.

Suyef glanced back over his shoulder at me. "Trust me, the pull is very strong in waters this deep. Look at how fast the water is moving past us. Stick your hand in. Feel the tug downriver."

"There's got to be some trick we aren't thinking of," Quentin muttered, turning his back to the river and looking around.

I turned and looked with him, but everything appeared ordinary. A smooth cliff face soaring high over us, smaller rocks strewn all along the river's edge, gravel and debris from the river gathering in the crevices. Nothing strange jumped out.

Quentin stepped near the cliff face, extending a hand to brush at a slight bump in the stone.

"Do you see something?" I asked, moving to stand next to him.

His hand still touching the rock face, he looked over at me. "This part doesn't feel right."

"Doesn't *feel* right?" I asked, ducking my head around to examine the bulbous bit of rock face he referred to. It jutted out like a bubble pushing up through a piece of cloth. "It doesn't look any different." I pointed up along the cliff face. "There are several like this one."

"Put your hand on the rock next to it; then slide it over."

I did as he suggested. The cliff face felt rough and damp, giving it a smooth, slick feel despite the myriad of tiny pockmarks marring the surface. As I slid my hand over the bulbous bit, the dampness vanished. I moved my hand all the way across the rounded face until it encountered the damp slickness again.

"It looks the same," I whispered, running my hand across the face.

"But it's not," he said, looking up at the cliff. "So, the question is, why?"

"To hide something," I said, drawing a circle with my finger around the edge of the strange-feeling surface. "It's not large, about the size of a . . ."

My eyebrows shot up. Quentin grinned as he pulled out his padd.

"Of this?" he asked, holding it up to show it did indeed fit inside the invisible circle. "Maybe a screen like this one."

"So, how do you access it, if it is there?" I asked, tapping at the surface in multiple places and peering closely at the rock face. "There's no trigger or latch."

Quentin tried holding the padd up, screen side out, to the rock face, but nothing happened. "Worth a shot," he muttered, pocketing the device and shifting to stand squarely in front of the dry surface. He leaned in close, his face inches from the rock.

The surface melted away in a flash to reveal a screen. A beam shot out at Quentin's eye and a vertical line of light slid across his pupil before he could even blink. The screen flashed several times, then went dark.

"Um, what just happened?" Quentin asked, blinking his eyes and looking at me.

"Your eye was scanned." I described the light.

"But nothing happened," he stated, leaning back down close to the screen. No light appeared. "Why scan me if you aren't going to do something, you infernal machine?"

"Maybe it did and you aren't the right person," I suggested, shrugging.

He pointed at me. "You leaned in almost as close and nothing happened."

I shook my head. "I'm just telling you what happened. We're all guessing here."

Quentin's jaw clenched as he glared at the now-blank screen.

"You okay?" I asked.

"Technology I can't figure out irks me," he muttered, tapping a finger to the screen. Nothing happened. "It's like it's mocking me."

"You know it's a machine, right? It's not sentient."

He turned his glare on me. "I've had enough experience with these networks to doubt that premise."

I pointed at the blank screen. "You're going to argue that thing's not only sentient, but mocking you? Why?"

He shrugged and kept quiet.

"Just because you can't figure out how to work it doesn't mean it's conscious and doing it on purpose." I leaned close to him and dropped my voice to a whisper. "It just means you don't know everything."

He grimaced. "I don't have to know everything." He tapped the screen one more time, then turned to face the river. "Just how to find out the unknown parts."

"Says the guy just trying to argue the computer's alive." I smiled and turned to look at the river.

I made light of it, but my father's wariness of the network terminals came to mind. He'd acted very much like someone or something was using them to spy on people. My eyes moved back to the now-blank screen, and I wondered just what my father knew that made him think that.

Quentin just shook his head and crossed his arms over his chest. I chuckled and stepped near the water's edge, taking in the beautiful sight. The sand-colored cliffs soared over the water rushing past my feet. The sound of water bubbling and flowing filled the air, and an unfamiliar scent tickled my nose.

"What is that scent?"

"You're smelling life and death," Suyef muttered, waving a hand around at the canyon. "The water brings life, but too much life brings festering and decay." He pointed off to our left, where a pool of water stood separated from the river. "Life and death, all in one place." A green substance floated on the water, and what looked like a green sponge grew on the sides of a rock near the still liquid. "That's what you're smelling."

"It smells . . . oddly old," I said. "Strange that a place with this much life would smell old."

Suyef pointed up the canyon. "Something's coming."

I turned my head and followed his finger to see what could be a boat—but not really much like those I'd seen in pictures—appearing from around the edge of the large island that separated the river. Silver in color, it sat low in the water and seemed just large enough to hold all three of us. No one was in it.

"Where did it come from?" I asked.

"How it's moving is probably a better question," Quentin said, stepping closer to the water and squinting to look at the craft. "It's got to be coming from the tower."

I frowned at his response and tone, but he wasn't looking at me. "Why?"

"Where else would it be coming from?" Quentin asked, glancing at me with a questioning look on his face.

"You're jumping to a lot of conclusions here." I indicated the boat. "You're probably right, but it's annoying."

He shrugged. "If I'm right, does it matter?"

Suyef looked over at him. "Don't be immature."

"You aren't that much older than me, Suyef," Quentin said, glaring at the Nomad.

"Then act like it." Suyef glanced at me, then looked at the boat. "You summoned it."

"I did?" Quentin asked, glancing at the rock face. "You mean when that thing scanned me?"

"It's the only logical conclusion to jump to," Suyef said, smiling at me.

"But why me?" Quentin asked, stepping up to stand next to me, eyes on the boat. "She leaned in just as close. Why not her?"

"Sounds like a good question for whoever lives in that tower," I said.

The boat did come to us. Suyef insisted on examining it from front to back, looking for anything out of the ordinary. I almost asked how he would know if there was something strange about the boat, then stopped myself. He'd probably seen them on his shell. After a few moments of examination, Suyef climbed in the boat and waved us in after him.

"Passes your inspection?" Quentin asked, a smile on his face as he climbed in and held a hand out to me.

A grunt was all I heard from Suyef. As soon as we all climbed aboard, the boat shifted out into the water, returning back the way it came without turning around. We seated ourselves for the ride, my companions leaning over and staring under the water for something. Quentin glanced at me when I leaned over and arched an eyebrow.

"I'm looking to see if something is pulling or pushing us under there," he said, pointing at the water racing past us.

"And?"

He shrugged. "Can't tell."

I nodded and sat back, tilting my head to look up at the massive formations of rock towering above us. The boat cut across the river, ignoring the strong flow of water pushing against it. Caught up in looking at the giant cliffs to either side, we'd moved to the far side of the river and past the large island much sooner than I expected. Our launch point was hidden from sight. Turning my head to the front, I caught a glimpse of our destination: a platform just above the rushing water, reaching out into the middle of the river, held up on what looked like pillars. Above, the rock tower burst out from the cliff face, a giant dagger slicing up into the sky.

The boat came to a halt, resting alongside the platform. Suyef climbed out first, testing the surface before putting his weight on it. At his nod, Quentin followed and helped me out. At the end of the platform stood a closed door, a single panel mounted to the left side. The air was quiet, save for the sounds of the river flowing past.

"Before I go near that panel, you two go try it," Quentin said, pointing toward the screen.

Suyef, shaking his head, stepped forward and stopped near the panel. I moved up next to him and watched him tap the screen. Nothing happened. He waved a hand over it, pressed his hand flat, and even pushed on it with not a small amount of force. The door remained closed. He arched an eyebrow at me.

"Try looking at it."

He frowned.

"Lean down, let it see your eyes."

He shrugged and leaned over, placing his eyes near the panel. No beam of light shot out as had happened before. He stepped back and nodded at me. I tried the same steps and received identical results.

"It doesn't work for us," Suyef called back to Quentin. "Your turn."

He eyed the panel, shifting back and forth. Finally, he nodded and stepped forward. He wasted no time, leaning over and letting the panel get a clean shot of his eyes. Nothing happened.

Frowning, he stood up, muttering, "Well, so much for that."

"Try touching it," Suyef said.

Quentin placed his palm on the screen. It didn't change. He tapped it with his index finger, sliding it around the edges. He leaned down close to the screen, examining it.

"It looks exactly like the other, but it's not doing any—"

The screen flashed, changing from its normal gray color to orange. Then a voice very similar to Dyad's spoke, saying, "Voice imprint recognized. Processing."

All three of us stepped back.

"What happened?" Suyef asked. "What'd you do?"

"Nothing," Quentin insisted. "You were standing right there, watching me."

The screen blinked, changing to green. "Voice imprint confirmed. Access granted."

The door slid open, revealing a dimly lit hallway, gray in color, leading to another door several paces away. None of us moved.

At my glance and a nod at the door, he shrugged. "You got me."

"You got something you want to tell us?" I asked.

"I've never been here before," he protested, shaking his head and staring at the screen.

"It seems okay, but at this point I'm not sure what to expect," Suyef stated, stepping into the entrance and looking around. "Clearly, someone wants you to get in."

"Clearly," Quentin muttered, pushing past Suyef and walking into the hallway toward the other set of doors. "And I'm going to ask him why."

"So, the technology just let you in?" I asked, waving a hand at the recording device. "Just opened and you didn't question that?"

"You heard me," Micaela said, glaring at me. "I questioned him."

"Did you believe him?"

She shrugged. "Not really, but I didn't have evidence to the contrary. All we knew was someone had keyed the devices to respond to Quentin."

I frowned. "Seems awfully convenient, that happening."

She nodded. "We all thought the same thing." She let out a long sigh. "Still, I had my own part in what happened next."

CHAPTER 42

THE TOWER

The technology continued to react to Quentin as we entered the hallway. The lights, dim when Suyef walked in, brightened the instant Quentin pushed past the Nomad. He paused a few paces from the doors, nodding at Suyef to approach first. They remained closed. When Quentin stepped near, they slid open without a sound to reveal an elevator identical to the one we'd ridden at Mortac's prison facility. As we gathered close inside, Quentin's face furrowed into a look that might have been funny under different circumstances.

"You okay?" I asked him as the lift rose inside the tower.

He shrugged. "Confused, curious. Okay is in there somewhere."

"You noticed the entry panel's voice, yes?"

He nodded. "Probably a voice pattern whoever lives here likes."

"And you've never heard it before?" Suyef asked, eyes roaming around the small lift.

"Besides in the wolf, no."

"Well, it's obvious someone was expecting you to come," I said, nodding at the doors. "Judging by the reactions of all the technology."

"But who? And how?" Quentin asked.

"Maybe the wolf had something to do with it?" Suyef offered. "She could have recorded your voice while we were in the cave."

"That answers the how, possibly, but not the why."

I smiled. "You didn't ask why."

He grimaced. "It was implied."

"Oh, so now we have to keep track of what you imply as well, huh?" I asked, arching an eyebrow.

He rolled his eyes and looked at Suyef. "This doesn't concern you?"

"Of course it does," the Nomad replied, shrugging. "But there's nothing to be done about it."

"Considering how wary you've been of some of the places we've gone, your comparative lack of concern strikes me as odd."

Suyef jabbed a finger at him. "You've caused me enough trouble; it's about time having you around benefited me a bit."

Quentin stuck his tongue out at the Nomad, and the conversation died as the lift came to a halt. The doors slid open to reveal a large, circular room with a high ceiling. A window with a massive balcony stood to the right, with views of the Central Mountains in the distance. A long table built into the wall filled the left side of the room. It ended at another set of doors opposite the lift we'd just left. In the center of the room lay a circular platform, and just beyond that platform stood a network station. Quentin darted around the room to the panel and tapped the screen. Nothing happened.

"That's new," he muttered.

The instant he spoke, the panel lit up. The voice spoke again.

"Welcome back, sir. I trust your journey was a success."

Quentin glanced at us as we moved to stand to his right. "Our journey was eventful."

"Systems check has been completed per your request. All systems go. Your grav-board is fully charged and calibrated."

"What's a grav-board?" I asked, looking around the room.

The computer did not answer.

"It seems to be keyed to respond only to my voice," Quentin said, tapping the panel. "And the touch interface has been locked."

"Would you like to reactivate touch-screen mode?" the computer asked.

"Yes," he answered.

"Please enter your personal passcode." A small panel flashed up on the screen. "Please enter your personal passcode."

"Well, now you're stuck," I muttered, moving away from the panel to examine the table. "Suyef, what do you make of this?"

On the table lay a long, flat board, tips curved upward on either end. It was silver in color. Next to it, I saw what looked like a cloth belt, with small circular panels inlaid around the belt's outer edge, and a magnetic clasp.

"Any ideas?" I asked the Nomad, who leaned over the table to examine the items there.

"That could be the board the computer mentioned," he said, moving back and forth along the table, eyes darting over to look at the belt. "But this. Quentin, does this look familiar?"

Quentin stepped over, his eyes widening. He parted his cloak and removed an identical belt from around his waist.

"That's the belt your father gave you, yes?" I asked. "When you were a kid?"

He nodded, holding it up next to the other. The two were nearly identical.

The computer spoke again. "Sir, I've detected a fully recharged control belt new to the system. Would you like to sync to this new one?"

We all turned to look at the panel.

"Um, sure," Quentin said, stepping back to the panel, belt still in hand.

I looked at Suyef. "What's a grav-board?"

"I have a guess," the Nomad whispered, "but if I'm right, this is Ancient technology."

"Literally?"

He frowned.

"Was it designed by the Ancients?"

"Oh yes. They used to make these. Most were lost ages ago." He leaned over the board, sniffing it. "This one is very old."

"You can tell that by sniffing?"

He shook his head. "I was sniffing for anything out of the ordinary. Ancient devices are infamous for having no smell to them. Not even a metallic one."

"And?" I asked, hiding a smirk as the Nomad continued to sniff.

"Nothing. If this has been used recently, it's been cleaned." He stood up. "I'm wondering if this belt controls the device." He looked over at Quentin. "How did you do that?"

Quentin stood tapping away on the panel. He glanced over at us, a sheepish grin on his face.

"Everything else was keyed to react to me, so I tried the one passcode I might use for this, and it worked," he said, looking back at the panel. "Not that that's helping me much. This is just another access panel to the network. There's no local drive visible. And this place's connection to the network is weird."

"Define *weird*," I said, moving toward the balcony to get a look outside.

"Not sure. It's slow. Much slower than it should be."

I stepped outside to the edge of the balcony and grasped it with two hands. The view stunned me. The Central Mountains rose high in the distance, and between our location and those mountains several different offshoots of those peaks rose out of the vast wild land we were lost in. In various places, clouds floated over the Wilds and something bright flashed out to strike at the jungles. To the east, the fog remained over the river. To the west, the end of the river we'd just crossed burst out at the head of the canyon it had cut into the landscape. A wave of dizziness overwhelmed me when I looked at the base of the tower. More flashes of light struck the distant jungles. When I turned to ask Suyef what it was, my eyes caught something moving above the distant Colberran peaks. I squinted, trying to get a better view, but couldn't make out any details.

"Suyef, what do you make of this?"

He joined me on the balcony, following my finger pointing to the north. "A ship of some kind, hovering over the city."

"Seekers control all of those on this shell," I muttered, my eyes locked on the distant object. "That can't be a good sign, can it?"

"It could be anything," he said, shrugging. The sound of his voice said he didn't believe his own words.

"Could that ship be coming to look for us?" I asked.

He nodded. "It's a possibility. They're going to need a more robust search party. This region is massive."

"This cursed machine is busted or something," Quentin said from inside the room.

"Could the connection be filtered?" Suyef asked as we moved back in to stand next to Quentin.

"Filtered? As in to keep content from reaching here?"

Suyef shook his head. "No, more along the lines of hiding this terminal from the network."

"Ah, you mean masked," Quentin said, snapping his fingers and nodding. "That's possible. It would account for the sluggish response to network queries. If I could find something local, even a local process to run, I could test that theory."

"You could make one," I suggested. "These things all have a sandbox state you can access."

"No." Quentin turned away from the panel. "What I need is to find the local files."

When he moved out of the way, I stepped to the panel and began my own search. It took no time at all for me to bring up a sandbox program to work in. My intent was to create a code to dim or brighten the panel when a finger tapped the window. Once done, I tested it. The screen's illumination went up, then down, with a touch of my finger.

"Local process works," I muttered. "No detectable lag."

"So, the problem is external to this station, at least," Quentin stated, moving closer to me.

I opened the controls for the network link and zoomed in to check for the same broken link we'd found on Quentin's padd a few days before. It was a long shot, I knew, but worth a check.

"No, all the symbols are correct," I said after a few moments scanning. "It's not the shield."

"So, maybe he's right." Quentin nodded at Suyef. "Maybe it's masked."

Silence fell on the room. Quentin turned toward the platform dominating the center of the room. "Any guesses what this is for?" he asked, stepping near the elevated floor.

Suyef shrugged, shaking his head. "Could be anything. Try asking your newfound friend."

"Okay, let's stop right there," I stated, holding up my hands and stepping away from the panel. "Am I the only one concerned here that he managed to gain access to someone's private terminal system?"

"Sure, it's odd." Quentin moved around the platform, eyes never leaving the floor. "Doesn't mean we can't take advantage of it."

"And it's getting pretty hard to trust you about this whole place," I said, glaring at him.

That got his attention. He looked right at me.

"What are you saying?" he replied, his eyes flaring as he spoke. "You still think I've been here before?"

"The evidence is leaning that way, yes." I pointed at the panel. "How else do you explain that thing being locked using your preferred code?"

"Coincidence?"

I frowned. "You don't expect me to believe that, do you? You don't even believe in coincidences."

"Don't really care what you believe!" he yelled, his face turning red. "All I know is the truth. I've never been here before."

Suyef stepped toward Quentin. "Neither of us can prove you have, but the evidence is mounting against you."

"I don't know who runs this place or what they're trying to prove, but I've never been here before," he said, his voice lowering at the Nomad's calm demeanor.

At that moment, the computer spoke. "Sir, your presence near the transport platform has been detected. Do you wish to travel?"

Instinctively, all three of us moved away from the platform. Quentin bumped into the table as he did.

"Sir, your presence near the grav-board docking station has been detected. Do you wish to activate and make use of the device?"

Quentin pushed himself up from the table and turned to look at it. "Guess that answers your question, Micaela."

"That thing said a transport platform," Suyef said, pointing at the panel. "Ask it where it goes."

Quentin did so. The computer responded: "The destination has not changed."

"That didn't help," I muttered.

"Computer, can I change the destination from its current one?" Quentin asked.

"At this time, there are no other destinations in range of this platform."

"Computer, please identify the current destination," he ordered the machine.

"Nomad tower."

We both looked at Suyef, who mouthed the computer's words.

"Any idea where that is?" Quentin asked.

"It's got to be on your shell," I said. "Why else call it that?"

"It could just be a name for another tower on this shell," Suyef said, pointing at the platform. "I'm not familiar with this mode of transportation."

"I've never heard of it, either." Quentin moved around the edge of the device. "But that doesn't mean anything. There's so much we don't know about the Ancient world and their technology."

Suyef shook his head, pointing at something on the side of the raised floor. "This isn't Ancient. Or at least not completely. They don't have these kinds of grooves in Ancient technology."

I looked down at the edge of that side of the platform and saw the grooves he meant, where the metal had been fused together. "How is that accomplished?" I asked, leaning down to look at the metal. "There isn't even a gap."

"Someone's been scripting," Quentin surmised.

I looked up at him. "You mean someone scripted this thing from scratch?"

"Or took something else and altered the coding enough to make it work how he or she wanted it to," Quentin said, nodding. "Still, that's an impressive bit of scripting."

"But that's Ancient?" I asked, nodding at the grav-board.

Suyef nodded. "Both in make and age. That thing I'm familiar with, if in passing. Ancients used them to build the citadels."

Quentin moved over to the table, picked up the belt, and held it up next to his own. "Suyef, you don't suppose these are gravity-beam generators?" he asked, waving the Nomad closer.

"I'm not sure. It's possible. They look like much smaller versions of what you'll find on the speeders."

Quentin stood staring at the table for a moment, then set the belt back down. "Computer, has my belt been synced?"

"Affirmative."

"To what?" I asked.

The computer didn't answer, so Quentin repeated my question.

"To the grav-board, sir. The new belt is now the primary control device, per your request."

Quentin started putting his belt on, then began removing his cloak. "Computer, how do you activate the belt?"

A wary feeling filled my gut. "What are you doing?"

Quentin shrugged. "Testing a theory. Computer?"

"Secure the clasp, sir. As always."

He finished pulling his silver cloak off and donned the belt over his dark-blue shirt. He settled it just above the utility belt holding up his brown trousers. The instant the magnetic click engaged, Quentin looked around the room, his eyes wide.

"Oh, wow," he whispered, reaching out his hand and grasping at something only he could see. "Oh, wow!"

The wary feeling rose to grab at my throat. "What is it?"

"I think I'm seeing the beams this thing produces," he said, walking around the room, turning in circles, eyes moving all around as he did. "I'm not sure what they're doing, but they're there. All around." He moved his arms about, pointing, grabbing at air. He paused, looking at the table. "And if I focus on something, several larger beams move to point right at it."

"Point at it or grab it?" Suyef asked.

Quentin shrugged. "I don't know how to tell." His head tilted to one side, and his eyebrows furrowed. The board quivered, shifting toward him. "Whoa!"

"What did you do?" I asked, moving away from him and the table.

"Not sure. I focused on the board, and the beams moved to touch it. Then I imagined it coming toward me, and it did." He looked at the belt, running his hands along it. Quentin focused on the board, and, a moment later, it shifted back to where it had been. He looked around the room, grinning. "This is an impressive bit of technology. I can't even feel the beams."

Quentin turned around in the room. "They just move wherever my focus is. This is amazing."

"Quentin, you need to take it off," I said with a little more force. "It could be dangerous."

He wasn't listening. He continued to spin, laughing, then holding up his hands at us as he stared down, concentrating on the surface just beneath his feet. He squatted low and leapt as high in the air as he could. As he reached the apex of his leap, looks of glee and shock flashed across his face as he crashed back to the floor. He fell backward onto his posterior and cried out in surprise.

Suyef and I didn't move. Quentin looked at his waist, shaking his head.

"Why didn't that work? That should have worked," he muttered, pushing himself up to stand.

"What were you trying to do?" Suyef asked.

"To hover, to use the beams to push up and hold myself in place."

"You did it wrong," Suyef said, waving a hand at him. "Try again."

"Wait, you're encouraging him?" I asked, feeling a bit betrayed by the Nomad. "He needs to get that thing off him. We don't know anything about it. You just found the stupid thing, and now you're trusting your life to it."

"Actually, I've had this one for more than ten cycles," Quentin pointed out.

"And you never figured out how it worked, and now you're suddenly going to trust it?"

"Hovering a few feet off the ground isn't that much of a risk," he replied, focusing on the ground. "Now let me try this again."

Suyef shrugged at my glance and resumed watching Quentin. I threw my hands up in defeat, crossed my arms over my torso, and glared at Quentin.

The look was wasted on him. The next moment, he squatted and jumped. This time, he did slow for an instant before falling back down. He expected the fall and landed on his feet. He shook his head and leapt once more. He slowed noticeably this jump, so much so that his landing had almost no impact on him. He wasted no time jumping, and, much to my disappointment, he succeeded.

Quentin hovered in midair, a boyish grin on his face, hands held high over his head in victory.

I held up my hand, and Micaela stopped, arching an eyebrow at me across the table.

"I have some questions," I said.

She nodded.

"Are you going to explain how he got access to the panel?"

She shrugged. "I could tell you, but it's not important. Yet."

"Not important?" I asked, not bothering to hide the incredulity in my voice.

"Yet," she said again, then held up a hand to forestall my response. "I'll get to that part, trust me. This will all make sense, eventually."

I frowned and glanced over my notes. "This entire scene seems a bit too weird."

She nodded. "I agree. I thought so then as well. I tried to say something, but, as you'll see soon enough, events spiraled out of control quickly." She took a deep breath, letting it out as her eyes drifted off to stare at a wall over my shoulder. "Very quickly."

"Do you need a break?" I asked, feeling a kink twisting at my neck.

She nodded, and we stood up together.

"Maybe I could come back later?" I suggested, waving a hand at my notes and the recording device, still active.

She shook her head. "We're coming to a crossroads. Trust me, you don't want to stop now."

We returned to our work a short while later, having watered and fed ourselves from the supply of food made from the Queen's reforging device. She kept her supplies in a small kitchen for one of the few things, according to Micaela, the Queen enjoyed: cooking.

"I think she finds it calming," Micaela said as we ate. "It's simple and has an end point. She values that, considering how old she is."

I spent a few moments collecting my thoughts while staring out the window at the core. The story was building to something, to something Micaela claimed she needed to tell me. Still, something felt off. Something about what was coming in the narrative bothered her. I mentioned as much when we sat back down.

"Yes, very much so," she whispered, a far-off look cast over her face. "But it was necessary. Very necessary."

"What was?"

Her bright eyes—silver and blue mixed with just a hint of green, masking a very reserved, quiet intelligence—focused on me. Her jaw set visibly as she took in another deep breath.

"Another loss."

CHAPTER 43

FALLING

Quentin spent the next several minutes playing with his new toy. He experimented with changing his elevation, shifting around the room, even flipping. He only did that a couple of times, however. He seemed to have an issue with spinning too fast. Luckily for him, he wasn't too high in the air when the first bout of vertigo struck him and he lost control of the device. Still, I'm not going to say it didn't please me when he fell on his posterior. Hard.

"That'll take some getting used to," he muttered, pulling himself up and rubbing the bruised area.

I glared at him and opened my mouth to retort, but he continued.

"Computer, display any records you have on the grav-board and its use," Quentin said, head tilted up to the ceiling.

"Those files are not available from this location," the voice answered. "Access to citadel database is required."

"Can you connect to the full network?"

"Not at this time," the computer replied. "Access has been restricted."

"By whom?"

"You, sir."

Quentin frowned, looking at me. "By me? I've never been here before."

"If you say so, sir."

"Well, turn it off," he said.

"The restriction cannot be lifted at this time. Please try again later."

Quentin closed his eyes, hand going to his temple as he spoke. "So, if the restriction was put in place by me, can't I lift it?"

"The restriction specifically blocks any cancellations by you until the restriction period ends."

Suyef glanced at Quentin. "Sounds like 'you' wanted that block in place for a set period of time."

Quentin nodded. "Computer, when does the restriction end?"

"Information about the restriction is locked at this time. Please try again later."

He shook his head, throwing up his arms. "Fine, forget the restriction. Do you have any records on the use of the device in this facility?"

"That information is restricted."

His frown deepened. "Let me guess. By me."

"Correct, sir."

"That's getting annoying," he said, looking at us and waving at the panel.

"If you're telling the truth, why is she convinced you've been here before?" I asked, nodding at the panel.

He shrugged. "Case of mistaken identity."

"It must be," Suyef stated, pointing at Quentin's waist. "Remember, she didn't recognize his belt. He's had that most of his life, and, if he's to be believed, he's worn it most of that time. So, it would stand to reason that had he been here before, she'd recognize that device."

"Unless he took it off," I pointed out.

"I haven't been here before," Quentin said, his tone firm.

"Ask her when you last came here," Suyef suggested.

"That information is restricted," the computer said to Quentin's request.

"Is any information on the person who lives here available?" he tried.

"That information is—"

"Restricted," he said with the computer. "I know." He sighed, one hand covering his mouth. "The network here is weird; you saw as much, Micaela. Whoever put those restrictions in place may have dropped the filter on the connection to mask it. That would slow it down a lot."

"Why mask it so?" I asked, then held up a hand. "No, never mind. That's obvious." He nodded at me, so I said, "To hide it from the rest of the network. Pretend it's not here or that it's a different location."

"You should be familiar with the concept. Although your father never made use of it, so maybe not."

"It's a lot harder when you're using a network hub that's hard-wired into the main water lines," I said, pointing at the panel. "This one isn't, or we would have seen a water line coming to the tower outside."

"It could be buried," Quentin suggested. "There's an entire side of this tower we couldn't see from the direction we approached."

"Yeah, the south side." I pointed out the window at the mountains to the north. "All water pipes spread out from the north to the south. They don't turn."

"Computer, can you display a map of this region?" Quentin asked the panel as he walked closer to it.

"Displaying map now."

We gathered around as the image appeared. Quentin grabbed the image with two fingers and zoomed in by sliding them away from each other.

"That's us, I assume," he said, indicating a red dot on the map near the edge of the shell. As he zoomed in even more, the terrain became visible and the tower stood out. "Look there, to our west." He pointed out a line leading from the Central Mountains. "That leads to the edge of this canyon." He tapped the end of the pipe. "My bet is that's where the river starts."

"It flows over the edge?" I asked.

He nodded. "Never seen a waterfall before, have you?"

"In pictures only."

Suyef grunted. "If you ever get to my shell, you'll see many of them."

"We passed one when I went to meet his council," Quentin said. He directed a meaningful look at me. "Stunning sight. If there's a waterfall over there, considering how high those cliffs are, it must be amazing." He released the map and left it on the screen as he stepped away, eyes never leaving the panel. "This lockdown is frustrating. So much we could find out, just by knowing the simplest things."

Without thinking twice, I moved to the panel, opened the sandbox, and executed a simple program my father had taught me.

"What's this?" Quentin asked, moving closer to me.

"A program that will allow me to see active processes on the local system," I muttered, eyes never leaving the coding in front of me. "So we can analyze their functioning capability."

"For what purpose?" Suyef asked, stepping near on the other side.

I chuckled. "When you're managing the primary water supply for an entire settlement, you have to make sure it's functioning at peak capacity all the time. My father perfected the art of examining these programs without messing any of them up or interfering with their work." I looked over at Quentin. "And it lets you examine things from a different angle."

He snapped his fingers. "Which is how your father found the problem. Ingenious. Trick the computer into thinking you're just practicing in a sandbox, giving you free access to examine an entire string of complex active coding, even if it's protected."

I nodded. "It doesn't always work. And you need the right kind of program to be able to do it." My fingers tapped the panel. "This is mostly his work." Something twisted at my heart, a memory of a happier time, of sitting in front of a network station with my father and Donovan. "His, mine, and Donovan's."

I shook my head and focused. My mind needed to be here, now, not in the past. Still, even that thought made me feel guilty.

"So, what are you trying to do?" Suyef asked.

"Examine the programs to see if there's a way to unlock this station," I muttered, pushing my feelings into a back corner of my being and focusing on my work.

Quentin and Suyef fell silent, freeing me to focus. It didn't take long to identify which program was the guilty party. I recalled all the work my father had taught me about the water program and brought it to bear on this. After several minutes of balancing code, with a constant stream of Quentin muttering to himself just low enough my ears couldn't make it out, I finally did it.

The panel blinked and reset to the home screen.

"Nice work!" Quentin exclaimed, patting me on the back.

Suyef gave me a slight nod as Quentin stepped near the panel. "Computer, when was I last here?" he asked.

"You never left, sir."

He looked over at us. "I think this thing's busted." He tapped around a few things, shifting files here and there, scanning through data logs a bit before shaking his head. "Whoever lives here wanted to make sure we couldn't figure anything out about this place. Every log has been wiped."

"To what end?" I asked.

He shrugged, searching for several more moments before giving up and moving away from the panel past the balcony.

"To hide it from us, why else?" he asked.

In the distance, the ship circling over the Central Mountains remained in sight. Was that another near it? I turned to mention it to Suyef and saw Quentin walking toward the table.

"What are you doing?" I asked, the wary feeling returning as he approached it.

He lifted the grav-board, eyes combing it over. "Just had a thought."

I watched him nervously as he lowered the board to the floor and stood over it. Suyef suddenly hissed, drawing my gaze. He pointed at the board. I looked back to see it had risen several inches off the ground, floating just before Quentin. He looked up at me, grinned, and stepped on the board.

"Quentin, don't," I said, moving forward to grab at him.

My hand just missed his arm as he rose toward the ceiling high overhead.

"Oh, wow, it's so much easier," he exclaimed as he moved in a circle around the room. "The control is so much better." He shifted until the board was parallel to the wall, and moved up to the apex of the room. Near the top, he flipped upside down and crossed over to the other side before coming back down. "It's like the board gives the belt focus. Something to hold on to." He flew a few circles around the room, then stopped before the balcony. "And the vertigo is gone! When I flip like that, the change is gone because, to me, the board is down."

A sense of dread rose into my throat along with a bitter taste. "Quentin, don't do it."

He looked back at me and broke into a wide grin. Without a word of warning, he shot out of the window.

I raced over to the balcony to see him falling toward the ground, along the tower's wall. My hands gripped the railing as he neared the base of the canyon. At what looked like the last second, he righted himself and shot off down the canyon, following the river. A breath I'd been holding without realizing it rushed past my lips. In the distance, the speck that was Quentin disappeared into the fog.

"Such an odd thing to watch from this perspective," a faint voice said from behind me.

Suyef and I spun to find an old man standing just inside the room. Bald on top, with white wisps clinging to the sides of his head, he had a face that was wrinkly and weathered, lips dry with age. His eyebrows were as bushy as the hair coming from his ears, and he stood with a hunch to his back. He wore a raggedy, gray cloak under a myriad of cloth strips sewn to it. Each strip was a different color, and below the cloak he had no shoes on feet that looked as weathered as his face. He clasped his hands before him and watched me with bright-blue eyes that twinkled in the core-light.

"Who are you?" I asked, but he ignored me.

"Yes, odd thing indeed," he said, smiling in a very fatherly way at both of us. "You seem to have found your way inside." He sniffed, looking over his shoulder. "Hope that beast of a woman got you here without too much trouble."

"Do you mean Dyad?" I asked. "The wolf?"

"Oh, is that her name now? Dyad?" He rubbed the end of a small stick to his forehead, as if scratching an itch there.

I frowned at the forearm-length bit of stick. "Where did that come from?"

The old man looked at the object in his hand and cocked his head to one side. "Where did *you* come from, my dear?" he asked the stick. "You mustn't act so around guests." He looked over at us. "Please forgive Stick here; she's a bit cranky these days. Usually doesn't let anyone see her."

"She's a stick," I said. "Since when do sticks have dispositions?"

He grinned at me, winking. "This isn't any ordinary stick," he whispered, shaking the small, tan piece of wood at me. "And mind you, don't say anything nasty about her when she's around. The results, for me, will be weeks in the offing." He sighed, rolling his eyes as he caressed the wooden twig in his arms like a baby. A moment later, he looked up and smiled. "Why hello, nice to see you here. I see you made it without any trouble. Did your guide cause you any problems?"

Suyef moved to stand partway between the old man and me. "We went over this already, sir," the Nomad said. "Dyad, your wolf, brought us here."

"Which one of you came up with that one? It's pretty good." I raised my hand, and he smiled. "Oh, that's right. Silly me." He stepped back through the door, waving us after him. "Come in, come in; let's wait for the other to get here."

"The other? You mean Quentin?" I asked, stepping toward the door. "Who are you? How did you know someone else was with us?"

The old man froze, turned partway back toward the room. One hand shot up to point at the table. The other smacked himself in the forehead.

"Water above, I did it again." He shook his head, turning to look at Suyef. "My mind's not what it once was. Keeps glitching all the time. Can't keep things in order anymore." He glared at the Nomad. "If memory serves, you're not going to like this next part." He moved near the panel, and his eyes widened. "Oh, dear, yes, you have opened it." He shook his head. "It's just like I maybe think I recall it happening."

A frown twisted my face as I tried to make sense of his words. His hand shot up to point out the balcony. Spinning, thinking it might be Quentin returning, I saw nothing.

"Oh, there they are," the old man hissed. "Forming up. Just on schedule."

Suyef nodded toward the mountains at my glance. I moved back out to the balcony, where I saw that more ships had begun joining the original one in the distance.

"Sir, do you know what's going on up there?" I asked, looking back at the old man.

He shook his head. "War, damnation, the end of times! I think. Memory's going. I've been here so long." He let out a long breath, and his entire frame deflated as he did. "So very, very long."

I moved closer to him, drawing his eyes. When he turned to me, a sad look came over his face.

"And you, dear, are going to *hate* what comes next." He shrugged, shuddering as he did so. "What to do, what to do. Eh, Stick? Can't be helped."

Suyef paused in the entrance, glancing around the room and the balcony. "What will we not like?"

"No, no, *you* will not like it," the old man said, stepping near the Nomad and tapping him once on the chest. "She will hate it."

The feeling of dread returned. "What will I hate?"

He shook his head some more. "It all makes sense now. I always wondered. Nothing for it, though." He pointed into the distance. "Is he still out there? The other one. Come now, out with it. You accessed my panel. Mind's not what it was, but I know what that means. Well, he took the board, yes?" At my nod, the old man stepped toward the balcony's edge, a wistful look on his face. "I do miss that thing. Haven't ridden it in cycles. Stands out too much. Can't be seen on it where people might recognize it. Makes them talk about things better left dead."

I moved closer to the old man. The Nomad shifted to stand between us and the room within.

"Are you okay, sir?" I placed a hand on his shoulder.

He tensed under my touch but didn't pull away. His eyes closed, and he took a deep breath.

"I forgot what that felt like," he whispered. "So long, so, so long."

"How long have you been here, sir?"

He laughed. "The answer would make you think me crazy." He barked another laugh. "As if the talking to a stick didn't already, yes?" He shook his head, still laughing. "Crazy. That would make this so much easier." He looked back at the Nomad. "Yes, I see now. It all makes sense." He looked back at me. "Trust me when I say this. I'm very, very sorry."

"Sorry for what?" I asked, my head cocking to one side and shaking. "For being a bit crazy? I didn't say that. You did."

He shook his head and looked off the balcony. "There he is. Riding my board."

My eyes shifted down out of the tower and saw a speck moving back up the canyon. "He'll bring it back, and I promise you he won't leave with it."

The old man laughed, a soft noise that barely escaped his lips. "If only those words were true," he whispered.

He reached up and took my hand from his shoulder, holding it between his two mottled, wrinkly, but gentle hands. He looked at them for a moment, and a tear rolled down one cheek.

The old man moved faster than I would have given him credit for. One hand shot out toward Suyef, and the Nomad cried out, arms spread out to either side as he was knocked backward. The old man turned to face me, a confused look on his face.

"I don't know what happens next," he whispered, hands held out toward me. "I can't remember."

I dodged him and moved toward the entrance but hit something solid. The old man's hand was held out, fingers twisted into a knot. I tried to move back, but the air felt thick and heavy. My legs and arms wouldn't move.

"I don't know what to do!" the old man cried out. "Stick! Help me! It has to happen. I remember it happening!"

Suyef appeared from inside the tower, staff in hand spinning to strike. "Release her."

The old man moved to catch the staff, and whatever the invisible force was that held me threw my body up against the wall, smashing the wind from my lungs.

"No!" the old man yelled. "You can't interfere!"

Suyef spun into my periphery, then vanished, soon replaced by the old man.

"You can't stop this!" he cried out. "It must happen!"

Whatever was holding me jerked my body away from the wall. Suyef tumbled past me toward the tower entrance as I kept moving away from the wall.

"You mustn't interfere!" the old man screamed, a look of pure agony on his face, one hand pointing toward Suyef. "It's the only way!"

The next instant, the barrier along the edge of the balcony slammed against my legs. The old man cried out "No!" one last time. After that, I fell into thin air.

Micaela stood and moved toward the bathroom.

"Wait, what happened?" I asked, hands spread out to either side.

She paused and looked back. "When?"

"What do you mean, when?" She arched an eyebrow. I looked down. "Apologies, High One. After you were knocked from the tower, what happened to you?"

"I fell."

Quentin wasn't in his room when I woke up the next day. In fact, he was nowhere to be found. Suyef sat in the living area, consuming a nutrient pack and reading something on a padd. The sight gave me pause.

"I don't recall ever seeing you read anything," I stated, moving to stand next to him.

He shrugged, keying the device off. "He's not here."

"Where is he?"

He pointed down the hall to the balcony. "He came out here and demanded his grav-board." He leveled a gaze at me. "He hasn't asked me for that thing in a long time." He motioned for me to sit. "In fact, the last time he rode it was the day he died."

"Clearly someone resuscitated him," I pointed out.

He shook his head. "You keep thinking of death in such a linear way."

"There are other deaths than the physical? Is that what you mean?"

"Oh, he died physically. But, more importantly, something that makes him who he is died that day." He pointed at me. "And whatever it is you're doing to get him to talk is reawakening it."

I shrugged. "All I'm doing is listening."

"And asking questions. You're an audience. It's something he's needed for a long time." He set the padd down. "Before the day he died, he'd spent so much of his life hiding. Holding everything in. Letting it build up inside." He pointed at my travel sack. "He needed to do this sooner. It may have prevented what happened." He shrugged. "Maybe. I don't know. The point is, this is helping."

I smiled. "It's a good thing you convinced the Queen to let me do this."

"I did nothing of the sort," he commented. "You did by choosing to listen to me."

I lifted my travel sack and held it open, showing the box still sealed inside. "Why give this to me?"

He didn't take his eyes from mine. "All you need to know is that I don't know what you're talking about. The sooner you realize and remember that, the better off we'll all be."

I went to the balcony some time later and found Quentin standing on the same spot he'd been the day of my arrival, returned from wherever he'd gone. The grav-board lay behind him.

"This is it, isn't it?" I asked.

Quentin turned to look at me, eyebrows arched.

"The grav-board you found." I pointed at his waist, where the belt with its circular panels was just visible. "And your father's belt."

He looked out into the expanse. I paused, uncertain of what to say next. A frontal assault seemed best.

"When Micaela fell from the tower, did you catch her?" I asked, holding my breath.

He let out a long breath, shoulders slumping as he did.

"Barely."

CHAPTER 44

FLIGHT

The sensation of flying out of the tower was very different than what I expected. The grav-board changed it. You see, we all know what falling feels like. It's tumultuous, nerve-wracking, spine-tingling. All of that. Those feelings all coursed through my body as well, but so did a sense of control. The board gave me a feeling of gravity in a situation where I was playing with the very laws of the same. Needless to say, my mind took a few moments to adjust to the changes.

Unfortunately, the adjustments in the tower didn't prepare me for the fall *out* of the tower. As the canyon and river rushed closer, I tried to focus on the ground far below, as I had in the room. I tried to push against it using the beams. For some reason, they wouldn't focus. As the ground rushed toward me, I looked at my feet and saw the tower racing past. A thought occurred to me as panic began to overwhelm me: the surface was technically beneath me. I focused on the structure and saw the beams sharpen and lock on to the rock face. What came next is hard to explain. I imagined myself slowing. That seemed to be how the board worked, once you adjusted to it. I would imagine where I wanted to go and it would reach out for any surface within optimal range and make it happen. However, if I overfocused on something out of range, it stopped working. It was a delicate balance of keeping your present state in contact with a potential future state.

That understanding all came later. For the moment, I hung suspended about a hundred paces above the river. It seemed strange that the feeling of dizziness and nausea didn't come, seeing as I was standing sideways in air. I rubbed a foot back and forth on the board. The board didn't move at a foot stomp. It appeared as solid as ground to me. Looking down at the river, my eyes followed the canyon. With a thought, the board shot off down that direction, the orientation shifting to match the surface below. My eyes roamed far ahead, focusing on a canyon wall, and the board started to sink. I quickly brought my attention back to what was closer, and it stabilized. Through trial and error, I made my way quickly down the canyon and around the bend. When I looked back, the tower remained just visible over the canyon wall. A moment later, the fog swallowed everything as my momentum carried me into it.

The loss of sight was very disorienting. The board shook as my certainty wavered. Luckily, my momentum carried me close enough to one side of the canyon to have a surface to focus on. I shifted closer to it and looked around. If the board was dependent on my line of sight, that seemed a major design flaw. I peered into the fog directly ahead, looking at the far side of the canyon. At that action, the beams sought out the far surface, but none came into sharp focus. I took that to mean they didn't lock on to it. Something looked different about the color of the beams. I glanced back at the few holding me in place just off this wall. Sure enough, the color was different. Those locked on to the wall were sharp and bright, those roaming around more diffused and dull. I moved away from the wall and saw the colors diffuse on the locked beams. At the same time, those reaching out to the far wall became brighter.

A laugh escaped my lips. It was an ingenious solution to flying blind. This knowledge enabled me to move into the fog and my mind to grow accustomed to reading the information the beams provided. At the fork in the canyon, I turned south, following the fog and river out to the shell's edge. As the end of the river neared, I slowed. The fog dissipated quickly, and the expanse beyond came into view. My heart pounded in my chest, and my breath quickened as the abyss of our world became clear. Far below, the core shone bright, its light the only source of illumination this world knew beyond machines. Far in the distance, a massive shell continued in its orbit below Colberra. Suyef's home, and the only other continental mass visible to Colberra at that time. As I floated there for a moment, memories of my life there flooded through me.

With a shake of my head, my attention refocused on the river, and I spun in place to look around. The water cascaded over the edge, falling about a hundred paces toward the core before vanishing. Curiosity pulled me down to the very edge of the landmass beside the river to follow the water. The entire world flipped upside down with my shift from a point parallel with the top surface to a similar position under the shell. The bright light forced me to shield my eyes. The landscape under the shell was as alien as Suyef's landmass had once been. Jagged dagger edges of rock shot out from the surface, slicing through the air toward the core below. Nothing here resembled the sweeping desert plains that made up the Outer Dominance regions above. And I saw something else extremely odd.

The river that plummeted over the edge turned back in toward the bottom surface. It flowed into a massive lake, filling a bowl in the mountains just near the end of the shell. Another river poured out the far side to fill another giant lake. Everywhere I looked under the Colberra shell lay lakes, all feeding from the river pouring over the edge.

"The water isn't being wasted," I said out loud to no one. "It's all under the shell!"

Excited by my discovery, I moved back above the surface and shot over the mountains. Flying along the river toward the tower, I became filled with eagerness to share my discovery with Suyef and Micaela. Approaching the structure, mind equal parts distracted by the water and focused on keeping the grav-board operating, I almost didn't notice something falling out of the tower. It took a moment of confusion as to what was happening for my eyes to make out any detail.

My momentum carried me close enough to see it was a person. I saw a flash of red hair and realized it was Micaela.

I would have screamed had there been time to think about it. The world tumbled around me—the tower, then the Central Mountains shifting back and forth into view as my body flipped over and over. With each flip, the river raced closer. I tried to call out for help but found breathing to be difficult. I tried to catch sight of Quentin, to wave for help, to slow my turn. Nothing helped. The river grew close, and images of my family flashed through my mind: my brothers, my sister, my parents. Looks of betrayal contorted their faces into something ugly, looks that said, "You were supposed to find us, not to die on us." A cry built up in my gut, and I finally screamed, a howling, guttural sound of anger and sorrow that tore through my throat and echoed off the canyon walls.

As my body flipped one more time, an object moved above me. Another flip took it from my sight, but I knew it had to be Quentin. As the river raced even closer, something pulled at me, tugging at my torso. My body turned again, and he came into sight, moving in right over me, board between us, eyes locked on to me. He held a hand out toward me as he closed the gap. I expected to turn one more time, but whatever he was doing was definitely pulling on my body. The passing terrain slowed, and Quentin approached me.

I started to reach a hand up as he made a motion with his, kind of a twisting flip of his palm. On cue, my body flipped in the air to look down at the now slowly approaching river. Something wrapped around me—his arms engulfing my torso. My fall slowed to a halt. My heart pounded in my chest as I struggled to control my breathing.

"I got you," he whispered in my ear.

A second later, we shot off down the canyon. I gripped his arms as we moved.

"Amazing isn't it?" he yelled over the wind howling in our ears.

My jaw clenched tight, preventing me from speaking. Ahead, a turn in the canyon approached. Quentin shifted, and we moved up the rock wall, rising higher in the air. The edge of the mountains spread out before me, the great expanse beyond that. We slowed to a halt, and something firm appeared under my feet. I looked down to see the grav-board there. A long breath rushed past my lips, and tears poured down my face. My legs gave out, and my body collapsed back against Quentin.

"Please, take me down!" I cried out.

Quentin shifted the board, and the ground came closer. My hands gripped his arms until the board touched down, allowing me to fall to the ground and crawl away. I curled into a little ball, eyes squeezed shut, sobs racking my body. My head shook, trying to block out the images filling my mind: of me falling, of me hitting the ground, of my family, staring at me, disapproving looks on their faces.

"What happened?" Quentin asked. His hand touched my shoulder. "Did you jump off?"

I shook my head, covering my face with one hand. My mouth opened to speak but couldn't. My body began to tremble uncontrollably.

"Micaela?" he asked, shaking my shoulder. "What's wrong?"

I didn't answer. I just shivered and cried, wishing to be left alone but unable to speak. After a few more attempts, he stopped talking and just sat there, one hand on my shoulder. His touch helped me to calm. It's hard to describe. His touch gave me a point to focus on. His hand brought me back to a semblance of reality. My breathing slowed, the tears stopped, and the shivering faded. I lay there for a bit, just taking long breaths. He remained, silent, one hand on me.

After several moments, I pulled my face from under my hand and said, "Thank you."

"For?"

I shrugged. "For being there."

He chuckled. "That was my promise, wasn't it?" he asked.

I nodded. "Bet you didn't expect that to happen when you made it."

"No, flying through the air to catch you was definitely not on the list of things that I thought might be required of me," he said, removing his hand.

I turned onto my back to look at him. "There's someone up there. An old man. He attacked us and th—"

Quentin frowned and looked back at the tower. "Suyef?"

I glared at him but shrugged. "I saw him fighting the old man, but he fell. Then I just—"

Quentin stood up and held a hand out to me. "We need to go back."

He didn't notice my second glare as he pulled me up. He already had the board in hand and was preparing to take off.

"There's something else," I went on. "He kept apologizing. And saying strange things."

Quentin listened to my recounting of the man's words, his face twisting into a deep frown.

"He's acting like he knew this was going to happen," Quentin muttered, looking at the board. "And this is his, huh?"

I nodded. "And he said that what happened next I was going to hate. He repeated that, emphasized it."

"That definitely makes it look like he knew what was coming." Quentin looked up at me. "And how you would react. But you said he was confused at the end?"

"Very, like his knowledge ended just before he attacked us."

"Yet another person acting like he knows us," Quentin whispered.

"That's at least three."

Quentin stared at me, frown remaining. "Well, this makes what I found seem unimportant." I arched an eyebrow at him, and he chuckled. "You use that look well."

I scrunched my nose. "What did you find?"

He pointed toward the expanse. "The water isn't falling off the edge. It's being pulled under the shell to form massive lakes there."

It was my turn to frown. "How is that possible?"

He shrugged. "The gravity well the citadel generates operates on a flat plane. It's possible it's designed to duplicate the effect under the shell."

"On purpose?" I asked.

He shook his head. "I don't know. It might be a happy accident. Either way, the water pouring over the edge isn't being wasted. And it looks like it's been flowing that way for a long time. Those lakes are huge and probably deep."

"And inaccessible." My eyes wandered to the board. "You went over the edge with that thing?"

He nodded, one hand running down the board's surface. "It took a bit of effort, but I figured out how to make it work." He grinned. "Good thing for you. I must admit, as rough as that was on you, catching you was quite the learning experience."

I glared at him, then paused, turning my head to look at the tower.

"What?" Quentin asked.

My gaze shifted back to him. "This is a bit of a stretch, but that may be why he did that."

"Why who did what?" He looked back at the tower. "You mean the old man? Is he the one the wolf brought us to?"

"He specifically waited until he knew you were coming back up the valley," I said, pushing myself to my feet and eyeing the board.

"Before doing what?" he asked.

I opened my mouth to tell him what he'd kept me from saying before, but something behind Quentin drew my attention. Far in the distance, more ships were amassing. If that was a search party, it looked like it was almost ready to start looking for us.

"Can you get us back up there?" I asked, my previous thought forgotten for the moment.

He nodded, jumping up and holding out a hand to me. I stepped closer to him, and he turned me to face away, wrapping his arms around my stomach.

"At first, this will feel odd," he said. "Once the board is under us, the odd sensation goes away."

I smiled, patting his arms. "Which sensation? The hug? Or something else?"

He gave me a slight shake; then we lifted off the ground. I cried out involuntarily.

"Whoa, that's very odd." We hovered a few feet off the ground. "Give me a little bit of warning."

"Micaela, we're taking off," he said, shifting as the board rose under our feet.

That comment earned him a smack on his hands as we shifted in the air. He was very right about the sensation changing once our feet touched the device. It created a feeling of the ground under us, even when we moved. This produced a quandary in my brain as it adjusted to the feeling of standing on something solid while shifting through the air like a piece of cloth caught in the wind. Below, the landscape moved away and past us. The wind whipped wisps of my hair around and tugged at my clothing.

My eyes moved around the shell below. "*Odd* is a good word for this."

Ahead, the tower loomed high. The balcony was just visible as we approached. Quentin shifted and brought the board around the back of the tower, moving to where we could see the balcony. Suyef stood, frozen in place, staff held up over his head midstrike. There was no sign of the old man.

The board came to a stop in front of the balcony but didn't approach. I turned my head to see Quentin's head turned to look back to the north. Then the board shifted away from the tower.

"What's wrong?" I asked, thinking of Seekers coming for us.

"Look over the mountains," he whispered, pulling one arm free and pointing.

I followed his point and nodded. "Yeah, there are more now. I mentioned them before, remember?"

We were too far away to make out details, but the fleet of ships looked massive. As we watched, more continued to rise and join the others already airborne.

"Those ships can't be up to anything good," Quentin said, spinning the board and darting back into the tower.

We landed with a thud on the balcony, and Quentin pushed me toward the railing, where I ducked. He stepped near the Nomad.

"Can you talk?" he asked Suyef.

"Yes, just go inside. Once he sees you back with her, I'm free."

I glanced at the room. "Is he in there?"

"I assume so. I can't exactly look."

Quentin moved past the Nomad and stepped into the door. "Hey, you, old man. We're back."

I pushed myself up and hurried over to stand behind Quentin. The old man stood at the panel, busily tapping away at something.

"Hey, old man!" Quentin called, stepping toward him.

The man looked over, saw me, and grinned. "See, Stick, just as I told you. Fine and fit as fadiddle."

Quentin stumbled to a halt, glancing at me. "Did you do that to Suyef?" he asked.

"Course I did it, sonny," the old man said, cackling as he tapped his head with the small stick. "Mind you, didn't care for that bit. But it made sense, it did."

"How does throwing me from a tower to my death make sense?" I asked, moving to stand behind Quentin opposite from the door.

"You didn't die, now, did ya? And I didn't throw you. Well . . ." He grinned at me, showing off a horrid set of teeth. "Not on purpose. And anyways, you didn't die, right?"

"Only because he caught me."

The old man cackled. "Yep, just like he was supposed to. Learns fast, don't he? My mind used to be that quick. Back before . . . before . . . well, something or other."

Quentin pointed at Suyef. "Do you mind?"

The old man looked out the door. "Oh, him. Promise he'll behave, and I'll loosefy him."

"Promise he'll what?" I asked. "He's not a trained animal. Let him go."

He waved a hand at me. "All right, all right, don't get your wad all up in a britches."

I opened my mouth to ask what that meant and heard Quentin chuckle. "Something funny?" I said.

The old man waved a hand at Suyef, freeing him.

Quentin shook his head. "His words. They're backward sometimes."

Suyef, now free, rushed into the room toward the old man, the staff he'd been holding returned to wherever he kept it. The geezer held up his stick to fend off the charging Nomad.

"Now, now, you promised!" he cried out.

"Suyef, hold!" Quentin barked, his voice reverberating through the room.

His hands inches from grabbing the old man, the Nomad froze, head turning to look at Quentin. "You'd better have a good reason for stopping me from throwing him off the balcony."

"Information," Quentin replied. "Old man, there are ships massing over Colberra City. Can you show us a closer view?"

Suyef, the old man forgotten, spun and raced out to the balcony.

"Really, of all the questions you could ask, that's what you start with?" I asked him, watching Suyef move.

Quentin shrugged. "He may be more forthcoming with things that don't pertain to him."

The old man stood there, eyes locked on his stick. "It's come again, Stick."

Quentin glanced at me, nodding his head at the stick. "Why is he talking to that thing?"

"He didn't say. He seems a bit—" I pointed a finger at my head and rotated it.

"The thing is, he looks a bit like someone I met once," Quentin whispered, moving closer to me. "An old, crazy coot near my settlement on Suyef's shell. No one talked to him, and he wore a cloak similar to that one." He shook his head. "Not as colorful then, though."

"Maybe he added more?" I offered.

Quentin nodded and turned to the old man. "What's your name, sir?"

"What's that?" he asked, looking round the room. "I do believe the lad asked a persninent question, Stick. We should reward him!"

"Persninent?" Quentin glanced at me, rolling his eyes. "You're making words up, old man."

"Who you calling old, you cognizant twit?" he cried out, waving the stick at Quentin.

"And now you're using the wrong words," Quentin said, chuckling. "What is your name, old man?"

"Ah, ah, too soon for that bit of knowledge, now isn't it? We wouldn't want to screw with continuity, now would we?" the man answered, wagging his index finger at Quentin. "Plus, you've got somewhere to be, if memory serves."

Quentin frowned at me, then looked over at the balcony as Suyef returned.

"That fleet of ships is preparing to move," the Nomad said, looking at the old man. "He been of any help?"

Quentin shook his head. "Old man, we need to know what those ships are doing."

The old man glanced at the panel. "You'll find your answer there in about"—he squeezed his eyes closed, mouth hanging open—"a minute."

"A minute? A minute exactly?" Quentin asked. "How the heck do you know that?"

The old man waved his stick at Quentin. "Don't you get all cranny with me, Big Nose. Mind you ridicule your elders."

My mouth dropped open as my head cocked to one side. The man's words were just impossible to keep track of.

"You do realize you're using the wrong words, right?" I asked.

He favored me with a very fond smile. "Good to see you, too, my dear. Oh, wait." He paused, looking about the room. "What time is it? Have we met already?"

"Yes, right before you knocked me off the balcony," I said, pointing out the open door to the sky.

He grinned and clapped his hands together, the stick having vanished to who knew where. "Ah, that's grand. Glad that's done with. Nasty business that, but had to be done." His eyes settled on Quentin. "I believe you're supposed to ask me a question now."

At that moment, a panel appeared on the screen behind the old man and a frozen image of a familiar figure standing at a podium filled it.

"Colvinra," I whispered, pointing at the screen.

CHAPTER 45

NECESSARY

Before anyone else had a chance to speak, the image began to move and the Questioner's familiar voice filled the room, continuing a speech clearly already in progress.

"To borrow the words of other leaders from our ancient past who faced a similar choice, I say that this attack made it clear, beyond all doubt, that the Nomad and red-dragon movements are willing to use any force available to them to harass and do further damage to our people."

The sound of cheering and clapping interrupted the Questioner. He waited for the sound to die down before continuing.

"The red dragons, the Nomads, and those that have betrayed us have engaged in a struggle against the free peoples of Colberra. We must therefore make it clear that Colberra will honor the principles of our people, and we will respond to this act of aggression perpetrated on our soil. We were at peace with the Nomad nation. One of their own serves in our elite Seeker corps. Alas, that mattered not.

"It will be recorded that the distance from the Nomad shell to Colberra makes it obvious that the attack was deliberately planned well in advance. The attack a few days past on the prison facility in one of our Outer Dominance provinces has caused severe damage to Colberran citizens, to facilities, and to our forces.

"As the newly appointed commander of the Seekers, I have directed that all measures be taken for our defense. And always will our people remember the character of those that brought this onslaught to us."

The sounds of a crowd cheering his words filled the chamber. I turned to look at Quentin, who stared at the now-frozen panel. Suyef moved to stand next to Quentin.

"We're going to war," he whispered.

"He's referring to the Intershell War, isn't he?" I asked, interrupting Micaela. "The recent one?"

Micaela nodded. "The one that changed everything."

We both looked out the window. In the distance, where once we might have seen several shells orbiting at this altitude, we saw only one.

"The Queen's managed to keep our shell out of the fray."

Micaela shrugged. "Does it matter?"

"It might. She's trying." Micaela remained quiet, staring out the window. "So, the war. You three started it."

Her head nodded, a slow, deliberate motion. "So many people, dead." She closed her eyes for a moment. "It's ironic that the very reason the Ancients founded their civilization, to provide a better alternative to war, would only make the same that much easier all these centuries later."

I stared at her, my mind spinning at her words. "How is it you know so much of a time we've lost so much knowledge of?"

She shook her head. "I started a war."

Quentin turned away from the panel to glare at the old man. "You knew he was going to say that."

The old man looked confused. "Something's about to happen. Something. What was it?" he asked, looking about the room. "Stick? *Stick?* Where have you gotten off to?" He spun around the room, empty hands patting at his brightly colored robe. "Blast it, you piece of fabricated wood, don't you go vanishing on me now."

"Old man!" Quentin yelled, reaching out to grab him. "Hey, I asked you a question."

The old man moved with surprising speed. As Quentin's hand came near his shoulder, he ducked away, twisting his body out of the grasp of the younger man.

"Ah, ah, don't you be accosting me. I won't be privy to your games."

"Games?" Quentin glared at the old man. "You think this is a game." He pointed at the now-frozen screen open on the panel. "That man is threatening an invasion of another shell under false pretenses."

The old man grinned, sidling toward me and whispering, "Oh, he's doing more than threatening."

He shied away from my outstretched hand. "Quentin's just trying to ask you some questions," I said.

That comment earned a glare for Quentin from the old man. "This one could do with a good beating, if you ask me. Teach him to mangle his manners. Respect his inferiors!"

I smothered a smile at his misuse of words. "Did you know that speech was coming?" I asked, nodding at the panel.

The old man squinted toward the screen, running a hand through the wisps of hair clinging to his forehead.

"I remember . . . something," he whispered. "Something . . . big. I need to say it. Can't remember what, though." He tapped his forehead with the stick, then jolted and stared at his hand. "Where'd you come from, you blasted machine?" He brandished the stick at me. "Stupid thing has a mind of its own sometimes."

"Bah!" Quentin exclaimed, throwing up his hands. "He's useless."

He flung a hand toward the grav-board, leaping onto the device as it moved toward him. Astride the board, he flew out the door and stopped just beyond the balcony's edge, hovering as he stared back toward Colberra. The old man watched him on the board, a strange look on his face, still tapping his forehead with the stick. Emotions twisted his visage into something I was unable to wrap my brain around. Shaking my head, I walked onto the balcony with Suyef. There we followed Quentin's gaze toward the Central Mountains.

"They look like they're getting ready to do something," Quentin muttered from just off the balcony. "How many would you say?"

Suyef whistled as he squinted at the horizon. "Thirty big ones, maybe more. A lot of smaller ones."

"That's most of the Dominance's big ships, then." Quentin glanced over at the Nomad. "He's going to invade your shell, isn't he?"

Suyef nodded.

"Which end of your shell is nearest Colberra?"

Suyef let out a deep breath, looking at me. Something filled his eyes, something sad, reserved.

"Your outpost is right in their path," he whispered, looking at Quentin.

I looked between them, confused. "Wait, the one the Forces occupied? Colvinra wouldn't dare attack an outpost full of Colberrans, would he?"

"You heard his speech, Micaela. 'Those that have betrayed us.' Those are very specific words." Quentin shook his head, gaze returning to watch the amassing fleet. "He's convinced the

Expeditionary Forces are in on this. Worse yet, he may have convinced the Central Dominance leadership of the same."

"Why would they approve an invasion without evidence?" I asked. "What proof could he have?"

"Does he need any actual proof?" Quentin shot back at me with a glare. "The Colberrans don't think for themselves anymore. Not in the Central Dominance. They are spoon-fed what information the Dominance feels they need and nothing more. That speech had all you needed to know in it." He pointed at Suyef. "Even a Nomad to link them to the attack."

I glanced at Suyef. "And you did fight against the Seekers."

The Nomad nodded. "If he managed to capture video of me doing that, combined with what was happening to the Colberran prisoners . . ."

We all three turned our gazes back to the fleet. As we watched, the ships began to move in turns, gliding through the air to rise higher above the mountains.

"They're moving to maximum altitude," Suyef stated. "Preparing for the intershell trip."

Once they reached a predetermined point high above the mountains, the ships broke formation one at a time and moved closer to us.

"Why are they coming this way?" My eyes stayed locked on the approaching fleet.

Suyef leaned closer to me, his voice dropping. "This end of the shell is nearest mine. To get to the Nomad shell, they must cross over us."

The giant ships came into greater focus. They were long, sweeping machines, their noses and tails ending in identical triangular points. Flat along the sides, they had superstructures dominating the topside. The largest of them had three of the hulking towers, the smaller ones two. All along the upper sides, what looked like rectangular turrets, multifaceted triangular-shaped emitters attached to one side, rose up from the deck. Some were large turrets, each with four of the emitters, and those lay near the ends of the ships. Along the sides of the superstructures lay several smaller turrets, most with two of the emitters. The turrets also lay along the bottom of the ships, coming out of bays that opened in the hull.

"Are those pulse emitters?" I asked, pointing at one of the ships as it neared us.

Suyef nodded. "Focused energy beams." He looked over at me. "Lasers." He pointed up toward the top of the nearest large ship. "And those rectangular boxes installed near each of the super-structures? Rockets, if I'm not mistaken."

"What's a rocket?" I asked.

Quentin turned his head to say, "Propellant-powered weapons that explode on impact."

"Propellant? You mean fuel?"

The Nomad nodded.

"Where did they find fuel for that? It doesn't exist anymore."

Quentin turned a curious look at me. "Matter reforgers."

The ship glided past us, followed by the rest.

"Why aren't they attacking us?" I wondered out loud. "Surely they can see us from there."

Suyef waved a hand at the sky. "The shield keeps them out as much as it keeps the Wilds in."

As he spoke, a mass of clouds burst up all around the tower just below where we stood. I heard a crashing boom split the air and saw a flash illuminate the clouds beneath us at the same instant.

"Lightning," Suyef said at my glance. "Electrical charge in the clouds jumping back and forth."

"And that sound is . . . thunder, yes?" Another rumble echoed around us. "We studied weather patterns once in school. Always wondered why my father insisted on that one."

The ships streamed past overhead as the storm raged below. They made no noise as they passed, not that we could have heard over the thunderous symphony the storm made. Lightning flashes lit up the ships as they flew past, all heading out over the shell's edge. We watched until the last of the ships had gone past. Quentin floated there, facing the direction the fleet had gone. His face wore a mix of emotions. His fists clenched and unclenched; his jaw ground together, then loosened. His eyes darted back and forth as he watched the ships vanish. He turned his gaze toward the tower.

"Computer," he called, gliding back into the room and jumping off the board. "This transportation device. It goes to the Nomad shell, yes?"

"Affirmative, sir," the very cold-sounding feminine voice responded. "As it always has."

"Quentin, what are you thinking?" I asked, feeling a tingle go up my spine and the hair on my arms stand on end. I could think of very few reasons he would want to travel to the shell the Seeker fleet now soared toward. None were good.

"Computer, can it transport all of us at once?" he went on, ignoring me as he donned his Seeker cloak again.

"Negative, sir. Individual transport rings only."

"How long will the trip take?"

The computer took a moment, then responded, "Ten minutes at current distance."

He nodded. "Prep the rings for transport." He looked at Suyef. "Those ships will take at least thirty to make the same trip, yes?"

"Quentin!" I walked over and grabbed his arm, turning him to look at me. "You can't do anything. You saw all those ships."

"I can try to warn them." He looked back at Suyef. "Thirty minutes?"

Suyef frowned, glancing at me, then back at Quentin. "Those are warships. Overestimate their capabilities to be safe."

"Right, so I'll be cutting it close, especially as I don't know where this thing is taking me," Quentin muttered, waving a hand at the platform.

"Even if you do make it to them in time, what can you hope to accomplish?" I asked, trying to get him to look at me. "You saw all of that weaponry."

The old man began wringing his hands, eyes darting around. He started muttering, but not loud enough for me to make out his words.

"They can get away from the settlement, at least," Quentin insisted, ignoring the doddering old man and pointing at Suyef. "Ask him. It's in a very indefensible location. Probably the only reason the Nomads let the force have it. If I can get there before those ships, some of the people might be able to get away into the nearby mountains."

"Assuming you can get there before the ships do." I pointed in the direction the ships had flown. "They've got a head start on you, and you don't know where this thing is taking you."

"Something, oh, it was something important," the old man whispered. "Have to say it. What was it?"

Quentin glared first at the old man, then at me. "It's worth a shot. Unlike you, I've got a chance here to do something."

I felt every hair on my body bristle. "How dare you," I whispered. The mere thought that he would say such a thing sent a jolt of anger through me like none I'd ever experienced. "I would have done anything to stop them being taken from me. Anything!"

"Course, it probably wasn't that important," the old man continued, oblivious, it seemed, to what was going on around him. "It must be, though, else why would I remember needing to say it. Some word, that was it. Just one word. Stick, what was it?"

Quentin, still ignoring the old man, waved a hand at me. "I'm not saying you didn't try. Didn't mean that at all. But you didn't have a chance. I do."

"Dangerous?" the old man blurted out, waving the stick at us. "No, it's always that. Imminent? No, we're past that. I mean, you could still say that, but that's not as applicable now."

The anger didn't subside with Quentin's explanation. It sounded very much like a cover-up for his previous statement.

"Against a fleet of warships?" I asked, arching my eyebrows and pointing out the window. "You think you can do something against a fleet of those things?"

The old man went on, saying, "Impossible? No, we've done that enough times to know that word's meaningless. Well, to us it is. Some others, maybe not."

"Like I said, I can try," Quentin whispered to me, his eyes roaming over to the old man.

"Maybe if I remember to whom I need to say it," the old man said, looking around the room. "Oh, hello. Didn't see you there. Have we met?" His eyes settled on me, and they widened. "Ah yes, we have. So sorry for what I have to do next."

I leveled a finger at him. "Don't even think about touching me again."

His face brightened, a toothy smile splitting it. "Oh, goodie, we're past that one. Haven't been looking forward to that, I promise you. Wasn't even sure how it was supposed to happen." He looked at Quentin and Suyef. "Laddies, I believe you were about to do something. Forget what, but go on. Nothing to it."

Quentin shook his head and stepped up on the platform, his hand held out to summon the board to him. "Computer, activate the transport ring."

"Quentin!" I jumped up to grab his arm and pull him back down.

A solid-metal ring lifted from the floor, knocking me back to fall at the old man's feet. He leveled a sad look at me. On the platform, the ring rose to Quentin's waist, then began to rotate and flip around him in several different directions. As it did, he lifted off the ground, allowing the ring to pass under his feet. A door spun open in the floor, and he dropped from sight. The instant he was gone, the doors slid shut.

I pushed myself to my feet and saw Suyef stepping onto the platform. "What are you doing?" I asked the Nomad.

"Someone has to keep him out of trouble," he said. When nothing happened, he looked down, confused. "Why isn't it letting me follow him?"

"Maybe it has to come back first?" I asked, looking at the old man. He seemed preoccupied with something on the end of his stick. "Old man, is there only one ring?"

He looked down his stick at me. "Course not. What kind of a useless invention would that be?"

Suyef pointed at the panel. "See if you can activate another ring."

I jumped up and moved to the panel. "I don't even know what I'm—" My eyes caught sight of a program flashing off. On a hunch, I dragged it into my sandbox program and examined it. "Yes, yes, this is the control program." I traced up the columns with a finger, quickly translating the complex symbols. "Attitude. Speed. Targeting," I muttered while reading, trying to find the necessary sequence. "Everything looks fine. It should be working."

Suyef, still standing there, shook his head. "Clearly, it's not."

"How in frag's sake do I make this thing respond to me?" I hissed, touching the screen to throw the program out of my sandbox. A thought came to me. "Maybe if I . . ."

My fingers raced across the screen, tracing new symbols in the sandbox. I drew as fast as possible, keenly aware of the time ticking away. Once the completed symbols were sorted into a new column, they created new bridges and added an entirely new command to the structure. When it was finished, I saved the construct and returned it to its active state.

"Computer, recognize new voice control," I stated.

The screen blinked. "Control recognized. Welcome, Micaela."

"Wait, how did that thing know your name?" Suyef asked.

I ignore him. "Prepare another transport ring for current platform occupant."

"Destination?"

I looked back at Suyef. "The Nomad tower."

A ring appeared, and, just as before, the door opened, and the Nomad dropped from sight. My eyes locked on to the floor, a feeling of dread, fear, and curiosity welling up in my gut. Despite my misgivings, my choice to act had just committed me to this course of action. No turning back now. The old man nattered away behind me, whispering to himself.

"Couldn't have been for them. Didn't have time to say anything. Must be for her, but what?"

"Computer, another ring for the Nomad tower." I moved up onto the platform, turning to face the old man. "What's your name, old man?"

"It's not far, I say," he muttered, waving a hand at me.

"Nidfar?" I shook my head at the strange sound. "Is that your name?"

His eyes focused on me. "How'd you know that?"

"You just said it."

"No, you asked me how far, and I said, 'Not far.'" Nidfar glanced around the room. "How'd you guess my name?"

"I thought you said Nidfar. Is that your name?"

He smiled. "Pleased to meet you." Nidfar snapped his fingers. "Aha! I remember."

The ring rose out of the floor. All sense of weight vanished as it began to spin.

"What is it, Nidfar?" I asked, watching the ring around me.

His eyes widened as he saw the device. "Shhh, don't say my name. He might hear you!"

"Who might hear me?" I pointed at the room. "There's no one here."

"Never let him hear my name," Nidfar insisted, waving his hands around his head and just missing clocking himself with his stick. "Never let anyone know you know it."

The door in the floor spun open.

"Old man, you wanted to say something to me," I reminded him as the door revealed a dark tunnel.

"Oh yes, Micaela, yes!" he cried out, hopping back and forth from foot to foot and clapping his hands. "I remember now."

He jumped onto the platform, his face mere inches from the spinning ring.

"What happens next is necessary!" he yelled.

The next instant, the ring dropped into the darkness, taking me with it. His last word echoed after me as I fell.

"Necessary!"

CHAPTER 46

WAR

"What did he mean, necessary?" I asked, holding up a hand to stop Micaela.

"Exactly what it sounds like. What came next was very necessary."

I shook my head. "No, did he mean the trip? Did he mean the ring taking you somewhere, like you weren't going to like it?"

She smiled. "No, that was oddly pleasant and terrifying at the same time." She took in a deep breath and let it out, eyes wandering off to stare out the window. "No, he meant what happened after that. The whole sequence of events that came next." She chuckled, shaking her head and grabbing at a strand of hair, fiddling with it. "To be honest, he could have meant everything that happened after that."

I jotted a few notes down for questions later, staring at the mess of random scribbles. "One other question," I said, eye darting to a recent note. "How'd he know your name?"

She arched an eyebrow and shook her head.

"Nidfar, the old man. How'd he know your name?"

She smiled. "You ask the most random, yet piercing, questions sometimes." She shrugged, and said, "Suffice it to say I wondered that myself. I remember very clearly I'd never told him. We sort of went past that kind of introduction when he knocked me off the tower, and the conversation spun out of control once we got back." She nodded at my device. "The only answer left is just to assume he heard it in conversation. Quentin called me by name at least once in that room, and the computer had also just identified me."

"That, too." I waved my stylus at her. "Did you ever figure out how the computer knew that? Could he have had something to do with it?"

Her eyes narrowed. "Another piercing shot. I'll say this: I know now how the computer knew my name. And no, Nidfar had nothing to do with it."

I stared at her, contemplating pressing the question. She was dodging the matter. Either she knew more or at least suspected more about the old man.

"So, this Nidfar, why do you think he was so particular about his name?" I asked, deciding to move on.

She chuckled. "Because Nidfar is Nidfar, and there is no rhyme or reason to what he does."

Though she said it with a laugh, the feeling didn't touch her eyes. Indeed, the humor left her as the words faded and her eyes wandered back out the window.

"There's more to this old man than you're telling me." I jotted down his name and put a question mark next to it.

She nodded slowly. "Very much so." Her eyes focused on me. "But only because of where we are in the story."

I waved a hand at her. "So, you fell into darkness."

Darkness swallowed me. The wind rushed past, and what little light followed me down from above vanished when the door spun shut. My braid whipped around behind my head, which at least told me I faced down as the device fell. The ring shifted to one side, and my body orientation moved with it. The wind kept hitting me in the face. Just as I began to wonder how long this tunnel was, a door spun open, and the ring shot out into the expanse below the shell.

The bright light from the core shone up at me, blinding me and forcing me to squeeze my eyes shut and cover my face with my arms. I turned my head upward and opened my eyes slightly to adjust to the light. The underbelly of Colberra moved away with some speed. A wild expanse of fingerlike mountains jutted down toward the core, a forest of gigantic stalactite-like structures slicing through the air below the shell. Near the edge of the landmass lay massive lakes of water filling in the gaps around some of the rock structures. The device turned the next moment, and my gaze moved away from my home shell.

The Colberran fleet lay spread out before me like an approaching swarm of dragons. The massive ships soared through the expanse, gliding on wings jutting out from the sides to give them balance. Giant doors had opened in the sides to allow the wings to slide out. My ring overtook the giant machines strung out in a long train bound for a massive landmass in the distance.

The Nomad shell.

I'd heard tales of the size of Suyef's shell, read about it in my studies, yet the sheer hugeness of the landmass awed me. It dwarfed Colberra. One entire end of the shell stood at an angle, tilted up toward the water shield above: the crashed shell. The closer the ring flew toward the mass, the more the destroyed landscape reaching out before me from the upper end of the sloped shell came into detail. It ended in the far distance at a glistening, shining body of blue that dominated the center of the supershell. The world's only remaining sea.

As my ring raced closer to the upper end of the supershell, huge mountains rose up all along the nearest edge to greet me. Partway up the shell, what looked like a massive Ancient city structure rose from among the peaks: one of that shell's two citadels. The ring dropped in elevation, taking the citadel from sight. The shell's edge loomed close, and, far off to my left, a peninsula extended out at the uppermost point of the landmass. Perched precariously near that point lay an outpost: Quentin's home.

Behind me, the Colberran ships began to approach the shell. As they did, their wings retracted, the gravity beams locking on to the supershell's mass and guiding the ships closer. The ring turned, and the landscape shifted below me. The device flew down near the shell's edge and moved away from the peninsula toward what looked like another massive rock tower similar to the old man's. The ring raced closer, and I began to ponder how it would stop. As the possibilities began to bubble up and form, each one worse than the last, the ring slowed and dropped closer to the mountain-ous terrain. Just when the ring looked to come down for a land-ing in a windswept ravine several chrons' march from the tower, a door spun open, and the ring moved down into another tunnel. Darkness swallowed me as the ring reoriented my body. The air shifted, and then another door opened above. The ring rose into a room identical to my departure point, the door spun shut, and my body weight returned. The ring lowered out of sight, and I looked around while my hands adjusted my clothing to rearrange any windblown dishevelment that had occurred.

"Quentin? Suyef?"

"Over here," Suyef replied from this tower's balcony.

I rushed over to find him standing there, Quentin hovering on his board just beyond the balcony's railing.

"You're still here?" I asked.

He shrugged. "Just trying to get my bearings."

"The ships are amassing just off the shell's edge," I warned him. "They're close enough to use their gravity beams."

"Then let's not waste any time," Quentin muttered. He looked at us and concentrated. "This will feel a bit odd."

My feet lifted off the ground without warning, as did Suyef's. Quentin, using his belt, lifted us off the platform and brought us to either side of him. I grabbed his arm and planted my feet on the board. In the next moment, he shifted down, the balcony shooting up above us. He brought the board to the base of the structure and landed near the entrance, a door cut in the side of the mountain the tower rose from.

"Now what?" I asked. "You going to carry us all the way to your outpost?"

Quentin shook his head and pointed behind me. Two speeder bikes of similar design to those used by the Seekers sat parked near the entrance. Suyef grunted and moved toward the mounts.

"I can't ride one of those," I said, looking back at Quentin.

He'd already moved off, floating up to hover above a nearby boulder. I glared at him, but he didn't look down at me. His eyes were focused on the mountains in the distance. Spinning around, I rushed over to where Suyef had mounted one of the speeders.

"I can't pilot one of these."

He shrugged. "Get on."

I refused to move. "We have to talk some sense into him."

He nodded in Quentin's direction. "You think anything you say is going to stop him?"

Quentin had moved off down the valley, away from the tower. Shaking my head, I mounted behind Suyef, and we took off after Quentin's descending form. The wind whipped at my braid and scarf, which I secured under my armpits while huddling close to the Nomad.

"He'll listen to you," I called into Suyef's ear.

"Why all this concern?" Suyef called back.

I paused, thinking about it. "I don't know."

That much was true. It was hard to pinpoint when it had happened, but suddenly the thought of either Quentin or Suyef being in danger gave me pause. It was a very familiar feeling, one I'd first experienced when Jyen had been taken. Somehow, without my realizing it, these two had slipped into a place that previously only my family had occupied. And, also previously unaware of it, I'd taken to that role again. That of a mother protecting her family, even if it was a chosen one. That thought really gave me pause. When had these two become my chosen family?

Suyef shifted the mount around a boulder, jolting me back to the present.

"It doesn't matter!" I yelled at him over the wind. "The point is, he's being rash. He's going to get himself hurt. Or worse. You need to try to talk to him."

"I think it does matter," he called back. "And unless you figure out why, you're not going to convince him of anything."

That made me pause. Suyef was right, although I didn't realize just how right at that moment.

"You two are all I have left at this point," I said, leaning near his ear. "Besides my father, and I don't know how to get to him." I waved a hand out ahead of us. "I'm here, alone, on a strange continent with only you two as friends."

Suyef reached back with his hand to grab my arm as I pulled it back.

"That is what you need to say to *him*," he said, but he held up a finger after letting me go. "But I don't think you'll dissuade him." The Nomad shook his head. "What comes next I believe is necessary."

A chill gripped my spine. "What did you say?"

"What happens next is important."

"No, you said *necessary*." I repeated his original word, leaning closer to him. "Necessary."

He shrugged as he piloted the speeder down a gully between two mountains. Quentin darted down across the same gully ahead of us, cloak whipping in the wind around him.

"Either word, it's the same thing."

I stared at the Nomad for a moment. The words of the old man echoed in my memory as the speeder shifted about under Suyef's command, jostling me in an effort to keep up with Quentin.

"What happens next is necessary."

Those words occupied my mind, which tried to find their meaning. I didn't have to wait long.

We darted through the brown rock ravines, slicing between the peaks all around us. As we flew, I kept a wary gaze out for gaps that might reveal what was out there. Somewhere, the Colberran fleet was forming to move in the same direction as us, if they hadn't already. Ahead, Quentin moved across the terrain, darting back and forth, vaulting off tall rock formations, flipping once or twice. All the while, he never slowed, keeping us moving in what I assumed was a westward direction.

"Are your cardinal directions the same here?" I yelled into Suyef's ear.

He nodded. "Except for between the Shattered Citadel and the Great Sea." His body tensed as we dropped off a ledge. "The fool is going to be the death of me."

The mount's gravity beams caught us as we came down near the ground, our forward acceleration slowing in the process. Once the beams had purchase, Suyef opened up the throttle, and we surged forward. For a few seconds, we neared Quentin enough to see him execute an impressive flip off another ledge and bring the board back down below him in time not to lose any acceleration.

"Hate to admit it, but he's getting better," Suyef called to me.

I groaned. "Being able to fly on that thing isn't going to help him in a battle."

Suyef shrugged, guiding the mount around another large rock formation and down into a widening valley that opened up to the north and south.

"Where we're going, there might not be a battle." Suyef accelerated in the open terrain, pressing forward across the valley to gain some ground on Quentin as we neared the mountains looming in the distance.

"You don't sound confident of that," I said, gripping his torso and pushing a strand of hair from my eyes.

He grunted. "With Seekers, you can't ever be sure."

The valley floor began to climb the slopes before us. Quentin, halfway up the peaks and heading for a gap just off to our left, pulled away from us. Suyef leaned forward and gave the mount more speed. The wind whipped around us as we soared past rocks and stunted trees. So far, save for the preponderance of mountains, the terrain looked very similar to Colberra.

"Your shell doesn't look that much different from mine," I called to Suyef as we reached the same gap Quentin had already vanished into.

He nodded off to the north. "It is in that direction. Beyond these mountains and closer to the Shattered Citadel."

The speeder shooting out from the gap stopped me from asking why it was called that. Suyef reversed the gravity beams on the top of the mount to stop it, and I clenched tight to him as we decelerated, squeezing my eyes shut until we stopped. Quentin hovered just ahead of us. I opened my mouth to call out to him, but the words never came.

The mountains ended just behind us, sweeping off to our right to form a bowl around a flat piece of terrain. The land sloped down from where we were to meet the peninsula visible during my flight to the shell. It rose from the lowest point of the bowl, sticking out into the expanse. Situated precariously on the edge of that peninsula sat Quentin's home.

And there, floating above like a swarm of the pesky locusts we so rarely saw on our shell, hung the entire Colberran fleet.

No one moved, save the swarming ships. An eerie silence hung in the air, no one daring to make a sound. My eyes darted to Quentin to see him inching forward, hands gripping into balls at his side.

"Don't do it," I hissed at him, keeping my voice as quiet as possible. "Don't, Quentin."

He moved a few inches more. His face wore a torn look. The ships, still keeping their distance, moved about in what appeared to be a random pattern, the larger ships circling over the outpost, the smaller ones around them. Several looked to be holding off the edge, and more seemed to be just visible below the edge.

"Quentin, you're too late," I pleaded with him, reaching a hand out. He looked like he didn't know what to do. I tried to use that. "They don't need a warning. They probably won't even fire. They haven't yet."

He didn't move, either way. One hand unclenched a bit.

"Think about it, Quentin." I felt bolder. "They don't need to attack their own people. It's pointless. They have to know they didn't do anything. It's not necessary."

I regretted that last word the instant it left my lips. As the old man's warning echoed in my head, every Colberran ship opened fire on the outpost.

The shock of the attack stunned us. No one moved for a few moments. Down below, rotating turrets on the bottoms of the ships spun about, unleashing laser after laser onto the outpost. The larger ships all dipped to one side, allowing the weaponry on the topside to bring more firepower to the attack. The smaller ships circled the edge, swooping low to the ground and pouring their own blasts into the side of the compound walls.

At first, the walls seemed to hold. That kind of firepower would prove too much eventually. Even as we watched, the exterior walls started to fall back in on the compound, and here and there a building collapsed under the barrage.

"They're attacking the foundations," Suyef hissed, shifting in his seat and looking about the valley. "They'll bring the structures down on top of the people."

Suyef's words jolted Quentin into action. He leapt forward, sailing off down the valley in the direction of the battle.

"Quentin!" I cried after him, jumping off the mount and cupping my hands to my mouth. "Come back!"

He didn't hear me. As the Colberran ships continued to pour their firepower into the outpost, Quentin sped across the plain, hugging the ground.

"What's he going to do?" I asked Suyef. He didn't answer. Spinning around, I jabbed a finger in the direction of the battle and yelled, "We have to stop him!"

"Or help, at least," he said. "Wait here."

"No!" I yelled, freezing him before he could even move. "I'm going with you."

"I can help him better if I don't have to worry about you," he hissed, starting to move.

I grabbed his hand. "Suyef, I need to help. I need to do something this time."

"You're the one who didn't want him charging in there, and now you want to go in after him?"

I pointed down the valley. "He made his choice. Now we need to help him."

We held each other's gaze for a few tense heartbeats. Suyef finally nodded and held a hand out to pull me back on the mount.

"Your choice."

The mount surged to life, racing down the valley. Ahead, Quentin reached the outpost as laser fire pelted the ground all around from the smaller ships strafing the exterior walls.

"What are they shooting at?" I asked Suyef as we raced toward the battle.

Even as the words left my lips, the answer became clear. The ships flew low, their lasers raining destruction down on the outpost. As the walls and structures buckled, people appeared, fleeing the scene. When they broke free from the structures, the smaller ships poured forth a deluge of lasers, driving the people back into the outpost.

"Barbarians," Suyef growled as he turned the mount to follow the bowl of the valley around the battle.

"Where are you going?" I craned my head to catch some sight of Quentin. "Suyef, we need to get him out of there!"

He ignored me, piloting the mount around the edge of the valley just where the ground began to slope up to the peaks in the distance. As we moved, more of the exterior walls began to collapse, and, for an instant, I saw something flitting along the structures like a small insect. Could that have been Quentin, or just a figment of my imagination? It was impossible to tell.

The mount stopped, jerking my attention back to Suyef. "What are we doing here?" I asked. "Did you need a better view?"

He didn't answer. Instead, he held a hand up, some kind of weapon grasped in it. With a squeeze of a trigger, a bright flaring bolt shot high in the sky.

"Hold tight to me, Micaela, or get off now," he whispered.

Confused, I gripped his torso tighter. "What was that?" I craned my head to see the pulsing flare wink out.

"Help."

I frowned and looked down at the battlefield. Nothing had changed save for more walls had fallen.

"What kind of—" I never finished that thought. All around us a reverberating blast echoed across the valley, a roar that filled my ears. Several of the mountain peaks exploded outward, rocks tumbling into the valley. Something moved out from the smoke and dust emanating from the former peaks. Several things, actually.

A cloud of dirt rolled down past us, forcing me to shield my eyes. As the dust began to clear, another fleet even more numerous than that fielded by the Colberrans swept into view.

The Nomads had come to the fight.

CHAPTER 47

SPLITTING

The sight of the Nomad ships should have given me hope or buoyed my spirits. It did neither. Instead, as the ships surged into view, a sense of dread took hold of my heart.

I hardly had time to notice that feeling before the battle began in full. Overhead, the mighty airships swept down the valley to engage the Colberran fleet. From where we were, there seemed to be little difference between the two fleets save that the Nomad ships all lacked the tall superstructures the Colberran ships sported on their topsides. They did not lack for firepower, however, and they brought all of it to bear on the ships attacking the outpost. The Colberrans reacted quickly. Several of their larger ships climbed higher above the outpost, shifting to direct their weapons at the new threat. As the Nomad fleet closed, laser blasts filled the air, beams of light splitting out from each ship, trying to connect with a target. Some struck home, hitting an enemy ship. I expected damage, but, as the blast dissipated, a shimmering, cloud-like substance faded from sight as a sound similar to the thunder in the Wilds echoed across the valley.

"Shields? The ships have shields?" I asked. "Doesn't that require a lot of power?"

Suyef nodded. "Most likely powered by Ancient generators."

"Thought the Colberrans didn't like using that stuff," I muttered.

"If it gives them an advantage, the Seekers will use anything."

As the battle unfolded, something shifted near us. Another force arriving drew my attention from the battling fleets: an army of Nomads on speeders. Suyef raised an arm to a nearby squad, and our mount took off for the outpost. As one, the Nomad speeders raced across the valley toward the stricken structures.

"What are we doing?" I cried into Suyef's ear, clinging to him as laser blasts detonated above us.

"Going to rescue the people in the city."

"Why?" I leaned over to get a view of our destination, riddled as it was with fire from several Colberran ships still holding their ground over the outpost. "Why do you care?"

"Because they're innocent pawns in this fight," he said, gunning the speeder forward.

I clung to Suyef as we neared the outpost walls. Pieces of the wall lay strewn on the ground we flew over, and an acrid smell filled my nose. Blasts from attacking ships echoed all around, some detonating against the walls we neared, most against ships overhead. Off to our left, a smaller Colberran ship, riddled with fire, crashed into the valley floor.

We crossed into the outpost, and smoke swallowed the battle above. The Nomads scattered in all directions once inside, bringing their speeders to whatever semblance of shelter they could find. Suyef brought us near one of the larger structures and stopped. He motioned me off, and, once he'd parked the speeder, we ran over to a crack in the structure.

"Anyone here?" he called into the darkness.

The only answers he got were a muffled cry and someone hushing what I assumed was a child.

"They think you're the attacker," I said, grabbing at his cloak.

He nodded and pulled the cloak off, tossing the silvery material into a fire. "Go in there, and convince them to come out. Quickly."

I hesitated for a moment, then nodded and squeezed into the fire into a dark space. The thought of that kid perishing in this structure drove me forward past my doubts. At first, it was impossible to see much in the dim light. With every blink, my eyes watered from the smoke in the air.

"Hello? I'm here to help."

"Who are you?" someone asked from my left.

"A friend," I answered, pointing at the door. "With lots more friends. The Nomads are here to help you."

"Why would they help us?" a gruff voice asked from the other direction.

I shrugged. "They just risked a lot of their people to get into this place to help you get out." I pointed at the ceiling. "And they have an entire fleet up there attacking the Colberran ships firing on your outpost."

"Why are they attacking us?" a kid asked in a sniffling, trembling voice.

An adult hushed the child before I could try and explain how his country had betrayed him and his family. The kid looked to be barely five cycles old, with big round eyes and eyebrows set so high on his forehead he looked perpetually surprised.

"It doesn't matter," the gruff voice said from behind me.

A tall man leaned out the crack in the wall. He shook his head and moved away from the light, heading farther into the structure.

"The buggers are pulling people out and taking them away," he said, motioning everyone to follow him. "We've got to get farther in so they don't find us."

"You're hiding from them?" I asked. "They're here to help you."

"They've ignored us most of the time we've been here," the man said, his voice firm as he paused to glare at me. "Rude, aloof, isolated. Any time we deal with them, they act like it's a bother."

That said, he turned and disappeared farther into the darkness. Most everyone there moved to follow him. The mother holding her wide-eyed son did not. She stood motionless, eyes on me.

"You're sure they'll keep us safe?" she asked.

I shook my head. "I don't know what will happen, but they're here to rescue you." I nodded into the darkness. "It's at least a better chance than staying here."

She looked after her companions, her hands clinging to her son's cloak, eyes darting around as she struggled to decide. Finally, she nodded and moved toward me.

"Get my son out of here, please," she begged me.

She and her son followed me, and we moved toward the crack in the wall. Suyef waited outside, leaning near the wall, a curious look on his face.

"She's the only one who would listen," I said, nodding at the mother and her son as they stepped out of the building. "The rest think it's a trick."

He nodded and motioned for us to follow him. "Their choice."

"You're not going to try to help them?" I asked, grabbing his shoulder.

"You can't help people that don't want it," he said, nodding at the mother. "We can help her."

Part of me wanted to fight him, to make him go help the others. I never got to decide.

As we stood there, me gripping Suyef's sleeve, the woman clinging to her son, a laser blast struck the building overhead. The blast sent a shock wave out in all directions, knocking us to the ground. All the air expelled from my lungs when my body hit the ground, and my vision went blurry from the impact. I struggled to breathe and clear my vision. When my sight returned, I looked up to see a chunk of the metallic building break free. It swung down, a small piece of piping still holding it in place. It dangled there as the entire wall shifted and leaned out over us.

"Suyef!" I cried out the instant my lungs took in air.
The piece of wall broke free to fall straight down toward us.

We all scrambled backward on the ground, trying to get out from
under it. As it plummeted, something tumbled away from it and
my heart stopped. It was a body knocked from the upper levels.
The chunk of wall crashed down, ripping pieces off the structure
as it went. At the last instant, a small round object shot out from
the smoke and hit the piece of falling metal square on the side. The
chunk of wall careened off into the smoke to land harmlessly out
of sight. Blinking through the smoke, I just made out Quentin hovering there on his board, a look of concern on his face as he used
the gravity beams to bring the person he'd caught to the ground.

"You okay?" he asked me as he landed.

I nodded and looked around. Suyef was helping the mother
and her son to their feet and guiding them to his speeder. The body
Quentin had caught wasn't moving. I stepped near and felt the
man's neck. When Quentin knelt next to me, I shook my head.

"He's gone."

The mother shielded her son's eyes from the sight, and no part
of me could blame her. It was the first dead body I'd ever seen this
close. It felt as disturbing to look at it as it had been to see the bodies exploding when they hit the ground at the prison battle. This
one wouldn't be my last that day.

"You got her?" the Nomad asked, pointing at me.

Quentin nodded. "Get them out of here. We'll go find more."

The Nomad mounted his speeder and helped the mother climb
on board behind him. Her son squeezed in between them, and the
trio lifted off moments later, the son looking back—at us or at the
body, I'm still not sure. Quentin moved in front of me, distracting
me from the boy.

"What were you thinking?" I cried out, smacking Quentin's offered hand away. "Flying off like that in a battle."

"You're welcome," he muttered, extending his hand.

I glared at him, then at his hand before taking it and standing up. "This isn't over," I warned him.

He grinned. "Clearly. Come on."

He lifted me onto his board and moved us off into the thick smoke. As we rose, the battle overhead came back into view. Fires raged on several Colberran ships as laser blasts lanced out from the embattled hulks. Despite their numbers, the Nomads seemed unable to dislodge the Colberran fleet from their attack. On the ground, several speeders loaded with rescued citizens raced off toward the mountains. Some of the Colberran ships seemed to have noticed the rescue. One ship poured a deluge of laser blasts after a squad of speeders racing off into the desert. One of the fleeing mounts did not make it. Before the ship could destroy any more, a Nomad ship swooped in to silence the laser battery's assault on the speeders.

"Don't the people on those ships realize what's going on?" I leaned back against Quentin, his arms wrapped to hold me in place.

"Maybe. Maybe not." He darted back down into the smoke, concealing the sight, if not the sounds, of the aerial battle. "They're Seekers, remember. They've been trained for cycles to follow orders and believe what the government tells them."

I shook my head. "But attacking someone who's retreating from the field? That's low."

Quentin spun low around another structure. "They're Seekers."

"That doesn't explain this," I muttered more to myself than to him.

He brought us down near a smaller structure on the outskirts of the outpost. The Colberran attack had already moved farther into the larger structures, having all but destroyed this building.

Once on the ground, Quentin let go of me and, with a motion of his hand, peeled part of the wall away.

"Does the hand motion help?" I asked, nodding at his belt.

"It gives me something to focus with," he said as he walked toward the building. "Anyone here?"

A muffled cry answered him. We moved into the dark structure to find two men lying near the wall, both injured.

"Micaela?" Quentin asked, pointing at the men. I nodded, moving toward them. "I'll get some help."

He leapt into the air with his board. The man closest to me, long hair smeared with sweat and blood across his face, stared openmouthed at the retreating Quentin.

"How'd he do that?" he whispered.

"Magic." I knelt to examine the other man. "Sir, can you hear me?"

The man nodded, his eyes squeezed shut, his hands grasping his left thigh. A closer look revealed a nasty fracture just below the knee.

"Does anything hurt besides that?" I asked, leaning close and feeling his forehead.

He shook his head and wheezed out a groan of agony.

"What about you?" I asked the first man while grabbing a piece of cloth lying on the ground and looking for a splint.

He shook his head. "Minor wounds at most. It looks worse because I was lying under him. Blast knocked us off the wall." He coughed and spat some nasty-looking fluid. "Dragged him here to hide."

I braced a piece of metal next to the man's leg and splinted it in place. Noises outside the structure drew my attention as my hands finished tying off the splint. Two Nomads jumped off their speeders and rushed into the structure. Moments later, the two men were mounted up behind their rescuers and racing off into the desert. There was no sign of Quentin, so I moved away from the building toward another, looking for more victims. There was no one there, so I moved farther into the outpost.

"Micaela!" Quentin called out from behind me.

He rose from the building he'd left me at. I waved at him, calling him over.

"Come on, there's more over here," Quentin said when he picked me up.

We soared up over the smoke, toward the far side of the outpost. A massive Colberran ship, crippled by fires fore and aft, wavered in the air just to the north, its massive laser batteries still raining fire down on the outpost.

Quentin noticed my gaze and nodded. "Yes, that ship isn't going to stay up much longer," he said, bringing the board back down, the smoke concealing the flaming hulk from my view.

"What will happen if it crashes?" I asked as we landed near another large structure that was riddled with cracks.

"If the Ancient reactor on board is damaged when it comes down, a whole lot of bad." He looked at me. "And let's not discuss what might happen if those missiles carrying all that fuel explode with it."

He motioned for me to follow and approached a large crack in the wall. His board had shrunk in size in his hand.

"How'd the board do that?" I asked.

He glanced at me, then the board. "I'm not sure," he said, shrugging and motioning me into the building.

"They wouldn't listen to me," he said. "Can you go convince them to come out? I'll round up some help."

I plunged into the pitch black as Quentin leapt up into the smoke. The darkness inside brought me to a halt while my eyes adjusted. As I waited, the ground shook, minor tremors reverberating through the structure.

"Hello?" I called into the darkness, a sense of urgency filling me. "Hello?!"

"Who's there?" a quiet, female voice called back.

"My name is Micaela. We're here to help," I replied. "We can get you out of here, but you need to come out of the building."

It took several more moments of coaxing before the entire group decided to trust me. We sent them off on speeders to safety and moved on, repeating the process as fast as we could move. At the third building we came to, Quentin paused near the structure, his head cocked to one side.

"What is it?" I asked, leaning close and looking around.

"Shhh," he hissed, waving a hand at me.

My eyes darted around, my ears listening for something new. All around, lasers made their impacts, people cried, structures groaned, but nothing else. Quentin, on the other hand, sensed something else. He spun around, eyes looking up at the battle. The blazing hulk of the stricken Colberran ship we'd seen before appeared through a small gap in the smoke.

"She's coming down," Quentin said.

As he spoke, the ship began to shake, list to one side, and lose elevation. Quentin pulled me behind part of a fractured wall. We watched the doomed ship plummet toward the shell. Smoke shifting in the wind obscured her from view, but we all knew when she landed.

The impact was deafening. A flash of light momentarily blinded us, but we could still hear the blast. Smoke rising up from the burning outpost shifted as the shock wave blasted in all directions. Pieces of the ship shot high in the sky when part of her exploded, landing all around us. One part of the outpost, battered from all the laser blasts, gave out and tipped over to fall on top of the stricken ship.

Just as I thought it was safe to move again, the ground began to shake. My eyes couldn't focus on anything around me. The wall we hid near jolted and shifted as the ground beneath our feet rocked and swayed. I fell backward into Quentin, and we tumbled into a twisted knot of arms, legs, and cloaks. The ground continued to shake, and then a sound that, at the time, I did not recognize filled the air. Now it's very familiar to me, and it is probably one of the most terrifying sounds one might hear in our broken world.

The sound of the shell splitting apart.

CHAPTER 48

BROKEN PROMISES

Quentin didn't hesitate. After extricating himself from my legs, he leapt onto his board, lifting me up after him. We rose above the smoke billowing around us. Down below, the outpost lay almost destroyed; buildings lay toppled and mangled. On the north side of the outpost, opposite the expanse and astride the base of the peninsula the outpost had been built on, lay the inferno that had once been a Colberran ship.

"They're shifting," Quentin said, pointing up at the ships.

The Nomad and Colberran fleets remained fully engaged with each other. Several Colberran ships were in ruins, still floating somehow but no longer contributing to the fight. The Nomad ships ignored them, focusing their firepower on the remaining threats. The Colberran ships, once focused over the outpost, were moving.

"Are they driving into the Nomad fleet?" I asked.

Quentin turned the board in place, scanning the entire battle. "Yes, and all those ships they kept out of sight. Look."

Remembering the ships just visible below the battle, I looked out into the expanse. Some were rising now to join the fight, pouring in on either side of the outpost to form two new battle lines. The ships already above the outpost pushed inland, forming another line. The Nomad ships, still the more numerous, bowed back into the shell but did not break.

"What are they doing?"

The Colberran ships merged into one solid line encircling the peninsula.

Quentin exhaled behind me. "Rockets," he whispered.

"Excuse me?" I asked.

"They haven't used their rockets yet," he said. "Not one rocket has been fired."

A thought occurred to me. "You said those were explosive on impact, right?"

He nodded.

"Quentin, those ships under the shell!"

He blurted out something that didn't sound pleasant, spinning the board and moving out over the edge, staying low enough to avoid the laser blasts still being exchanged above.

Once we neared the edge, the peninsula just behind us, we paused to look down. Far below, the core shone and the sheer drop made my stomach churn. Quentin turned us back around to look at the shell, and I forgot about the open sky below us. The line of Colberran ships continued, matching the line above almost exactly. Some Nomad ships had moved out to engage the few Colberran ships just visible along the edge, but none had moved below the shell.

"Are they going to fire the rockets into the shell?" I asked.

He didn't answer. Instead, he moved us back up near the outpost. The Colberran ships executed another coordinated shift, forming a double line: one engaging the Nomads, the other behind that front line. That interior line proceeded to roll over, bringing the topside of the ships down toward the shell. The rectangular-shaped launchers Suyef had highlighted opened up, and a myriad of projectiles launched from them.

"Oh no," Quentin whispered.

The barrage of rockets barreled into the ground all around the outpost, detonating with a force I did not realize was possible from something so small. As the shock wave moved past us, several more waves of rockets followed, hitting the same line. The explosions ripped through the shell, and the outpost began to shake.

"Are they—" I began, but never finished the question.

Quentin surged toward the outpost. As we descended, several Nomad mounts caught in the attack were flung into the air, their riders falling to their deaths. Closer to the structures, most of the Nomad mounts in the area hung in the air, their riders and passengers watching the attack. The Nomads watched with stoic faces, but their passengers were shaken by the sight. I saw many looks of terror mixed with uncertainty as we landed near Suyef.

"They're trying to knock the outpost off the shell," Quentin said.

The Nomad nodded. "We'll have to risk the rockets," he called into a device in his hand.

In answer, mounts raced off in the direction of the battle. Rockets continued to pour into the crack forming around the peninsula, joined now by lasers. The Nomad ships, having realized what was happening, had shifted several of their ships to try to shoot down some of the rockets with their laser cannons. They weren't having much success, from what I could tell.

"Micaela, come on," Quentin called to me, waving me after him. "We have to check for more survivors."

"Quentin, we need to get out of here." I pointed at the battle. "They mean to destroy this place. We've done all we can."

"There are still people trapped inside!" he yelled, waving an arm at the wreckage. "My people. I've got to help them."

I ran up to him, grabbing his arm as he made to turn. "You can't do anything for them," I insisted, tugging him away from the outpost and remembering those first people we'd tried to help. "They don't want to be rescued."

"I'm going to try," he said. "Not all of them are that stupid."

I looked back into the outpost and shook my head. "Yes, I think they are," I said, my voice quiet.

He lifted off the ground, pulling himself free from my hand. Just as he did, a laser bolt detonated into the nearest structure, flinging Quentin to one side with its shock wave. He spun out of control and came close to crashing into another building.

"Quentin!" I cried out, running toward him. "Are you okay?"

He lowered to the ground, holding his head. I moved in front of him and looked into his eyes.

"My head is ringing," he whispered.

His pupils were fully dilated.

"You've got a concussion." I pulled his still-floating form away from the outpost. "Come on, we need to get out of here."

He shook his head, then groaned. "No, they need us," he whispered, tugging halfheartedly against me.

I put my arm around his torso and steered him away.

"Yes, they need help, but so do you, and you won't do any good in this condition," I said.

A pair of Nomads landed nearby and stopped when I waved at them.

"We need help," I called to them. "He's been hurt."

One of them dismounted and helped me situate Quentin on the back of the other speeder. Then we mounted his speeder and moved to the north, skirting the outpost and looking for a gap in the rocket and laser barrage. Just above us, I noted the Nomad ships had given up on shooting the rockets down. Instead, they were pouring their firepower into the most damaged Colberran ships, trying to take enough of them out to break the front line and get to the line attacking the peninsula.

As we neared the northernmost edge of the outpost, the flaming wreckage of the downed Colberran ship came into full view. The heat from the inferno made my skin tingle and dried my eyes

out in an instant. Our Nomad pilots steered us to one side, bringing us closer to the flames.

"What are you doing?" I asked my pilot, shielding my face with
my scarf.

"They're not firing this close to the ship," the Nomad called
back to me.

My hand began to hurt from holding the scarf up, so I wrapped
it in one end and held the scarf back up over my head. He was right,
as no rockets or lasers landed this close to the fire. As I looked up,
the reason why became clear to me. The smoke here was so thick I
could hardly see the battle.

At that moment, the other Nomad cried out. A split second later,
the Nomad I rode with gunned his mount forward to soar past the
flames. Clinging tightly to my pilot, I turned my head back, searching
for the other mount. He raced to keep up with us, but what I didn't
see made my heart stop.

Quentin was not on the mount.

I grabbed at the Nomad, pleading with him to stop. He didn't listen. Craning my head the other direction, I tried to look back into
the flames to see where Quentin had fallen. The Nomad steered
the mount toward the west, giving me a good view of the wreckage, but there was no sign of Quentin. We came to a halt near what
looked like a gathering point: a small hill the battle hadn't touched.
As soon as we stopped, I leapt from the mount and raced to the top
of the hill, shoving past several Nomads and refugees.

I stared at the battle below, squinting to try and spot Quentin.
A Nomad nearby tossed me a spec device to scan the battlefield.
With it, I looked around the wreckage and the ground near it. No
sight of him.

"Blast him, where is he?" I whispered, turning the device back at the outpost.

"My lady, he jumped off," a Nomad said to me.

I glanced over to see the other mount pilot standing there, shoulders slumped, brow furrowing. "He didn't fall off?" I said.

The Nomad shook his head. "He pushed himself up to stand. I tried to pull him down, but he jumped up into the air and disappeared into the smoke."

"Blast him and his board!" I hissed, targeting the specs at the outpost.

Sure enough, just on the edge of the outpost, near a precarious-looking building, Quentin huddled down on his knees. He seemed to be pulling something from under one edge of the building.

"You idiot, what are you doing?" I called out to him, not caring he couldn't hear me. I grabbed at the Nomad. "Please, go get him!"

He shook his head. "We can't. It's too dangerous."

I shoved him toward a mount. "Then show me how to fly that thing. I'll do it myself."

"What's going on here?" Suyef's voice asked from behind me.

I whirled on him, pointing back at the outpost. "The idiot is still down there trying to rescue people!" I yelled. "Go stop him!"

Suyef grabbed the specs from me and looked down at the outpost. He hissed, and I knew he'd spotted Quentin.

"He's pulling someone from the building," Suyef said.

All around him, the Nomads gathering murmured as one.

"Don't just stand there admiring him!" I yelled at them. "We have to help him!"

Before anyone could move, an explosion filled the air. As one, our eyes turned skyward to see yet another stricken Colberran ship begin to teeter precariously in the air near the edge. As we watched, the ship pulled out of the line, diving toward the already-crashed form of her sister ship.

"What are they doing?" I whispered to Suyef, my eyes locked on the falling ship.

"Sacrificing themselves," he said, placing a hand on my shoulder.

The ship, rocked by more explosions inside, convulsed as it fell, crashing down into the other flaming hulk. Another blast filled the air as the ship exploded on impact, sending debris skyward to strike at other ships still battling. I shielded my eyes from the blast but squinted to look back down at the outpost through the specs I had yanked back from Suyef. Quentin, having spied the falling ship, had crawled inside the fallen building. He stuck his head back out, then crawled from the structure, pulling at someone behind him.

The entire peninsula began to shake, trembling, so I couldn't focus on Quentin anymore. I lowered the specs to see the far end of the peninsula jutting out into the expanse begin to dip toward the core.

"Oh no," I whispered, and felt Suyef's grip tighten on my shoulder.

The ground cracked, echoing across the valley.

"No." I felt something twist inside as the peninsula began to shake. "All those people."

The peninsula dipped farther, breaking free from the shell. Colberran ships continued to pour lasers into the gap forming in the shell. I lowered the specs as my emotions began to roil inside. I gritted my teeth, trying to keep my face straight. It was happening again; yet another person was being taken from me. So many people were being taken.

Suyef's hand gripped me, and I was vaguely aware of a sound coming from the Nomads behind me. A chant.

The peninsula, outpost and all, began to dip out of sight. More cracks echoed across the valley. The chant from the Nomads climbed in volume, reverberating through Suyef's chest into my back.

The air went silent, the laser and rocket barrage coming to a halt. Even the Nomad ships stopped firing. Everything paused. Everything stopped, including the chant. Even I stood still, though inside I boiled over what was happening, over all those people falling to their deaths. Of Quentin falling to his.

"Those people are monsters," I whispered, and felt Suyef's hand squeeze my shoulder.

The peninsula broke free, falling from sight toward the core, taking Quentin with it. I stood in silence, watching as the outpost fell from sight. But inside, I wasn't silent. Inside, another part of me had ripped away. Inside, I screamed.

"No!"

EPILOGUE

Micaela stopped talking. She stood and walked over to the window. There she remained in silence for so long I thought she'd forgotten about me.

"Do you need a moment?"

She shrugged. "I've had so many of those it won't really matter if I have more."

I stood, setting my stylus down and moving to stand next to her.

"So, what happened to him? When he fell?" I asked.

"He fell."

"Like you did when you fell from the tower? Only he had his belt and board."

She looked over at me, a hard look.

"I'm sure that came in handy," I stated, turning my eyes to look out the window at the nearby shell, as her gaze made me feel uncomfortable.

Micaela let out a long sigh. "The answer you seek is on that shell over there. Go find it yourself."

"What answer?"

She turned to walk toward the door I'd yet to pass through. "To what happened to him."

"What's over there?"

She didn't answer.

When my ride landed on the nearby shell, what I found left me speechless. Barren of almost any feature and equal in size to the green-dragon shell, the shell's surface was mostly flat. It was possible to see almost all the way across to the other side. What Micaela had sent me to find was very visible.

Strewn out before me lay the wreckage of a destroyed Ancient outpost. Pieces of boulders lay piled all around the ruined buildings. Sheets of metal wall stuck out of the shell's landscape like daggers fallen from the sky. Near the edge, an unusually large piece of landmass lay partway over the expanse below. One piece of the outpost was still attached to that large chunk of rock. Every piece of metal bore dozens of scorch marks, and the chunk of land lying over the edge was riddled with holes.

I ran a hand through my long hair, confusion taking hold. Was this the outpost Micaela had seen fall from the Nomad shell? It had to be. What were the odds another outpost would be so damaged from laser fire and have fallen to crash on a lower shell? Still, this gave me no answers. Just more questions.

As I turned to go back to the dragon shell and question her, my foot brushed against something soft. A piece of cloth jutted out from under a rock. I leaned down and pushed the rock over, yanking the cloth free. I shook the dirt out of it, then froze.

It was a cloak, torn and dirty. Despite the damage, I recognized the silver material.

Micaela still stood by the window when I returned, holding the cloak in hand.

"This was his, wasn't it?"

She nodded.

"You knew this was there." I tossed the cloak onto the table, eyes never leaving her. "You know he didn't tell me what happened next. Do you know what happened to him?"

"He made a choice," she said. "True, he did it to help others, and in that I can't find fault. But still, he made a choice."

"To go back?" I asked.

She nodded. "To go back alone."

"You know you couldn't have helped," I said.

She shrugged. "Doesn't mean I didn't want to try. We all did. But we were helpless." She looked away. "And then he was gone."

She closed her eyes for a moment. When they opened, a quiet rage filled them and gave me pause. Her jaw clenched as she took a breath. When she let it out, the angry edge wilted away.

"Again, I can't fault his choice. But there's a pattern with him. Sure, he's loyal, sometimes to a fault. But he's also stubborn and, at times, impulsive." She held up a finger. "Once or twice, I can forgive. But he's done it time and again. He promises to stay, that he's not going anywhere. Then he leaves. There's always a reason, and most of the time they are good ones. But that doesn't change the fact that he leaves. Just like everyone else." A single tear crept out one eye and rolled down the side of her nose. "I've been alone for so long."

Micaela turned to look back out the window. I opened my mouth, then closed it, uncertain what to say.

"High One, what happened to Quentin?" I asked, my voice barely louder than a whisper.

She lowered her head, hands clasped in front of her. "You heard me. He's gone."

"But how?" I moved closer. "Clearly he survived. Did he just not come back afterward? And you know where he is now. How is he gone?"

"Like they all are," she whispered. "Even though he promised me, he ended up just like my family." She looked me square in the eyes. "He died."

I left my room and stepped into the living area to find it empty. My review of my notes with Micaela from weeks before had kept me awake and occupied all night, prompted as it was by Quentin and Suyef's tale of the battle. As such, I wasn't sure if anyone else was awake yet.

"Suyef?" I called out. "Quentin?"

No one answered. I frowned, moving into the hallway and going into their rooms. No sign of them. The balcony was empty as well. I climbed all the way up the tunnel and searched as far as my eyes could see. Nothing.

"Why just leave?" A few moments later, I sat at the table, a near-empty hydration pack in my hand. "Quentin, I get. He's done this before. But you, too, Suyef?"

I shook my head, looking around the room. My travel sack sat on the table, and the box just peeking out caught my eye. Still closed. Under it lay Suyef's note. I pulled the paper out with one hand and read it again. My other hand pulled the box free of the bag, my thumb picking at the magnetic clasp.

"This hardly qualifies as my most dire need."

I set the note down. What could possibly lie inside this box? What object could be so central to controlling the network? So dangerous even the Queen would not speak of it? And why entrust it to me? Why not keep it with them until we found the other two items? I looked around, pondering the possibility that one piece lay hidden somewhere around me in this place tucked away from everyone and everything. I glanced down at the note.

"Because you trusted them," I said to myself. "They knew you would. So, what do you do now?"

I lifted the clasp, moving my hands to either end of the box. "Only at your direst need." Shaking my head, I lifted the lid and looked inside.

TRANSCRIPT OF LOGWYN'S INTERVIEW WITH QUENTIN

Attached is a transcript from my initial interview with Quentin. I've included just a sample, as his rambling tends to go on forever. I provide this simply to give you, the reader, an idea of what it was like interviewing him. Audio of this sample will be provided soon.

I need, that over there, yes, that window. Move here. Why are you moving like that? No, don't touch that. Okay, there. See that out there? Look, out the window. What do you see? Yes, yes, all that. Man, your brain is full. I know someone who can help you with that. Well, I used to. Somewhere. What happened to him? Ah, never mind.

    Empty sky. That's what I meant. Now, what's out there in the empty sky? Shells! Lots of them, with millions of people living on them. Millions. Think about that. Even after what all this world went through, we've still managed to repopulate all these shells. Testament to the Ancients right there. Not that they stuck around to help us. Useless ketches. What's the point in building all this amazing technology, then leaving us to figure it out alone? Anyway, I digress.

Point is, all of those shells are really far apart. You could fly around and around, again and again, big giant circles. Course, how would you know where you'd been? You could fly the same orbit over and over and not realize it. Maybe you could leave a trail. Some kind of colored smoke. But it would dissipate. That's useless to you. What's that? The computers? How would you communicate with them? Still, the ones on ships could do the plotting. So, there you go. Just use a ship with a computer. Problem solved. I like having you around. Quite useful. Help me stay focused. What was I saying?

Oh, circles. Big, giant circles going around and around, and you could miss all of the shells. How, well, sometimes people get a bit too overfocused. Ignore what's right under their noses. Hard to miss a giant piece of rock floating in the sky, but still. This is a big world in here. So, yeah, you could miss them. And traveling from shell to shell. How would you do that? With our ships? The gravity-beam-driven ones? No, you'd need another form of propulsion. And fuel to sustain it. What'd you say? Balloons? Yeah, but those are susceptible to wind. You could end up anywhere, going in circles and out of control. Up into the water, even. No, there's a reason we keep balloons tethered. Safer that way. Go look up your history. We learned that lesson the hard way.

So, yeah, our ships just travel to close shells. Ones we can see. Ones we can get back from. Don't want to lose home, right? Home matters. It's important. You need it to live, in this case. If that shell you're going to is moving on, yeah, we need to get back. If that shell goes too far away, you're stuck once it's beyond your ability to fly back from it. So, that's why intershell travel is unheard of.

So, that's where the Expeditionary Forces came from. If you have a problem like this, what else would the government do than start an entire organization funded just to do one thing. Sounds very government-like, right? Waste a ton of money on a very limited thing that will probably just end up costing you a fortune and give you hardly anything in return.

Still, some people wanted to go, wanted to explore other shells. And they knew they might be gone a while. Maybe forever. Planned it that way, even. Facing that, you'd have to be a special kind of someone. Funny, never thought of them that way, but I guess my parents are special. Very much so.

EXCERPT FROM *FALL*,
SEQUEL TO *RISE*

Scribe's note: The following events occur directly after the events chronicled in *Rise*. In summation of the narrative, the Colberran fleet's surprise attack on the Expeditionary Forces' outpost located on the Nomad shell sent Quentin and the entire outpost tumbling toward the core. Micaela and Suyef remained on the shell post-battle. In summation of the interviews, Micaela had just informed me of Quentin's demise, and Suyef and Quentin had vanished from their hidden home. That left me with no clue where to go except the still-closed box entrusted to me. I opened it, in search of answers.

A stick.

The box lay open on the table before me, Suyef's note underneath it. Inside lay a stick, smooth and round on one end, broken and fragmented on the other. The wood bore a light-brown hue, was smooth to the touch, and had only two slight bends in it, breaking up the otherwise straight lines. The fragmented tips along one end were very sharp. Nothing else lay inside.

"What is this?" I whispered, staring at the item.

A memory bubbled to the surface. A memory of a man and his stick. Pulling at my notes, I flipped through pages of memories, of a story as convoluted as my notes. It took several moments, but I found what had piqued my interest. The list of names the Queen had given me and a note from a session with Quentin, all quickly jotted down. A simple phrase next to one name: *Nidfar. Ask about Stick.*

My eyes shifted back to the open box. Could this be his stick? The one he'd spoken to? The one Micaela and Quentin both insisted he'd had with him each time they met him?

I flipped through my notes, searching for more information. Page after page, memory after memory. Theirs and my own. As the images their words had created in my mind flitted to the surface, images of them sitting before me, their stories pouring from them, mixed in. I shook my head for focus, eyes darting back and forth until finding the sought-after notes.

I scanned the words of Micaela's first encounter with the old man. The crazy old man that had also once lived near Quentin's home. The crazy old man who talked to a stick.

"This isn't any ordinary stick."

I'd written those words down exactly, circling the contraction. What could that have meant? I scanned over the page again and found something else.

"Piece of fabricated wood."

Another circle lay around the word *fabricated*. My eyes darted to the piece of wood laying before me. Being fabricated wasn't necessarily strange. Most wood was fabricated from matter reforgers. Still, the words made me wonder if there was something more to this stick.

My eyes shifted to Suyef's note, then back to the box. Yes, there was definitely more to this stick. Something powerful. Dangerous.

Something worth hiding.

I tucked the stick back into the box, closing and returning it to my sack before sitting back to ponder my next move. Quentin and Suyef remained absent. Waiting seemed the best option, but there was no telling how long they could be gone. I considered for a moment going back to the Nomads in hopes they might be able to tell me where Suyef had gone. That was probably useless. They'd been less than helpful the first time. What motivation did they have to do more now?

Pondering my limited options, eyes scanning my notes, I heard a sound nearby. A shuffling, like feet not lifted from the ground. A sniffle. Someone was crying?

"Quentin?" I called, moving toward his room, my notes and sack gathered into my arms.

No answer. Just another sniffle. I moved down the hall and stopped in his door. It wasn't Quentin. Sitting on the bed was an old man, hair barely clinging to the sides of his head, a cloak made of many colorful strips of cloth hanging from bony shoulders. His eyes were locked on the sketches of Micaela, and he held something in a fist just visible to me at his side. A strip of gray cloth. The strip Quentin had torn from my cloak.

"Nidfar?" I asked, my voice a whisper.

He shuddered, head jolting around. Bright-blue eyes locked on to mine, and his fist clenched tighter on the cloth.

"Who is it?" His voice croaked as he spoke.

"My name is Logwyn," I said, stepping into the room.

He shifted on the bed and moved away from me. I froze, not wanting to scare him. His eyes darted over my shoulder at the door. As I followed his gaze, it dawned on me he might feel trapped with me standing in the room's only entrance. To help soothe him, I moved to the side, allowing him to leave if he chose. His eyes followed me, darting once at the door, then back to watch my movement.

"Do you know the Dragon Queen?" I asked.

His eyes widened at the name, but he didn't speak.

"Do you know her, Nidfar?"

"Shh!" he hissed, waving the hand clenched around the cloth at me. "Don't say that name!"

I looked around. "There's no one here but us."

His eyes, wild a moment before, locked on to mine. Strong, clear, blue eyes.

"In this place, he is always here," he whispered.

I pressed my lips together, nodding once. He calmed, lowering his fist. My eyes followed his hand.

"Are you going to use that?"

He looked down at his hand, opening it to see the cloth. "Maybe. It's not as bright as my others."

My eyes darted over his cloak. The gray cloth would indeed be plain among the myriad of colors he'd attached to his garment.

"Why all the colors?" I asked, thinking that might be a less volatile subject.

He shrugged. "Seemed a good idea. Now I like it."

His fingers played with the cloth in his hand, his eyes staring off at the wall over my shoulder. As he sat there, the box in my sack came to mind. Questions formed, questions for him about the object inside that box. Suyef's words held me back. Could I trust the old man? Was it his? Was my need to know driving me to do something I shouldn't?

The old man shuddered where he sat, shaking his head and focusing his eyes on me.

"Well, hello, have we met?" he asked, his voice cheery, a smile splitting his face. "I'm afraid my memory's not what it once was." He tapped at his forehead with his balled hand. "Glitching and messing up." He looked at his fist and saw the cloth there. "What have we here?"

He held up the gray cloth, eyes darting up and down, his nose sniffing. "Hmmm, lower-shell fabrication, if my nose is near the mark." He licked the cloth, smacking his lips together. His hand balled into a fist around the fabric, one finger pointing at me. "Several decades old. Inherit that cloak, did you?"

I frowned. "You can tell that from licking and sniffing it?"

He grinned. "Nope, made it all up."

I shook my head and looked at my notes. I held them up and showed him the pages.

"Do you know what this is?"

"Paper?" he asked, his face splitting in a toothy grin.

I glared at him. "Do you know what's on it?"

His eyes narrowed. "What do you take me for, a saysoother?"

"You mean soothsayer," I said, smiling at his mistake.

"S'what I said, witnit!"

I smothered another smile, trying to keep my face as calm as I could. "So, what is this?"

He shrugged. "A waste of valuable paper, it looks like." He leveled his finger at me again. "Hope you got the necessary authorization to use all that. Had to cost a fortune in reforge credits, I'd wager."

I started to say they hadn't come from the reforger, but stopped myself. The first page hadn't; the rest had. I shook my head, waving the pages at him.

"I've got your name in here," I whispered. "Written as clear as day."

That got his attention. He sat bolt upright, looking around. He pointed at the sketches.

"It was that girl, wasn't it?" he said. "Blasted, I told her not to go blabbing."

I shook my head. "Micaela didn't give it to me," I stated. "The Queen did."

His eyes widened. "She mentioned me?"

I nodded. "Gave me your name herself."

His face transformed before me, a glorious smile melting into place, dancing in his eyes, his mismatched teeth jutting out.

"She mentioned me," he whispered.

"The Queen gave me a task and said you were one of the only people who could help me," I went on, embellishing a bit, as it seemed to buoy his spirits.

He looked at the papers. "That's what all that is, isn't it? What she needs help with?"

I held them up. "These are my notes on it. I have a padd I'm recording it on as well."

His head moved up and down in a methodical manner, his empty hand patting his cheek as he stared at my notes.

"And you want me to talk? You said record, so I guess you mean my voice?"

I shifted the papers under my arm and pulled the padd from my sack, careful not to reveal the box just yet.

"On this, yes."

His eyes narrowed as he pondered the device. "Is it safe?"

"The Queen assured me it was."

He glared at the device. "Has it been isolated? Domain blocked or masked? Does it have connectivity of any kind? Can you detect any packet transfers? Any pings?"

I held the device out to him. "Feel free to check her work. I trust the Queen when she says something's safe."

His eyes locked on to the padd. "She assured you?"

I nodded. "She's very thorough. Very capable. If she said it was safe, it must be."

We fell silent after that, him watching the device, me him. I shifted the padd in my hand and looked around.

"So, you want me to talk." Nidfar pointed at my papers. "And you want to take notes. But you haven't told me what you want me to talk about."

I eyed him, contemplating what I should say. How I should say it. "What was necessary?"

Necessary.

A lot of things are necessary. Food, water, love. We know life is full of these things. But there are more. Moments that make us, break us. Lessons. Successes. Failures. The things that fill pages, that people want to read about. The things that make us real.

When Micaela stepped onto that platform, so much flashed through my mind. Whereas before that all had been chaos, a swirling surge of memories boiling over my head as I struggled to stay afloat, the sight of her standing there brought a moment of clarity. A vision of defined purpose. A point on a map guiding me home.

And it was all summed up in one word: necessary.

So, as the ring took her from sight, I called after just that one word. Hope filled me she would make sense of it. I couldn't say more. Not for lack of time, which was obvious. But for lack of knowledge. So much unknown to me. What might happen if I said to much? What events might change? A singular struggle I alone have faced for so long.

No, not alone. This hasn't been just my struggle. The Dragon Queen, as eternal as the water above shines a crystal blue, yes, she's struggled against this along with me. Rather, she's struggled in her own way. A point of disagreement between us. A wedge, so small at first, driven deep with the blows of time's infinite, omnipotent hammer. A gulf as vast as the atmosphere is empty. But I digress.

Unlike the Queen, I've spent all this time trying to have as little impact on the world as I can. Still, I knew the time was coming when that would be impossible. When Micaela and her companions would walk into my tower and set in motion a series of events so powerful the world still hasn't stopped shaking from them.

How do you tell a person she must go forward? She mustn't turn back. How do you say all that without saying anything at all?

You say it in one word: necessary.

And you trust the person to figure it out.

I held up a hand to stop the old man.

"Are you claiming to have lived as long as the Queen?"

He grinned at me, a toothy thing that made him look even older than he already appeared.

"And how old is your Queen?"

I frowned. "No one knows. She's been around longer than our history records."

"Yet your people call her eternal, yes?"

I nodded.

"Without evidence? Does she ever confirm this descriptor?"

I shook my head. "It's rude to ask such things."

He wheezed, his chest heaving with what sounded like a laugh. "Why, because she's your Queen?"

"No, not just that. She's a lady. It's rude to ask."

He pointed at me, a knobby, wrinkled finger with a jagged, torn fingernail on it. "You're a scribe. It's your job to know such things. Does this stop you from asking?"

I shook my head.

"So, why haven't you?"

I paused, contemplating his words. "I haven't had the need to."

His eyebrows raised as his finger pointed up to the ceiling. "Haven't needed to. So, in all the time your people have kept their history books, no one has ever needed to know?"

"I don't know, maybe it's protected information."

He nodded. "Possibly. Or it's not there because no one knows."

"What does this have to do with your age?" I asked, feeling my face heat up.

"Simple. If you can't say how old she is, how can you say how old I am?"

"You're the one claiming to be that old!"

He shook his head. "No, I said I'd struggled long in this fight. Just like her." He locked his bright-blue eyes on me, finger pointing at my face. "You assumed. Stop doing that. You've been doing it most of your life, and it's done you no good."

My eyes narrowed. "How do you know so much about me?"

He grinned. "To quote one of the greatest fictional characters of all time, 'spoilers.'"

Once Micaela left my tower, I knew one thing was certain. What came next was going to be rough on her. The battle at the outpost didn't have a good ending to it. It wasn't an ending at all. Just another beginning. And the chapter that came next for her was a dark one for sure.

You have to understand the predicament I was in. I knew what was coming, but the details were relatively unknown to me. It was like being able to see a painting from a distance. It's possible to make out major features, but the particulars are lost over the gap. I'd had so long to prepare for that day, but something had kept me away. Something inside pushed me not to look, not to fill the gaps in my knowledge. To stay in the dark. Maybe I was protecting myself. Maybe protecting her and her companions. I don't know.

What I did know was I couldn't follow. Not right away. What happened at the outpost had to happen free of outside influence. So, I waited. I paced the tower, talked to myself, talked to my stick. For once, the infernal thing stayed around. It's quite annoying misplacing something as simple as a stick when you need it. But let's leave Stick out of this. I've got a feeling the thing's annoyed with me right now, as I haven't seen it in a while.

Once all the ships were past, I began to ponder going. The platform beckoned me. I could check if the Nomad tower was empty. The computer could tell me that much. So, why didn't I? What held me back? Dread. What came next filled my memory, and part of me dreaded witnessing it again. So, I stood there, waiting, contemplating, hemming and hawing, waffling, and several other *-ings* for good measure. It all amounted to avoiding, and I knew it.

Something happened that compelled me to move. As my feet carried me around the chamber, my pacing led me out to the balcony to check if the attacking ships were truly gone. A quick glance out to the south showed the fleet vanished from sight, off to their deadly appointment. That meant little to my dilemma. What lay to the north, on the other hand, did. When my gaze turned to the mountains, the sight of more ships amassing over the citadel greeted my eyes. Many more ships than the fleet already on its way to the Nomad shell. A massive fleet that filled the sky above the mountains.

An invasion force.

A chime rang from inside the room, beckoning me to the panel. I tore my gaze from the fleet and moved nearer the network station.

"Computer, what is it?"

"Incoming message, sir."

I looked around, licking my lips. "From where?"

"Attempting to identify. It would appear someone has found a way to send a message from the network to your isolated system."

"Put it on screen."

The computer complied, and a new panel appeared in the center of the station. A very familiar face greeted me.

"Ah, there you are," the face from long in my past said. "My, time hasn't been friendly to you, has it?"

I felt my heart race, despite the fact I knew of his presence. "Rawyn," I whispered. "How did you find me?"

The man frowned, his still-young-looking face wrinkling as he did. "Technically, I haven't a clue where you are. I've been trying to find how you and your infernal beast allies communicate without using the citadel network, and I stumbled across your connection." He leaned close, his cold, black eyes gazing at me. "I know you're on this shell, and if I had to guess I'd say in the Wilds." He chuckled, leaning back. "Where you are is of no importance. Well, no, it is. The fact that you're here and not elsewhere will make what comes next much easier."

"You know you can't stop the events coming."

He waved at me on the screen. "Don't talk to me about temporal mechanics. You're not going to stop me again."

"I didn't stop you last time," I whispered.

"Yes!" he hissed, hand slapping down onto a surface out of my sight, his eyes flaring wide. "Yes, you did." He paused, taking in deep breaths to calm himself. "The two of you did. You locked the system away. She told me."

"Who told you what?" I asked, shaking my head in confusion. "The Queen won't talk to the likes of you."

"Oh, not your precious 'Queen,'" he said, fingers wiggling to emphasize the name as he spoke. "I'll deal with her soon enough." He pointed at me through the screen. "You know who I'm talking about."

I glanced at the screen around his face. "If you've convinced Celandine to help you, then your problems should be over."

He laughed, his head shaking, hair falling into his face as he did. "You know full well no one controls that woman. Not when she has the entire citadel network at her disposal." He leaned in, voice dropping to a whisper. "Let's just say she and I have common interests. And one of them is you." He grinned, an evil thing that transformed his face into something truly hideous. "Well, no, not you. Rather, your stick."

I clutched at the object of his interest, safely hidden behind my back. "You know there's no controlling this thing. She barely tolerates me."

"Yes, Celandine did mention that little irony." He shrugged. "That's your problem. Mine is simple. I want it. I'm going to get it. And I know full well that some time soon, your precious little Micaela is going to find it. I thought she already had it, but clearly she would have used it against me if she had."

I held my breath, wondering what he knew. My fingers wrapped tight around the piece of wood in my hand.

"When she does, I will take it from her." His face loomed large on the screen. "And when I do, everything will change."

His voice fell so quiet I barely heard what he said next.

"And then I will kill her."

"Wait, you were holding the stick when this happened, yes?" I asked, interrupting the old man.

He nodded, smiling at me and saying nothing.

"So, if you had it, how was Micaela going to find it?"

Both eyebrows on the man's face rose, and he remained quiet. I shook my head, scanning my notes, trying to make sense of the conversation he'd just shared with me.

"You said his name was Rawyn?"

He nodded.

"Is this the Rawyn? The one all our history books mention?"

No answer.

"The one that vanished just after the world was split apart?"

He just sat there, not saying anything.

"Are you going to answer any of my questions?"

"Are you ever going to learn to fly?" he asked.

I leveled a finger at him. "The issues of my past are not what we're talking about here."

The old man leaned toward me. "The topic of our conversation is as intricate and complicated a matter as your failure."

My heart raced in my chest as I held his gaze. Through clenched teeth, I whispered, "I tried my hardest that day. Harder than at anything I've ever done." A sigh shook my body, a shiver running from my neck to my toes. "The blessing wasn't meant for me."

A tear rolled down his face, catching in the wrinkles and hanging there for a second just next to his large nose. It fell a moment later onto his cloak.

"My dear, the 'blessing' is meant for everyone," he whispered.

A NOTE TO THE READER

My thanks for backing this novel on Inkshares. It means so much you took the time to support this dream of mine. When you finish, I would love to get feedback. E-mail it to me at Colberra@gmail.com. I would also love it if you prepared a review to post to vendor sites once the book is released. If you can't wait to read the next installment, be sure to go to inkshares.com and preorder *Fall* as soon as possible. Thanks again for your time and your support.

ACKNOWLEDGMENTS

My thanks and gratitude to all that supported me in this.

First, to God and Creator, the Great Writer. This wouldn't have happened without you.

Second, to those that supported me as I wrote and edited *Rise*. Specifically, to my artist, Chris McElfresh. Thanks for the sounding board and all the creative work you've helped me with. I'm so glad we got your cover on the front! To Laura Kenney, I appreciated so much all the editing work you did on *Rise* and *Fall*. To Jess Chancey, the "voice" of Logwyn and by far my most avid and critical beta reader. To put it bluntly, Logwyn would not exist had you not been pushing me with questions and more questions and even more! To Jerry Fan and Kalvin Fadakar with Jukepop Serials, who supported *Rise* in its first run. Thanks, guys, for giving me an avenue to get this out there and learn what I'm doing. To all of you Tadpooligans and the many friends, family, and strangers that became backers and supporters on Inkshares, this is as much your success as mine. I can't express how grateful I am you all stepped up and took a chance on this project, especially those of you that I "bugged" multiple times.

Third, to Inkshares, the *Nerdist*, and Girl Friday Productions. This novel would not be here had Inkshares not begun this amazing project, nor without the *Nerdist* sponsoring the contest. The time and effort the people at Girl Friday Productions have invested in the production is humbling. Don't think we don't appreciate what you do. Job well done, Matt, Jeremy, Avalon, Emily, Ryan, Matt, and Paul.

To my family. To Kiddo: every time I found you sneaking peeks at my story as I edited, tapping me to not move on, begging to have a copy of your own, and especially how you didn't complain when Dad had to go hide in the basement again—all of that made this so much more worth it. You're in this grand story, and someday you'll figure it out. And to my wife, Michelle, the inspiration for Micaela. My most critical reader. You've read all the bad and now the good. You never stopped supporting me and helping me. This story would not be what it is now without your constant support. To see and hear your words of support for what it's become, knowing how discriminating you are in saying such things about stories, made all this worth it. I never would have been able to do this. I love you forever, beautiful.

ABOUT THE AUTHOR

© Donna Arendes 2016

Based in Germany, Brian Guthrie is a serial author of science fiction, fantasy, and more. His first novel, *Rise* (book one of a series of four debuting September 2016), won the Inkshares Nerdist Contest. His second novel, *After Man* (coauthored with Michelle Guthrie, book one of a trilogy slated for release early 2017), won the Inkshares Geek and Sundry Contest, making him the first author on Inkshares to win two contests. He has completed *Rise*'s sequel, *Fall*, and has plans for an anthology piece, some historical fiction, and much more. He is married to Michelle Guthrie and has a rambunctious young daughter and two cats.

LIST OF PATRONS

This book was made possible in part by the following grand patrons who preordered the book on inkshares.com. Thank you.

Ariel Brayboy IV
Brendan Thompson
Crystal Turney
Angela Emmons
Jessica Chancey
JF Dubeau
Joey Lambert
Justin Speck
Kimberly Burns
Laura Kenney

Melissa Barnes
Michael James
Michael Misha Huls
Michelle Guthrie
Peter Osborn
Philip W. Kaso
Ryan Duehr
Sierra Guthrie
Tim Kaso

INKSHARES

 Inkshares is a crowdfunded book publisher. We democratize publishing by having readers select the books we publish—we edit, design, print, distribute, and market any book that meets a preorder threshold.

Interested in making a book idea come to life? Visit inkshares.com to find new book projects or to start your own.